MW01435008

The Cure

Robert W. Rand
&
Maida Sussman

tomoko,
THANKS FOR BUYING
25-OCT-2009

Llumina Press

© 2008 Robert W. Rand & Maida Sussman

All rights reserved. No part of this publication may be reproduced or transmitted in any form or by any means electronic or mechanical, including photocopy, recording, or any information storage and retrieval system, without permission in writing from both the copyright owner and the publisher.

Requests for permission to make copies of any part of this work should be mailed to Permissions Department, Llumina Press, PO Box 772246, Coral Springs, FL 33077-2246

ISBN: 978-1-59526-903-4 (PB)
978-1-59526-904-1 (HC)
978-1-59526-905-8 (Ebook)

Printed in the United States of America by Llumina Press

Library of Congress Control Number: 2007909433

For our parents,
who pushed us into the world,
making us the risk-takers we are today.

Prologue

Chapter One: *New York City*

JUNE HAMELS WALKED SLOWLY down the familiar street. Eleventh Avenue in Chelsea had been her home this past year—quite literally; the street was her home. Her only home, now. At least she could be near the water, if you could call the Hudson River water. She would go there, crossing the West Side Highway at great risk to both her mind and body, and watch the ducks navigating amongst the trash—the spent milk cartons, the boxes. All that packaging. Then the produce! Cabbage, carrots, potato peels, all traveling with a speed so determined, so grandiose, and with a distinct air of exclusion, as if on a luxury yacht, far from her reach. What stopped her from diving in for that food she couldn't be sure. She was hungry enough. Could she even swim that fast? The ducks were easier to catch, but they were full of parasites and disease. *Foul fowl*, she thought. On the better days, with perhaps an apple in her hand, when the trash flow ceased and the traffic slowed, just sometimes, and only if she were feeling optimistic about her circumstances, she would stay to see the sunset.

She sidestepped a pile of feces—animal or human, she couldn't be sure—and clasped the shoulders of a man slouched in a doorway.

"Wake up, Charlie. Jesus."

Charlie's eyes opened, barely, crusty mucus keeping them partially sealed.

"Hey, it's dollface." Charlie's voice was scratchy, congested.

"Dollface yourself." June brushed soot and dirt off the bum's greasy jacket just as Charlie started to slouch back into a corner. She righted him again, and he began to hack. Violently.

"You're sick again. Goddamn it."

"It was cold the other night."

"Where's that scarf I made you?" June looked around the sidewalk hovel. No scarf. Just cardboard and a plastic grocery sack riddled with holes. June looked inside the bag. One comb, one plastic razor, and some dirty lozenges missing their wrappers. Charlie's eyes were closing again, so June shook him awake.

"Hey, hey!"

Charlie re-emerged.

"Get yourself to the free clinic. You might need antibiotics. Here," June reached into her jeans pocket and retrieved a crumpled ten-dollar bill. She molded Charlie's hand around the worn currency. "You've gotta get there yourself, though, okay? I can't take you this time." June was beginning to feel vaguely unwell herself. Charlie nodded and closed his eyes again. His forehead was sweating. A fever. A determined fly clung to his nostrils, searching for moisture. She swatted it away.

June stood and was dizzy for a moment. *Low blood sugar*, she thought.

She walked along carefully. She would go to the corner market at 28th Street and 10th Avenue for a piece of fruit then back to the house. The house was not a home, perhaps a shelter. It *was* shelter, after all. She walked slowly, passing multi-million-dollar loft spaces housing blue-chip art and the upwardly mobile young people of New York, who could have been her classmates had she finished high school and gotten a good job, maybe even on Wall Street. Ironically, money had robbed her of all that. But things could turn. In fact, they would turn. She was sure of it. Despite her ravenous hunger and increasing dizziness, June could appreciate that is was a perfect, warm, spring day, with a slight breeze from the west. The small buds on the trees sang of their green futures. She was sure she heard a lawnmower—or a leaf blower?—in the vicinity. The city was abuzz with activity. A wave of happiness passed though her; she was so glad to be alive today. June paused, catching her breath, and looked into a new shop, spotting couture shoes from Europe, sans price tag. They cost more than a month's rent in this town, as if she could afford even that. But maybe one day soon, she could. The posh shopkeeper glared at her. She knew she didn't look so good—when had she last showered? But she knew she didn't look wretched, either. As she turned back to the sidewalk, she felt a sudden severe pressure in her ears, as if someone had suddenly poked her with a sharp instrument. She looked around as if searching for an explanation, but the disorienting pain disappeared just as swiftly as it had arrived.

She continued slowly on her way, the market in sight, but as soon as she regained her pace, she felt a powerful onset of nausea, as if she had eaten bad food. Had she? Where *had* she been last night? And how did she come to be walking in her neighborhood? It occurred to her that she had no idea. She stopped walking, alarmed to not be able to recall where she had come from. Charlie—yes, but what before then? Violently, she doubled over in agony, dry-heaving, knees on the uneven pavement. If she could just make it around the next corner, to where she and her friends squatted in the old, abandoned fire station, she could get some help. But could she even make it there? The pain in her ear returned, traveling around to behind her eyes with a fierce agony that stunned June. *It must be food poisoning*, she thought, attempting to right herself, but crawling instead.

June finally made it to her feet; none of the passersby tried to help her. Now she hated this city as much as she had felt its poetry moments earlier. Very slowly, she placed one foot forward, then the next. One foot forward, then stumbling. *I must try again.* The same foot. Forward. People around her were blurs, swatches of color, like digitized images that didn't resolve—suits, briefcases, sunglasses, the wind, a leaf. *Slowly, slowly.* Walking much slower seemed to help. She sensed a loss of consciousness was rapidly approaching, but she was conscious enough to tell herself to stay focused. She broke out into an intense cold sweat and felt her body swaying, as if it was as dizzy as her mind. She grasped her soaked shirt and tried not to panic, taking deep breaths. She tried to concentrate on keeping upright, getting to safety. June was tall, fair, and naturally blonde, with a dancer's physique and an elegant air. She was seventeen. People who met her thought she was a model, not a homeless street kid. At least, until they smelled her.

At this moment, however, she was sure she looked like a lunatic—a strung-out junkie. She finally reached her corner, and the big iron door to the fire station was in sight. The building was a turn-of-the-century, red brick two-story, once a city treasure, but now a squatter's haven, thanks to various historic preservationists and homeless advocates. The city had wanted to destroy the building! What nonsense. *Two more steps…*

June held out her trembling arm and laid her finger on the buzzer, pressing it with all her might, letting her exhausted body rest on the large, cold door. She let it buzz and buzz and buzz, the buzz vibrating through her arm and into her brain, which was tingling, and from there it traveled into her tongue, which vibrated in sync with the doorbell and felt like it had swollen to twenty times its size. Was it even still in her mouth? If she'd had the energy, she would have reached to her face to check. She tried to catch her breath, but it kept itself at a heavy, imposing distance, like that sumptuous produce showing off in the river. Her lungs were leaden. The air weighed a million pounds. She felt the door slide out beneath her, saw the approaching floor, and sneakers next to her temple. The cold concrete against her steaming, red face was a relief. She hoped that, in her delirium, she was actually at home.

Greg let out a shriek when June's body tumbled to the floor in front of him.

"June!" He immediately crouched down and held her head in his hands, patting her sweaty face, trying to revive her. Her eyes were open, eerily looking out at him, but with no recognition. The others came running—some teens, some even younger—summoned by his scream.

The county emergency room was packed when the ratty bunch gathered in the waiting room. Two of them made the rounds, asking other poor people for spare change, a departure from their usual routine, which included hitting up sympathetic nouveau-riche yuppie types. Greg saw another two of his young friends handing people brightly colored flyers and vaguely wondered what trouble they were getting into. But he couldn't be their big brother now. Greg paced with anxiety, running through various scenarios that could have led to June's condition.

None of them added up. He'd last seen her four days ago, at the fire station. The next day, she went out with the others to pick up tricks and look for change. But June was always careful and safe. She was just surviving. She wouldn't have picked up just any guy, Greg was sure of that. With her great looks and figure, she could afford such a luxury. She hadn't come home that night, which didn't seem too odd at the time. He had gotten worried after a day or two.

Now, an ER tech was before him, interrupting his thoughts. Greg saw the man's tired face, his scrubs, and the clipboard, which all added to his panic.

"You are the," the tech consulted his notes, "the admitting contact for June Hamels, is that right?"

"Yeah. Where the hell is she?"

"I'm afraid I have very bad news. She didn't make it." The tech watched the poor guy's face. He'd done this so many times he no longer struggled with the facts. As he saw things, people lived, and then they died.

Greg went completely numb; he was unaware that he was shaking as he spoke. "How? What happened?"

"Cardio-respiratory arrest from an irreversible coma-induced stupor. In other words, a heart attack after a coma. Our best guess—drug overdose. Unfortunately, we see this frequently with the local homeless population. We tried our best to revive her."

"What?" Greg wanted to punch the guy for his crack at the homeless and his casual attitude, and his arm twitched slightly, involuntarily, as if he would. "But that's—that's—" Greg struggled to calm himself, relaxing his tense fist. "Well, that's impossible."

"I'm afraid not. We were going to draw blood to check for drugs and take an x-ray to look for head trauma—a car accident or something—but she expired before we could. Since she seems to have no legal family, she'll be a coroner's case." Greg's face went from white to whiter.

The tech continued his explanation. "The county will do some further investigation if they see a reason. Chances are they won't. We're pretty backlogged with cases, as you can see." The tech gestured to the triage room behind the glass, where chaos ensued. Ambulance sirens signaled the arrival of another disaster. He saw Greg's utter despair and actually felt sorry for the guy. He looked smart, but young. Probably had no family himself, and no money.

"Look, I know it's hard to take. But what you can do," the tech reached into his scrubs pocket and pulled out a blank index card, on which he began writing, "is follow up with the coroner's office. They should know something in the next few days, and it might be helpful for them to get some info from you. They like getting cases that aren't complete Jane Does. Here's their number."

Greg stood, motionless, speechless.

The tech patted him on the shoulder and said, "I'm sorry. Good luck," and then he began to walk away. It was strange that he felt sorry for the man. *Must be time to take a vacation*, he thought.

"Good luck?" Greg said aloud. He lunged forward, arms open, about to tackle the guy to the ground. But four sets of little bodies got in the way, surrounding him.

"C'mon, Greg, let's go."

Greg stood, watching the man with the clipboard disappear behind a steel swinging door.

"C'mon," repeated one of the youngest kids, the one they called Beans, who picked up the courier's bag Greg always carried, stuffing away the neon-bright flyers he'd been handing to people. Then he took Greg's hand and led him out of the ER, to the fading light of day.

Chapter Two: *Monday, Westside Los Angeles*

ONE, TWO, THREE, BREATHE right. One, two, three, breathe left. Flip, turn; push off. The bottom of the pool needed painting, a distraction. She emerged and took a deep breath for the next series. Fifty fresh meters stretched out before her, the sun in her eyes. The pool was deserted, her favorite. Her mind settled, and she was at the end of the length without having made another list in her head, without having made a plan, without thinking, just breathing. Some people called it "the zone," but she thought of it as woolly space. It was only in this quiet, muffled, meditative mindset that she could experience what she thought of as real peace. No what ifs, no should haves or could haves. No decisions to be made. After about 300 meters, she might get a breakthrough—an idea, unbidden, perfect, and seemingly flawless. Or a solution to a problem she didn't realize needed an answer. But not always, and maybe not today. *Must not have any expectations.* She took another deep breath and turned for the next set of forward crawl.

The lists were back, then her mother's voice, then another list for Culinary Classroom. Her mother's voice, telling her not to worry so much; she'd find her thing in life. Then the lists of supplies to pick up for the today's gardening demo and meal plan for the working poor lunch in Central Park in two days. A new design for the next schoolyard garden. That was only in two weeks! Better get a move on! Flip. There might be tangelos at the market today. She could mix those with the young limes in the school's garden—maybe a new dessert?

If only she could admit to herself that she wasn't there yet! That she just hadn't found that *thing*. But she had put so much time and effort into this one. And she loved good food—who didn't?—so it seemed a natural fit to share the pleasures of food with children. And the progress with the kids was extraordinary. Northern California had shown the world that organic farming in schools could change children's lives—if only by exposing them to fresh, local, organic, sustainably harvested produce on a regular basis. With children's diabetes on the rise, it was a great place to start. Her Culinary Classroom foundation worked with state authorities and other private foundations to repeat those gardening successes in Los Angeles. One, two, three, breathe right. One, two three, breathe left. Flip, turn, and then—ahhh!—a reassuring "click" in her left foot. The tiny bones that gave her so much trouble were back in place from the gentle pressure of the push-off. That should work for a while, until she could get to her regular physical therapy appointment.

At the end of the lane, Therese Edwards hoisted herself out of the pool and stood near the edge, leaning on her good foot as always, breathing heavily from her half-mile swim. While she didn't feel her mind had rested, her body now could. *I'll get you next time*, she thought, addressing her brain. In the search for inner peace—well, there was always tomorrow. She removed her swim cap and goggles, squeezed the excess water from her long auburn curls, and looked out over the sparkling outdoor Olympic-sized pool of her alma mater, catching her breath.

Could you call it your alma mater when you didn't exactly finish? She looked now, as she had many times in her fifteen years of swimming in this pool, at the UCLA Bruins timing scoreboard that hung proudly above the entrance. She hadn't been on that team, of course; she'd never been good enough. On the other hand, she wasn't a joiner; she knew that much about herself. But she had enrolled in undergrad at fifteen, pre-med even, then the youngest student ever. Now there were kids who were nine, eight, even seven enrolling. And graduating. Well, she had finished her undergrad and two years of medical before she'd gotten too irritated with the politics to stay. It was always something, with her, wasn't it? A professor who rubbed her the wrong way, a policy she'd disagreed with. She'd stayed enrolled at least in one class all these years, if only to continue to have access to her favorite pool.

She headed for the showers, anxious to warm up and rinse off the harsh chlorine. It was a chilly spring morning, and despite ten extra pounds that she kept meaning to lose, she was covered in goose bumps. *Never trust a skinny cook.*

After showering, she emerged from the campus building and walked down a flagstone path, a slight limp to her gait. The wind jostled the tree branches above her head, and small purple wisteria blooms sailed down, almost marking a path to the street. She put her good foot out to cross the street then heard the distinctive honk of the 1972 Jaguar Series Three E-Type roadster just as it pulled up to curb. The top was down, and there was Carlo behind the wheel, a smile on his face as always, fresh from his daily intense workout.

"You know you don't walk. I always pick you up."

"I didn't see you in front. Besides, I thought the walk might do me good." Therese slid easily into the passenger's seat of the small car, as she had maybe a million times before. Carlo engaged the loud clutch, something she could only hope to do one day—if her left foot could be re-engineered. He swung the car around in a u-turn.

"There was a new guard on duty at Gate 2. I had to, ah, make her acquaintance." Carlo smiled sheepishly. He was beyond handsome: tall, with a sculptured face and Mediterranean skin. If he weren't practically her brother, Therese would have had a crush on him. As it was, she knew his good traits—and his faults. He was, after all, human.

"Let's head downtown to the Grand Street Market. I need to pick up some things for tomorrow's demo."

Carlo made a tipping-of-the-hat motion and turned left onto Wilshire Boulevard. Traffic was building up already, although it was barely 7:00 a.m. Cars flooded into the university hamlet of Westwood—students, professors, doctors. At a light, Therese inhaled the smell of thick Turkish coffee from one of the many Middle-Eastern joints. It gave her an idea for a white chocolate dessert bar she might make. With a bit of anise? Cardamom? Mmmm, yes. And maybe some light almond cookies on the side.

Deftly, Carlo maneuvered away from the sea of cars and took a right onto a residential side street. They sped through what had once been considered a middle-class neighborhood—small, mission-style bungalow houses meant for university families—but which now cost a small fortune. Carlo took a left to avoid Century City's mall, then a right and another left, spitting them out onto Olympic Boulevard. Now they would make up some time. Century City Hospital whizzed by on their left, and now, provided there were no accidents, they would cruise against commuter traffic through Beverly Hills, Miracle Mile, Hancock Park, and Koreatown. Maybe they should stop and grab a Korean breakfast? Therese began to ponder the possibilities: noodles, mung bean pancakes, or both? Green light after green light, the street became a true boulevard, its center aisle overflowing with mature landscaping.

The tall buildings surrounding them cast the street in shade; Therese wrapped her scarf around her neck.

"There," gestured Therese, pointing to a non-descript mini-mall. "Can you pull in?" Carlo got into the right lane just in time to pull into the tiny parking lot. Therese gathered her wallet from her bag and looked over at Carlo, who was shaking his head slightly.

"Noodles?" Therese enquired with an optimistic enthusiasm.

Carlo winced. "It's not even eight o'clock in the morning."

Therese got out of the car. "They're really good! C'mon, try something new for once. They have lots of vegetarian options." Carlo had sworn off eating anything with flesh after his short stint as a homicide detective; after the gruesome scenes he had witnessed, he could barely stomach the sight of blood. Still, he was a natural cop—always seeing clues where other people saw concrete or cars.

"No, thanks!" Carlo laughed and watched Therese go into the shop, the giant brass bells on the door announcing her presence. The sign for the place was a jumble of unintelligible Asian characters. The glass doors were steamed up, so Therese became a blur on the other side. Carlo looked around. He was always nervous in these neighborhoods; Therese was too outgoing, almost fearless. There was one other car parked in the lot. A drug dealer's by the look of it—tinted windows, low riding. The little shops in the mini mall were all covered with a thin layer of soot and grime, as if a diesel semi had idled nearby for hours on end. A wino leaned against the trash dumpster that marked the entrance to an alley. *Good. Out of easy view.* A modified Honda Accord thump-thumped down Olympic behind him. He glanced in the rearview in time to see it speed by, all chrome and mufflers, then a Mercedes S-Class close behind it, changing lanes to pass. Another ghetto vehicle, then another, then two BMWs, then a Maserati. This town was crazy! When he was coming up, those cars would never mix. The world had really changed. Maybe it was the nature of LA. Whatever it was, he just didn't get it.

The clang of the brass bells brought his attention back to the Korean greasy spoon. "Therese, don't," he called as inconspicuously as possible, but it was too late; she was heading for the wino. When did she see him? *Damn.* He got out of the Jag and stood to watch her hand the wino a big white bag of what he presumed was "breakfast." With an unsteady hand, the wino reached out to take the bag, and Carlo nearly reached for his firearm, strapped, as ever, to his belt, hidden from view by his leather jacket. *Relax*. Therese turned and smiled at Carlo, who got back in the car, shaking his head.

"See?" smiled Therese as she opened the Jag's heavy passenger door. "My fellow Angelinos can appreciate this fine, native cuisine." Seatbelt on, she reached for her chopsticks, and they sped away, the low, sharp, spring sun in their faces.

Chapter Three: *Coroner's Office, District 7, New York City*

IT HAD BEEN a normal Monday morning at the morgue. Dr. Burt Colins, City Coroner, stripped away his sterile scrubs and headed out to the sink area, away from the cold, reeking surgery "theater," an old-fashioned name for the operating room that had stuck over the years. There was certainly a lot of dark drama that took place there, but thankfully, not today. Just bodies. Lots of them. Just a shell that we rent for a very brief time. That's all they were to Burt. Besides, the job had to be done. He could take pride in that.

At the sink, Burt peeled off his latex gloves and began to scrub, reflecting on the morning's events. Two simple bullet wound deaths, one spinal cord death via car accident, and one cancer victim, homeless, covered in tumors. All bodies accounted for, all things in their place. He was drying his hands when the double-thick plastic doors to the surgery room opened with a loud swoosh—plastic against concrete.

"Burt, hang on there; we got one more coming out of the Tank, and the scan's got a picture you're gonna want to see."

Burt walked back into the room, not bothering to drape up. The Tank—their specialized examination machine—was buggy sometimes, but Burt seemed to have a knack for getting it to behave. He joined his colleague at the Tank's workstation, which consisted of two big monitors and a computer keyboard.

"What do we know?" Burt began, picking up the clipboard on the cadaver and scanning it. He read aloud, "County body, 'estimated cause of death: cardiac arrest.' Okay—cardiac arrest, so what gives?"

"Here, watch this. I've done it once before, and the night tech ran her last night. When I saw the image corresponding to cause of death the first time, I thought I'd better double check."

The tech hit a button, and the prone cadaver entered the scanning chamber via a stainless steel conveyor belt. Because they were so overloaded with cadavers, each incoming body was run through the Tank, an advanced full-body scanner, which "examined" bodies faster than any human could. The machine was a large rectangular box finished in a gray fiber carbon, and it lay horizontally on a table, resembling a coffin. Like other medical scanners, it provided accurate imaging to diagnose diseases, but unlike other systems, it used a unique combination of computerized tomography (CT) and magnetic resonance (MR) technologies, generating detailed, sixty-four-bit images.

And the Tank was more than just a powerful imaging tool because it was linked to a large database. The database connection allowed the Tank to interpret the raw pictures, eliminating the need for full-time staff radiologists, although the radiologists contended nothing could replace their experience. Atop the scanner sat multiple monitors, some of which displayed data, others sharp pictures of the inside of the corpse—spleen, liver, kidney, brain, heart, and skeletal bones. The Tank spit out reports that, ninety-five percent of the time, gave the autopsy staff all they needed to make a report of the cause and time of death.

Burt was lobbying hard for the county to buy a second Tank, but at $4.5 million a unit, he knew he was dreaming. They were lucky to have one, so Burt encouraged the small staff to treat the machine with great respect and care. Everything seemed to be working as usual. The body emerged from the Tank's inner chamber, and the belt stopped moving. The computer analyzed large amounts of graphical data and communicated with its database servers, which sat somewhere in New Jersey.

They waited for the computer to finish. It always seemed an eternity when you were in a hurry, but all things considered, it worked remarkably quickly. Burt paced; he was anxious to get to his weekly meeting with the chief, for which he was now late.

"Don't you know the saying, 'A watched file never downloads'?" joked the assistant.

The answer they were awaiting arrived in the form of a picture. Burt studied the image on the screen. An arrow pointed to a clear hole in the base of the cribriform plate, the area that connected the bridge of the nose to the nerves of the olfactory bulb, the nose's smell center. The text at the bottom read: "Cause of death: Cardiac arrest, secondary to meningitis with massive cerebral edema."

Burt sputtered, "Meningitis? Jesus. If that's the case, we need to sample the spinal fluid right away and make sure we don't have a contagious body in the morgue." The assistant nodded an acknowledgment.

Burt leaned in closer to the monitor, his nose practically touching its surface. "And what the hell is that hole?"

"I know. Weird, huh? We'll get that spinal fluid sample right away and see what kind of bug shows up in it. As for the hole, you got me there. Surgery?"

"Can't imagine what else. Did they know she had meningitis and were trying to stave it off? Or did they cause it? Let's put her back in the freezer for safekeeping. Maybe I'll open her up if she's not infectious; see who got to her before we did."

The two men stood transfixed by the image on the screen, deep in thought. Finally, Burt hit a series of command keys on the keyboard, then pushed the green PRINT button on the machine, and it responded by displaying a long progress meter at the bottom of the monitor. The Tank would now send a huge print file—about two gigs—to the large plotter printer in the back room. A highly detailed scan like this one would take a few hours to print.

Burt hurried to the chief's office and took a seat. The chief was on the phone, as usual, talking to some city administrator about money, money, and more money. Burt was used to the city system; it was how they trained you here. There was never enough money or time, so you just did your best and hoped for more in your budget next year. Sometimes you had to cut corners and make tough decisions, but Burt took pride in his strict work ethic, and he believed he'd made all the right choices. The chief put down the phone in exasperation, almost knocking over an industrial-sized container of small cream mints, the kind you saw at the front registers of Indian buffet restaurants.

"That was it—the zinger. They mean it this time, too, Burt." The chief took a big swallow of tepid coffee laced with two artificial sweeteners and a heap of non-dairy creamer. After awhile, Burt reckoned, you could get used to anything that came in a foam cup. The chief looked more like a desk cop than a highly experienced surgeon, and that was why Burt had done everything in his power to remain on this side of the desk.

"What do you mean, 'It'? No second Tank in the works?"

"A second Tank? Please, I might have to lay people off, Burt. This is really serious. Thank God I retire in six months." The chief popped a handful of the mints in his mouth. One fell undetected into his shirt pocket, which was already nearly overflowing with pens and note cards.

"They always say that, you know. We'll find a way to keep—"

"No, really; we're getting a quarter of what we expected. That's a quarter, not half, not even a third, for chrissakes."

"So what should I tell people?"

"Well, first thing, no more goddamn scans. CT, PET, MRI—any of 'em. You know what a good MRI costs out there in the world? I'll tell ya. $5,000.00! That's before someone even reads it; then we gotta pay him. That's why we have the Tank, which I may have to sell, if I can find someone stupid enough to buy one. And stop sending high-res images to the Tank printer; you guys print those pictures as if they were free. No special blood work-ups from outside vendors, no special pathology, either. Basically, no outsourcing. If we can't do it here, we can't do it. Period."

Burt took this in like the professional he was, but was relieved he had just sent the last scan to the printer before he met with the chief.

"Got it, Chief. I understand, and I'll spread the word. But I have another thing that needs your immediate attention. According to the Tank, we've got a case of meningitis on the floor."

The chief went slightly ashen. "Meningitis? We haven't seen that in a few years. Just what we need with that audit coming up on Friday. They'll love that! Who is the deceased?"

"Homeless, but we have a name, no family. The Tank says she has it, but the techs are doing a lumbar-puncture now to confirm." Burt watched the chief swish his coffee around in his cup, thinking hard.

"How the hell does the Tank figure out a corpse had meningitis?"

"Brain inflammation, I guess. I'll look into it more. Should we issue a bulletin to the local hospitals? She came from County."

"I'll issue the warning today to be on the safe side. Let's proceed as if she is contagious and follow our normal disease control procedures, until we know for sure that there is no contagion. And let me know if that damn Tank is on the fritz, not that we can afford to fix it. I must say, I hope it's wrong about her."

Burt stopped in the kitchen for a cup of coffee. The chief's mention of layoffs and selling the Tank rattled him. He couldn't imagine his job without the Tank—they'd come to rely on it so heavily, and he'd championed it for so long. But if it was broken—if the Tank was wrong about the meningitis—would that call into question all recent diagnoses? Just what the higher-ups at internal assessments would love to get their hands on, especially after the scandal last year, in which a junior tech got the identities of two corpses confused. The audits had been fast and furious since then, and it practically took an act of Congress to get any real work done these days. Another serious audit would be a disaster.

And then there was the meningitis, an audit trap waiting to happen if the body was contagious. But, then again—how unusual. The mystery of it made his pulse race, reminding him why he'd gotten into this line of work in the first place—why he bothered to get up at 3:30 every morning, just to "cut up dead people," as his teenagers liked to say. No, it wasn't every day you had a problem like that. He tossed the remainder of his lukewarm, acidic coffee down the drain. He would prove the Tank was right, he thought, and he would help stave off any possible infection from the meningitis. What auditor could question him then? They'd be congratulating him, instead.

"It won't be before five p.m., that's all I can tell you," explained a patient woman on the other end of the phone. Burt was in his office now, and it was only eleven a.m.

"There's no way to run the lumbar faster? If it's meningitis, we would be required to shut down the morgue, and that will take some coordination."

"We'll work as fast as we can, and I understand you'll need to control any possible spread." Normal working hours for the staff coroners were five in the morning until three, but if Burt learned of contagion, he could call the staff back in.

"Well, I'll be here. Please call me as soon as you know something." Burt hung up and paced in his office. He could hardly wait to open the body of June Hamels and see that hole, but he couldn't do so until he knew if she was contagious or not. Nothing to do but wait.

At 12:30, after lunch, he went into the Tank's back room, where the film plotter sat. *The scan should be done printing by now*, he thought, eagerly anticipating the fine detail the picture would show him. But as soon as he opened the door, he could see something was wrong. The plotter was not in motion. A piece of film was sticking out of the plotter; it looked like it was stuck. Half of it was in the machine, half was hanging out, already printed, waiting to deposit itself in the tray below.

"Shit," complained Burt, looking around the machine to diagnose the situation. A red light blinked next to the power icon on the front panel. Burt walked to the back of the plotter, but it was plugged securely into a 220-volt wall outlet. He hesitated to turn it off and on again; it might zap the data from the printer's memory, and he'd have to start the lengthy process all over again, and that was now a no-no. He retrieved the owner's manual from a nearby filing cabinet and looked up the blinking light in the Troubleshooting section. He read, "Either the power was interrupted or the data cannot be sent to the printer." They'd not experienced any power outage that Burt knew of. Must be the Tank couldn't send the file. But why?

Burt left the back room and moved to the Tank itself. He was alone in the surgery theater. He looked at the Tank's monitor, which was frozen. He moved the mouse, but it did not respond. "Damn thing crashed," he said with a sigh, and then, as he had done many times before, he unplugged the Tank from the wall and plugged it back in. The Tank's green lights flashed in confirmation, and its fans began to whir. At the monitor, Burt was informed that the Tank was rebuilding its database indexes and backing up all data. "This may take several hours," a dialog box announced with a picture of a clock, its arms inching slowly clockwise.

"Okay, I can take the hint," said Burt to the machine.

In his office, Burt busied himself with a backlog of paperwork for the next four hours—it could have easily taken him another four to finish the stack—and then returned to the surgery theater. He strode up to the Tank's monitor and was shocked to see a red dialog box on the screen that read, "Fatal error-703. Database could not be rebuilt."

"What?" screamed Burt to nobody. Could not be rebuilt? Did that mean the data was gone? He knew they kept disks for each patient's Tank data in their respective charts, and he had June's. Maybe he could load her data back in?

He retrieved June's data disk from his office and inserted it in the Tank's drive. He heard its drive readers crunching away at the disk. He received another dialog box. "System error-532. Disk cannot be read."

"No, no, no, no, don't do that to me." Burt leaned on the machine and looked up at the ceiling.

He would have to call tech support.

Who were in New Jersey.

And were closed.

Burt slammed the phone down for the second time that day, but then it rang, as if having a conversation with him.

"Yes?" he answered, eagerly.

"Dr. Burt Colins?"

"Yes?"

"This is Steve from TriLab. I'm calling about—"

"The meningitis, yes. What is it?"

"Meningitis, yes. Infectious, no."

"Phew." Burt let out a sign of relief. The Tank was right, and the morgue didn't need to be shut down. No investigation would come his way.

"But—"

Burt interrupted him. "Can you fax over the full report?"

Burt yanked the stuck piece of film out of the plotter. He held it up to the light. It was only about half-complete, showing the top half of the brain. Well, it would have to do. He was not going home now, not after waiting all day. Now the question that he wanted to answer was: what was that damned hole doing there? Since the Tank couldn't tell him any more about it, he'd have to find out the old-fashioned way.

Burt strode to the cold room and pulled June's body out of the freezer, then switched on the massive caged mercury-vapor lights over the autopsy table. They slowly came to life, hissing and sparking in protest; it was only five in the evening, not five in the morning, their usual waking hour. The purple tint the lights cast did nothing to make the job any easier. He switched on the ultraviolet ventilation system and geared up in a disposable surgical gown, surgical cap and mask, and of course, double gloves.

The ventilation system was warmed up now; he could feel the air moving about the room. But of course, he could still smell the reek of formaldehyde, which never left him. The air had circulated though a large filtration system, which used UV rays to kill most, but not all, bacteria emanating from the corpses. Many a coroner had contacted tuberculosis this way, but so far, Burt had been lucky. Next, he switched on the audio recording system, and microphones descended from a panel in the ceiling. He would note his findings aloud, making a recording of the autopsy, which might be needed if there was a trial, although this was very rare. Usually the tapes were used for teaching, if they were ever dug out of the vaults.

Burt reviewed the corpse's thin chart before he began. This young lady had undergone a Tank scan, which had ruled out a number of diseases and conditions, including internal hemorrhaging in the chest and abdominal cavities. No fractures were seen in the bones, and the soft tissue did not show evidence of malignancy in the female organs, which were actually quite normal. There was a slight bruise on the head, evidently from a fall.

The preliminary Tank report in the chart noted that the brain was swollen, especially the temporal lobes, which had herniated into the incisura opening, causing severe brain stem compression. This Burt concluded, had lead to the cardio-respiratory collapse and her death. The Tank was probably right about that.

Was the swelling from drugs, as the ER paperwork hypothesized? A toxicology blood panel had not been done in the ER. That would be the first order of the day. With a swift and practiced hand, Burt drew blood from the cold arm and placed the tubes in a stainless steel box with a latched lid and identification number.

But Burt doubted the blood panel would turn up anything that would cause this much brain swelling. Studying the incomplete printout of the Tank scan, he confirmed that the skull showed no fractures or brain tumors, at least that he could see. He saw the top of the strange hole in the right cribriform plate, where the olfactory nerves entered from the upper nasal passages to go to the olfactory bulbs, but he could not see far enough down to confirm that. The olfactory system delivered smell signals to the temporal lobe of the brain. Burt racked his own brain, trying to remember what else he knew about the olfactory system, but all he could remember was that smell was the one sense that didn't work when asleep. That was the reason smoke detectors were so loud—your brain wouldn't help you smell smoke in the middle of the night, but your ears would hear the alarm.

Perhaps the girl had undergone surgery for some odd nasal tumor, but that seemed unlikely, since she had been homeless. The Tank report told him the lateral and third ventricles were slightly enlarged, due to the pressure between the third and fourth ventricles, including the Aqueduct of Sylvius. The Tank had reasoned, and Burt tended to agree—since he was not, by any means, a brain specialist—that the cerebrospinal fluid could not circulate to the brain surfaces to then be 'injected to the venous sinus through the microscopic vileae of the arachnoid,' whatever those were. *Time for an anatomy refresher.* The fluid in the ventricles that he saw on the Tank printout appeared cloudy, as if there was an intra-ventricular hemorrhage, or perhaps, as the Tank had concluded, meningitis.

Burt now read the faxed, detailed lab results from the lumbar puncture, which showed polymorphonuclear white cells with cocci bacteria, the type of bacteria that makes its home in the upper nasal passages. Spectral analysis of the fluid had ruled out any type of viral encephalitis. There was a note at the bottom of the report, stating that further tests were being done to discover if the bacteria had been of the arnaltic or anaerthic type, but this required a culture of forty-eight hours. Damn! What the hell did that mean? It hadn't even been twenty-four hours. That meant he couldn't get inside the skull. For all he knew, the body could still be dangerous, and he couldn't take the risk. He would have to wait until tomorrow after all. Why hadn't the lab made that clear when they'd phoned?

With a sigh, Burt moved the body back onto a gurney that would fit inside the freezer. At least he could get the blood work done and have a more complete picture. But that defect in the skull bothered him because he couldn't place it. He turned the head around to one side and studied the back of the neck, parting the hair to see the skull. There was no outward sign of surgery; in fact, Burt couldn't see any scars anywhere on the head or neck.

Any brain surgery carried with it the risk of meningitis or other infections. Could've been cosmetic surgery, even. If a hole was made in the cribriform plate, as the Tank report said, but Burt could not confirm, spinal fluid could easily have leaked through that hole and infected her brain, killing her within hours of the surgery. But he just couldn't know until he'd gotten to see inside the skull itself.

Burt sighed with exhaustion. He replaced the body in the freezer and closed the door, then remembered the audiotape was still running. "Today is Monday, May 1; time is 6:20 p.m. Patient #76549, June Hamels, age seventeen, died in the county ER on Sunday, April 30, at 7:35 p.m. The preliminary cause of death is cardiac arrest, secondary to severe cerebral edema, caused by non-infectious meningitis. Final cause of death to be determined after exam and lab tests are completed." He switched off the machine and stood, thinking.

He left a note on the freezer door that contained what had been June Hamels. "Do not remove this body until further notice." He signed and dated the note. Freezer space was limited, but all he needed was about twenty-four hours.

As Burt drove home, his eyes throbbing with tension from the long day, it struck him—were there other holes on the head or neck that he had missed? Perhaps he should have searched further—shaved the head, even. Had he been so busy covering his ass with the auditors that he had overlooked something on the body itself? He would check first thing tomorrow. Then he had another idea. Why not ask plastic surgeons and neurosurgeons what kind of surgery could have required a hole in the cribriform plate? Good idea—as long as it was wrapped up by the time internal assessments decided to show up.

Chapter Four: *East Los Angeles*

THE FIRST GRADERS WERE crowded around Therese, all kneeling next to the plot of earth in the school's courtyard. It was lunchtime, and most of the school's population was making its way to the cafeteria to try a new menu item: naturally raised turkey chili with beans grown in the schoolyard. This group of seven-year-olds was in "harvesting" rotation, so it was their turn to reap the rewards of the school's collective hard work.

"So what you want to do is just grasp the shoots from here, see?" They all crowded around to see better. The first crop of arugula had done well in this shady spot of courtyard. Its tall green leaves almost reached the kids' knees.

"Okay, now everybody pick some." Therese got out of the way of the little hands. Therese moved to the picnic table to begin setting up the sandwich supplies she'd picked up earlier today: olives, goat cheese, chives, olive oil, salt, and pepper. She sliced a baguette from her favorite French bakery and assembled the utensils.

"Miss 'Reece, I got mine," a boy tugged on Therese's shirt.

"Okay, let's all try it. First of all, what is this thing called again?" Therese sat down on the grass and crossed her legs. Various forms of the word were called out.

"Recuerdas? Do you remember? Ar-oog-ga-la."

"AAAR-oooooool-gala," they chanted back.

"Great! Now let's describe it. Tear off a little bit and lets smell. Mmmm!"

The kids made exaggerated smelling sounds. "Can somebody tell me what you smell?"

"Poison!" shouted one.

"No!" countered Therese.

"Spices!" called out another.

"Right! What else? Does anybody smell something nutty?"

"It's *piemienta*," said a little girl.

"Right. Pepper. Peppery. Let's taste it now. Everybody wash your leaf in the bucket of water." This was their favorite part! The water went sloshing, and inevitably, the bucket was toppled, to everyone's delight.

"Everybody chew!" More exaggerated chewing. "Ick," said one, who spit his into the grass.

"I like it. It's fresh," said another. Some made faces, but most chimed in with some remark: "It needs something else," or "It's strong, Miss," or "I never tasted this before."

"Come over here, and we'll make our lunch with this arugula." Therese went to the picnic table, which was sheltered from the sun by the branches of an old walnut tree. The kids ran over, chanting, "A-roo-ga-la, a-roo-ga-la."

"Who can tell me what we have here for our sandwiches?"

"Veo el queso."

"You see cheese? Okay, what kind of cheese? Let's taste it and see." Therese handed out small pieces as someone else called, "Aceitunes."

Therese translated. "Olives. Good, Marie."

"Salty!" "Weird!" "I don't like it."

"Goat cheese. Quese de la cabra. Yes? It's delicious, no?"

"Cabra! Baaaaah."

"That's a sheep, dummy."

"Okay, that's enough name calling. Has anybody ever pet a goat?"

"Ci, ci; en la casa de mi abuela."

"Help me with abuela. What's that?"

"Grandma, Miss," said one with exasperation.

"Okay, thank you. Now, everybody take some bread, and let's make sandwiches. Hagamos los emparedados."

The kids dug into the supplies and olive oil, salt, and pepper were flung here and there. The kids were hungry, though, and seemed satisfied enough with the new food. They had probably all had most of these foods at some point, maybe even from their own gardens—arugula was practically a weed in southern California—but they probably hadn't had it with goat cheese. They sat in the grass, munching away, juice boxes nearby. Right on schedule, Dr. Rodriguez appeared in the courtyard in denim overalls and a kerchief around his neck. His face was aged from the sun, and he was older than she'd remembered—could he be 60, 65 now?—but his spirit was young.

"Hola, good afternoon. Cuál está para el almuerzo hoy?" What's for lunch today?

"A-roo-ga-la and la cabra," smiled one child, looking up into the sun at the local professor.

"You're eating a goat? I don't think so." Everybody laughed. "Goat cheese," he corrected. "Right?"

She nodded. "Everybody, say 'Hola' to Dr. Rodriguez."

"A chorus of 'Holas' serenaded the scholar.

"Dr. Rodriguez is going to talk to you about botany today."

Dr. Rodriguez began his talk as he unpacked small trowels and gardening forks from a box nearby. "Who can tell me what a doctor is?"

"He takes your pulse," answered one.

"You go when you're sick," said another.

"That's one kind of doctor, yes. A medical doctor. But there are other kinds of doctors. Like me. I'm a doctor for the plants. A botantist. *Doctor para las plantas*—"

Therese watched in delight as Dr. Rodriquez took more tools of the trade from the box and passed them around. The kids howled when a can of worms emerged. Now finished with their sandwiches, he got them all to imitate the growth of a tree, crouching down and slowly rising to greet the world. Next, it was hands-on time, and of course, the children were up to their ears in mud in no time. He went over the qualities of good soil, discussed the job of worms (*Gusanos!*) and covered ph—acidity and alkalinity. The kids ran their fingers through their fingers as he discussed how soil, water and sunlight delivered nutrients to the plant.

Therese had the supplies cleaned up by the time the lecture was over and the kids were due back in class. They washed their hands under the outdoor tap and fell in line behind the school monitor just as the bell rang. Therese overheard, "That's a root; I told you," and "No, that's a stamen, dummy." Dr. Rodriguez straightened up from the flowerbeds, which he had hastily tidied, refilling large holes dig by curious hands.

She shook Dr. Rodriguez's hand as he removed it from his work gloves. "Thank you, so much."

"The pleasure is all mine. The parents have the hard job now—keeping worms out of the house!"

"It's been years since I've seen you. How is your family?"

"Everybody is fine, just fine. We have good health and two boys whose biggest problem is paying off their student loans. What could be better?" He smiled and Therese saw that his face had aged. He held her hand in his and patted it gently. "And what about you? Your father? I know he worries about you."

"Oh, I'm fine. Really." She smiled back at the doctor, who had helped her father with the cultivation of an exotic plant once, many years ago. The result had been bigger and more successful than either of them could have imagined. She guessed that the last time Dr. Rodriguez had *needed* to wear work clothes had long ago passed. He looked down at her hand.

"No wedding ring yet, I see."

"No, not yet. Who knows. I'm trying to keep an open mind. And you know, it's so hard to—"

"It's this damn modern world." Dr. Rodriguez's face clouded over. "When we were young, much younger than you, we didn't think about love so much. We met a person from our hometown and got busy. Nowadays, well, I don't like it! It's fine for you to be doing odd jobs and all, but really, you must think about the future. You should be thinking about marriage and children. Therese," he paused, and with true concern added, "you can't do this forever."

I can't? thought Therese, cringing at the notion that there could exist a time when she wouldn't be able to work on multiple projects simultaneously, much less simply work. Her foot throbbed, as if in response. She smiled anyway. If only he knew what the dating world was like! Surely then he would prefer she be alone. Therese had recently dated a man who turned out to be gay and another who had hidden the fact that he was married. "Dr. Rodriguez, I know. It's just tough to find someone special enough."

"Don't settle, my dear. Don't settle! But you must look around you with fresh eyes. I know your father will only accept the best candidate, and surely there must be one!" Therese smiled outwardly, but noted with sadness that Dr. Rodriguez had no idea that neither of her parents had ever been very involved in their daughter's life. Of course, they cared for her, but their own lives had been so demanding, and now, with Mom gone…

Therese handed the doctor a check from her pocketbook. "Here you are. A little something for your time."

"Nonsense," said the doctor, who ripped up the check. "There's nothing I wouldn't do for you or those kids. You know that. But promise me something."

"What's that?"

"The next time I see you, you'll be married."

Therese laughed. "I'll work on that."

"Promise?"

"I promise."

"Good." He kissed her on the forehead. "Let me help you clean up."

"No, really. Carlo will be along in a few minutes."

"You rest that foot."

"I will. Goodbye, Dr. Rodriguez."

"Goodbye." He donned a large, brand new sombrero that he must have forgotten was part of his costume earlier and left the courtyard.

Therese did as she was told, propped her left foot on the picnic table, and closed her eyes. From the open classroom windows, she heard children responding to lessons, papers shuffling, chalk on chalkboards. In the distance, she thought she heard the Jag's heavy metal door slamming. Carlo would have put her things in the small trunk for tonight's flight. She dreaded the thought of LAX right now! And that awful food and hideous sounds and diesel fumes. Still, the reward would be worth it. *Right*?

Chapter Five: *Chelsea, New York City*

BEANS HAD GIVEN Greg the idea. On the awful night after June left them, when they all returned to the abandoned fire station that they called home, Beans retrieved his flyers from Greg's bag. Absentmindedly, Greg read the words on the pink neon paper. He must have read them five times before he comprehended them. Now, Greg was paying attention.

"Beans, where did you get these?" Greg asked, astonished.

"At the hospital. Some nice lady gave me five bucks; said she'd give me more if I handed 'em out to all the people in the hospital. What do they say, Greg?" Beans, a skinny, scruffy, filthy eight-year-old, was wearing an ear-to-ear smile, pleased at having earned so much money for such a simple task.

Greg shook his head in disbelief. He forgot Beans could not read. He tended to forget he was the one with the college degree, not them.

"It says, 'Free Lecture—Know Your Medical Rights.' Then it goes on to state a date, which is tomorrow, and place—Central Park—and hey, these people are also offering free lunch!"

"I wanna go!" piped up one of the youngsters, followed by a chorus of "Me, too" and "All right!" from the excited, dirty bunch now gathered around him.

"Guys, you stay here, and I'll investigate tomorrow. I promise to bring you back some of the free grub." Greg studied the flyer as if it was a ransom note, examining the font and paper, as if was somehow linked to the mystery of June's death. The timing couldn't be better. Greg needed an arsenal of information about how to find out what killed his friend. Greg usually knew about these events; he thought he knew about every free service in New York City. He had needed to know where to get help—as a homeless adult, Greg had been stabbed, beaten, robbed, and had twice been sexually assaulted. But he, by some disgusting luck, was still alive. June was not. He would do anything to reverse that, if he could.

The next day, Greg marched down the marked path through Central Park. It was a picture-perfect spring day in New York—a blue sky with a few soft puffy clouds, a gentle breeze, and water trickling nearby, but Greg ignored these facts, since the blissful weather only reminded him of the weather on the day that June had died. In fact, everything reminded him of her, and this realization overwhelmed him. He just couldn't believe that the hospital had been so aloof. What kind of city was he living in? What kind of world? As he had many times, he felt vindicated for having chosen to be an outsider in his life. June's death was proof. The system just didn't work. These thoughts made him see red all over again, and he felt his blood pressure rising as he arrived at the event.

A big canvas sign read, "New York City Works: Free Lecture Today on County Medicine." All the chairs were taken, so he stood in the back. If he couldn't sit on the aisle, he wouldn't sit—too hard to get away. His eye throbbed in the midday sun, still sore from getting between two fists in a public bathroom. Wrong place, wrong time. At least he had been paid to keep his mouth shut, and handsomely, too; what he had seen could have been all over the tabloids today. Greg was still surprised to find celebrities looking for kicks in park bathrooms. Did they not have enough money to find thrills elsewhere? The memory of this most recent episode between the haves and the have-nots made his blood boil anew, so he exhaled deeply and clutched his tattered notebook.

Therese watched from the back row of chairs as the seats began to fill up. She was pleased to see the people streaming in; she hadn't made too much food, after all. Volunteers were setting up cold drinks on a large folding table, pouring ice into coolers, coordinating the placement of boxes of Culinary Classroom bagged lunches that Therese had made fresh that morning. Therese greeted a local alderman as he made his way to the small stage. A long table was set up there with a series of microphones, which would be necessary today. There was a large turnout. This shouldn't have been any surprise, since healthcare for everyone—much less the homeless or mentally ill—was in a dire state these days. She silently counted her blessings for her almost perfect health and access to quality healthcare. She felt guilty for a moment, but then that moment passed, as it always did when she reminded herself why she had set up Culinary Classroom in the first place: to give others the skills for better health that didn't cost much, if any money at all.

But still. Therese Edwards Franklin was the daughter of a billionaire, and there was nothing she could do that would ever balance that absurd inequity.

She felt a man's eyes on her, and she looked over her left shoulder. There was indeed a man there, leaning precariously against her snack table in a purple windbreaker and dirty jeans. Greg sneered at her from behind a swollen face and shaggy beard. She smiled thinly and turned back to face the stage.

The first speaker began, addressing the availability of free medical information on the Web, in public libraries; patients' right to copies of medical records; and informed consent, the document that patients must sign before a medical procedure. The next speaker, the radiologist, defined basic terms that every patient should know, like, "Radiologist: the specialist who reads and interprets films taken of the patient; pathologist: the medical physician who reads slides of stained tissues or blood under a microscope and classifies them; surgeon: a certified physician who specializes in working with his hands to remove disease from a patient; anesthesiologist: a certified physician who specializes in administering chemicals to a patient to produce loss of sensation with or without producing loss of consciousness; CT scan: a radiographic, three-dimensional image of the body structure constructed by computer software from a series of cross-sectional images. He showed examples of different kinds of films and passed them around the audience, who held them up and turned them one way, then the other, trying to make sense of the blotchy black-and-white forms. Their plastic corners flapped distractingly in the breeze.

Next, the admitting nurse covered emergency room procedures and stressed the importance of preventive medicine, highlighting the free checkups program run by the city. The lecturers were engaging and spoke in laymen's terms, and before Therese knew it, the Q & A had begun. She glanced over at a volunteer from the city, who was checking his watch and smiling. Everything was running on schedule.

The Q & A brought up good issues. Which immunizations are free, what are the hours and locations of soup kitchens, why is the wait at the ER so long? Therese was moving over to the table to set out the boxed lunches when she heard the next question.

"Okay, smart guys, answer this. What would put a young, drug-free, healthy person that happened to be homeless into a deadly coma, followed by cardiac arrest?"

Therese looked back at the crowd, startled by the gravity and tone of the question. The person who had spoken was the strange man in the purple windbreaker. He looked about to explode with rage, and the sudden silence that fell over the crowd gave his question an added tension. The panel stood surprised for a long minute or two until the radiologist took the microphone.

"Well, many things, and I'm afraid there's so many I wouldn't know where to begin. Without the medical records, it'd be tough and even unprofessional to speculate. You should seek the patient's doctor out and—"

Greg threw his notebook down and yelled, "The patient died at County, and there is no doctor because she was homeless, remember? We're here today because we're homeless. And she had a name: June Hamels. She was seventeen. Nor is there a no family to give a background or incentive for anyone to find out what she died of; at least, that's what they told me when my best friend died on the ER table last week. The coroner hasn't bothered to return my phone calls."

The crowd was silent, except for an obviously drunk man who called out, "You tell 'em! Damn pigs." A strong volunteer was on notice, watching both men carefully. Instinctively, he moved forward, ready to restrain anyone. But the drunk wandered off, grabbing three sack lunches as he went. The radiologist cleared his throat and collected his thoughts, beginning slowly.

"Of course, I understand. I know the county system can be frustrating, and that's why we're here today. I'm terribly sorry about your friend, and surely, there is some logical explanation. There is free county counseling available to you; why don't you speak with the panelist from Admitting after the session?" The radiologist pushed the microphone away and leaned back in his chair.

"You piece of shit! Counseling! You think that's what I need? I'd like to see how you'd react if your goddamn daughter turned up in the morgue tomorrow." The volunteer did not wait another second. He grabbed the guy in purple with an impressive maneuver akin to a wrestling hold, and before the guy could blink, had him restrained, one arm forced up the middle of his back. The volunteer led him toward the tent as the other attendees scattered, grabbing sack lunches and bottled waters.

"Get the fuck off me, you bourgeois jerk," screamed the man in purple, as he struggled to get free of the stronger man's hold.

"Hey," shouted the volunteer next to his ear, making him jump. "It's me or the cops. They're seconds away. You decide, okay? I think you'll be happier with me." For emphasis, he ratcheted the purple man's arm up even higher, producing a painful groan. "Now, I want you to get away from here, you understand? Don't hassle anyone else, just get the hell away from here; otherwise, I'm gonna call over the men in blue. You got it?"

"Yes," muttered Greg demurely. The volunteer let the man's arm free, and instantly the man in purple took a swat at him, clocking him solidly on the jaw. When the volunteer moved to hit back, the man in purple took off, running at an impressive speed, grabbing two sack lunches on the way; the volunteer was too shocked to move. He held his jaw in his hand as red began to seep through it.

"Shit!" spit the volunteer, crouching down to let the blood run from his mouth onto the green grass of Central Park. Therese and the other volunteers came running, a doctor from the panel close behind.

The ambulance had come and gone—the volunteer inside. Now the site of the lecture was only empty water bottles and crumpled-up pamphlets. Therese and the other volunteers were picking up trash when Therese realized she was in need of a bathroom, but the Port-O-Potties had already been picked up and whisked away. She left instructions with the volunteers and went in search of a park toilet, glad for a break from the site of that near-disaster. She was grateful for the volunteer's bravery. What if that man in purple had gotten violent with a speaker or her? What would she have done? When she was sixteen, Carlo had accompanied her as a bodyguard everywhere she went—of course, that wasn't what her family had called him. They had a euphemism, like "helper" or "driver." But she didn't like that arrangement, for although she knew her father had her best interests in mind, the presence of a "bodyguard" made her feel watched, tracked, and hunted. But worst of all, it made her feel different.

In the park's public toilet, she was rummaging through her pockets for tissue when she heard a moan through the cinderblock walls. Startled, she flushed and moved quickly to the sink to wash her hands. Over the trickle of water, she heard the moans again, which she now recognized as someone being sick. She turned off the water and looked around the women's stalls, which were empty. The awful sound got louder, more urgent, and vibrations bounced off the concrete block walls eerily. Therese steeled herself and stepped gingerly out of the women's room; she stood near the men's room entrance, hesitating. She was too curious to stay outside, but too foolish to stop and consider the danger. She poked her head around the concrete barrier that divided the two rooms and peered inside.

The man in the purple windbreaker crouched on the dirty floor, his head in his hands, recovering. A patch of sun from an overhead window let her see him quite clearly. His body trembled with every exhalation. She watched and wondered. He had been violent, but he didn't strike her as a druggie or a criminal. Would he hurt her if he caught her watching him in this vulnerable state? Was he mentally ill? Paranoid? Did this dead friend of his even exist? And then, he started to calm down, the last muscle spasms choking their way out, and she saw him reach in his windbreaker pocket and retrieve a handkerchief. He blew his nose loudly, and then she cleared her throat.

"I'm sorry about what happened back there."

He spun around quickly, making her flinch. "What the—" shouted the man, spinning around like an animal faced with a predator. Therese's legs trembled, but she held her ground, digging her toes into her shoes. His face softened slightly when he registered who was in the doorway. "No, it's me who should be sorry. I only wish I was." He blew his nose again, and Therese could see red splotches on the handkerchief. He had been beaten up recently; that was obvious.

"Are you—are you okay, now?" offered Therese. What a bad question that was. This guy's life was not going to get better anytime soon. But the loud vomiting had shaken her, and she didn't know what else to say.

"I'd be a hell of a lot better if you'd write me a nice, fat check," he sneered.

Perhaps he was just a bum after all, reasoned Therese. She turned and began walking quickly away. God forbid he starts talking about suing someone for the volunteer's manhandling. She should have never walked into that bathroom! How stupid she'd been!

"That was sarcasm, if you didn't notice," he shouted towards her as she retreated. He came out of the bathroom and began to follow her. She stopped and turned.

"Don't even think about following me, you creep. I'll have the cops here before you can catch up to me in your sorry state!"

"Hey, I'm sorry; that was my brand of humor, that's all. I don't want a check from you. I know that's what you folks like to do, though. It makes you feel better. Less guilty." He kept walking towards her, and Therese moved away, slowly, now very conscious of her lame foot. How far could she run, if she had to? Best not to have to.

"What do you mean it makes 'us feel better'?" Therese posited, stalling, already knowing the answer.

"Hey, I know what it's like. My father was a rich bastard, bless his soul in heaven, but look where it got me." He sat on a tree stump and looked up at her, the sun and tree limbs making a crown of jewels on her head. "Nowheresville. So powerless it makes me puke."

He had struck a chord, and he knew it. Therese stopped moving, sat down on a bench, and sighed, crossing her bad foot behind her good one, an age-old habit. Therese studied his face. A streak of blood was creeping again from one nostril. He had been good looking, once. Something about his anger made her want to know more. Had an injustice truly been committed?

"So what about June?" she asked in a quiet voice. She didn't want to talk about the perils of money. She could see he was pleased someone had remembered the poor girl's name, but the thought of her also gave him a pained expression.

"I know I got out of control. But I just know something isn't right."

"She was homeless?"

His voice was quieter now, respectful. "She was, yeah, on the streets since her folks were killed about three years ago. Some bad drug business, I knew, and blood money was involved. She was running, scared they'd come after her. She ditched the cash her folks left her and went underground. She didn't really have anywhere safe to go, so she just started living with us."

Therese let that sink in before she said carefully, "Was she, well, was she a drug-user?"

"No, not June. She was straight as an arrow. The doctors at County guessed drugs had been involved, but I'm sure she wouldn't have done that. At least, not voluntarily." He paused, and Therese saw him glance at her Culinary Classroom badge before he asked, "Do you know how I can find out what really happened? I mean, without any money? Is there some society or something that would help me investigate? There must be some test that could be done on the body, while it's just sitting at the, at the—you know.

"I mean, I suppose I could lobby harder for the coroner to give me some facts, and maybe they haven't gotten to her. But, if I had more, well, legitimacy in their eyes, I could probably get her body to somebody who could, I don't know, run some tests or something. I can't stomach the thought of her being prodded and split open, but I need answers. Do you think the county coroner will get to the bottom of it?" A light of hope had come into his eyes.

Therese felt a frown form. She doubted the city would bother with a homeless girl. The man in purple continued before she could reply.

"See, she wasn't just any street kid," he began with enthusiasm, eager to tell someone who seemed to care, even a little, about the faceless young woman. "She was going to go to Harper's in the fall after taking the GED. She was smart. She had a gift for drawing. She made us all laugh, and she knew how to do—hell, it seemed like everything. Computers, electronics—she built things from crap we found in dumpsters. It can't be as if she never existed; it's just not right. She was, well—you know."

Therese filled in the blanks. Obviously, he had admired her, maybe even loved her. Therese was getting interested, but why? She had no reason to go out of her way for this violent young man; hadn't she done enough already, getting up at four a.m. to cook? She knew she was overreacting, but lately, she suffered from helping too much, or not having enough boundaries, or not doing exactly what was right for her or something like that. She felt the need to stop herself from immediately volunteering to help—it just didn't seem like a real career anymore. On the other hand, she wasn't very good at doing anything for any length of time. First, it had been med school, then veterinary, then teaching, and now gardening and cooking.

The man was right; it was easy to write a check, and that had appeal. The fact was, money mattered. She wanted to avoid getting involved in this person's life, though. She sensed she could get too involved in his loss, and then what? He probably needed a support person—a friend, even—and she couldn't be that, didn't want to be that. She hardly saw her own friends! Well, maybe she didn't make enough time for them. Anyway, she certainly didn't want to get emotionally involved. But hadn't that been the reason she'd been bothering? What a mess! She looked into the man's eyes, one bruised and nearly swollen shut, and saw him as a person, not a thing to be fixed. She felt ashamed.

"What's your name?" she asked.

There was a pause while the young man evaluated what was happening. Greg paled, and his eyes darted around. He cracked his finger knuckles mindlessly. Had he said too much? Too late. She got up from the bench and extended her hand.

"I'm Therese. Therese Edwards. I'd like to help you get those tests done." She announced it with a smile, hoping to gain his trust. She could do it with just a few phone calls. She'd start with the coroner. Certainly ascertaining cause of death shouldn't be too difficult, and she couldn't imagine it would even take any money—probably just time and diplomatic skills the young man obviously lacked. She'd have an answer for him by the end of the week—Monday at the latest, she was sure.

"I'm—well, I'm shocked. I can't tell you how, er, what a relief that is. I'm Greg," he countered with an awkward handshake. He wasn't used to such respect, except among his own ranks. She handed him her card.

"Here's all the info about me and the foundation. There's a lot of phone numbers, e-mail, mailing address, and a Web site. How can I contact you?" Therese knew he probably had no phone, but she also knew people appreciated being treated equal, because she did, too. After all, when it came down to it, they were, right? If only she could get to a place where she actually believed that.

"There's a payphone near me. Here, I'll just jot it down." Greg made some notes in his notebook about June and tore the sheet out, handing it to her. She folded it carefully and put it in her pocket.

"How about I call you at a predetermined time—let's say a week from today to be safe, at noon?"

"Great, I'll be there." He stood up, his lean frame towering over hers, but she was no longer afraid of him. "And, uh," he struggled, "thanks."

"You're welcome."

Therese turned and walked back to the lecture site, and Greg watched her go, her hair backlit by the sun. A cloud arrived, and the sun faded. He looked up at the sky, which was no longer blue, but a dirty, hazy grey. *Thank god*, he thought. He collapsed in exhaustion on the grass and closed his eyes.

Tuesday. Coroner's Office, New York City

Burt slammed down the phone in his office, again. He could not believe the flippant message he had received from the morgue's night staff. They'd cremated all the bodies from yesterday! Another screw up! Even after his explicit orders to keep the meningitis body! Talk about incompetence. Now how could he prove the hole in the cribriform plate had led to meningitis? Damn!

Wait a minute.

Burt sat in his chair, trying to focus. Maybe this was a blessing. Wait. If there was no body, and the body wasn't contagious, at least according to the high-level meningitis report, then what was the problem? Sure, he might not know what happened, but did it matter? The girl had no family, and this was one less line item to be investigated by the friendly auditors.

Problem solved. Another item scratched off the list. Put in its place. Done.

Burt heard his name paged from the surgery theater and went off to organize the next bit of chaos trying to muddy their orderly world.

Part I

Chapter Six: *Bethesda, Maryland*

0.0657 WAS JUST NOT 0.0656*, no—not the same any way you looked at it.* Richard Weigand, PhD, vacillated between the numbers as he sat in the lab with his staff. While they worked on the assays, he reviewed the latest data set from the tests they were constantly running. Potency and quality, parts-per-million and sterility; Richard always concerned himself with the details. Details were what he knew best. These details would constitute the twenty-first paper Richard's name would appear on since he started his career at the National Institutes of Health (NIH) seven years ago, and he was proud of that work. All who knew him called him a workaholic; he called himself a good scientist.

"Richard, come look. Richard, hey, Richard!" called one of the staff. He lifted his head of overlong, sandy brown hair from the figures to see the entire lab crowded around an open window looking down onto the common. Martine waved him over, her pretty smile alight with childlike glee. "Come *zeee* this!" she said in her Filipino accent. He raised himself off his uncomfortable, too-tall lab chair slowly, waiting for them to stop moving. The sound of all the footsteps made him need to take a deep breath. He moved hesitantly, slowly, and kept his distance; he hated being too close to people, especially groups of people. Standing, he was a solid six feet, his legs and torso well proportioned and his body fit, thanks to genes, not regular exercise. He craned his neck above the other heads now crowded around the window. He should have known before he looked down, and he supposed a part of him did know. A press conference was getting started—an army of cameras, flashes flashing like supernovas, and Donaldson. Dr. Donaldson, of course, the director of the NIH and thus, Richard's boss. His statement was beginning. Richard watched Donaldson's mouth move, as if in slow motion, and listened to the words he knew were a long time coming, but which made his entire body ache with dread. The flashes burned Richard's sensitive eyes. He turned away and closed his eyes, listening instead.

"The National Institutes of Health has always been at the forefront of medical research in this country. And I am extremely proud of the work done here, for it serves the nation in a noble and ethical manner, bringing safe, cutting-edge drugs and therapies to our citizens. But because we are a federal entity, we are bound by the ruling of federal mandates, often directed to us directly by the president of the United States."

Someone muttered, "Did he just say 'directed to us directly'?" Richard felt his anxiety rise. This was not sounding good. He heard Martine sigh and Ravi utter, "Please, man, give us a break! Why won't he fight for us if he believes in us so much?"

"Shhh!" Richard admonished. It was hard enough to filter all the environmental noise: the hum of the lights, the pipes carrying water, the blinds on the windows clanking quietly in the breeze.

Donaldson continued from the lawn below. "As you know, there is great debate regarding the ethics of research involving human embryos. Over the past weeks, the directorship of this institution have been in close contact with members of Congress and the president himself, in order to find a compromise between the current administration in Washington and the pursuit of excellent health sciences in this nation. I myself have gone before a special panel and testified to our policies and procedures. However, today the president and Congress made their final decision. The NIH shall immediately cease and desist performing any research using human embryos. All NIH research utilizing stem cells derived from human embryos or other harvested human precursor cells is hereby cancelled. This decision is in no way reflective of the quality of the science performed by every member of our distinguished staff. Thank you, ladies and gentlemen."

The press questions began immediately, fired off like automatic weapons. Richard tried to block them out by covering his ears, but the effect was like turning the volume from ten to eight.

"Dr. Donaldson, do you expect that stem cell trials will be conducted elsewhere, in other countries, giving that country an advantage in the development of life-saving drugs?"

"The United States of America is and will continue to be the most innovative, forward-thinking, aggressive drug researcher, providing the highest quality, lowest cost, most effective drugs in the world..."

Richard opened his eyes and stared blankly out at the lawn. His face was reflected in the window; his eyes, a transmutable hazel, glowing with green from the well-tended lawn below. But he didn't notice this or the dark circles under his eyes, and he turned back to the room, away from Donaldson, into his inner lab office, which he had soundproofed with materials used in professional sound recording studios. He rested his head on the desk there and closed his eyes again. *Time to think now.* He tried to process the path his life was now taking, but could not focus on it—a microscope tube locked at the wrong height. But the writing had been on the wall for some time now, and that reporter had hit it on the head. Without noticing he was doing so, Richard rose and wandered out into the corridor, the heavy lab door sliding closed behind him, bringing him back into his environment. When did this place start feeling so tomb-like? He started the long walk to the cafeteria. Martine ran up behind him, brushing her hand against his arm, which he quickly withdrew to prevent another such occurrence.

"*Reechard*, can you believe it?" Martine gasped. With her accent, it sounded so dramatic, and the sound irritated Richard. But he knew Martine meant well. She had been a loyal and dedicated lab assistant over the past year. He owed her some support. They walked side by side, and he tried not to think about the spot on his arm she'd touched.

"I can believe it. But you know what? It doesn't really matter in the long run. We'll focus on oncology again, and that's rewarding, too. It's not like you'll be out on the street." He hoped he sounded positive enough. Casual. Normal.

"But *Reechard*," she began, and he managed to smile as she dragged out the syllables of his name. "You have worked so hard on all those papers, especially this new paper. You have been building a career on these stem cells, and the work is so promising. How can they look the other way?"

"They have no choice, I suppose. The work was getting too promising, and it got noticed. Now that's a compliment, isn't it?" He thought he should be happy to see a smile spread across Martine's delicate face, so he smiled back, and they turned into the bustling cafeteria.

They took their places in line and picked from the same uninspired grill offerings as any Wednesday, then fought for a free spot at a table. Martine chatted about her husband and two new cats, as if their world had not just been turned upside down. Richard found it hard to concentrate and be friendly because, although he had seen this coming, he was still shaken by the moratorium on his research, and the cafeteria was just loud enough for him to hear almost nothing—a skill he had practiced since childhood. While Martine continued, Richard thought about how Donaldson had indicated this would have to happen—and they had all been following the debates in Congress. Private companies would snatch the stem cell work up—it had too much financial promise to be abandoned. And the NIH had published everything for them—for free—they just had to read it and copy it. Then, of course, there was the emotional promise to consider—after all, stem cells could potentially cure Parkinson's and MS, maybe even some cancers. That was just the thing that made it so appealing to the press, and suddenly, right-to-lifers were obsessed with stem cells. Richard couldn't get caught up in that—the emotional side. That is, he couldn't feel it, couldn't truly empathize, because his brain didn't really work that way; at least, that was what the specialist had said—Richard himself had never noticed. The problem with emotions was that they tended to not be based on facts. The relevant fact of this matter that the emotional public failed to grasp was that the NIH was never in the business of using aborted human fetuses. They were only using frozen fertilized eggs left over from fertility clinics. Hardly dramatic, yet Donaldson hadn't even tried to fight.

"Richard?" Martine tried to catch his eye. She had asked him about ice cream. He had obviously been paying less attention than normal, less than he'd realized.

"I'm sorry? Oh, yes, I would like to get dessert. Sorry. I suppose I'm a little distracted. Just thinking about that last test. I'd like to finish it tonight and put the paper together anyway, just for completion's sake. I was thinking about staying late."

"Staying late, again, even now?" Martine was what Richard was told was *incredulous*. "You are amazing! I would go home after lunch, if I were you."

But you're not me, thought Richard. *You're nothing like me. Nor is Donaldson.*

"You know, I think you are too good. You know what I mean?" asked Martine.

"I don't, actually," he replied, with his usual honesty.

"Some people in the department—I mean, I think you are aware of this—well, they look bad next to your hard work."

Richard knew whom she meant: the senior scientists, mostly, who got the press and credit for the big breakthroughs, but didn't participate in the real lab work, without which there would be no breakthrough. It wasn't that Richard wanted fame and attention—certainly not any attention, but he had come to expect some recognition; the senior scientists got it in the form of financial "incentives" from the private drug companies. He had worked too hard on the stem cells—on his own initiative—to get nothing now. He was at a real roadblock and sensed a change was in the air, but what that change was he couldn't picture. At all. He had always thought he'd be a career government researcher. He didn't like the notion that plans might need to change. When he was invited to the NIH right out of school, he'd been glad to have a solid place to spend his time. After all, it was a prestigious post for any aspiring researcher. But seven years later, even he had to admit the routine was not enough for him. Was this dissatisfaction? Probably. The papers were published and the work continued, but he didn't see any real change in the medical world. An ocean separated his ideas from clinical applications, where they mattered.

But he decided to try to put a positive spin on his words. He wanted to protect the dream that something real, and maybe even good, could come out of the long hours. A piece of him still believed it.

"That's their problem. It doesn't matter who does the work, just that the work is good and the drug companies are interested in the work. And if I raise the bar of what's expected, well then, the bar should have been higher. There will be a payoff in the long run, and when a new and great cancer drug is released, it won't matter who was in the lab at all hours for ten years—just that someone was. What a great thing to be a part of!"

"Are you interviewing for Donaldson's post?" joked Martine, an invitation to leave serious conversation. They spent the rest of lunch debating the virtues of soft-serve versus real ice cream, Richard quoting fat content and facts from fluid dynamics, Martine pretending to be interested.

Chapter Seven: *Four Seasons Meeting Room, New York City*

"EVENING, GENTLEMEN—AND LADY," began Stuart Franklin as he stood in front of the gathered board members, all but one of whom were male. The female board member always gave a smile with this acknowledgment. They were all dressed alike again. They looked like a foreign army in their navy blue jackets and forgettable ties. They hated it when he wore his khakis, as he had today. He looked more like a graphic designer than a businessman. With a tanned and youthful hand, he brushed his still-blond hair to the side of his head; he was proud of his Paul-Newman good looks. Every one of these board meetings was a test of his mettle—still, even after fifteen years as chairman and CEO. His defense, and way of maintaining power, was to stay current, young, and ravenous, like the wunderkind he'd been—the one who'd revolutionized the drug world by doing things differently: faster research, more efficient production, higher quality. Under Stuart, BioSys Pharmaceuticals Inc. had grown over 200%. Still, the room was tense. Stuart had to put them at ease, had to charm them. Again. He fought back the fatigue that welled up behind his eyes. He took his place, standing at the head of the table.

"I want to begin tonight's meeting with news from our friends at the FDA," he smiled, opening his arms widely. Everyone in the room chuckled, since the board was anything but friendly with the bureaucratic agency. Stuart had made a career out of challenging the governmental body and winning. BioSys had a love-hate relationship with regulators. On the one hand, it was important to have a central body for safety, but on the other, Stuart believed their bureaucracy stunted drug innovation. He raised his fists with exuberance.

"We've been green lighted to start Phase I ABT-55 trials in September!"

There were cheers, although they were tempered. Everyone knew this could change tomorrow, on the FDA's whim or a discovered mistake. But they also knew Stuart had pulled many strings to get that date; it was now barely April.

"The production folks are going to be working around the clock preparing everything for September. We're conducting additional animal tests now, just to keep the FDA happy. But we all know the drill. We'll have to put the pressure on at just the right moment, and they'll give in. I'm absolutely confident that the Phase I trial will prove ABT-55 safe in humans. We've done exhaustive internal animal safety studies, as you all know. I believe the reports are back in the BioSys library for your reading enjoyment."

More laughter from the room. Stuart's staff always provided the board with thorough scientific reports. Of course, the board couldn't really understand them, but they were kept in a stack in the library anyway.

"As you know, ABT-55 is a remarkably benign chemotherapeutic agent—"

"It's a goldmine!" someone interjected.

"It'll be a goldmine for the first quarter of next year, certainly, just when we'll need it. And, it's so simple, that's the beauty! I promise you, we can make that date, and we'll be seeing returns immediately."

Paul Westin, VP of Operations at BioSys, stood up. He had been one of Stuart's most loyal friends—and challengers—over the good and bad years at BioSys. "I hate to burst everyone's bubble, but I did actually read the first series of animal testing reports. What about the monkey that died?"

Damn it, Paul, why did you have to do that now? It was just like Paul, although Stuart was usually grateful for his precise observations. But today, the remark seemed cutting and mean. Stuart was under enough pressure keeping drugs coming out on schedule and keeping the board satisfied with the company's stock value.

"Well, as you know, Paul, it's a dose-escalating study, so the point of testing is to determine the range of lowest-to-highest dose. We give the subject more drug as the trial goes on. One monkey did die, it's true." Stuart heard someone muttering about the poor monkey, and then someone else in reply: "Fuck the monkey, you idiot."

"But that's part of the testing procedure. It expired because of too high a dosage, not from any adverse events that might be expected at a normal dosage."

Silence. Stuart thought he had read that, but now, actually, he couldn't remember. Did the monkey die of liver toxicity? Hemorrhage? Stuart hoped he had said the right thing.

"Thank you," Paul said finally, and he sat back down.

Stuart felt oddly shaken because he could not remember. *Stop worrying*, he thought as he tried to check his composure. They'd be on to another topic soon. He was right.

"And the Swedes?" asked another board member.

"Ah, the 'takeover,'" mocked Stuart, his fingers forming quotation marks in the air. A large European conglomerate had been speculating in the trades about bidding for BioSys. Stuart felt a 100% return of his confidence. Back on reliable ground. His charm with the press and the company's relations was something he could always rely on.

"If I've said it once, I've said it one time too many: We're not for sale. Period. Please put it out of your minds!"

"But do you intend to even meet with them? Putting them off might equal fear in their minds. The press would be all over it," noted the female board member. She was a newcomer to the board and always worried about bad press. She was smart to have this concern—their stock seemed to rise and fall with just the mention of the company in the *Wall Street Journal*. And now, with so many people trading online—people who didn't understand the biotech market—the fluctuations were getting serious.

"Well, I'm not sure I'm worried about looking nervous to the press. It'll pass. We've been in this situation before, during the recession. But now we *are* the market. In fact, I'm glad you brought the subject up. Let me show you this," Stuart put a chart up on the large easel. "A new chart, from yesterday's numbers. Risalin, up sixty-five percent in the US alone. Monoplor, up eighty-eight percent worldwide. Even Grensin, on the market for six months, is dominating its stiffest competition. BioSys overall has sixty-five percent of the oncology drug market share. That's sixty-five percent. We've continued to grow every year since the country came out of the recession. It's a different market now, thanks to us." Stuart took a sip of water. *They love me*, he thought.

The woman was satisfied, and Stuart saw glimmers of smiles among the board members. He was off the hook for now. He had impressed them again, that was what was most important. He had to keep their reins as short as possible for the good of the company and his power.

The meeting was adjourning. Stuart caught Paul's gaze as he left the room, but he had work to do, so he did not stop and chat with Paul as they often had in the past.

Paul gathered his things to leave the meeting. He knew they all respected Stuart. They had watched him emerge as a rising star of the pharmaceutical world with the drug Fensor, an anti-depression drug developed just for cancer patients, which he had marketed, quite ingeniously, at a small biotech company in the Midwest. When the FDA tried to recruit him as an administrator, he turned them down because he wanted to keep drug development in the fast lane. The young Stuart lost respect for the FDA after being embroiled in a political nightmare surrounding the first sales of Fensor. It took guts and integrity to face-off with the FDA, and that's what Stuart had. Because of that, BioSys was now a household name, a real brand. The good publicity had translated into serious dollars. Paul hadn't meant to be difficult, but he wanted to make it clear that he knew Stuart had been bluffing. Stuart had always been a good actor, a persona, a good face for the public. But Paul knew that the dead monkey had gone into cardiac arrest at a low dosage; ABT-55 wasn't ready for a trial.

Chapter Eight: *Bethesda, Maryland*

***IT WASN'T THE SAME** as stealing, really, when you thought about it*. And Richard had thought about it, from every possible angle. There were all kinds of forms at the NIH. Forms for moving computers. Forms for medical exams. Forms for escorting visitors. Forms for becoming an escort. Forms for requesting a different parking spot. He'd checked. There was no form for this. He made his way down the familiar winding, dingy corridor to his NIH office. He had been working steadily in the lab all afternoon since the Big News, and still no one from management had bothered to contact him. He was on his own to find a new project, he supposed. Well, he had another project—it just wouldn't be taking place here.

The fluorescents buzzed and zapped overhead, so easily heard late at night when everything was still. The poor lighting made his wrinkled lab coat appear green and putrid. He looked down at his hands, which carried reports from a recent test. His father's hands. *Tell me I am not becoming him! The man wouldn't know how to read a control chart if it hit him the face.*

He reached his office and unlocked the door, revealing a small and stuffy, but extremely tidy room. Medical journals and article reprints were stacked neatly on bookshelves in chronological order. Three-ring binders with large, typed titles on their spines lined the other shelves. Another bookcase contained gadgets and computer accessories, along with a newly framed achievement award, which he hadn't had time to mount on the wall. Besides, almost everyone got that stupid award.

He walked though the office to another door behind the desk. From his key ring, he drew a second key. The complex of buildings at the NIH was so sprawling that almost no one kept track of it completely, especially in this old building. Most people had been moved to newer facilities with better computers and high-speed, fiber-optic Internet connections, but this space had been written off. Because of the lack of storage, most people were on their own when it came to rooting out extra space. Richard had commandeered this office two years ago, when he saw the potential to convert its back room into badly needed specialty freezer space. However, in typical bureaucratic fashion, the plan to supplement Richard's group with a bare minimum of freezers had been derailed by "lack of funding," and no one wanted to bother improving space that would soon be abandoned, anyway. However, the department had purchased and forgotten one freezer, and here it sat. Richard flicked on a bank of fluorescents, pulled out yet another key, and used it to unlock the freezer. Richard was thrilled with his own private minus-80° centigrade freezer; it had come in handy. He opened the thick door and the familiar, intense cold hit his face. He quickly grabbed a small Styrofoam box and closed the freezer door with one swift motion. He filled the box with dry ice at the carbon dioxide tank.

He glanced up at the wall clock as he replaced the lock on the freezer, then carefully positioned the box under one arm and moved out of the spare office, turning off the lights and checking the self-locking door. He took a moment to roll up the printed sheets of data that he would also need then exited the main office. The door locked itself behind him.

He made his way out of the complex. The bus stop he normally waited at was outside C-7, a fifteen-minute walk. But tonight, he wanted another bus. He estimated the time of the walk to be about twenty minutes then he'd switch to the outer-city line. He hoped his contact would be waiting for him, all according to plan. *No, it was not the same as stealing,* he reminded himself. For a crime to have been committed, someone would have to know about the stem cell line Richard had created, now in the foam box beneath his arm. And no one did.

Chapter Nine: *BioSys Headquarters*

BIOSYS'S HEADQUARTERS WAS LOCATED in Research Triangle Park, North Carolina. The vast campus-style complex stood on fifty acres of land. Over thirty buildings housed one of the most powerful drug companies in the world. They manufactured and researched many of their products here to maintain control and quality assurance. Furthermore, BioSys had branch plants in other countries, located there to take advantage of local medicinal plants—and local workforces—that performed best in their native lands. When Stuart became chairman and CEO, he had insisted on the highest measures of quality, since even one quality-assurance oversight could result in an injury or worse, death, and bring the company to its knees. But at the same time, he believed in the power of local enterprise and felt himself altruistic for creating jobs where there previously was none. He liked the word *globalization* and used it whenever possible, especially when speaking to the members of the board. He had even received a knighthood for the economic growth he had brought to the British colonies. The workers there addressed him as "my lord." Think of what he had done for the lives of those utterly destitute people! It gave him a rush of adrenaline every time he thought of it.

Stuart parked his electric, aqua blue, three-wheeled Corbin Sparrow in front of a BioSys office building and took a flight of stairs to a basement, then followed a series of underground corridors and fire doors to access his secured private elevator. The complex was designed with utmost attention to security detail. Every department could exist as its own contained entity for a number of days in case of a fire or terrorist act. Stuart arrived at his personal elevator door, which today was guarded by his loyal security chief, Frederick. He placed his warm hand on the hand geometry recognition pad. It beeped in acknowledgment. Stuart sighed and caught his breath as Fred stepped out of the guard tower.

"You look like you've been running. Everything okay?"

"I have been putting in some long hours, but it's just because I'm excited." Stuart noticed he was sweating.

"Tough day? Already?"

"Well, maybe I make it harder than it needs to be." Stuart smiled, wondering why such a comment had slipped from his mouth. He must be more composed in the future. "What are you doing here today, anyway?"

"The guard on duty had to run an errand, and I knew your schedule, so I came to meet you myself."

They rode the elevator in silence up to the thirty-eighth floor. Stuart had known Dr. Frederick Thiessen since his own early days at Harvard. Fred, in his argyle sweater, had taught him introductory pharmacokinetics, which was all the science Stuart could tolerate. His heart was in the business side of the drug world. When Harvard tried to take away Fred's tenure because he had gotten romantically involved with one of his male students, Stuart rallied his classmates, and with Stuart orchestrating, they made a convincing presentation to the university regents about Fred's good character. True, Fred had made an error in judgment, but he was a man of integrity and honor. It worked, and they had been friends ever since.

The affair soon fizzled, and Fred never fell in love again, nor did he have a family. So, when it came time for Fred to retire, it seemed natural to bring him to BioSys. Stuart asked him to choose what he'd like to do, and since Fred had become very interested in artificial intelligence, they decided to give him the chief of securities post. Fred liked the idea of protecting Stuart's enterprise after Stuart had protected his teaching career. Usually, Fred oversaw the work in the intelligence center located on the floor below Stuart. Fred knew all the inner workings of the company; in fact, he'd planned and implemented most of the current security and operations protocols. Fred's team had installed BioSys' vast array of cameras, tracking devices, and even voice-recognition technologies, all designed to protect company secrets. Because it was hard to draw the line between security and quality of manufacturing effort, Fred had also been instrumental in planning shop floor operations down to the second, and all of the company's interactions ran like a state-of-the-art bullet train. It had never occurred to Stuart until now that because of this level of security and coordination, he had very little privacy. And today, he just wanted to be alone, off-camera.

"Kind of you. I hope I'm not taking you away from anything."

"Not at all. The flights are covered, we're not expecting any shipments, and the usual staff has their eye on escorting visitors."

The elevator opened into Stuart's top-floor executive suite.

"Thanks, Fred," said Stuart, stepping off. Fred gave him the thumbs up. Something about Fred's meeting him at the elevator wasn't quite right. Stuart felt uneasy, and he was still sweating. A lot. He strode down the hall, which was bright already. Floor to ceiling windows revealed views of the BioSys lake, golf course, and airport. Stuart paused to mop his brow with a silk handkerchief retrieved from his blue jeans pocket.

Stuart's staff gathered around his office door as he approached; it was their usual Thursday morning meeting. The anticipation of the work yet to accomplish—as fast as possible—made him feel at ease again. Better than sleep!

"Go, Caroline," said Stuart as he unlocked the office door with an electronic fob.

"Two things. The scientists from Australia—they need to be here by end of this week."

"Send a plane." They all followed him inside the sprawling office, which was more like its own wing than a typical corner office suite. Stuart flicked a switch, and the automatic blinds that covered the huge windows began to rise silently. The early day's sun crept into the office, and the A/C kicked on, almost silently.

"Got it. Also, the CEO of GreenLabs wants to meet about foreign sales of Grensin." A staff member passed Stuart an espresso cup, a small biscuit resting on the saucer. The others sat down in oversized leather club chairs or on the sofa. Some drank their own coffee; others took notes.

"Can you put him off?"

"Have."

"Okay, but make it end of next week if you can."

"Understood."

"Next, Jimmy." Stuart slammed his strong coffee in one gulp, and it made him sweat even more.

"Two problems with ABT-55. Snags on animal testing for liver toxicity and motor dysfunction."

"Okay, whatever you need to do, make it happen. We have our eye on a September Phase I clinical trial. How's the press release coming?"

"There's a copy on your desk now. As for the September date, Basic Science tells me it's going to be close on their end, and administration tells me we also have a problem with our contact at the FDA. I don't know if September is a realistic time frame."

"Is it Dr. Thomas again, slowing things down?"

"It is. He swears it's nothing personal."

"Right. Sure. Have admin put in a 44RC request for a new, objective review." Stuart walked over to the corner and opened a small refrigerator, from which he retrieved a cold bottled water. He wanted to hold it to his head, but settled for opening it and taking two giant gulps.

"The routine."

"You betcha. How else would we ever get anything through that office? What a joke. Anyone else?" Stuart surveyed the faces. They all shook their heads no.

"Great. Can you all hold the calls, please? I need to get some work done."

They took their leaves, and as usual, Stuart left his office doors open to survey the office outside. He liked to interact with the staff, build their trust, and create an open, ideas-minded environment. At least, that was what HR promoted. In the background, muffled phone rings and working chatter could be heard. In his office, the plasma flat-screen TV displayed live stock figures. Stuart dove into a pile of documents, including the ABT-55 press release. He thought about looking over the monkey studies that Paul had reminded him of at the board meeting. He would call Basic Sci and have them brief him instead. As CEO, he must provide a clear, consistent message when it came to minor problems with drug development. In his head, he rehearsed his position on ABT-55. He decided to ignore the issue of the dead monkey, for the time being; he had other performances to give. Discreetly, he wiped his brow.

Chapter Ten: *New York City*

AT EXACTLY 2:45 A.M., Richard's cab pulled up to the receiving dock of a major New York medical center. The big metal doors started to rise, and Richard asked the driver to pull into the covered dock area. The man was waiting for him, as planned. Richard hopped out of the cab and handed him the box.

"This needs to go right into the minus eighty-degree freezer."

"I understand," said the man, as he held up the freezer keys.

Richard got back in the cab and asked the driver to continue.

Several hours later, Richard walked into his apartment in a shabby area of DC. He had once lived in a restored ivy-covered brownstone, but that had all changed. He crossed to the phone by the worn armchair in the corner. The tiny apartment had been neglected by Richard's long work hours and was more utilitarian than charming. A dusty, unused upright piano stood in the corner, one of the only pieces of furniture, and as such, its bench was piled neatly with books and papers. The noise of the never-ending nightlife in the street below could be heard from the closed, double-hung window. Richard dialed hastily.

"Hi, Dad. It all went fine. Speak to you soon."

Richard collapsed in the armchair, exhausted. He rubbed his eyes, inserted foam earplugs that he pulled from his shirt pocket, and fell into the sleep of the dead.

Chapter Eleven: *BioSys*

STUART HAD BEEN ABSORBED in work for many hours when he looked up from his desk. The cleaning crew had arrived and were plugging in a vacuum in the hallway.

"Hi, Elsie," he called out to the custodial woman who'd been trying to get him to leave at five for years now.

"Mr. Franklin, still here? What a surprise!" They both chuckled. "Does your family even know you still exist?"

"Oh, damn; that's right! I was supposed to call Hattie." Stuart reached for the phone and began to dial. Then he stopped. He hung up the receiver and picked it up again, floating his index finger over the dial, staring hard at it. He dialed "2-5-2" quickly then stopped and hung up yet again. He closed his eyes and mumbled some numbers aloud to himself.

Stuart got up and paced around the office. Then he moved to the desk again and dialed. He spoke quietly, conspiratorially.

"Yes, please—Franklin, first name Stuart. Residence. On Rosarita Lane. Thank you. Oh, forget it; I've got it. I've got it, no need. Thank you, anyway." He hung up quickly.

"Jesus," muttered Stuart. He grabbed a legal pad and wrote his own home phone number on it, then sat down again. He reached for a giant marker, traced his number in large, heavy strokes, and taped the piece of paper to the desk. He dialed. He tried to prepare a carefree, normal tone as the call connected, but all he could think about was the struggle it had been to remember his phone number, so he hung up before there was an answer.

Stuart swiveled around in his armchair. The panorama of the BioSys campus was arresting at dusk. Clouds floated over the expanse of golf course; there was still enough light in the sky to outline them. Why had he never noticed how painterly it all looked? The twinkling lights, blinking on and off, as if holding a conversation, the remaining light of the night sky silhouetting the lab towers—the grounds were at peace, yet humming along in the quiet of the early night, like a steam engine tunneling through the Great Plains. "8-2-9, 7-3-4-6," he announced aloud, and then again for good measure, "8-2-9, 7-3, 4-6."

He felt he might cry. But then it was too late; he was crying. What was happening to him? His emotions were completely out of control today, and he was so hot. He closed his office doors, then ran into his large full bathroom and locked the door. He turned on the tap, full. He sat on the floor and wept. He had never felt this way before: helpless and pathetic. He was terrified that the cleaning crew might hear him. His heart beat so hard he saw his chest heaving. Was this a panic attack? He unbuttoned his shirt and fanned himself, then took a deep breath.

Using up his last stores of energy, Stuart picked himself up off the bathroom floor, splashed cold water on his face, turned off the water, and strode out of the bathroom. He moved to his desktop computer. Stuart composed a quick email to the important members of his staff. "Guys. Need to take a few days off. Something's come up. I'll be checking my voice mail on the GPS. Thanks in advance for handling everything." To Caroline, he emailed, "Caroline, please arrange a company plane for my use midday tomorrow. Going to NYC; be back in a couple days." As he shut the computer down, he felt better, in control, certain of himself. He buttoned his shirt and tucked it back into his jeans.

Chapter Twelve

BUT THE NEXT DAY, the deep melancholy returned. From his orchestra seat at Lincoln Center's Rose Theater, Stuart listened, enraptured, to each sorrow-filled note from the stage. Eve Klein played jazz standards at her piano with her usual creativity and style. Stuart had watched her for many years now, and there was nothing "standard" about her interpretations. She had pared down her band for this performance—just a trumpet and a percussionist. She wore a satin purple gown, and her eyes sparkled as her confidant fingers danced on the keys. In these moments, Stuart was sure the world existed for him only. This scared and enthralled him at the same time; he did not like that something had any power over him. But the escape into music was just what he needed.

The performance carried Stuart back to the old study on Greenwood Avenue. He was ten, and his twin brother sat next to him on a piano bench. They played a simple duet, which had been a struggle for Stuart, all thumbs. At sixty, Stuart could remember this moment perfectly—the creak of the bench, the notes melding together. It was a moment of truth for him, just like when he bought his first sports car. But those days at the piano were merely a memory; Stuart was forced to give up the piano that summer. His brother died later that year of tuberculosis. He couldn't remember what became of the piano. They had moved into a small apartment about then; the family was just getting by.

It was spring again, a time that always gave Stuart the blues. It made him remember the drudgery of his studies, years of campuses and business school, and then many years spent witnessing the blossoming of the buds from the wrong side of a library window. There had been no time to wonder what went on in the world as he worked, and he hadn't cared. On the other hand, it had been spring 1969 when the FDA accepted his first drug for review. His exceptional career was birthed, and it had been the beginning of finding the next thing, then the next—each achievement almost embarrassing compared to the next idea. He remembered his beginnings with loathing—if only he had known then what he knew now!

But since Stuart thought himself a man of exceptional reason, he pushed away these memories, this sentimentality, and he then, as applause jolted him from his thoughts, noticed he hadn't thought about it, the problem, in the last hour. The sudden remembering was painful, like the memory of a death or other tragedy—it was always there, just below the surface, dreadful and bleak and unalterable. That was the worst part. It felt unchangeable, fixed, impossible to undo. Stuart faced the problem and reflected. At first, it had seemed like a little thing—they had all been understandable accidents; after all, he was a busy man with many acts to juggle, and he liked it that way. But then the events started to pile up, like snow in a whiteout, submerging him—the lost wallet, the wrong road taken, the birthday gone unacknowledged. Stuart sensed in himself a black place, a repository, just out of reach.

More applause signaled the end of the concert, so he stood in ovation with the others around him. He chastised himself. Why hadn't he been paying more attention? Damn it, these concerts were the few mental vacations he allowed himself. He gathered his things to leave. He was sweating again and exhausted—too exhausted to go backstage and speak to Eve, as he usually did. He didn't even want to watch her take her second bow. He wanted only to be alone. He clutched his cashmere overcoat, palms inexplicably sweating, and made his way towards the exit.

A thought arrested him. Where was his car? Did he arrive by train? His driver? Why could he not recall? In a panic, he exited the hall quickly, weaving through the other concertgoers, and emerged onto Broadway at West 60th Street, traffic whizzing by. He looked up the street towards Columbus for a clue. The night had turned stormy, and the cold windy air hit his wet underarms, sending a chill throughout his body. He donned the expensive coat.

Stuart walked around Lincoln Center, which took quite some time, and then walked it again. It began to pour rain, giant drops of the stuff hitting the pavement like exploded water balloons, and Stuart was without an umbrella. He saw no sign of a familiar hired driver, yet stood anyway on the curb, in case he had asked the driver to arrive after he would have visited with Eve. But he was freezing now and only getting wetter, so Stuart hailed a cab.

"The Plaza, please," he barked to the driver, all frustration now. He leaned back onto the cold vinyl seat and added, in a collected voice, "It's this goddamned weather."

The cabbie responded, in a thick Brooklyn accent. "You know what they say, mister. Spring showers—"

"Make me glower." Stuart smiled thinly. Conversation closed.

"Yeah. Whatever." The cabbie rolled his eyes and shrugged, staring the meter.

As they drove through the crowded wet streets, Stuart made a note to phone Eve. He must see her soon—he needed to be near her. He tried to keep calm by focusing on the streaky reflections the traffic lights made on the wet windows, but his heart thumped, and his fever soared. His body's engine was revving, trying to restore itself to normalcy. *But would it win*?

The next morning, Stuart sat at the ornate desk in his pied-a-terre condominium residence at the Plaza. A pencil was wedged over his ear, his eyes intent on the laptop screen. The sun had been up for some time now. He knew, because he had hardly slept, so troubled was he about *the problem*. His fever had been subdued by eight capsules of ibuprofen, and Stuart had confirmed that he had made not plans with any driver the previous night. So it wasn't exactly the same as the other episodes, he reassured himself. He clicked and read, clicked and waited. The printer printed sheet after sheet of information. The desk was being put to good use. There was a knock at the door, but Stuart didn't hear it and kept reading about vitamin E and antioxidants, synapses and plaques. The knock persisted.

"Mr. Franklin?" an accented voice called from the hall.

Silence.

"Mr. Franklin?" the voice called louder. Stuart finally reacted.

"Uh, yes. Come in, please."

Stuart's breakfast arrived from the Oak Room downstairs. The bellhop, in a formal white coat, was an extremely tall man with ebony skin and long fingers with buffed fingernails. The servant began to set the table for a meal. From a gilded tray, he placed the food out—a stunningly colorful fruit salad, a basket of fresh-from-the-oven croissants, an order of eggs Benedict, and a giant glass of milk. "Did I order this much? My."

"Should I take this away, Mr. Franklin?" The bellhop motioned to the tray of untouched supper from late last night. His accent was east African, tainted with British.

"Oh. Yes, please."

The servant gathered the plates and loaded them onto his tray, then stood, waiting. He towered over Stuart, so he could easily see the laptop loading a web page, which read *The Alzheimer's Foundation of America*. The first paragraph on the screen read:

> Alzheimer's Disease (AD) is a neurodegerative disorder associated with a gradual deterioration of cognitive functions, personality, and behavior. Impairment of recent memory is commonly the first symptom of the disease attributable to neurochemical and pathological changes in the medial temporal lobe...

"My grandmother, she had dat." The bellhop motioned to the screen with his free hand.

Stuart looked from the bellhop to the computer, processing. "Oh. Really? Well, I don't. Just doing some research."

"She didn't know us. Any of us. In dee end, I mean." Stuart didn't reply, so the bellhop continued. "You've hardly eaten, sir. Best to try to eat somesing."

"Yes," muttered Stuart absent-mindedly. He stood, finally tearing himself away from the computer. "How kind you are."

Stuart tipped the bellhop, and he left, struggling through the doorway with his oversized frame and the giant tray. Stuart noticed running sneakers under the tuxedo trousers. Stuart took a few sips of the glass of milk then he pushed the food aside and wrote on a tablet of Plaza stationary. "SYMPTOMS: memory loss, loss of appetite, trouble hearing, fever, confusion." Stuart sat back at looked hard at the list. Then he added, "Depression?"

He needed to make a plan. If he was exhibiting signs of Alzheimer's disease, he must determine it for himself. He couldn't go to a doctor without word getting around. No, that was out of the question. No one must know; of that, he was certain. Not even the bellhop. At least, no one should find out before the release of ABT-55. That would be certain death for the company and a great risk to his fortune. In that moment, Stuart decided no one would find out, ever. Why should they?

There must be a way to keep this under control, mused Stuart. He rose to lock the suite's door then he refocused his attention to the blinking cursor once more.

The morning turned to midday then evening was upon him, though he hardly noticed, since he was so engaged in what he had discovered. He pushed aside the sheets of paper he had printed out about genetic testing, vitamins, diet, reading, lewy bodies, and chemical markers, and turned back to the screen. He had heard of stem cells, of course. The entire science and biotech world had been heralding them for the last seven years. They were the hottest science buzzwords since "gene therapy." But what was actually being done with them, and how did they really work? Stuart summarized what he had learned about two important concepts on a nearby steno pad.

First, he learned that stem cells grew in many organs throughout the developing human body, and in the embryo, these cells were programmed to grow into different tissue types. A kidney stem cell would support a kidney; a heart stem cell would support the developing heart. The cells were unique and special because they could renew themselves and differentiate into other cells. In theory, scientists could harvest the cells and apply them to a failing kidney or heart. Stem cells could be found throughout the adult body, even in blood, skin, and other tissues.

Stuart got up and paced. He had read about stem cells and their potential applications to heart disease and diabetes all day. One article he found even suggested possible applications for Parkinson's disease and Alzheimer's disease. And why not? If you could flush a sick kidney with new cells and see cells being repaired, why not in the brain, as well? Why did stem cells in the brain stop repairing things around middle age? Did he just need a fresh supply of them? Well, of course! It was simple. Once in the brain, the cells could replicate and repair infinitely, thus potentially making a "new brain." It was like what nature did, season after season. He looked out the window down into Central Park, onto the tops of trees, all rejuvenated. Re-injected with life.

It sounded like a work of fiction to Stuart, like a modern retelling of *Frankenstein*. It also sounded too simple. A new brain! Still, what other hope did he have? The current Alzheimer's drugs were close to useless.

The stem cell papers that interested Stuart—the ones about potential applications of stem cells to the brain—all had one author's name in common. A PhD's name. The papers were highly scientific and seemed thorough, but involved advanced science with which he had never been familiar; he needed help reading them. He needed help.

Chapter Thirteen

STUART SPENT THE NEXT two days thinking and sitting in parks. At the end of the second day, Stuart found himself in alone in an old church off Fifth Avenue. It had been years since he stood in a Catholic church, or any holy house, for that matter. He had been cynical about organized religion, rooting instead for a vague faith in mankind, if he even thought about the subject at all. His years of studying science and business flashed before him, and he felt a new reverence for nature's creations. *Should I pray now?* he thought quietly. He was so emotional these days! He was shocked at the flood of feeling that rose in him every few hours, as his fever did, only worse.

He was surprised to find himself actually standing by the altar, gazing heavenwards. He felt his throat close up as a panic seized him, so he took a seat in the second row pew. He felt delirious, capable of any irrational act—make it go away! Make the fear go away. He rested his head on the pew in front of him for support as he knelt. When he closed his eyes, he could see his world and all he had worked for—his staff, the campus, the recognition—slipping from his grasp like a dropped glass full of red wine.

And yet, just as he had these feelings, new emotions arose, as if they had entered with the wind though an open window. As they came to him, he named them: fear, anxiety, calm, hope, then fear again. He felt like a canvas of many colors, all jumbled together, like a child's chaotic finger painting. And buried somewhere, underneath the confusion of colors and patterns, was his old self, a simple, bold stripe of a single color.

He stood with the strength of this newfound old Stuart, the clear-thinking one. Of course, there was a solution to all of this. Stuart grasped this vision just long enough to seize upon it, and he finally saw that he was anything but powerless. With new clarity, the thoughts came swiftly and in order. He saw a plan. It was time to act.

Stuart left the church in a hurry, but with a quick glance back at the altar.

Chapter Fourteen

RICHARD WAS STUDYING the young stem cells plucked from his NIH freezer when the phone rang. Usually, he let the group's assistant pick up, but today he knew the assistant was off helping in another department. There just weren't enough bodies; it was almost impossible to hire anyone these days. The interruption irritated him.

"Dr. Weigand here," he answered briskly.

"Dr. Weigand, hello, finally. You're a tough man to find. My name is Stuart Franklin; I'm CEO of—"

"Of BioSys, of course," Richard finished the sentence for him, and then immediately regretted interrupting such an important man. A thousand thoughts ran through his head. Why was Stuart Franklin calling him? He put his work down to free his hands, for some reason—an aid in concentration.

"Yes, that's true. I'm flattered that my name precedes me. I'm calling because I've come across some of your stem cell papers. I found your work quite inspiring, and I'd like to meet with you about them."

Richard was flabbergasted. He'd worked so hard and gotten so little acknowledgment, and now a pharmaceutical giant was calling him? It didn't seem possible.

Silence.

He wondered if the caller were a prankster, or a phony, or worse—a spy. No caller ID on this phone, either. He held his finger over the phone's cradle, about to terminate the call.

"Look, Dr. Weigand, I wish I had time to convince you, but I don't. It's urgent that I meet with you." This was even more suspicious; in fact, NIH personnel were trained to report exactly this type of phone call, in which the caller claimed to need to meet urgently.

The press had only been interested in the celebrity scientists when the big stem cell story broke, and now most stories were just political ones—what was ethical, what was not; should human fetuses be used to advance science? If the caller were from BioSys, what would that company want with science their own labs were probably already experimenting with?

"I'm sorry, but I can't talk to the press—"

"Good lord, I'm not the press! Okay, I'll prove it to you. You are a scientist, aren't you? No question about that—" Richard heard typing, fast and furious, in the background. "Okay, are you near an Internet browser?"

"Well, I guess I could." Richard looked around him. He was alone in the lab; it was lunchtime. Richard cradled the phone against his shoulder and opened a browser on the computer, closing the technical data he had been reviewing before the call. "Okay, where are we going?"

"Type in this URL: https://BioSys.com/cgi-bin/decrypt.pl?/. Note that this is a secured page that would not be known to just anyone, let alone the press."

"Okay, I'm there. It wants a key."

"It better. Check your email." Richard did, copying and pasting the key from a new email. Up popped a table of 2006 financial data, with the BioSys logo in the header. Richard's eyes showed his surprise.

"Convinced?"

"Yes, I'm sorry; it's just that, well, contacting me directly seems, well—maybe contacting my boss might have been more…appropriate."

"It was hard enough to find you, much less find some bureaucratic paper-pusher. Am I wrong? Besides, I don't need to talk to anyone but you. And before someone sees what's on your screen, quit your browser, if you don't mind. The data is confidential."

Richard exited the browser application, and sighed. "You're right about my boss. He is an administrative type. And you must understand—we have data and intellectual property to protect. I have to be sure."

"Of course. No one knows that better than me," Stuart said as he typed again.

Richard got up and paced as far as the receiver's cord would allow. "So, what is it you're proposing?"

"I want to meet with you. In person and in private. I can pick you up tomorrow, if that works with your schedule."

Richard thought about the data he was running. He didn't like interrupting a process; it was too confusing to pick up later in the middle, and control could be lost. He could stay late and finish it tonight…

"Since you're in Bethesda, why don't I have a jet meet you in the morning? Can you take the day off? I'd like to meet at BioSys's Anegada headquarters; that's a place we won't be interrupted. It's a matter of utmost confidentiality."

"Ana—what?" Richard restored the Internet browser and brought up a search engine.

"Anegada, in the British Virgin islands."

"Oh." Richard typed in the island's name and hit "Enter." He got many returns, one at the top with the header "Anegada—the Drowned Island in the BVI." Didn't sound appealing, but still, it was a real place. "Of course, I understand. What time?"

After the call, Richard wandered absentmindedly over to the window, gazing out at the lawn where just yesterday he had seen the press corps and Donaldson begin to take his livelihood away. He took a deep breath, forcing his heart rate to slow. He leaned on the windowsill, hands shoved deep inside his lab coat pockets, and thought about what this extraordinary phone call could mean for him.

And for his father.

But he would have to see him later. For now, there was data to collect.

Richard walked back to the computer and sat down. He opened his data program again, and then paused. He wondered…

He opened the Internet browser again and typed in the URL Stuart Franklin had given him moments earlier. Richard had an excellent, photographic memory and typed it in exactly as it had appeared. The browser helped him by populating the rest of the URL from its memory. He hit the Enter key, ready to enter the username and password again. But a dialog box appeared with a 404 error: "The page requested could not be found."

He checked the address again. He was sure it was correct. He reviewed each letter. No extra spaces. No extra slashes.

"Shit!" Had he been hoaxed after all? Richard stood up and stared at the screen. Then he sat back down, moved his cursor to the end of the URL, and backspaced, taking out the last section. Hit Enter. Still, no document found. He kept backspacing, stopping at each break—each break, he knew, represented a folder in a directory on a computer—but still, nothing. Either someone had taken the machine offline, or someone had served the folders temporarily, in order to fool…

Richard closed his data program again. There was no way his tests could be concluded today, not now, now that perhaps he was about to get on a plane with a journalist, a spy, or even a kidnapper. He didn't have to get on that plane tomorrow. But he was curious. Funny that someone would go to such lengths to lure him. He wanted to know who that person was.

And if he was kidnapped? What was he worth to the NIH? Probably not much scientifically, anymore, but perhaps a lot in terms of public relations. He thought about the bills that came in the mail. The answering machine with no calls to answer. His father, the only person who might notice he was gone…

Richard pushed the odd thoughts from his mind—and this was not difficult. He opened his Internet browser once again. This time, he did a search for Stuart Franklin.

Chapter Fifteen

RICHARD WATCHED THE TWIN-ENGINE JET APPEAR—a beacon in the inky sky. The tarmac was deserted, the pavement cold beneath his feet. He checked his watch. The plane was right on time. Only thirty minutes or so until dawn. Richard had gotten familiar lately with sunrise and sunset times, his internal clock having been reset by his recent late night run into New York City. He hadn't realized the plane would be a small, private jet, and as it neared, he saw only one person aboard—the pilot. The engines spun down, and the pilot disembarked and walked around to meet him. The pilot removed his glove and reached his hand out to Richard.

"Dr. Weigand, nice to meet you."

"Yes," Richard replied, surprised to see Stuart Franklin himself extending his hand. Richard had studied his picture on the BioSys website yesterday.

"Stuart Franklin. Thanks for coming out so damn early. We'll have a great view of the sunrise as we head south. As I mentioned on the phone, we're going to a favorite spot of mine in the British Virgin Islands, a tiny island called Anegada."

Richard studied Stuart's face. He seemed younger than his experience—blond and tanned. In a leather jacket and blue jeans, he looked like an adventurer, not a stuffy billionaire. Richard decided he ought to like him.

But then they moved to board the plane. Richard had never been in a small jet before, despised enclosed spaces, and was certainly not used to being as close to another human being as the seating would obviously require. His heart began to race.

"Well, actually—I—well, you see, I can't actually get in the plane with you."

Stuart stared back at him. Silence.

"I mean, it's so small, and I can't—I mean—"

"You're a man of science, no?" Stuart passed Richard a large aviator headset and ear protection.

"Well, of course." Richard noticed his hands were shaking, but he did not feel them doing so.

"Right, then. Science makes the plane work. You know that."

"I do, but I don't even know you, and it's dangerous, and who knows what might happen."

"Aha, I see." Stuart smiled. "It's a control thing. Listen. I've got an idea."

"You do?"

"Sure. It's simple. You'll just have to fly it."

Richard blanched. "I'm sorry?"

"C'mon. It's easy. I'll show you how."

"Are you crazy? I don't even have a driver's license."

"Well, you'll see what you're missing, then."

Richard paused. He had to admit that he did like the idea of flying the plane himself.

"Do you have a gun?"

"A gun?" Stuart laughed and raised his arms in the air. "Look, you can search me if you want."

Richard stuck his hands firmly in his pockets. "That's okay. Just asking."

"Well? Are we leaving now, or are we going to miss the sunrise?"

In the passenger's seat, Richard strapped himself in as tightly as possible. The takeoff was so smooth that Richard wasn't sure they were even airborne until he noticed the lit-up dials flip wildly in response, an eerie effect in the dark cockpit. Outside, the stars righted themselves in the sky. Richard exhaled.

"You ever been to the Caribbean, Richard?" Stuart's lips moved, but Richard heard him though his earphones, another disconcerting effect.

"I've never been away from the east coast!" said Richard too loudly, forgetting about the headset's microphone.

Stuart laughed comfortingly and patted Richard on the shoulder. Richard tried not to flinch.

"Well, you're in for a treat. Enjoy the trip. We're headed about one hundred miles east of Puerto Rico."

It became obvious that Stuart was a capable pilot, and Richard's heart rate gradually normalized enough to notice that the view *was* stunning. Richard had never thought much about the view from a plane.

The highest building he'd ever been in was the Empire State Building, and that had been when he was a small child, just after his mother died. But now—perhaps it was the time of day—he saw the earth from the sky, as if for the first time. Still, he tried not to lean on the door. Or move. At all.

Stuart pointed out his favorite sights as they flew south. They followed the coastline and watched the small coastal towns waking up. They spotted eddies in the current, a group of seals, and fishing boats returning from night hauls. A couple hours later, they headed further east into the Caribbean. The water was startling in its clarity, and shimmering blue. It was beautiful, but Richard reminded himself to not get carried away. Surely, there was some catch coming, and it might be this plane hitting the water. But before he knew it, they were landing in the middle of a hand-cleared runway of packed red dirt, in the middle of a tall crop of tropical plants.

"This is one of the fields where we grow purple cornflower for the production of Monoplor. BioSys practically owns three of these islands. The British do a good job of preserving them. In fact, this island has a stupendous national park, with habitats for flamingos and ospreys. If you like the outdoors, well, this place has it all—hiking, caves, rainforests, and of course, surfing."

They deplaned, a wave of sea air greeting them, Richard's knees shaking. Richard had never touched alcohol, but could see its allure now. Stuart led them to a waiting jalopy. "We just have a brief drive to my estate, Eastwind, where we can sit and talk. This island is small—only about fifteen square miles."

"Beats downtown Bethesda at lunch hour," remarked Richard as he looked around at the deserted airstrip. He was warming to this place, if only because it was open, he was no longer airborne, and strange bodies did not surround him.

They drove on dusty, unpaved streets and then turned into a long, elegant gravel driveway. Again, they were in the middle of what felt like an orchard or grove. The trees were dense, but the sun trickled in. The day was beginning to heat up, so the shade was welcome. They emerged from the grove in front of a tall, wooden, two-story house that resembled a plantation, with a big front porch, colonial-style windows and columns, and huge wooden doors decorated with ornate carvings of sea creatures.

Inside, everything seemed unusually grand and large, and Richard, a tall man, felt as if he had shrunk on the plane ride. Entering Stuart's house was like entering a museum, and Richard wanted to examine everything—gilded mirrors, chandeliers, and recognizable fine art. A large Picasso hung in the entryway; a collection of Miros lined a hallway. He stopped at each piece of art and got close enough to each surface to see paint strokes. Stuart smiled and led them—slowly, as Richard stopped many times—to a large central living room with a massive table in the center. A huge, shiny ceiling fan with wooden blades turned slowly overhead. At the table, they sat in oversized wicker chairs with feather cushions. Almost immediately, a native woman in uniform presented tall glasses of iced tea with large green mint leaves and a tray of finger sandwiches, tropical fruit, croissants, and other pastry. Then they were alone in the giant room, and the house was silent except for the whir of the fan and the faint patter of the servant's footsteps trailing away.

"So," began Stuart, "you're probably hungry. Have some breakfast." Stuart motioned to the tray, but Richard was looking up at the big ceiling fan.

"How does that stay in the ceiling? It looks too large to be supported by a normal beam."

Stuart looked up at the ceiling. "Well, I don't know. I never really thought about it, to tell you the truth." Stuart poured them both some iced tea.

Richard continued to look up, following the lazy movements of each blade, distracted by its slowness. He perceived the almost strobe-like effect created—light, dark, light, dark. "That is not a normal fan."

Stuart sat back in his chair and surveyed Richard. Was he just one of those eccentric, highly intelligent people one heard about, or was there something else going on? No matter.

Stuart cleared his throat, which had the desired effect, bringing Richard back into his realm. "You must be wondering why I've brought you all the way out here. I didn't mean to be mysterious, but I needed to maintain a certain level of, well, discretion."

"Yes, I was wondering about—" Richard motioned with his hands in the air, searching for the words. "All this." He took a sip of the iced tea, trying awkwardly to navigate around the sprig of mint.

Stuart leaned forward in his chair, placing his hands on his knees. "Well, as I mentioned on the phone, I read your papers with great interest. Stem cells—progenitor cells, the cells responsible for entire organs, hearts and kidneys, skin, even. That these things have been discovered and isolated, the fact that you can see them grow—well, it's remarkable!" Stuart took a sip of his tea, pausing his speech. Richard studied him as he lifted the glass to his lips. He was outwardly handsome, a bit weathered from time spent in the sun; his face was chiseled, yet just imperfect enough to look—normal. Richard didn't know how else to describe it. But somehow, underneath his confidence and his dress shirt, he didn't seem to be exactly the man who had just deftly piloted a plane to a remote island. The room was still quiet.

"I'm fairly certain I have Alzheimer's, you see."

"Alzheimer's?" As he said it, the wheels began to turn in Richard's brain. *But what do I know about Alzheimer's?* He looked blankly back at the powerful CEO, who continued calmly, without any more gravity than if he had been speaking about Petri dishes. Stuart rose, crossing to the large French doors that led out onto a flagstone-paved verandah. He turned back to Richard, hands clasped behind his back, an old technique he had learned from his father, who had been a door-to-door salesman during the Depression. "*Always stand before you ask. And always tuck your head down, just a little. Makes you look humble.*"

"Let me get right to it. I'm interested in a venture—a business venture. Hopefully, a venture with you. I'd like to undergo one of your proposed stem-cell implantation procedures." Richard's face showed shock and surprise, so Stuart held up his hands in a disarming gesture. "I understand you haven't done it on humans yet, but I would provide you with testing facilities, a state-of-the-art lab, human subjects, and all the supplies you'd need." Richard could hardly believe what he was hearing. He was afraid he hadn't understood correctly and felt his face flushing.

"And of course, a generous salary," continued Stuart, misinterpreting Richard's blush. "You could hire your own people." Stuart sat back down in the deep chair, its wicker creaking under his weight. His pitch now out, Stuart paused to let the idea sink in.

Richard looked up at the ceiling. "Well, it's possible, of course. I mean, scientifically." He watched the large fan spin lazily overhead, its blades making constant shadows on the ceiling. "How far along is your, uh—your—" Richard, having spent most of his adult life in a laboratory, had never developed much in the way of clinical skills, a fact he was very much regretting after he spoke those clumsy words.

"My disease? Early." Stuart fetched a remote from a nearby console table and turned the ceiling fan off.

Richard recovered. "Thank you. That was really distracting me. It's interference—light interference." Richard sat back in his chair, more focused now. "You mentioned human subjects. I don't know much about the world of human clinical trials. My career has mostly involved mice and primates, but I do know that work on humans can't be done without a considerable amount of formality and structure—a hospital or university set up to review the protocol, recruit the subjects, and oversee the research."

"But Richard, look who you're speaking to! My company is one of the largest 'structures,' as you say, that one could hope to find. Hell, we develop new drugs for clinical human use every year."

"Of course, of course," said Richard, not entirely convinced, but then again, what did he know about the private sector? "So, somehow, we would work with BioSys."

"Yes, exactly. A simple R & D setup, that's all. But listen, Richard, before we go much further with this discussion, I'm going to have to ask you to sign a confidentiality agreement. You understand. Intellectual property and all. Yours and mine. You have the science, but I have the idea about how to use the science. And the money."

From a nearby desk, Stuart retrieved a pen and a triplicate form and handed it to Richard for his perusal. It was titled *Non-Disclosure Agreement,* a form Richard had seen many times at the NIH. It was covered in legalese, but the summary was bolded near the bottom signature line. "I agree to not disclose any items discussed at the meeting on (DATE) at (LOCATION) between Stuart Franklin/BioSys and (PARTY) to anyone at any time unless summoned by a federal court of law of the United States of America."

Stuart filled in the date, place, and Richard's full name, and then signed the form. Stuart passed Richard the pen. Richard thought about the ramifications of signing. And then an image of Donaldson on the lawn appeared, the flash bulbs going off, and the fact that Donaldson hadn't even bothered to speak to him, still, after all that work. *Worst case*, he thought, *there's always Dad's lawyer*. Richard signed.

"Now, with that business out of the way, how about a boat tour of the area?"

Richard could only smile, visions of a brand-new, sparkling lab floating before his eyes, a treasure chest. As they stood, Richard looked up again at the fan.

"You know, you should really get that looked at."

"Yes, I'll do that," remarked Stuart, barely listening.

On the small, inconspicuous motorboat, Stuart drove at a fast clip, the sea spray meeting Richard's dry skin. It was strange, thought Richard. Two new modes of transport in one day. Unlike the small plane, the boat calmed him—all that open space. About five minutes out, Stuart turned the boat then slowly maneuvered it into a cove. "It's quiet here," explained Stuart as he cut the engine. The sun was making its way up in the sky, but a large rock formation provided shade and clear, almost motionless water. Both seated now, with only the surrounding tropical fish to overhear, Stuart outlined his ides for a new, secret company that would exist financially outside of BioSys, but be physically located within it, here, in Anegada. Stuart was emphatic about the secrecy. Richard would not be able to tell anyone about his venture, and his staff members would only know about their own jobs, not the overall mission to successfully implant viable stem cells into Stuart's ailing brain. There were many details to work out still, but the offer was a dream come true for Richard, and Stuart knew it. He'd researched everything Richard might need—equipment, staff, subjects, money. Stuart had almost thought of everything.

"Well, there's something I'd like to mention. My father is a neurosurgeon; although he doesn't practice much anymore. His—"

"License has been suspended; yes, I know. I also know he was a pioneer in micro-neurosurgery and stereotactic procedures, the cornerstones of modern neurosurgery."

"Yes, that's all correct," replied Richard, wide-eyed at the interest the powerful man had shown in his life. "He's always been a risk-taker. He's taken patients most surgeons would pass on, and some people think that's hurt his career. He just wants to make a difference, you see—in his lifetime." Aloud, the last words didn't sound as convincing as they did in his head. He should have let his father say them himself.

"Of course! Who wouldn't? I'd like him on the team, if you think that's the right move."

Richard was obviously relieved. "He's my only family, you know."

Stuart stood and made a show of coiling anchor rope. “Without risk, there is no big payoff, Richard. You found that working for the government, I suppose, while walking down the straight path.” Stuart paused and looked beyond the cove. “But you know, on either path, well, there are always hard decisions to be made. You can’t avoid that.”

Richard didn’t know how to respond to this, never having worked anywhere else and not understanding Stuart’s philosophy. So he looked out at the blue water, too; it was bluer than he had ever seen—a living cliché. Its clarity almost shocked him. In the distance was the island from which they’d sailed. It looked to Richard like one of the landscapes in a glass dome that tourists purchased, preserved in surreal perfection. The hills of neighboring islands were covered in plants and flowers, like glimmering emeralds. He imagined he could move to paradise. The job offer was almost a miracle, and its locale was an Eden.

It dawned on Richard that he had been thinking only of himself. “Can you tell me a little more about the human subjects?”

Stuart sat back down. “Alzheimer’s patients from a teaching hospital that BioSys funds. I just set up a little protocol, as R & D, you see. It’s common practice when dealing with cancer, so why shouldn’t it be the same for those suffering from dementia? In the past, we’ve also used prisoners—with their full informed consent, of course. We get the subjects we need; they get funding. That’s how it works.” Richard had never worked directly with people, only monkeys, and so had never heard of this practice. But, he reasoned, it seemed logical and convenient.

“What about some kind of oversight committee or review board?”

“Oh, we’ve got all that; don’t worry. Sure, they’ve tightened the reins over the years, but we’ve bounced back. We do a lot of work here in the British Virgin Islands because the political climate here is more research-driven.”

Later that day, Stuart sent Richard back to DC on a commercial jet from the main island, Tortola. In his first-class seat—thankfully, no one beside him—he replayed the other conversations he’d had with Stuart. Richard was scheduled to deliver his decision about the venture in forty-eight hours, so the plane ride home seemed short; he needed time to think. He absentmindedly accepted a glass of champagne.

The comment Stuart made about working in the British Virgin Islands had stayed with him. Reading between the lines, Richard could see that BioSys did their research in the islands because there were fewer regulations. Well, if BioSys was already in that business and making drugs sold in the United States, things must be legit. Other pharmas no doubt did the same things. Still…

Richard now realized they hadn't discussed where they would get the stem cells for this venture: Richard possessed only a small supply of a potentially difficult type of embryonic cells. That could be a problem.

He also realized only now, after some reflection and another glass of complimentary champagne, that they would need more people for this venture—specialists, like expert radiologists, lab technicians, and surgery staff. How would they be part of the team without giving away the secret? Perhaps Stuart had already taken care of that.

The opportunity seemed perfect. Was it too perfect? As the plane landed at Ronald Reagan International Airport, he had a vague notion that he should research BioSys more carefully before accepting, but he knew in his heart that he would find nothing to discourage him. He needed an outlet for his work, he needed the money, and he needed—what? Recognition? No. Something else. The sales pitch he had just been presented, the plane, the lush island, the money, had been carefully planned, and it had worked, in some way. Richard was vaguely aware of having been manipulated, but also proud to have been fussed over, for once in his lonesome life. He and his father would obviously accept.

His father…

The next morning, Richard took a late morning train into New York City to confer with his father.

Bob Weigand, MD, maintained an office at a large New York medical school and hospital. Although he no longer practiced there, he had many colleagues who supported him—protected him—and enjoyed having him in the building for his stories and advice. Bob was famous for the large amounts of time he spent with his peers consulting on difficult or unusual cases. He loved his work and son equally.

Today, Bob Weigand was not in his office, but in the university's largest lecture hall. Richard hustled over to the student center just in time to hear his father's opening remarks. The place was nearly full, so Richard learned against the rear wall of the large auditorium. He could see Bob down at the lectern, commanding and confident. He glanced at the programs stacked on a chair near the entrance: "A Short History of Stem Cells." Richard reflected that the history was actually quite long. It was just like his father to try to sum up a complicated matter into digestible pieces, leaving the details to others, like himself.

"Stem cells, as you all know," began Bob, clearing his throat, "is the hot science topic of our time. Today, we'll discuss what the fuss is all about."

Richard heard a rustling of paper and notebooks, a sound that had once comforted him, but now, he wasn't so sure about papers, abstracts, and peer reviews. What had they really done for him, or his father, for that matter? Well, they had brought Stuart Franklin to him, at least.

"The term 'neurogenesis' is derived from two Greek words: 'neuro,' indicating neurons, the basic building blocks of the brain; and 'genesis,' of course connoting a beginning stemmed from some union—Adam and Eve, life, Earth, or even the beginning of time. But why is the term important for us today? A short history of neurogenesis is worth examining as background for the study of stem cells.

"Up to twenty years ago, the dogma in neurology, neuro-anatomy, and embryology was that a person is born with as many neurons as he or she would ever possess. Those cells, once dead, could not be revived. Of course, we now know that to be untrue. The brain actually continues to produce healthy neurons throughout most of our lives, but it took almost twenty years and more than a few renegade scientists to prove it. Remember, a good scientist will always question dogma!

"The first, and considered perhaps the most unorthodox, was a man named Fernando Nottebohm, a zoologist preoccupied with discovering how and why birds sang. Fascinated by canaries and other singing birds, Nottebohm performed a long series of tests at Rockefeller University beginning as early as 1967. Quickly, Nottebohm determined that the birds could learn new melodies in different seasons—but how were they learning? With more research, he learned that, by administering male testosterone to a female canary, he could make the female's nuclei grow, doubling it in size. This contradicted what he and others has been taught—that the brain was static, incapable of producing new neurons. By the early 1980s, the idea had come to him. Could it be true that new neurons were born as old ones died?

"Again, this idea was revolutionary, and Nottebohm was discouraged by his colleagues. But, after more study, he and an assistant discovered, using a then-new radioactive tracer system, that the birds were indeed producing thousands of new neurons every day. Neurogenesis was definitely occurring."

Bob paused to take a swallow of water.

"Nottebohm's work eventually led to a major paradigm shift in the field of neurology, but skeptics didn't take his work seriously. They questioned his methods and couldn't accept the idea that perhaps what was true—if it was—in birds could apply to other species, or humans. His work was shelved, considered 'cute' and precious, but without broader application.

"In 1989, a curious young post-doctoral researcher in behavioral psychology named Elizabeth Gould became interested in neurogenesis when some of her work on stress in rats produced puzzling effects. In her study, she removed the adrenal glands of rats and watched the consequential rapid death of the rat's hippocampus—yet, upon examination of the hippocampus, she saw that there were the same number of neurons as before the damage. Why? She began to research neurogenesis.

"Gould then discovered another scientist who studied neurogenesis in the 1960s at MIT, Joseph Altman. Altman published several papers in reputable scientific journals about his discovery: that new neurons are formed in the brains of adult rats, cats, and guinea pigs. However, at the time, Altman's techniques were deemed primitive, and thus his results were open to question. Altman was ignored then ridiculed. He was a pioneer, but he was forgotten and forced to move to Purdue University when MIT would not grant him tenure. Purdue was lucky to have gotten him!

"Gould next discovered Michael Kaplan, a researcher at Boston University and later at the University of New Mexico who had used more advanced methods to trace new neuron development in the adult brain. His work met resistance, and he left the field.

"Gould finally began her own work. For eight years, she worked on neurogenesis, until she was out on research's furthest limbs. She moved to Princeton in 1997, and the work started to gel. She began to publish papers that showed neurons were produced in the hippocampus of tree shrews. Then a paper on New World monkeys showed adult production of new neurons. She repeated the work on Old World monkeys with success. By 1999, she had discovered that not only are new neurons produced in the adult primate brain, they even appeared in the neocortex, the area responsible for sophisticated thought and language. It was extremely controversial, and the traditional school took issue with her far-out results. Gould continues her work today and is one of the most sought-after researchers. She is the youngest tenured member of the Princeton psychology department. Her motto is to follow her scientific interests instead of the science community's latest dogma.

"Gould, of course, has a star counterpart named Fred Gage, whose name has become permanently linked to the arena of stem cell breakthroughs. No doubt, you know of his studies with the famous Karolinska Institute in Sweden and his work at the Salk Institute. He was the first to experiment with fetal cell transplants for use in Parkinson's models and the first to do conclusive testing in humans, which proved, once and for all, that the adult brain produces new neurons. For this, Fred Gage is famous, and rightly so.

"Gage also gives us the first use of the term 'stem cells,' which he defines as, 'A population of cells capable of extended self-renewal and the ability to generate multilineage cell types.' These are the progenitor cells—cells that make other cells—capable of neurogenesis in the healthy organ, tissue, or brain. What Nottebohm stumbled on in his birds was probably the bird equivalent of stem cells. You've all read about the great promise of stem cells for use in treating or curing diabetes, heart disease, Parkinson's, MS, and even Huntington's. But how do these cells actually work?

"Stem cells are unique because they undergo both self-renewal and differentiation. Adult mammal cells are capable of developing into a number of different cells with high telomerase activity. If cultured, these cells have been shown to be pluripotent and have long-term potential to expand without limits.

"There are two types of stem cells that matter today: embryonic stem cells and adult—already differentiated—stem cells. The former are derived from early human embryos as the fertilized egg begins developing into a fetus. At the embryo, or blastocyst stage—four to six days old—clusters of these cells are present. Extracted from this stage, the embryonic stem cells can be cultured indefinitely or cryopreserved in a freezing unit at minus 80 degrees centigrade.

"Adult stem cells are cells differentiated into the tissue types that can reproduce. For example, heart muscle cells for repair, pancreas ilet cells for insulin production, or neural progenitor stem cells that will develop into neurons and glia cells as identified by Fred Gage and others. These neural stem cells have been shown capable of repairing some areas of damaged brain tissue, especially in children or young adults. As one grows older, the supply of the differentiated stem cells grows less and less. Therefore, when neurons are damaged or destroyed in neurodegenerative diseases such as Parkinson's, the brain, in this case, has limited regenerative power. In young, healthy brains, these neural adult stem cells are found in specific areas of the brain, and these areas of stem cell production obviously warrant more research. Can they cure disease? Are they the 'magic bullet' the press has made them out to be? Only research can answer that complicated question."

Richard considered his father's statement. While it was true that more research was needed—a lifetime of it, probably—and while it was also true that Richard himself had helped his father with this part of the lecture, today it didn't sound right to him. Now that Richard actually had the chance to see his ideas through, instead of toiling in the lab year after year, only to have his funding cut, the sentiment seemed simply outdated.

"In conclusion to today's very broad introduction to the world of neurogenesis and stem cells, let me say, although it has proved complicated and politically impossible to perform stem cell research on human embryos, the work will continue all over the world. Great progress has been made via thoughtful in-vitro studies, like Elizabeth Gould's, which didn't even involve human embryos—and this work should and will continue. And the fact is, even if there were no debate in our press about the use of embryos for science, we'd still be faced with a giant problem: what is the role of science in our modern life?

"Thank you very much for your kind attention. There are reprints and references as usual at the back of the room. And don't forget—question everything."

The crowd applauded politely, but Richard was keenly aware that the lecture did not receive the hearty and robust applause that had characterized previous Bob Weigand lectures. Perhaps the news of the NIH canceling its stem cell research had tainted the students' impressions. Or, the kids might have been expecting the lecture to become a rally to protest the ceasing of research. It was hard to tell.

And then, another thought occurred to him as he stood against the back wall waiting for his father, the crowd dissipating past him. Maybe he was becoming a Nottebohm! How exciting that thought was! Richard waved to his father, who was still on stage. Richard felt a new determination as his mind raced through all the ways he would take this opportunity with Stuart to make the most thorough science possible. Stuart was right. Being at the NIH had bogged him down, taken his mind off the ultimate goals. He was sure they could pull it off and prove their methods sound. He might be leaving the NIH, but he wasn't giving up the world of neurogenesis, as others had. Let them laugh at his passion; let them cancel his research! They would be astounded when they met the new Stuart Franklin.

Richard and Bob walked to Bob's tiny office, chatting on the way about the finer points of the lecture. Inside, Bob's office looked, as usual, like a war room, the opposite of his own tidy quarters at the NIH. The cramped desk was a confused heap; the floor was covered in CT and MRI scans and stacks of selectively read newspapers and medical journals. The piles were so high that the publications slid off if you so much as brushed next to them, and then it was a struggle to not slip on their glossy covers. When there, Richard always had to fight the urge to haul in the nearest trash bin and start tossing everything into it. His father took a seat and began opening the mail, adding more junk to a pile.

"Another letter asking when I plan to resign!" Bob waved the letter in the air and let out a hearty laugh. Richard hefted a stack of patient charts from the only guest chair in the room. Since there was nowhere else to put them, he sat with them in his lap.

"At you again, are they?"

"They never quit. Claim they need the office space! Hah! This isn't an office, it's a closet, I always say. Anyway, wait until they hear my plan for the cells. Then they'll be begging me to stay."

"Well, you may not have to do that."

"Oh, no? Why's that?" replied his father, absentmindedly, still looking at his correspondence.

"You won't believe where I've just come from. I met a man, a powerful man." The phone rang, interrupting Richard, and Bob promptly answered the call. Richard listened to his father talk to a person calling for advice about a recurring glioblastoma. Richard knew those brain tumors were usually deadly and inoperable. His father listened carefully, sympathized, and gave suggestions regarding radical experimental trials that the caller might look into, even reading off two phone numbers, fetched miraculously from underneath a pile of something, with which the caller might get more information. He watched his father talk, as he had many times before. Bob was in his early seventies and sharp as tack. He still exercised at least three times a week, ate well, and read voraciously, and it showed. His eyes were alert and focused as he explained basic brain tumor therapies to the caller. He looked invigorated and engaged. A full twenty minutes had passed when Bob hung up the phone and Richard continued his exciting story.

"Now then, my boy. What were you saying?"

Richard recounted his day spent with Stuart Franklin on the tiny Caribbean island called Anegada. Bob was naturally astounded and enchanted by the description of the boat ride they had taken. Bob had always dreamed of having his own sailboat. Richard went over the specifics.

"If we accept, we would need to do a short trial on animals then start with humans, not unlike what you've been thinking about. Instead of grafting the stem cells like you're doing here, we can finally try to implant them. Stuart wants to test the most ambitious hypotheses we have. All in secret, of course, to protect Stuart. He wants everything performed with complete discretion."

"I understand," said Bob. "He sounds like a smart man. You've recounted the two keys: how we get the cells into the right part of the brain and how to monitor what they're up to once implanted. Where do they go? And how far will they travel in the brain? And naturally, the secrecy—he doesn't want anyone to know he's losing his memory. But who are the subjects?"

"Teaching hospital patients. Stuart has access to the hospital and access to subjects through other BioSys clinical trials, he says."

"Hmmm," sighed Bob, as he leaned back in his old, worn swivel chair. He rocked for a moment and rubbed his eyes. This was his grave-thinking pose. Richard watched his father, whose long fingers were cracked and worn, but tan and agile. Bob had been courted, once, by the most prestigious cancer research centers. He had seen all kinds of programs, clinical trials, underhanded procedures, and heroics. He knew his way around the ins and outs of the research world, but this was more than a break, it was manna from heaven. Richard studied his father's long nose. Bob's parents had been Ukrainian immigrants, and both Bob and he had the distinctive noses of their ancestors. "We'll need a contact there for follow up in the teaching hospital."

"Stuart said he'd handle all of that. In that sense, he'll actually be the trial's principal investigator and its key patient. He wants to undergo the procedure as soon as possible." Bob rocked some more.

"Of course he does. Of course." Bob got up and started to pace in the tiny space around his chair. "Sounds too good to be true, no?" It didn't feel good to hear this from someone else, Richard thought. But what other avenues did they have to run down? All they had now were a few stem cells. No patients, no lab, no help, and certainly no money.

"Well, I have to call him by end-of-day tomorrow and deliver our decision. Naturally, he's in a big hurry to begin. I can't see what real harm there could be in trying. We could always come back." Richard took a deep breath before he added, "And we could sure use the money."

The legal fees from the "accident"—or rather, malpractice, trial had bankrupted them, but Bob didn't like hearing that fact mentioned aloud. He always interpreted such acknowledgment as a son's cheap-shot criticism. But Richard's modest, government-strapped salary was all that kept them from poverty; the malpractice insurance had only scratched the surface and paid the victim's family. Bob's only income came from a few patients who insisted on paying him and a small stipend from the university. As things stood now, they would be making legal payments for the rest of their lives. They had no savings, and Richard worried about Bob's health; should it decline, how could he afford good care for him? The room grew tense as Bob continued to pace; Richard was sorry he'd mentioned the money troubles—they were like an armed intruder in the stuffy office. Nowhere to hide.

"Yes, the money," groaned Bob with the usual disdain for the subject. "More importantly, we have a chance to really shine here. I'm seventy-seven years old. I want to make a difference in my lifetime. Can't you understand that?" Bob had delivered this speech before, but today Richard really felt it, and so he didn't interrupt his father. Usually Richard suspected that his father actually wanted to become famous more than he wanted to be a humanitarian. But today Richard believed him; things had changed for both of them.

Bob continued, "Can you imagine the impact this work could have? Can you imagine the hope it will inspire? I've been talking about it for years now: a molecular-level solution. It could be a cure for Parkinson's, Alzheimer's, even cancer—who knows? Think of that, how big that is. Stem cells are the most exciting thing to happen to neurosurgery in my life, and no doubt for years in the future. Imagine replacing the dead neuron cells of the brain! We'd be helping nature perform its most awesome feat—neurogenesis! Look at this." Bob hastily grabbed a PET brain scan from one of his stacks. He held it up to the light from the desk lamp. The film showed a jumble of digital bits in rainbow colors. Richard saw spots of intense red, orange, yellow, green, blue, and then purple. "This is the brain of an advanced Alzheimer's patient. Notice the areas of blue and purple. There are many of them here in this cluster, in the hippocampus. Those are the areas lacking metabolic activity, as in: dead. It's quite widespread, as you can see. The areas that lean toward the red end of the spectrum are cells that are still metabolizing. Not so many, as you can also see. Mr.—let's see, what his name? There are so many, this is the problem. Ah, yes, Mr. Joe Harper. Mr. Harper is another victim of his own brain. But, if we could give him new neural stem cells that would grow and duplicate themselves!"

"Dad, I know all of this. And I'm glad you're as excited as I am. Maybe you could bring some of those films to show Stuart and give him a better idea of the magnitude of what he's proposing."

"Yes, I'll do that. Good idea." Bob sat back down again and moved his reading glasses up to his forehead. He looked tired. For an instant, Richard wondered if his father was up to the trip. What was he getting them into? And would it work? Suddenly, Richard felt incredible pressure. Why hadn't he realized sooner the enormity of experimenting on one of the richest men in the world? But then Bob broke the silence.

"So, when are we leaving?"

Richard smiled in relief. "I think I'd better start getting us packed. Stuart will collect us at the airport in a week." Bob's giant grin helped Richard mask his fear. But of course, they would try. They had to.

Chapter Sixteen

STUART FED THE NEXT document into the shredder. In his office that morning, he'd stumbled over the folder stuffed with his research on stem cells, including all the papers written by his new friend, Dr. Richard Weigand. Now was as good a time as any to get rid of them. The less Stuart Franklin was connected to this enterprise, the better. Not that he expected anyone to learn of it, he mused as he destroyed the last document. He wiped his hands together in satisfaction and moved toward the door.

Now, I just have to wait, he thought.

At his security facility, Fred's eyes scanned the monitors of his surveillance control center, and then back again. A movement caught his eye. He leaned in closer, his eyes straining though his drug store reading glasses. He recognized the figure immediately. What was Stuart doing in the basement of the furnace room? Fred, his mind on automatic pilot, noted the time and date, and watched his long-time friend and boss move into an elevator. Fred watched the image from the elevator's wide-angle lens. The elevator alighted; Stuart adjusted his tie and ran a hand through his thick head of blond hair.

Chapter Seventeen

RICHARD STOOD IN THE DOORWAY of his new lab on Anegada, in the British Virgin Islands. Movers and technicians worked busily, putting the last pieces of heavy equipment in place. The men were all locals and spoke little English, but Richard managed to direct the operation. He had been overprotective about the vials of stem cells, and his back still throbbed from insisting on helping move the freezer cabinet himself. He leaned now against the doorjamb for support, suddenly feeling exhaustion's pull. The last seventy-two hours had been full of details and decisions, pushing and pulling, yes-ing and no-ing. He let his eyes close for a moment then he remembered that Stuart was expecting him and his father for dinner at the sprawling plantation-style estate where Richard had been propositioned just a week earlier. He pushed himself off the wall and went next door to Bob's new office.

"Richard!" burst out Bob when he saw his son enter the office. Bob was spinning around in his new office chair like a kid, a grin of glee upon his youthful face. It'd been ages since he'd inhabited a proper office, and now here he was in a glorious suite with closets, filing cabinets, even his own bathroom. He spun around in the expensive office chair again. "Can I keep it?" Bob joked. When in a good mood, Bob made this type of remark about his son's financial support. Usually, the subject of money disgusted him. He had been burned by its power throughout his life—promised grants never granted, the never-ending chase for research money, the constant pull of purse strings from "benefactors."

Richard allowed himself a good laugh and sat down opposite his father's huge new maple desk. Bob had already begun to decorate the walls with his various awards, photos with proud patients, and an old portrait of Esther, Bob's long-dead wife and Richard's mother.

Stuart had directed that a wing of the BioSys research facility be converted for their use. The wing included a state-of-the-art radiology unit, a series of operating and recovery rooms, and a warren of lab space. The staff they had recruited would be arriving in the next couple of days. Richard had phoned an old colleague, an excellent radiologist who had gone bankrupt over-extending his company into the world of cutting-edge machinery. The man's multi-million dollar dream facility was now a wash, and he was anxious to investigate the new imaging breakthroughs that only big money could buy. The friend had agreed to the job offer without hesitation.

As Bob and Richard walked outside to their Land Rover, Richard heard the not-so-distant hum of a private jet landing, already a familiar sound on the island.

Chapter Eighteen

RICHARD, BOB, AND STUART were finishing their meals, which had been served on another giant table in an enclosed verandah at Eastwind. The grilled shrimp in banana leaves with mango salsa were delectable, fresh, and perfect. The verandah afforded a view of the sweeping estate grounds—Richard estimated at least ten acres. The island had just become dark, the kind of isolated darkness that makes a city person notice that stars do actually shine. Fireflies danced around the grounds, the only illumination for miles around.

"Well, we need to start with monkeys," Bob was explaining. "That should take about six to twelve weeks—"

"Six to twelve weeks! What about me?" Stuart was astonished and held his wine glass in mid-air, too shocked to move. Richard and Bob had expected such a reaction. Naturally, he would want to rush them, but they must convince Stuart that this was a risky operation, and they had not performed any primate testing themselves, let alone human tests.

Richard explained. "I know it seems like a long time, but it's actually a very abbreviated testing period. You'll see. And while we work on the monkeys, we can start growing the embryonic human cells we already have and testing them in-vitro."

"What kind of testing is necessary? I thought you had already done tests. I read your papers."

"Well, first of all, in the monkeys, we need to investigate numerous factors that will apply to the human use of stem cells. For instance, we need to test how the stem cells diffuse once in the brain," began Bob.

"And how far they'll travel," added Richard.

"Yes, and we'll be testing our delivery method as well," continued Bob.

"There are many technical factors, you see. After all, this has never been done. We'll give you updates just as soon as we get them."

"Tell me more about the testing period." Stuart was calmer now and admonished himself for his outburst. He knew this process, after all. Why did he think it could be different for him? He wasn't so foolish as to throw his life away by getting an overdose. *Could one "overdose" on stem cells*?

"Dad will start the monkeys, while I start in the lab. We figured the monkeys could come from your own research labs so we don't draw any attention to the project. Those monkeys have rights, you know!"

"Don't remind me. Our ABT-55 is currently working with monkeys, so your project will blend right in, no problem. Good idea."

Richard noticed a smile from his father. Because monkeys were expensive, Bob and Richard rarely found themselves in the position to call for their testing.

Base hit, thought Bob, who continued where his son had left off. "I'll test a total of twelve monkeys, broken into groups. I'll be conducting tests to determine safe dosage, rate of injection, location, method for injection, and collect data on adverse events. Then I'll routinely scan the monkey brains and watch for improvement."

"Do the cells really start working and growing that quickly?"

Richard replied. "We expect them to, yes. Improvement has been seen in previous mice experiments in a very short amount of time, even a few weeks. The cells grow quickly; that's part of their power. Think of the speed of a newborn's growth."

"Yes, I remember," trailed Stuart in automatic response, although he didn't remember—not because of his condition, but because when he'd had a newborn, he had never been at home long enough for any impression to form. For the first time in his life, he realized this. It had never before crossed his mind.

Hattie, the cook, presented warm berry tarts with ice cream and coffee to the group as Stuart leaned back in his chair, trying to recall just one mental picture of his newborn baby girl, without success. Richard continued, and Stuart focused again on the subject of saving his life.

"For the monkey trial to begin, I will first have to harvest embryonic and neural monkey stem cells from suitable fertilized monkey eggs. That will be quick and easy—we've already formulated those monkey cells once before. The monkeys will be divided into two main groups: those who receive embryonic stem cells and those who receive neural stem cells. They'll be further divided corresponding to the surgical approach taken. Dad will explain more of that later.

"After Dad implants the cells into the monkeys, I'll begin work on the human embryonic stem cell line I was working on when I left the

NIH. Because they're embryonic cells, it is difficult to predict when they differentiate and what triggers their development into hearts or kidneys or brains. I'll need a few weeks, at least, to test this particular human study. Of course, I've been already working on this for years, but never for human application. Depending on the results of the tests, we might need a new source of human stem cells soon."

"Where do we get them? From the subjects at the Alzheimer's hospital?"

Richard shook his head. "I'm not sure where we'll get a human cell source for the human tests. The purest source is the most controversial, and that's human embryos. Although this has been deemed the best method, it's also the most scientifically complicated. We don't always know how they will grow, or what they will grow into. At the NIH, we had access to reproductive clinics and donated embryos, but since these cells can be so tricky, we also experimented on other sources of human stem cells, some quite interesting—scalp, skin, and even bone marrow. In a perfect world, the best and most predictable alternative source of cells would be those harvested from young adult brains." Richard paused and sipped his coffee. He smiled and added, "But who wants to give up those? Not me!" Richard laughed. "And we're not sure how viable those are anyway."

Stuart did not laugh. "You said, 'In a perfect world.' That's what I want. That's what we're here for." Stuart's voice was tense. Had he picked the right group of researchers? Why did they not understand they could get anything—*anything*—they wanted? His face betrayed his sudden anxiety.

Bob looked at Richard, who was embarrassed, having unwittingly committed a faux pas. He would have a talk with Richard about leaving the delicate matters to him. Bob understood Stuart's desperation keenly, and spoke up to cover Richard's off-hand dismissal of any possible avenue of treatment. "They haven't yet volunteered to donate cells. That may not be true in the near future, when people understand their value. We'll make sure you have the best cells possible. We may even be able to use young adult cadavers, right, Richard?" prompted Bob.

"Of course, yes, there's been great promise in that arena. I should have mentioned that earlier. Quite a good idea." Richard wasn't sure why he was covering his tracks. Adult neural stem cells were the best source, but obviously off-limits. He couldn't think of anything less plausible than extracting stem cells from adults. Who would agree to undergo or undertake such a procedure?

Stuart nodded, apparently reassured. "So we see what happens with the cells you have. If we need new adult stem cells from skin, bone, or a cadaver, how do we pick the donor?"

"Younger adults would be preferable, that's for sure. Their cells are literally stronger," said Richard, back on track now.

"And those with smarter brains! Don't forget that," chuckled Bob.

"Really? Smarter? Is he joking, or will the intelligence of the donor actually affect my intelligence?"

"Well, yes and no." This time it was Richard's save. "Most serious scientists have only concentrated on restoring damaged neural functions, not making better ones. The work is hard enough to conduct, considering the ethical issues and expense. This isn't *Frankenstein*, but we're getting close to making you healthier, at least. Since genetic matter is being transplanted, it is possible that certain traits or abilities could be transplanted as well, but it seems highly speculative at this early stage."

Stuart let the matter drop, and a smile played at his mouth. "Well, let's make sure I don't *lose* any intelligence!" They all laughed.

"Now, let me show you what I envision for the surgical aspect of the human trial." Bob pulled a small pad of white paper he always carried from his coat pocket and began to illustrate, using a red felt tip pen.

"I would like to try two surgical methods, both of which are very non-invasive, very discreet. The first would be a transnasal stereotactic one—we'd use fiber optic cannula to deliver the cells, implanting them in the wall of the third ventricle, where we believe they will begin to do their good work. The second," Bob paused to flip to a blank sheet of paper, "is a transventricular method. Again, using the special cannula, we'd pass through the cisterna magna to the fourth ventricle then through the Aqueduct of Sylvius, into the third ventricle. Both methods would be outpatient procedures—the cells lie just beneath the wall, you see. Both methods would be almost non-invasive. With the transnasal approach, there would be no external signs of surgery. No incision in the scalp. And the transventricular would only result in a small scar at the base of the neck." Bob replaced the cap on the felt tip pen and smiled.

Hattie arrived with coffee warm-ups, and Stuart leaned back in his chair, resuming his role as host. "Let me tell you a bit about this stunning place we find ourselves enjoying. These islands were taken over from the Dutch by the Brits in 1666 and have remained colonies ever since. The governor here is a representative of the queen, which I find just fascinating, don't you?" Before they could reply, Stuart continued. "There is a legislative council, a bit like our Congress, consisting of popularly elected officials. Mostly, all this official activity takes place on the main island, Tortola. But BioSys didn't want to be in the center of things—easier to get things done when one is a little remote, you see. There is a great deal of folklore about this island. The shore contains very hazardous coral reefs, and as a result, there have been literally hundreds of shipwrecks just off these shores," Stuart motioned to the dark sea beyond the terrace. "There are swimming beaches, as well, but mostly, this water attracts divers and yachtsmen. If you've never dived, you must try it! I can arrange for a guide to take you out anytime."

"I'd hate to get shipwrecked," Richard said softly, the reality of his new remoteness sinking in. He had never been to an island before, and although he had enjoyed entertaining thoughts of the blue water, sandy beaches, and being away from crowds, the fact that there was no major airport or convenience stores to visit on late nights gave him pause.

They made a schedule for the next day's events, said good evening, and Richard and Bob made their way back to their Land Rover, identifiable by the giant BioSys logo painted on the driver's side door. Tiny torches stuck in the grass lit the long, stately gravel driveway. As Bob backed the car out of the drive, Richard noticed that the torches resembled emergency exit path lighting in airplanes. Eastwind estate receded into the distance, and they found themselves in the pitch black of the island. It had a been a grueling day, and Richard vaguely remembered the way back to their own hacienda, where they had been early this morning, only briefly, to drop their bags. It was so dark Richard had to struggle to make out the correct house number.

Their unit was nestled alongside the ocean amid a complex of similar vacation-rental condominiums. Theirs was obviously one of the largest and most luxurious, with many amenities and a patio that opened onto the fine white sand beach. The roar of the ocean filled the house as they entered, and Richard remembered he had left the patio door open earlier. Or had he? He was too exhausted to think straight. He stood and watched the view, too tired to get into bed just yet. In the far distance, he saw a lighthouse, its lamp making a hypnotic appearance every few seconds. He wondered how far away it was.

Tomorrow, he would get a map.

Chapter Nineteen

RICHARD LOOKED DOWN into the spinning centrifuge. He had given the harvested monkey cells to Bob that morning, and now got down to the human cell work at hand. His job was to begin converting general embryonic stem cells to neural stem cells—those that could potentially repair damaged neurons—in the next three weeks. He watched the stem cells spin.

Although Richard had been performing testing on embryonic stem cells for a few years at the NIH, he'd never been able to examine their human applications, only their basic science characteristics—what they were composed of, how stable they were, how they interacted with other cells. Now that he had a chance to actually place these cells in a human brain, he wanted to be sure he performed very accurate science to determine the viability of using them. With the assistance of his staff, he intended to create a highly organized lab study. Behind him, a large white board charted their approach.

The cells he had were embryonic, and for that reason, it was very difficult to direct and culture them to evolve into, say, heart cells, pancreas cells, or neural cells. But of course, Richard was only interested in cells that would evolve into brain, or neural, stem cells. Richard had developed sophisticated molecular technologies to divide the cells and find potential neural ones, and was now 90% sure that he had a sample of cells "programmed" to become brain cells, or neurons and glia. Richard couldn't be sure the cells would work as planned, however, until he saw them grow *in vivo*, in a live host. He didn't run the risk of creating a horrifying organ in the wrong spot, however; the cells would simply die if their surroundings were not correct. In other words, a brain cell would not grow in a heart, or vice versa.

He knew the embryonic stem cells could form tumors; he'd shown that to be true in earlier mice studies done at the NIH. This happened because the neural stem cells overproduced the glia, or supporting cells, forming potentially harmful teratoma tumors. Quite clearly, there was more work to be done with these cells. In a human brain, would the embryonic stem cells convert themselves into neural ones, or would they cause a tumor? It was difficult to know how stem cells would react in the brain. There had never been a precise way to study this. Although the teratoma-type tumors that the embryonic cells formed would be benign, he hoped to avert such an outcome, for obvious reasons. Alzheimer's patients had enough trauma—they shouldn't be forced to undergo removal of a brain tumor as well.

Richard delivered instructions to the staff, and then got down to work. It was well after dark before he looked up from his lab bench. As he turned off the lights to the lab, he wondered to himself if he had covered all of his bases. In twelve hours, Richard would have his answer. If the news was bad, he would always have tomorrow. He became aware of thinking this—that he'd always have tomorrow—as he turned off the lights and locked up the office. He didn't have that luxury anymore—funny, now, to see time as a luxury. This wasn't the NIH; better stop thinking that way.

Two days later, Bob performed a full day of surgery on his favorite twelve monkeys. He had gotten quite attached to them after profiling about two hundred monkeys in the last forty-eight hours. It had been quite a job to find twelve monkeys with some level of brain damage or brain trauma, as shown by CT and MRI scans. Bob had administered the stem cells to each monkey with loving care—after all, this was the beginning of his dream trial, and he was anxious to see the good results he expected. He had carefully plotted his two surgical techniques to ensure the easiest flow for the fresh cells. If all went according to plan, the cells would reach the monkey's area of brain damage, take root, and begin to differentiate, or reproduce, indefinitely. As instructed by Richard, six monkeys received monkey embryonic stem cells straight from fertilized eggs, and the other six monkeys received monkey stem cells already "programmed" to become brain cells. The operations were performed successfully and without incident.

Bob left the monkeys under supervision in a recovery room and sought out Richard. He found him in his lab, bent over some figures, a familiar sight.

"Great news, my boy!" boomed Bob as he swept open the translucent lab door. Richard jumped, having been deeply absorbed in his work.

"Dear God, what is it, Father?" Richard said, irritated. Bob was oblivious.

"Well," he patted Richard on the back with a firm hand. "The twelve monkeys have all received your stem cells without problems. They all left the operating room in good, stable condition and are resting soundly as we speak!" Bob beamed, and his enthusiasm proved infectious. Richard let a smile pass.

"Congratulations, Father. It's about time."

Richard glanced down at his paperwork, forming his thoughts. "I only wish I could share some confident news as well, but I can't. The results of my first test are not encouraging."

"Which test?"

"The initial test to see how successfully I can convert simple embryonic stem cells into neural ones. After twelve hours in this high-dose, molecular enzyme cocktail, I clearly see the beginnings of a benign teratoma tumor."

"Just like the mice we did last year at NIH."

"Yes. I took a slightly different approach this time, however, thinking I'd found a solution. I can't be certain this tumor would form in the human brain, of course; the *in vitro* tests are never quite the same as those performed in a body, but I'm discouraged."

"Is it possible that the dose is affecting the outcome? Perhaps you can't reproduce the way the cells would spread out, and too many potent ones form the tumor because they've nowhere else to go?"

"It's very possible. But we also don't know how far they will go in the real brain."

"The monkeys will show us more of that. We can inject a tracer that shows the path of new stem cells once they begin to travel and reproduce."

"Agreed. But I predict we'll see a benign tumor in at least one of the monkeys that receive embryonic cells."

"What do you suggest we do? How should we redirect the trial? And what shall I tell Stuart? He won't be happy, and he's already tense."

"Well, I can't do anything about controlling his reaction. Either I need more time to perfect the conversion process, or we move on to testing cells that are already neural—from adult cadavers, perhaps, as you brilliantly suggested the other night. We should do both, so we're as informed as possible. In the meantime, let's watch the monkeys carefully."

The two stood in thought for a moment. Bob nodded his head, moved toward Richard, and to Richard's surprise, gave him a bear hug. Richard tried to shrink away. He hated to be touched.

"You're doing a great job, my boy. Don't give up! And don't worry about Stuart. I'll deal with him."

Bob strode off, leaving Richard standing alone in his lab.

Chapter Twenty

THE NEXT MORNING, while Richard slept, dreaming of the calculations he'd written the day before, Bob summoned Stuart. Stuart drove them to an isolated purple cornflower field. Within a few minutes' walk from the car, the tall stalks surrounded them, making them invisible to any passersby. The early morning light shining on the plants created pools of shadows.

Stuart set a brisk pace. "Okay, Bob, no more suspense. I must confess; I'm worried sick about the new information on your wonder stem cells. I'm not sure I'm doing the right thing anymore." He struggled not to raise his voice. "It's been a lot of work to set all this up, and now all I can think about is Richard saying 'in a perfect world.' Jesus! I've got enough to worry about—and now I have to worry about you two not getting what we're doing here!" Stuart practically hissed the last few words, and his haggard appearance did nothing to improve the scene.

"Let me explain something to you," began Bob, with a confidence and authority reinforced by years of breaking bad news. They stopped walking and turned to face each other. "We've never done this on humans before, Stuart. No one has. We know of a few isolated trials that attempted to implant cells into a human brain, without success. Other scientists speculate that this approach is absolute fantasy—it might be possible one day, perhaps five or ten years from now—and they would call us crazy to try it now. Hell, they would incarcerate us for trying it. But we know we have a great shot at it. Richard is not just any researcher, as you know. He's working day and night trying to convert those damn cells. And he will get it right."

"I understand. But let me tell you something, Bob. I mean to make this work, for better or for worse. Money is no object. I want every option available to me—every one. If you think you need something, ask me. I'll get it."

Bob digested this, and Stuart saw the wheels turning.

"There is something, isn't there?" Stuart spoke slowly. "Something you need that you haven't mentioned. Am I right?" Stuart leaned into his words, looking deep into Bob's eyes.

"Yes. There is. We need to find more cells. And it's not going to be easy to get them."

"Just tell me what you need me to do. Anything, Bob."

Stuart and Bob began walking through the giant purple crops.

Chapter Twenty-One

STUART SAT IN HIS JET and began to rehearse what he was going to say. On his headphones, he listened to Ms. Eve Klein performing his favorite show tunes, humming along. The jet began its descent into JFK, and Eve's figure appeared in his mind, her long fingers passing over each key, like water from a great falls.

Now that the study was underway and Bob had reassured him about the abilities of the cells, he was relieved. *But what about intelligence*? That still nagged at him. He wanted to be sure that the embryos would not affect his mental capacity as Bob had joked. What if they could? Richard seemed to think it a possibility, if a remote one. If he only had one shot at this procedure, shouldn't he choose a donor more carefully? He shut his eyes and pictured Eve, her features coming alive though the language of the music in his ears. He knew just how he would talk to her—she was a mega-star, after all, and her ego required a special touch.

Eve, like other brilliant musicians, clearly lived in an abstract musical dimension, distracted by an inner music only she heard. Stuart had always been deaf to that world, the one in which falling leaves sang and hands spoke, but he knew it existed. If only he, too, were one of its messengers. Now that would be power, he thought with a smile.

Eve Klein. Stuart had first seen her in a small club in the Village. It was a tiny room, and she was doing basic jazz sets, long before she became famous for her interpretations. He still remembered being electrified by her presence, feeling alive for the first time since his early days at the piano. Her particular style had been transforming him ever since. That nigh, event in the dark, awful little place that smelled like cheap beer, he was drawn to her like a magnet, and he introduced himself to her. Over the years, he had been her greatest supporter, and at various times, a financial benefactor. In fact, without his support, he speculated that Eve Klein might still be performing in those dives, scraping by from gig to gig. *Now she can help me*, he mused. *She'll be happy to.*

At Lincoln Center that night, Stuart knocked on Eve's dressing room door. One of her personal assistants, who recognized Stuart as a regular visitor, let him in. Inside, the room was abuzz with other callers, flowers just delivered, and an interview in progress. Stuart took a chair and watched. He studied Eve, as he had so many nights before—her costume, her grace, and her consummate star-quality. Eve concluded the interview and turned to face Stuart. He approached and embraced her warmly.

"You were marvelous as usual! That moment in the encore, at the beginning of the first chorus, you really outdid yourself. A chill overcame the audience. It was enchanting."

Eve smiled graciously. "That part never loses its power for me, no matter how many times I perform it." She paused, reflecting on her automatic answer. She felt as if she was giving yet another interview, another performance. Would they ever end? How she longed for the days of playing for the art of it! She had known Stuart for many years now, and some years she saw him as a godsend, some years a pest. She had surmised he was a brilliant businessman, but this did not interest her. Lately, he had been so attached to her, calling her from all over the world. It was beginning to make her nervous. She considered making an excuse to hurry him out of her dressing room, but like the star she was born to be, she graciously tolerated him.

"I'm glad you enjoyed it," she smiled, surveying the intense face looking back at her with an odd expression. He was just staring at her, and it made her most uncomfortable. She found herself groping for something to say, but then suddenly his hand was on her shoulder. "Can we go somewhere—quieter—to talk?"

Without waiting for an answer, Stuart led Eve to a corner of the room and motioned for her to sit down, all the while a suspicious smile on his face. *Whom does he think he is, walking in here and shepherding me around?*

"Eve, darling, I've something very exciting to tell you!" Stuart sat next to her and leaned in closely. Eve moved subtly backward to compensate for the intrusion.

"Yes?" She prayed he wasn't about to make some kind of declaration of love.

"I'm planning on naming a new medical procedure after you! 'The Eve Klein cell transfer.' What do you think?"

Eve Klein felt a frown form on her mouth and fought it, smiling back at Stuart, aware that the photographer from *Vanity Fair* was still hovering nearby. "What kind of medical—what did you say? 'Transfer'?"

"Yes. It's groundbreaking. The procedure could reverse the effects of Alzheimer's disease!"

"Really?" Eve was actually interested now, having always had an irrational fear that she might succumb to this most unglamorous fate. She prayed for a dramatic and newsworthy death to strike her when not too old, and certainly not too young. A car wreck on the Amalfi coast would be fine, as long as her remains were not found and photographed. "But I don't have Alzheimer's. Why name it after me, dear Stuart?"

Stuart moved his chair closer to hers and gently took her hand in his. "Well, you see, I also have some bad news. You see, I'm developing Alzheimer's disease." He paused for effect and forced small tears to well in his eyes. As planned, Eve reacted with quiet—if not polite—shock, gasping slightly.

"As you know, the disease is quite incurable. There's a vaccine I'm taking that could slow down the disease and an experimental drug, too, but I'm doomed eventually. The good news is that at my company, I'm beginning a trial to test a new theory—one that has a good chance of curing me and millions like me!" Stuart smiled brightly.

"Why, Stuart, I'd no idea!" She placed her hand on his shoulder in an affected way. Part of her was sad, in the way that people felt pity for caged animals at the zoo, but Stuart's eerie enthusiasm confused her.

Stuart was pleased to see that Eve was taking this shocking news in stride, without an emotional scene. What grace she had! Other women might become hysterical. With confidence, he continued.

"But you see my dear, there's something I need to continue the project. Now, understand, this project could change the lives of many, many people whose lives have been robbed by this hideous disease. Millions of people. Think of your own life in thirty years. Can you imagine not remembering the notes to 'S' Wonderful'? Becoming completely helpless, needing tending every minute of the day, just to save you from yourself? It would make you sick with disgust, wouldn't it?"

"I know it's a horrible and undignified way to go, but what's any of this got to do with me?" Eve was losing patience, and she was irritated to see the journalist leave her dressing room. Stuart leaned in even closer and lowered his voice.

"Darling, this is where you come in. I'm coming to you today because I need to ask you a favor. Only you can help me—only the great Eve Klein, can help cure me of Alzheimer's."

"I can? But how on Earth?"

"That's the beauty of this; it's so simple! All you have to do is donate a few of your healthy brain cells to me! That's it. That's the Eve Klein cell transplant!" Eve's jaw began to open, slowly, as if preparing for a painful dental procedure. Stuart went on. "You see, with our technology, your young, healthy, brilliant cells could be transplanted into my brain, and my Alzheimer's could be destroyed! You wouldn't even know you'd had the surgery—it's very safe, and state-of-the-art, and the cells you donate will be replaced by your own healthy brain in a matter of weeks. It'd be painless!"

Eve stood up quickly with a fury that shook her entire body.

"What gives you the right? I can't believe you would even consider asking me such an outrageous thing! Have my brain split open and you reap the benefits? You must be crazy!"

Stuart stood and wrapped his arms around her, as if delivering comfort. She stood stiffly in his embrace. He was determined that his plan not be run afoul by a woman's first emotional reaction.

"Sssh, shh. Everyone will hear you. Please calm down. Please think about it." He felt her snaking out of his grasp and held her firmly by the arms, looking deep into her eyes.

"I've done a lot for you, you know. I wouldn't think I'd need to remind you. It's the least you can do for me, after all these years; surely, you must see you're somewhat indebted to me and—"

"Indebted? To you? That's utter nonsense." She paused, and this time, it was she who lowered her voice and leaned in close to his desperate face, her hand clutching his fine cashmere blazer. "I am the one thing you cannot buy, you hear me, Stuart? You'll never own me—or my brain cells, for that matter. Never. Now get out of my dressing room this instant, before I have you tossed out!"

"But, darling, it would be so perfect—" his voice trailed off and shook his head slowly, uncomprehending. He watched the lights sparkle in her long diamond earrings, the fire in her eyes, and beads of sweat, like dew, forming on her perfect throat, exposed by her chic formal gown. He would always remember her in that moment. He had her undivided attention, and it made his adrenaline surge. But she had turned him down! Didn't she know who he was?

He left the room in a blind fury. He spoke aloud, to no one. "You'll wish you had, darling; you'll wish you had."

Chapter Twenty-Two: *Four Seasons, New York City*

THE MONTHLY BOARD MEETING was to begin in twenty minutes. Stuart strode through the lobby of the posh hotel. At the end of the corridor, he saw waiters carrying the luncheon chafing dishes into the large meeting room. He was glad to be early—he needed a bit of prep time to consider his next strategy. The board mustn't ever consider him anything but a sharp man in top form. What a different life he led compared to his state at the last board meeting! He had been confused then, a heap of wild emotions—paranoid, even. At the next month's meeting, he reflected, he'd have had the cell treatment and would be well on his way to his old, shining self, the board none the wiser.

Stuart stepped into the meeting room. And there, next to the elegant long buffet table, stood Paul, helping himself to a cup of fancy loose-leaf tea. He wore a new silk suit, and his too-shiny loafers were deeply implanted in the plush carpet. Damn! He hated not arriving first—it destroyed his concentration. He didn't like seeing Paul there early, either, not at all. In fact, the sight of Paul in his tacky new suit made him nearly furious. What was he trying to prove?

"Stuart!" Paul turned, all smiles, and greeted Stuart warmly, then moved to the large oval table. Paul set his tea down then ostentatiously removed his suit jacket, draping it over a chair at the head of the table, directly opposite the lectern at the front of the room from where Stuart always spoke. Stuart gritted his teeth, fighting back invectives inspired by this display. It occurred to Stuart that he and Paul resembled two monkeys competing for territory. Stuart turned on his most confident CEO voice; there was to be no competition.

"Paul, how've you been? How's Carol and the family?"

"They're all super; thanks for asking. Listen, Stuart," Paul approached him, hands confidently thrust into finely tailored trousers. He looked ready to accept an award, a superficial smug smile plastered on his face. *What had Paul been up to—reading more monkey data?*

"I'm glad we have a moment of privacy before the others arrive. I've noticed you're becoming slightly, well—shall we say, slightly less involved in day-to-day matters at HQ. I know you want to be down in the islands to monitor the progress of ABT-55, so I wanted to offer you my services. If you need me to stand in for you, perhaps take meetings, speak to anyone, I hope you'll let me know."

Stuart stared back at Paul, trying to mask his disbelief. Was Paul vying for his position? But that was absurd!

"I mean, you've worked hard, very hard. Why not let someone you trust give you a little help? Maybe even help with, say, the FDA, if you ever need that. I know you don't have time to read all that paperwork yourself. Hell, how could anyone?" Paul's wide grin nearly showed his molars. Paul's attempt at a joke only echoed their mini confrontation about the dead research monkey a month ago, a jab Stuart did not miss. Stuart wasn't so mentally gone as to not take the hint. Did Paul really think he was?

My God! His worst fear was becoming a reality. He felt color rush to his cheeks but fought it. He knew how to handle this the right way. The way that gave him time to think.

"Paul, you're very kind, very kind indeed. I'll remember that." He almost laughed at his one-sided pun on the word "remember."

Thankfully, Paul let the matter of the "offer" drop as the other board members arrived. *Saved by the suits*, he thought. This time.

Stuart considered the meeting with the BioSys board as he sat in the back of his vintage Mercedes. His driver navigated deftly, as usual, through the late afternoon's Manhattan gridlock. After the humbling delivered by Eve last night and today's run-in with Paul, he had felt the need to bolster his character. He enjoyed standing in front of them all, delivering his words like the stock dividend hero he knew they perceived him to be. On a whim, he had suggested that BioSys donate their popular anti-nausea drug to cutting-edge cancer centers. Without blinking, he made an entire presentation about altruism. Of course, they had loved the idea of good PR. It only helped stock prices. *See if a dolt like Paul could ever come up with that one!*

The traffic was getting worse, and with a sudden turn, Stuart's driver made a clever detour. They sped down side streets through an evidently poor neighborhood. They cruised down unobstructed alleys and made incomplete stops at grimy neighborhood intersections. The driver's navigating led them to a busy intersection, where they joined other cars in line at a red light.

Out of his window, Stuart saw a group of ragged teens standing on the corner, jeering to the waiting cars. Stuart cracked his window, curious about the exchange.

"I'm only $25.00, and Sid here's in and out for $15! Now you can't beat that can ya?" The kids were laughing and seemed to be enjoying propositioning themselves to strangers. In disgust, Stuart sealed up his window. Traffic began to move. As they passed closer to the teens, Stuart got a better look at the frightful creatures. What wastes of precious life! The kids couldn't have been more than fifteen years old.

And then it happened in an instant, the way ideas used to come to him—complete and brilliant. Stuart turned his attention to his skillful driver.

These drivers—they came from a security firm. A private firm. They all had colorful backgrounds. That was actually a reason Stuart had hired the firm some ten years earlier. The drivers were all very capable men. Take Carlo, for example, back in LA with Therese. He was more than a driver; he was also a bodyguard, should such services ever be necessary. Carlo could handle any event that threatened his loved ones. Carlo had come from a tough neighborhood in East LA and grown into a star cop at a very young age—apparently too young for the job. But he was tough, and Stuart could offer him a much safer existence. With Carlo's street smarts, he had come to intimately know the ways of the petty criminals around him.

Stuart studied the driver with him today. He was about thirty-five and cut a mean, strong figure. One look at him revealed that he was a fighter. His Latino tough-guy good looks had no doubt helped him when he needed to smooth out the edges of life. In other words, people liked to do him favors. Stuart decided to speak to him before they got too close to the municipal airport.

As they crawled along the George Washington Bridge, Stuart leaned forward toward the driver, whose name he didn't even know. The sun was just beginning to set, filling the luxurious sedan with a golden glow that did not suit its driver, who wore big dark sunglasses.

"Look here. There's something I need you to do."

Part II

Chapter Twenty-Three: *Anegada, BVI*

RICHARD TAPPED AWAY on his computer keyboard, the sun setting across his desk. Now that the monkey tests were officially underway and he had concrete results on his "borrowed" NIH embryonic stem cells, Richard could get to the important and nagging question—how to make the NIH cells perform the correct function.

Richard organized his thoughts, devising new ways to perform molecular manipulations on the embryonic stem cells. He wasn't sure he could convert them to neural stem cells anytime soon, so he was also working on an adjustment that might prevent tumors from forming. This oncogenesis possibility might have unintended effects, however. It was impossible to know. That was a chance he'd have to take, since these were the only cells he had. Their entire study rested on the success or failure of these tiny proteins.

The new staff that had been assembled from various BioSys projects was quickly becoming indispensable. They worked tirelessly, setting up equipment and seeing to all the operative matters involved with any brain surgeries—monkey or human. Bob had directed them according to his judgment. Richard was very pleased with the caliber of professionals at their disposal, and since most of them were already BioSys employees, they were familiar with BioSys operating procedures and facilities. This took pressure off both Richard and Bob, for now they could concentrate on their research work. They had both put in many fourteen-hour days in their first few weeks, but were invigorated by the stimulation.

A knock at his lab door brought Richard back to the present. Through the glass, Richard and Stuart exchanged a wave, and then Stuart strolled into the lab, which was empty, the lab workers having left for the day at four.

"What's the latest with our brilliant Richard?" Stuart smiled and sat in a rolling chair. Stuart's tone was coy and his tone booming, both of which made Richard anxious.

Richard turned away from the computer and sighed, putting his hands on his knees. “Well,” he began, not sure where he was going or what Stuart was suddenly doing in the lab. Had he forgotten a meeting? “The embryonic stem cells are multiplying normally, but I’m still concerned about the potential for tumor growth.”

“Tumor growth? Why wasn’t I informed?” Stuart’s voice was edgy.

“I’m sorry; I thought you had been, from the papers I published on the mice. I wasn’t sure they would grow *in vivo*—we’re waiting on the monkey data to confirm that. Most likely, it would be a teratoma, a type of benign tumor—”

“Well, then, couldn’t it be treated or removed?”

Richard always got a bit tongue-tied when interrupted. Why couldn’t people let him finish? With some irritation, he replied. “Yes, it could be, but there could be brain damage. Increased intracranial pressure, potential stroke—”

“My God!” Stuart burst out.

The volume made Richard’s ears ache. “Stuart, I’m doing my best to make the cells convert properly, and we’re not sure the tumor would grow in a human brain. We need to make sure it won’t; that’s our only option right now. Please understand that this is very complicated, and we want to take every precaution. But some of the answers aren’t out there right now. As you know, it’s very difficult to get the embryonic cells to convert into the kind of cells we want. No one’s ever done it before for a human application, at least not with any success. And these things take some time.”

Stuart stood. “But time, my boy, is what I do not have.” Richard noted the use of the phrase ‘my boy.’ Perhaps he’d picked that one up from Bob.

“All I can tell you is that we’re working around the clock. I don’t know what else to do.”

“I do. We have human subjects ready and willing to be tested. The arrangements have been made at the teaching hospital. Why not start the trial now and see if tumors develop? Should one of them develop a tumor, we’ll remove it, simple as that.”

Stuart paused while Richard digested this.

“That’s a little soon, I think.”

“Well, you keep thinking, and I’ll have a word with your father. In the meantime, keep plugging away! You’re my only hope, you know.”

Stuart's tone had suddenly changed to one of affection. But his burst of anger and shortsightedness just a moment earlier was fresh in Richard's brain. *This was a lab, not a game show*, he thought to himself. Things must be tested, tried, and retested. He didn't like being spoken to in such a voice, and it didn't help him work any faster.

Stuart stared back at him with a glint of something unidentifiable in his eye. Richard tried to see things from his side. He didn't like anyone being unhappy with his performance, but it didn't sway him from the fact that science was methodical. Had he been too cautious, too conservative? Maybe he did need a jumpstart. But he doubted it.

Stuart delivered a firm but friendly pat on the shoulder, and left the lab as smoothly as he had sailed in moments earlier, almost like a ghost. Richard turned back to his computer to finish his lab notes. The sun had disappeared.

Alone in their vacation condo, Richard picked at his dinner. After three full days of test after test, he'd run out of ideas. Although he was making progress on an anti-tumor molecular formula, he knew that he needed months—probably years—to perfect the lab studies. He kept coming back to being pushed. He shouldn't be forced to rush; it just wasn't right. Although he'd been a good sport in the face of Stuart's tactics, his gut had been correct. He needed more time. A lot more time.

After the days of heel dragging at the NIH, he thought he would welcome the freedom that BioSys money bought, but instead, he felt a ticking clock. He had been a fool to think there would be no tradeoff. All the money in the world couldn't make him think any faster!

Bob burst through the front door. "Richard! We're back in business." A breathless Bob joined Richard at the dinner table.

"What do you mean?"

"Cells, my boy. We got 'em!" Richard's quizzical look prompted Bob to continue.

"Adult stem cells, that is—from an adult brain."

Richard's eyes widened. "But, how, from where?"

"There's a BioSys pilot trial using fresh cadavers—young cadavers, too. I'll be going first thing in the morning to remove the stem cells from the wall of the third ventricle, where we know they thrive. I'll bring them over to your lab in dry ice." Bob stood, a huge grin of satisfaction on his face.

"Now, that wasn't so hard, was it?" Bob strode off, leaving Richard speechless. After a moment, Richard let out a jubilant yelp to the empty room. The pressure to convert the problematic embryonic stem cells was off, for now.

Richard spent the next forty-eight hours testing the new cadaver human cells. His heavy disappointment from the prior days lifted, and he worked with unprecedented fervor. He felt more alive than he had in his entire life, and was glad to prove to himself that after all, he was up to the task.

He'd not much time for reflection, however. It was clear by the end of the first day that the cadaver cells could be easily formulated to migrate and differentiate through the brain and were potent. To his delight, Richard watched the stem cells continually divide, the miracle of neurogenesis taking place before his eyes.

With this good news, Richard began a battery of new tests, tests he'd always dreamed of performing. He utilized every instrument and every person around him. The lab hummed a like a beehive.

By the end of the second long day, there was no evidence of any tumor-forming agent in the Petri dishes. This was the outcome they hoped for. Richard sent the exhausted lab workers home, tidied his chaotic desk, and then shut his computer down. He was suddenly aware of an insistent hunger. He heard Bob in the next office dictating to a staff member regarding a post-surgical study of the monkeys. On his second wind, he nearly skipped into Bob's office just as he finished a dictation.

"You about wrapped up?" began Richard. He leaned on his father's desk and surveyed the room. In just two weeks, Bob had managed to make it his own. Articles were taped on the walls, the phone was off its receiver, and boxes remained unpacked—just the way Bob liked them. Richard noticed that Bob looked younger, engulfed in high energy that enlivened his face.

"I was just going to read this article about the stem cell debate raging on in our fair US of A in today's *International Herald Tribune*. Care to pull up a chair?"

Before Richard could reply, Bob added, "Listen to this headline, 'Today president rejects stem cell innovation.' It goes on. 'In a highly anticipated announcement today, the president brought to a close the nation's debate on stem cell use in the United States. After months of discussion in the House and Senate, the president finally weighed in on the issue, which he believes is a moral, not scientific one. A devoted Catholic, the president let the nation know today that he is pro-life, and thus, anti-embryonic stem cell research.' It goes on to tell us what we already knew. Research will take place in other countries before the US will touch it. So, *voila*," Bob motioned, indicating their present surroundings.

Richard was grateful to be out of that arena, he realized. He had tried to ignore the press during the NIH stem cell debates, because it was, after all, science that he cared about, not the mess others made of it. He tried to keep his hands clean of the politics. But he was not without ethics; he and his father had gone tête-à-tête on the subject more than once. Richard's grumbling stomach reminded him that he did not wish to have such a conversation now, even though his father was obviously in the mood to hash one out.

"Dad, the human brain cell tests are exceeding my wildest expectations. I think it's time to celebrate and take a moment to enjoy this paradise, don't you? I was thinking about going to the market and getting something to throw on the grill."

"Marvelous. But I'd like to get a couple more things done first, so why don't I leave the market tasks to you and meet you at home later?"

Richard was frankly glad to be have some time alone. He'd been so wrapped up in the ups and downs of the unexpected drama with the embryonic stem cells that he hadn't even made a trip into town. On his bicycle, he made his way to the small town square. It was dusty, but charming, just what he would have expected from a vacation on an island that had once been a spice-trading outpost for the British in colonial days. Tall, stately island women in colorful headdresses and scarves passed in front of him, barely taking notice of him, which he enjoyed. He parked his bike and adjusted the straps of his empty backpack. A breeze cooled his sweaty face.

The square's center was busy, but because no one was crowding him, Richard didn't mind. He was too hungry to let anything stop him from acquiring sustenance. Vendors hawked goods, priced to move, apparently, as the sun shimmied low behind them. There were three or more fishmongers, and an assortment of fruit, cocoa, and nut stands. Colorful and strange produce beckoned him with their new smells and textures, and before he knew it, his arms were loaded with purchases. He munched happily on a colorful thing that looked like a cross between an orange and a pear, its succulent juices streaming down his face. This island was blissful, after all. He hadn't stopped to bargain as the others around him had because, to his American eye, the prices were embarrassingly low. Richard had never been out of the US, and was experiencing an entirely new feeling—what it was like to be filthy rich.

Chapter Twenty-Four: *Friday, Santa Monica*

A FAINT RAIN TAPPED on the wood-shingled roof. Therese awoke slowly in her bed, grey light lingering in the skylights, her right leg tingling in response to the lack of circulation. She freed her leg from underneath one of Fancy's, the brindle-colored greyhound stretched across the end of the king-sized bed. Therese rolled over and sighed. The faint embers in the small corner fireplace crackled as a draft spiraled down the chimney. With a start, Fancy sneezed explosively then placed her front right leg back in its proper position, on top of Therese.

The stone floors were warm despite the chill in the spring morning ocean air. Therese opened the curtains, revealing a landscaped patio covered in a lattice of jasmine and early roses, vines tangled and woven, just the way her mother had planned. An azure pool was beyond, its surface reflecting the gently stormy sky, its shape natural and flowing, like everything about the house—no right angles. Her mother had been very specific about that with the architect. Curved walls, spaces cozy with wood beam ceilings and stones, as if it had grown naturally in this spot, borne of vines and rock, each room oriented to the spectacular wooded lot outside. And it did feel like that. Here, nestled in Santa Monica canyon among the old-growth cypress and avocado trees, one could forget the traffic and bad air, the concrete and steel. It was a hidden treasure. Visitors often missed the house entirely, so at one with the landscape were its wooden shingles and lime-leaf green windows.

Fancy padded along behind Therese and let herself outside via a motion-sensor operated French sliding glass door. Therese watched the dog from the oversized kitchen window, which glowed green from the spring rain's electric effect on the trees and shrubs that surrounded the house. Carlo had helped Therese build a large run for the ex-racing dog, but Fancy was more content curled up on the couch cushions, and only liked to run after the local rabbit population when they presented themselves. Therese watched as Fancy sniffed under a large planter for signs of rabbit then wandered off behind the hedges. Therese put the kettle on for coffee then retrieved Fancy's breakfast from the fridge: raw lamb, carrots, and brown rice. At the sound of the kettle's boil, Fancy trotted in for her feast, and Therese sat down at the large wooden table, ready to make a shopping list and sift through the mail.

Nearly all of her days had begun this way for the last five years.

That first year in the house was really a blur. But then she'd met Fancy, and they'd gotten into a routine, the two of them, and of course, the ever-present Carlo.

The mail revealed the usual sales correspondence, some addressed to her mother. With a slight pang, she tossed them into the recycling bin and opened her sketchbook to the drafts of the next schoolyard garden.

The drawings were due on Monday, and she had been putting off giving them the next round of thought. Her mother had been an aspiring landscape architect, and Therese had thought she could embody those skills, as if by osmosis. The fact was, she wasn't very good at it. True, the drawings would work. They were competent; she had learned the basics from her mother before the murder. But the ideas were less than inspired—the drawings practically clinical at this point. Therese made a few eraser marks and adjusted a flowerbed and a terraced water feature, then erased again. She comforted her inner critic by reminding herself that she had to draw things that the kids could participate in making; otherwise, there wasn't much point. Fancy's snout interrupted Therese's pencil, insistent and cold. Therese petted the silky hound, who whined quietly. *Cold*, thought Therese. She got up to start a fire, and Fancy ran to the patio doors and whined louder, then barked.

"What is it, Fancy Pants?" asked Therese, who looked outside to see what the fuss was about. The entire house was oriented toward the landscaped patio, so it was hard to miss any activity that occurred outside. Fancy was forever responding to every movement there—from a leaf falling to the gardener. Then she saw the problem. A large robin was lying on the flagstones, bleeding and struggling, a wing twisted under itself. Therese watched in horror as the bird tried to right itself, one wing flapping madly, the other useless. Fancy barked, more excited now, her deep-throated anxious tone echoing off the large boulders at the top of the bluff.

"Stop it, Fancy. Quiet!" Therese pushed past the hound, and squeezed outside, disabling the movement sensor so the dog was locked inside. The closed door muffled the dog's bark.

Therese approached the bird slowly, wondering what she could do. As she got closer, it flapped even more furiously, so she backed away. The bird managed to roll over, revealing a large pool of blood. The barking from inside turned into a growl. Therese turned to the dog to admonish it, just as a blur of wings appeared from nowhere. Jasmine buds fluttered down, ripped from their branches, a wing struck the patio, and then a streak of blood, mid-air. Therese finally registered the small hawk, its talons clutching the injured robin; in two seconds, it and its prey were gone, beyond the canyon, through he dense cypress trees, back from where it came, and once again, it was invisible to her. Perhaps to everyone.

Burt sat at his desk, poised to dial the phone. He had a stack of messages in his hand, and three of them were about his meningitis body, but the caller wasn't any of the specialists Burt himself had contacted; they had all called back already, and none of them had been any help anyway. He had ignored the new messages, since he had very little to say about the body. What's done is done.

However, the news of the meningitis event had traveled to internal assessments, who were now making the staff pull out paperwork on the all the latest autopsies to prove that the Tank was reliable. They were almost convinced, but hinting that minor findings were going to be documented anyway. They'd be written up on some technicality, you could be sure of it. In the meantime, IA had suspended use of the Tank. What a waste of an entire week. He was looking at another two weeks of paperwork to address the "minor" findings. Even if he'd wanted to, there was no way to get to the bottom of the meningitis mystery. The problem was the girl was dead, her body was gone, and she wasn't coming back.

With this sentiment firmly in mind, he began to dial the number of the insistent caller, one Ms. Therese Edwards.

Therese's cell phone rang from her nearby purse. She hurried to the phone, hoping it would be Carlo. She glanced at the number, eyes widening. Finally.

"Hello, this is Therese Edwards."

"Hello, Ms. Edwards, this is Dr. Colins from the medical examiner's office in New York."

"I'm very glad to hear from you, Dr. Colins."

"I believe you have questions about the body of one June Hamels. Are you a relative?"

"No, I'm—" What was she? "I'm an advocate for the young man who brought June to the ER."

"A lawyer, then?" asked Burt.

"No, goodness, no. The young man I'm helping is mourning the loss of his friend. He's tried to follow up her death—you see, he wasn't satisfied with the way he was treated at the county ER, and frankly, he didn't believe what they implied, which was that she had died of a drug overdose. I offered to make inquiries for him. He was upset and didn't know how to find out what really happened."

"How did you meet this young man?"

Therese felt Dr. Colins was probing. Or stalling? She looked out at the patio, at the remaining robin feathers matted to the flagstones. "He attended a seminar I sponsored. Why?"

"I just want to be sure you have access to him. You see, I don't have his phone number."

"Of course; that's because he doesn't have a phone." Therese was getting irritated, and she wasn't very good at hiding it.

"June Hamels died of cardiac arrest, I'm afraid, but it wasn't due to a drug overdose. Looks like she had a brain aneurysm, probably induced by biological stress. It caused a form of meningitis, which grew rapidly, infecting her brain, leading to the cardiac arrest."

"That sounds unusual. Is it?"

"Oh, certainly not, no, no."

"But I thought meningitis wasn't around anymore and hasn't been, well, for years."

"Well, there are occasional outbreaks, often in places where young people are crowded in small spaces together—camps, college dorms, that kind of thing." Burt cleared his throat, buying time. How to get the lady off the phone? He didn't want to mention 'surgery.' The line was silent.

"Do you mean she caught meningitis? I thought you said the aneurysm caused the meningitis. Has there even been an outbreak? She wasn't in a college."

Burt rolled his eyes and thought about simply disconnecting the phone. Shit! What had he gotten himself into? Like a conspirator, his framed county license caught his eye.

"No, there's been no outbreak. This was an isolated case."

"I see," said Therese, although she didn't see at all. "Where is the body now, doctor? The friend of the deceased would like to see the body properly honored." Therese lied, thinking instead of bringing the body to a pathologist of her own choosing.

"Oh, I'm afraid it's been cremated."

"Cremated!" Therese blurted in surprise. "But it's only been…" Therese's voice trailed off as she realized the body had probably been in the morgue for over a week.

"We just run out of space, you see, and because no family has come forward, our policy is to dispose of unclaimed cadavers as quickly as possible. Ms. Edwards, I'm sorry if that shocks you. I do apologize."

Therese recovered. "No, doctor, I understand. I wonder—well, I wonder if there are any other options without the body. We'd like to have something from the deceased."

"Well, there's simply nothing here. I don't know what—"

"At least the medical records, doctor."

Now it was the doctor's turn to pause. He cleared his throat and coughed before replying.

"Well, we are a public office, Ms. Edwards. You're welcome to view the records, but because you're not family, it won't be possible for you to have them." Burt reflected that there weren't any records of note, anyway, save the incomplete Tank printout, which would remain safely in his possession. He never imagined he could be grateful for the city's lack of infrastructure, until this very moment.

"I would. I would like very much to view the records. Just tell me whom to contact, and I'll arrange an appointment."

"No problem."

Therese wrote down the information and they exchanged curt goodbyes. She was surprised the doctor had discouraged her from obtaining June's information, but she supposed that was the problem with these agencies—no one wanted to do any work, didn't want the bother. Well, she intended to take those records away and deliver them to Greg, no matter what Dr. Colins said.

Therese sat back down in a leather armchair and stared into the empty fireplace. She closed her eyes and felt the day's ocean air on the breeze from the patio doors damp on her face. She pictured her mother sitting to her right in the empty armchair. What would she say? She could imagine it—her mother, forever young, blond hair perfectly bobbed, blue eyes sparkling. She'd be interested, curious. Maybe a glass of something in her hand. *What was that all about, dear*? she'd ask.

Therese would tell her mother the story of June's death and paint a picture of Greg as a sympathetic, smart person who just happened to have no permanent address. June had been young, not even out of her teens…

Maybe her mom would tell the story of her own near-death, giving birth to a stillborn sibling. *You were too young to remember, but you must always cherish each living thing.*

Or was it a car accident? The story her mother would tell of the near miss during the earthquake on the freeway—metal flying, cars raining down? She'd nearly died! *You must live every day as if it's your last!*

Therese would listen and nod, buoyed by her mother's strength and utter vitality.

But Therese had never been told those stories—not the childbirth one, nor the car accident—or the bit about cherishing life. She'd only created them as a child, a child who didn't comprehend murder. She'd pieced the real story together on her own, much later. For her mother *had* died, not *almost* died, as she'd fantasized as a lonely child. And not in childbirth, but at the hand of a startled burglar with a gun. And Therese *had* been too young to remember. They'd lived in a different city then, a different house with different plants and neighbors and street names. So she'd had to fill in the gaps the best she could—newspaper articles gathered from the library, case notes from the police. But those facts did not satisfy her, as they could not paint a picture of the woman her mother had been, so Therese had also combed though her mother's things—her diaries, her letters, the boxes in the closets—trying to get to know the mother who was taken from her over twenty years ago.

Therese paced in the empty house, the weight of her missing mother heavier today. Even though she tried to prevent it, she saw her mother at the kitchen sink, her mother in her favorite club chair; it happened sometimes, when she came home to all that loneliness. If only she could ask her mother what she thought, talk the facts over with her...

Her mother had been a journalist who wished she'd been an architect. She was a person of fact. She'd have asked for the facts, first. And so, Therese thought, facts were where she should begin. In the library, she switched on the computer and opened an Internet browser. She typed "aneurysm," hit the Enter key, and spent the next two hours learning about all the things that could go wrong in the brain's blood vessels, many of which were preventable, curable, and even symptomatic. Had June experienced any symptoms? Greg hadn't indicated that. Then again, maybe June had suffered a subarachnoid hemorrhage, which can be fatal in 50% of people. But what had the coroner said about meningitis?

"Hello?" It was Carlo, but Therese nearly jumped anyway. She heard him greet Fancy in the hallway and went out to meet him. He held up a craft paper sack and announced, "I brought dinner."

"Oh, thank goodness! How did you know I'd be starving and need your help?"

Carlo laughed and said, "Since when aren't you hungry?" and went to the kitchen sink to wash his hands. Fancy sat on the floor, awaiting her own dinner. Therese unwrapped the food—expensive vegetarian from the hot new Thai place in Brentwood—and set the table with porcelain chopsticks. Carlo handed her the dog's food from the refrigerator, and she placed it on the floor for the hound then the humans sat down to eat.

They both dug into their noodles and veggies, which were coated in a piquant and spicy lemongrass ginger sauce. "So," said Carlo between bites, "you mentioned something about help."

"Yes. What do you remember about human anatomy?"

"Jesus, Therese. We're eating!" Therese knew that whether they were eating or not, it'd be a difficult subject for Carlo.

"It's just that I'm trying to help a kid whose girlfriend died, and he can't figure out how."

"Who is this kid?"

"I shouldn't call him a kid; he's actually probably thirtyish. He's homeless in New York. He's obviously with it—he's not a criminal or anything. Anyway, his girlfriend showed up, after being gone over twenty-four hours, delirious, and died at County a few hours later."

"And what was wrong?"

"That's what we're trying to find out. The coroner said the girl died of meningitis."

Carlo was silent, appearing to concentrate on his food. Therese knew it'd be hard for the ex-star cop to turn down a mystery. "What reason do you have to doubt the coroner?"

"Well, meningitis isn't something you just get." Therese paused. "I've been researching it. And something about the man makes me doubt him."

"Something? You sound like an old cop. Using your instincts, are you?" Carlo teased.

"Well, I know it sounds crazy. But I have a bad feeling, and this guy, Greg, he's very sincere, and he's sure he didn't get the whole story. I mean, a healthy seventeen-year-old doesn't just drop dead of meningitis."

"True," concluded Carlo, slurping up the last of his noodles. "Well, there must be some records."

"There are. At the coroner's office in New York."

"So, when are we leaving?"

At the word "leaving," Fancy jumped up and nuzzled Therese's leg. "Not you, Fancy. Maybe next time."

Two days later, Therese and Carlo took a cab from JFK into New York City. By mid-morning, they were outside the office of the chief medical examiner. The plan was to have Carlo request the records—just in case there was any resistance. Carlo was, after all, a good-looking man with a LAPD badge. Therese had noticed over the years that service people—who tended to be women—responded much better to men, especially good-looking men in uniform.

The plan worked brilliantly: Carlo had simply walked into the records department and asked for everything. The staff didn't seem to have instructions to not give copies of anything he asked for. So Carlo requested the films, the chart, and all the reports. The helpful clerk even asked him if he wanted a copy of the "Tank data." Carlo had no idea what this was, but replied with an assertive, "Yes, please." The woman asked him if he was an investigator, and since he was indeed investigating informally, he replied, "Yes, I'm here in an official capacity." The woman didn't ask him for any identification. After paying a small fee for the copies, Carlo was out on the street with the records. Easy.

They sat in a café in Soho and took their time reading the file. It was thinner than Therese had hoped. With Carlo's experience, they determined that the top page was a preliminary death certificate, but under "Cause of Death," the entry was blank. They flipped through the other forms: one from the ER, stating the time and circumstances of June's admission. In the back, there was a paper report labeled TANK, PRELIMINARY—NOT TO BE USED FOR OFFICIAL RECORD. Therese skipped to the Conclusion section on the bottom of the second page, which she read aloud, "Scan with contrast of head reveals an abnormal gap (1.5cm x 0.5cm) in the frontal lobe, cause unknown. The margins of gap are clean and healing. Significant swelling of the brain and intracranial pressure are evident. No outside films available for comparison. Preliminary diagnosis: Cardiac arrest, secondary to meningitis with massive cerebral edema."

Carlo echoed, "A 'gap' in her brain? Part of June's brain was missing?"

"The coroner didn't mention any gap." She pulled the Tank disk out of a pocket in the back of the chart and studied it. It looked like a DVD. On it was scrawled 'June Hamels' Tank data COPY.'

"Do you know what this is?" She handed it to Carlo.

"Never heard of a Tank. But maybe this is just a DVD of the medical scans. It's all electronic these days."

Therese popped open her laptop and released the CD/DVD tray. Once the computer booted up, she anxiously examined the DVD's contents. It contained one huge file, about seven gigabytes, created, naturally, with an application she did not possess. She double-clicked on it anyway, just in case some miracle of computer-file conversion took place. She was prompted to tell the computer how to open it, but she knew she could not. It had a file extension she had never seen. She tried various applications without success.

"Damn computer! It doesn't know how to open it." Therese closed the paper file and shut down the laptop. Carlo took a long sip of his iced tea.

"Well, that's okay. It might not be important. Let's go back to the primary diagnosis—cardiac arrest."

"Yes. Strange, don't you think?"

"Not really. It's very common. In women, it goes undetected a lot. And if it wasn't caused by a heart condition, it could be drugs. Probably was."

"But how would that explain the meningitis?"

"That's where you lose me. I can't imagine—intravenous drug use? Dirty needles? I have no idea how meningitis is transmitted."

"I think this is the key," said Therese, holding up the DVD." Carlo shrugged his shoulders.

"I don't know. We have so little to go on."

"True. But what we do have is not adding up. The more I find out, the more suspicious I am about the death."

"But look at it from my eyes—no body, no witnesses, no police, not to mention a motive. Just one guy's feeling that something isn't right."

"One guy and one gal," said Therese, pointing to herself.

"Okay. And it's good to use your instincts. But from a law enforcement point-of-view, there's no problem to solve. See?"

Therese nodded. She did see. And she trusted Carlo, who knew much more about these things. But what was she going to tell Greg? The scheduled phone call was just two days away.

With a sigh, Therese put the DVD and meager medical file in her handbag.

"I know what you're thinking. What are you going to tell the guy?"

Therese smiled. They were getting to be like an old couple, practically finishing each other's thoughts.

"You got it. I'll think of something." Therese watched all the people rushing around outside and finished her tea. That was when she thought of Dr. Riley.

Dr. Riley had been a friend of the family since Therese could remember. He was a neurologist at UCLA and had helped after Therese's foot was slammed in the car door by her then-senile grandfather, who had forgotten Therese was in the car. Dr. Riley was able to revive most of the nerve activity, but her foot bones would never be the same. Surely, he could help her with the DVD. The next day, back in LA, Therese made an appointment to see him and was in his office a day later.

"Therese! How's the foot?" Dr. Riley welcomed Therese into his office with a smile and a hug.

"As good as can be. And how are you?"

Dr. Riley filled Therese in on all the misadventures of his twin grandchildren as an assistant brought them coffee from the hospital staff cafeteria.

"Dr. Riley, I wanted to talk to you about some medical records I'm trying to decipher. Do you think you could look at them? I don't really understand what I'm looking at."

"Of course," he replied, as he received the thin file.

"Okay, this is blood work. Everything normal there." He started to flip to the next page when Therese interjected, "No drugs, then?"

"No. No sign of drugs. This panel is clean."

Therese was encouraged by this bit of news.

"However, this does not look so good." Dr. Riley pointed to the conclusion on the Tank scan preliminary report. "This person died of cardiac arrest, secondary to meningitis? That's odd for, let's see—date of birth: unknown? How old was this person?"

"Seventeen."

"Hmmm. I see the problem."

"You do?"

"Yes, she got meningitis, and evidently it went untreated or treatment failed. The infection in her brain would have led to great suffering."

"What would the treatment have been?"

"Oh, I can't be sure, but I would think massive doses of powerful antibiotics."

"And what about that note about the gap in the frontal lobe?"

"Hmm, yes. That is interesting. Perhaps there was some history there—perhaps a benign brain tumor. It must have been an old wound because this report shows that the margins were well healed, perhaps even with scar tissue. I think that is unrelated to the cause of death."

Therese looked puzzled.

"I've got to get to my next patient, but let's send you down to radiology and see what films are on that DVD." Dr. Riley made a quick call and then hung up. "Dr. Wellman will be expecting you—third floor, East. Follow the signs to Imaging. Good luck—and stay off that foot when it bothers you, okay?"

Therese took a series of elevators and pedestrian overpasses and underpasses and finally found Imaging. Dr. Riley mentioning her foot had made Therese notice that was starting to throb. She asked for Dr. Wellman at the reception area. As she waited, she noticed a listing of staff, hinged on the wall artfully in metal block letters. Dr. Wellman was the chair of the department! In a few moments, a young intern showed Therese into the doctor's office. The office wall was covered in plaques, awards, and certificates, letters from what Therese assumed were former patients, and the standard family photos. A light box was mounted on the wall behind the desk for convenient viewing of films. Shortly, the doctor himself arrived. He was a hunched-over octogenarian, who despite his age and osteoporosis entered the room with a spring in his step and a smile on his face.

"Any friend of Dr. Riley's is a friend of mine," he began. He sat in his chair with some difficulty as the assistant stood by helplessly. "It makes my day to be able to talk to a young person. You know, when I was your age, I was—oh, who cares. It was so long ago!" The doctor laughed, a sparkle in his eye.

"Well, Dr. Wellman, I'm trying to help a young man determine how his seventeen-year-old friend died. She presented to the OR with a severe fever and convulsions. Unfortunately, she did not survive long enough to do many tests, but the coroner concluded she died of cardiac arrest due to meningitis. I was wondering if you could look at these films and tell me what you see." Therese held up the DVD.

"Oh, that is certainly interesting. Yes, yes, let's take a look at those," the doctor could not quite reach far enough across the office desk to retrieve the DVD, so the assistant intervened, offering to bring them up on the computer in the adjacent room. The intern left the room, and Dr. Wellman continued. "They don't let me do anything anymore! And then these computers, well, I've done my best to learn how to use them. I write my own emails, but sometimes I forget my password. Passwords, accounts, web sites! It has all gotten so complicated. When I was your age, we wrote everything—by hand, I mean. I had glorious handwriting! And letter writing was an art. Now I can barely read my own writing. Oh, well. Therese, let me give you a piece of advice: don't get old."

Therese smiled. "I don't plan on it."

The intern popped her head back in and looked worried. "Doctor, there's a problem with the DVD." She glanced at Therese.

"What do you mean?"

"We can't open it. It's some kind of old file."

"See what I mean?" The doctor winked at Therese. "Write it down. It'll be readable every time. As long as you can read your handwriting, that is."

Back in the Jag, Carlo took Westwood side streets, which led them to San Vicente, a tree-lined boulevard that ran down the center of Brentwood and headed west.

"I can't believe even UCLA can't read the Tank file," bemoaned Therese as they came to a traffic light. Middle-aged white women crossed the street—all shopping bags and hairdos. It was two p.m. on a weekday. One of the women, in a skirt far too short for her age, winked at Carlo, who waved back. Therese gave him a jab in the ribs as the light turned green.

"Is this Tank file really that important?" He looked at Therese, who was looking up at the tree canopy; she said nothing for a few moments.

"I don't know if it is or not. I just want to make something that seems complicated less so. If I can show Greg that June had a pre-existing problem—like a brain tumor—that would allow him to drop this whole thing."

"It sounds like it's your brain that could use a rest."

Therese smiled and closed her eyes for the remainder of the journey back to Santa Monica.

From home that night, Therese dialed Greg's payphone number. It was the agreed-upon date for the call, and she didn't have much to report, but she wanted to try anyway, now that she knew a little something. It rang a few times before being picked up by someone who said they would find Greg. A few moments later, Greg came to the phone.

"Hello?"

"Hi, Greg; it's Therese Ed—"

"I'm so happy it's you. What have you found out from that bastard coroner?"

"Well, some good news. It wasn't drugs."

"I knew that. I don't know why they lied to me. Did they think I wouldn't care about the truth?"

"I have no idea. But listen—had June undergone any surgery?"

"Surgery? No. Who would have paid for that?"

"Well, I don't know. Maybe old surgery—from her childhood? There are hints that maybe surgery caused the problem—I mean, the meningitis."

"No, that's impossible."

"She would have told you if she'd had epilepsy or cancer, right?"

"Cancer?" Greg was silent, taking this in. And then, "She would have told me, yes. We told each other everything."

"What about any symptoms? Headache? Nausea? Vomiting?"

"No, none of that. Look, she was as healthy as I am. And I am healthy, despite what you saw the other day. Does this mean a dead—I mean, that the trail's gone cold or whatever?"

"Not yet. Let me try a few more avenues, okay?" Therese forced herself to sound upbeat, and they said their goodbyes after scheduling another call.

For next three days, she called the coroner, but her calls went unanswered, and when took a redeye to New York and showed up in person, DVD in hand, the clerk informed her that the Tank was broken beyond repair and would almost certainly never work again. This seemed highly inconceivable to Therese, but worn out, she accepted the answer, certain she could find another Tank, somewhere—in LA.

But to her great surprise, she did not. She checked again at UCLA, USC—no one knew what the Tank was. And to her great annoyance, she had to admit that even she, with all her resources, was at a dead end, at least for now. It was time to return to work. The next morning, she awoke in her own bed, her dog by her side. In the kitchen, she watched Fancy forage outside. The robin blood on the flagstones was completely gone. Invisible.

Chapter Twenty-Five

RICHARD COULD NOT LIGHT the outdoor grill. He felt like a fool, standing there, making every attempt to get the gas range to light, but the wind and his lack of knowledge beat him. His dreams of freshly grilled yellowtail snapper were dashed, and awkwardly, he carried all of his newly bought supplies back into the villa, fighting with the tropical wind to close the sliding doors behind him. In the kitchen, he started the oven, setting the temperature gauge to "broil." He planned to have dinner ready when Bob arrived home, which he assumed would be any moment. He gave the snapper another glaze of a marinade he'd watched a woman in the market prepare and placed the huge and perfect fish into the broiler.

He assembled a basic salad, using greens he'd never come across in the States, although he doubted he would have noticed them, anyway. His trip to the market had opened his mind to an entirely new world of colors and smells. He wanted to explore them all, he decided. He nibbled on a green. It was slightly nutty and bitter, but tasty. He sliced a large tomato, watching the seeds ooze out of the ripe fruit. He dissected the entire tomato and examined its structure. He cut each piece of tomato into a perfect, bite-sized square, and then assembled all the squares in symmetrical piles on the cutting board. Next, a small red onion. He gave the onion the same detailed treatment and as he worked, he admired the vegetable's symmetry. Satisfied, he then opened a bottle of white wine that had been in the condo's refrigerator since their arrival, struggling with the corkscrew.

The cork safely retrieved in one piece, Richard decided some fresh air was in order. He moved to the terrace, where he watched a pale moon rising over the sea, the sky still bright blue. Leaning on the balcony, Richard studied the label on the bottle of wine. It appeared to have come from a local winery and bore the name "Franklin." Stuart's influence here was obviously quite far-reaching. Impressed, he took a sip of the wine, and then another. It was quite crisp, the perfect antidote to such a long hot day. Richard had little experience with alcohol, but the champagne on trip back to DC had inspired in him a curiosity about bubbly white drinks. The moon rose, steadily.

A loud, insistent bleeping jolted him out of his thoughts, causing him to drop the bottle and glass on the patio's bricks.

The doorbell? thought Richard in a panic, as he ran toward the front door to investigate, broken glass splintering underfoot. When he saw the smoke wafting from the kitchen, he put together the obvious. The smoke alarm was sounding. He ran to the oven and turned it to OFF, cursing the slowness of his own response system. His poor snapper was undoubtedly ruined. His ears pointed him to the source of the outrageous sound—a tiny white disc mounted on the ceiling between the hall and the dining area. Richard hastily ran to the front door and opened it wide, and then to the patio doors. He switched the A/C control to HIGH and burrowed in the broom closet for a stepstool. Surely, his ears were bleeding by now; the entire island must be able to hear it. Once mounted on the stepstool under the screaming white box, he attempted to twist the cover off and disconnect the alarm. But it was lodged in place. Try as he might, it would not budge; it appeared painted in place. He pushed the buttons on the casing, but they did nothing to stop the noise. With a firm grasp and even firmer determination, Richard pulled the entire unit from its ceiling mount. Down it came with bits of plaster and dust. Now the thing was in his hands, the alarm dismembered, but still sounding. He easily removed the battery from the underside and made it stop its bleating.

Peace at last! His head throbbed from the remarkably loud sound, his ears echoing with the noise. He came down from the stepstool and began to wave the smoke out the patio doors. He folded the stepstool, pondering how he might explain the destruction. Surveying the damage, he looked up at the hole he'd created in the ceiling. Now, with the dust settling, he saw a tiny flashing light in the hole where the alarm had been.

Curious, Richard mounted the stepstool again and looked into the crevice for a closer look. A tiny light there blinked on and off at regular intervals. Beyond the light, once his eyes had focused, he saw something unmistakable—a tiny, closed-circuit camera, and it appeared to be operating.

Richard and his father were being watched.

Richard stepped off the small ladder and looked again at the alarm he had dislodged and held it up to his eye. He could see the room perfectly through the cover! What appeared an opaque plastic cover was actually a clever transparent plastic. The battery and its wiring had been re-engineered to tuck into the lip of the cover, presumably to avoid blocking the lens of the camera device. Hastily, Richard located duct tape, and once again on the stepladder, replaced the alarm, taping it up as it had been, but with the tape covering the surface of the cover, thereby obscuring the lens.

It was refreshing to be working on something tangible again, thought Therese as she emerged from a meeting with the school district in downtown LA. She made her way underground to catch the subway. It was cool in the modern station, and clean. She rarely took public transportation, but Carlo was away for a while, visiting his family, so Therese took the opportunity to learn the relatively new subway system. It had cost LA a fortune and been mired in mismanagement and scandal, so she thought she ought to know if there was anything good about it. Besides, this line went by a great place for Korean BBQ, and Therese had arranged to meet a friend at the restaurant. The LED signage informed her that her train was "1 minutes" away from the station.

On the train, Therese took an empty seat next to a businessman. He was flipping through the *Los Angeles Times*. Therese herself had nothing to read, so she looked at the paper with him. As he flipped to a new page, she glimpsed an image in the section on his lap, an image that looked medical—was that a brain? She caught the words "new imaging tech" before he placed a different section of the paper on top of the article. New imaging—maybe the article would mention the Tank!

"Can I borrow the science section?" Therese pointed to the unread section of the paper.

The businessman glanced at her, barely. "I only take the train because there tends to be no one on it." He moved to an empty seat across the aisle. Angelinos were not accustomed to sharing their public space, having been raised in the relative private luxury of cars.

"It's just that I need to see something in that paper—you're not even reading that section. And it could be important."

"I doubt it. It's only the LA Times. Besides, you can get your own paper."

"It could affect someone's life. It'll only take a second."

"Please. Like that's true."

Therese made a mental note to remind people, like the botanist Dr. Rodriguez, why there were no men in her life.

The train pulled into a station, and the pneumatic doors slid open. Therese bolted up, snatched the science section from the businessman's lap, and leapt from the train onto the platform. The doors closed a second later. She waved to the businessman through the window as the train left the station; another passenger was laughing at him.

Therese sat on a bench to wait for the next train. Her foot throbbed from her spontaneous antics, so she propped it on the bench next to her and examined the pinched paper.

Her instincts had been right—this could be an important article. It was about a new form of medical imaging called fMRI. The article featured a large, electronic image of a brain. It showed areas of black, white, and gray. The copy below the picture explained how the scan could be useful in studying Alzheimer's disease, because it could represent the amount of effort made by the brain while remembering. The white parts showed, she surmised, areas of least brain effort. Those sections of the scan looked like nothing was there. What did that mean, she thought? She examined the article more closely, and then took the escalator upstairs into a dusky evening and dialed her mobile phone.

A week later, after a successful event in which she brought celebrity chefs into schools to cook menus created from the school's own gardens, Therese took the elevator to the imaging center at Stanford University in California. Therese had made an appointment with the school's leading radiologist, a woman who had been featured in the *Los Angeles Times* article. She had only gotten the appointment under the guise of wanting to invite the doctor to a Culinary Classroom event, and perhaps that wasn't so far from the truth. Therese felt the white lie was important—she might not have gotten an appointment so quickly without it.

A technician in a lab coat greeted Therese and escorted her down a long corridor. Various whirring and mechanical noises filled the echo-prone, cinderblock hall, which terminated at a conference room. Inside, Therese was introduced to the radiologist, who was a PhD in neuroradiology. Therese thought that title bode well for her case, for surely this woman would have at least heard of a "Tank." The doctor stood to greet her—a tall woman with tumbling chestnut hair and generous cheekbones.

"Thank you for seeing me today. I realize you must be very busy."

"Actually, this is a good time. Most of our computers are tied up processing data, and I needed a break, anyway." The doctor smiled; she spoke with a faint Russian accent. Therese explained her foundation's general mission to educate inner city youth about healthier eating and gave the doctor her card.

"I was wondering if you could visit one of our schools and perhaps teach the kids about irradiation of food crops."

The doctor laughed. "I don't know the first thing about that. I could perhaps discuss the effects of radiation on human anatomy."

"Of course, I realize—that must sound like a stretch."

"Is that really what you came all this way to ask me?"

"I'm afraid not. I didn't mean to be dishonest. I know you must be getting all kinds of crackpot calls since the article."

"Are you a crackpot?" The two women laughed together.

"No, although you may think I sound like one after I ask you some of these questions. You see, I was intrigued by your fMRI technology; I need some data analyzed, and I can't find anyone to help."

"Go on," said the doctor, stealing a glance at the wall clock.

"From what I've read, your fMRI technology is able to analyze data that could once not be captured. I was wondering if there have been any other recent technologies that have been revolutionary in the same way."

"Well, each imaging innovation has been revolutionary. X-rays, CAT scans, each one did something we could not do before. Which one did you have in mind?"

"Specifically, a Tank scan."

"A Tank scan?" The doctor raised her eyebrows. "I'm surprised you've heard of it."

"You have?"

"Well, of course. Tank technology could be considered a predecessor to our fMRI." The doctor looked at Therese quizzically. Therese could hardly contain her excitement and started opening her briefcase to retrieve the DVD.

"I wonder if you'd mind telling me where I can find a Tank. You see, I came across this DVD while trying to help someone, but I can't help him until I know what's on it and what this Tank thing is."

The doctor began to laugh. "You certainly won't find a Tank anywhere, not anymore. There were only a few built, and those were just

just prototypes. Here, let me see that," said the doctor, reaching for the DVD. "I guess this is what they say about getting your name in the papers; people crawl out of the woodwork." The doctor stood, more amused than dismayed at having been mislead. "Come on, let's go put this in my computer and see what we can do. I'm up for the challenge."

Therese and the Russian doctor made their way down a corridor. "Now, tell me a little about this person," said the doctor, gesturing to the DVD. Therese gave her the background, including the drug-free blood and the possible past surgery. They turned into an undistinguished office, and the doctor motioned for Therese to take a seat.

The doctor launched her own computer program and had the Tank file open in seconds, the doctor's system having recognized its type. The two systems were, remarkably, technically compatible. Therese stood up and watched over the doctor's shoulder eagerly, waiting for a picture to appear on the screen.

"This will take awhile; it has to be converted. Let me get it started, and then I'll give you a tour." The doctor made a few keystrokes, and then motioned for Therese to follow her. They walked down a busy corridor and past rooms containing various pieces of machinery. "Actually, I'm glad you came by with the Tank file, because we need to keep testing what we think we know, keep finding the boundaries of what imaging technology can do in the real world. We always need more data. Can I use this woman's Tank data for my own studies?"

"Sure; I don't see why not."

"Thanks, now we're even," smiled the doctor then her face clouded, slightly. "The only problem is that we've never really looked at data from someone so young. The computer may not like that."

"Why does age matter?"

"An fMRI, or functional magnetic resonance, is a revolutionary process because it shows areas of the brain that have to work harder to perform certain basic memory tasks. Most young people don't have anything wrong in that department, you see, so all we get is a lot of black area. But, what I'm hoping will work is that the machine can be set to better analyze those tiny areas of non-activity in June's image data. It may not work, but it could."

"It's amazing you can do all this without the living, breathing person here. And the scan was made after she died."

"True, but the program can reason, based on the anatomy of her brain, to a very accurate degree. And, actually, we do need a living, breathing person to compare the data to, as a control. Ideally, we need someone close in age to June." The doctor stopped walking, and the two women looked at each other, light bulbs going off.

"Okay, I'll volunteer," nodded Therese.

"Perfect!" The doctor smiled then continued. "I was hoping you'd say that. True, June was almost ten years younger, but you're both relatively young females. Now, I'll owe you. Here's the hitch—even though we're badly in need of this data, we can't run the exam on June's data or your own for free, and there's a grant that could cover the costs eventually but—"

Therese was grateful again that cost was no object. She interrupted the doctor. "It's no problem."

The doctor's eyes lit up. She had found a perfect subject. Maybe she should accept more calls from strangers! "It's not cheap. And we don't accept insurance."

"It doesn't matter." Not wanting to sound conspicuous, as she never did, she added, "I happen to have grant money myself right now."

"In that case, could we do the tests now? Do you have a couple hours free? We had a cancellation that freed up a test bay."

"Sure," shrugged Therese. "Why not? I'd be happy to help."

The doctor led Therese to the scan area, where she was asked to change into a gown, remove all metal objects, and relieve herself in the adjacent bathroom. A technician entered and gave her a series of instructions, then got her into place inside a long, thin, tubular table. He put a pillow beneath her knees for comfort and covered her in a blanket. The radiologist appeared and explained further.

"We'll only be imaging your head. Unlike a traditional MRI, you don't need to hold your breath or freeze. Also, there will only be small motor noise, instead of a roar. The process will take about one hour. And you'll only be exposed to a tiny amount of radiation—less than you would get from watching one hour of television."

Therese lay inside the pod-like thing and heard the distant hum of a motor start. Therese lay motionless in the pod, flat on her back, as the machine set out to work. The radiologist spoke to her from the operations room, behind glass, she reasoned, although from her position in the pod she could not see anything but the ceiling of the machine.

"If you're ready, we'll begin," stated the doctor through a microphone.

"Ready," Therese replied.

The test began. The doctor asked her a series of questions to "test" her memory. What was the doctor's first name, for instance, and what cross streets was the medical center located between? What color was the technician's shirt? Purple, she vividly recalled. Some questions were much harder, like the day she read the article about the new fMRI scan—when was that? Four days ago? Seven? She had been so busy working it was difficult to remember immediately. Did Therese recall the day of the week she read the article? She was glad to realize that she did; it had been a Monday. It seemed like hours between each question. The doctor informed her that the wait was necessary while the computer processed the data from her brain's activity.

It seemed well over an hour before the test was finished. Therese got dressed and was met by the doctor, who led her down a corridor to the blood lab.

"Now the lab techs will draw some blood for the genetic markers. This is part of the procedure, and it's not really necessary, since all we care about is the difference in the scans—between your and June's—but we might as well, since we'll get June's blood, too, from the coroner. It'll take a good five days, at least, before we can correlate all the results. The Tank file on its own will not help us much. Your scan will be ready sometime tomorrow. Next, we have to compare your brain's picture to June's Tank data, which we're converting and importing into our new software. I've already scheduled an appointment for you to return for follow up next Friday." The doctor handed her an appointment card. "After the blood work, please stop there," the doctor motioned down the hall, "to complete your billing information."

They said their goodbyes, each thanking the other profusely, and Therese surrendered her arm to the phlebotomist, who gave her an apple after he drew the blood. She then visited the billing office as instructed.

As the only child of a billionaire, Therese had never had to worry about money, and so she had devoted her life to those with less. At least, she thought that was why. What if her mother had been given more time? Surely, there would have been another child, maybe a brother. What would he have been like? Noble and caring, self-effacing and charitable? Or greedy and snotty? Maybe a drug addict or felon.

She had read stories about other children like her, born rich. Many did waste the money, squandering it to rebel, or took drugs to hurt themselves and their parents or to assuage their guilt. She did feel guilty, but had never been interested in doing anything illegal or illicit. She helped instead, or that was what it was called. She had given her time and effort tirelessly. She had seen children who lived from meal to meal, or worse, and the impact even one dollar had on them. But now, for the first time in her life, she truly understood the power of money as she looked at the bill for her fMRI.

She phoned up her personal banker and arranged for the instant wire transfer of $7,500 to be paid to Stanford Medical Center. She hung up the phone and was overcome with gratefulness for her health, her wealth, and her father.

Chapter Twenty-Six

STUART LOOKED UP from the financials he held in his hand. The flimsy fax paper began to wilt in his sweaty hand. He was back in North Carolina, reviewing the predictions for the third quarter earnings. The numbers were good. They were very good; in fact, Stuart had his suspicions about their goodness. While it was true that getting the public excited about a new drug could make market prices temporarily high, there was also the problem of overexposure to consider, not to mention market corrections, which were inevitable. Stuart crumpled the paper in his hands and tossed it into the garbage can, then put his phone on speaker and dialed.

"Paul Westin's office," answered a young woman's voice.

"Yes, and who is this?"

"I'm Tiffany, Mr. Westin's new administrative assistant. Can you hold, please?"

"No, I certainly will not hold. I'd like you to ask your new boss to get up here immediately. This is Mr. Franklin. I'm the CEO of this company, in case your boss neglected to mention that. I suggest you commit my number to memory so that the next time I phone you can address me by name. Is that understood?"

"Uh, yes, of course. I'm sorry, I—"

Stuart hung up the phone by pressing the speaker button. A dial tone ensued. Stuart looked out the window, wondering what number crunching Paul had done to get the predictions so high. Didn't the fool know that BioSys could never meet those predictions and they'd just look bad once the next quarter's real earnings came in? Those numbers must not be released to the press. What was Paul playing at?

Stuart waited and waited, but Paul did not materialize. The thought of walking around his own company looking for a supposedly loyal member of his staff irked him so he decided against hunting the man down, for now.

Chapter Twenty-Seven: *Anegada*

THE VIVARIUM SEEMED FILLED with screeching monkeys. The special lab arena seemed to be packed with them, but it was just the subjects' volume that created the illusion. In all, there were twenty BioSys monkeys; twelve were for Bob's use alone. Their cages were anything but cage-like. "Luxurious playpens" was a more apt description. The room was three stories tall, like a gymnasium, and featured a waterfall, real trees, and sophisticated motion-tracking computer devices that allowed digital cameras to record each monkey at any given location. Another computer controlled the vivarium's "weather," creating a very realistic rain forest, the ecosystem in which this type of monkey thrived. Every few minutes, the place was magically covered in a fine mist. Richard found the humidity hard to take and so had only visited the area once before; he preferred the cool detachment of his ordered lab.

But now Richard stood in front of a computerized panel with his father, Bob. A vast piece of Plexiglas separated them from their fellow primates and their wet world. From the computer station, they saw the latest stats on their monkeys—how they were eating, weight loss or gain, temperature, etc. Bob's team had been monitoring the twelve monkeys closely since their surgery four weeks ago. What made the monkey trial so perfect was the monkeys' pasts. They had all suffered head injuries of some kind, so they were ideal candidates for stem cell injection. Bob was taking weekly MRI and PET scans of the monkeys, which when combined, could show the progress of the stem cells.

With the assistance of a computer expert from the vivarium, Bob showed Richard his latest news. The man pushed a series of buttons, and the panel came alive with lights.

"You see, here is Hazel's last scan, taken yesterday. On the left you see her baseline MRI scan, taken before the surgery. Notice the areas of vast necrosis," Bob pointed to the area of damage in Hazel's small monkey brain, indicated by white areas. "And, here, on the right," continued Bob, "you see her brain today. In just four weeks, there is less dead tissue."

Bob asked the tech to bring up the PET scan results.

"Here is an even clearer demonstration. The PET scan shows metabolic activity, as you know. Dead areas are represented by the violet hues, and live functioning areas are indicated in the reds and oranges. Hazel's PET scan from yesterday shows less violet than in her baseline, it's as simple as that. Especially here," pointed Bob, "in the area of the right temporal lobe. This is very encouraging, because we know Alzheimer's sufferers tend to have necrosis in that area. And this display here," Bob continued, his voice full of excitement, "compares percentages of each wavelength per scan."

Bob read the comparison area aloud. "'Baseline, quadrant 1, right temporal lobe, 30 nanometers,' that's violet, the deadest area, '85%. Week 1 from the same area, what the machine calls quadrant 1, same wavelength, 82%, a small improvement. Week 2, 80%, Week 3, 75%, Week 4, 65%.' We know now that time is a measurable factor. It takes at least three weeks for the good stem cells to differentiate through the area and start to repair."

"It's remarkable," Richard began. "I didn't think we'd see such quick progress. What do you predict will happen after four more weeks? Will quadrant 1 be down to, say, only 40% dead cells?"

"I have no idea. But the other encouraging thing is that other monkeys that received treatment have basically the same results—give or take a few percentage points."

"Any sign of teratomas in the six that got embryonic cells?"

"Yes, I was going to point that out next. Our fine neuro-radiologist has been on the lookout for them. They're small," Bob pointed to a tiny area on Hazel's film. "See, you can barely make them out. Here's another view. But the tumor doesn't seem affect the power of the cells to repair dead area."

In the higher-contrast scan, Richard identified the suspicious tumor mass. "Can we get a sample of that? I'd like to be sure what we're looking at is indeed benign."

"Naturally; I'll do it tomorrow."

"On another subject, do all the monkeys have damage in the same area of the brain? I'm wondering if the stem cells stop at some places or move on."

"Roughly the same, yes. I rejected monkeys with damage in areas I knew I could not easily penetrate surgically. With these twelve, I had a pretty direct shot through the Aqueduct of Sylvius, down to the—"

"Okay, got it!" piped Richard. The thought of an open brain gave him the spins. Bob always forgot that Richard had never made it through an anatomy class.

A monkey approached the Plexiglas, as if making contact with Richard and his father. Richard bent down to get a better look at its face. The ape did not make eye contact for very long, but instead looked around.

"That's Cirrus," Bob said, "the eldest male in our group. He's smart, too, despite his brain damage."

Richard watched Cirrus stealing looks at him. The human-like features were always astounding to him, the long and perfect fingers a mirror of his own. The monkey's gaze was intense and distinctively thoughtful. Cirrus seemed to study Richard's sandy brown hair—so much lighter than his own fur. It was as if Cirrus was performing his own study on the humans. In an instant, however, the monkey changed his mind and trotted away, perhaps to go report on what he had seen. Richard watched a nearby camera pan, following the monkey's movements.

It was then that Richard was reminded of the disturbing discovery last week of a hidden camera in his villa. Were there more, he wondered? And what was their purpose? He had decided at dinner that night not to mention the camera to his father until he knew more about this strange little island. But now it occurred to him—that fan at Stuart's. It wasn't a fan, really. Was it?

"Let's see about reporting the good news to Stuart—back there," Bob gestured to an area behind the north wall. Bob escorted him out of the vivarium and into the ordered confines of the more traditional laboratory space behind it. To Richard's surprise, however, the room was more like mission control for a NASA expedition than any monkey lab he had ever seen. The room was vast, cool, and dark, lit only by small desk lamps and giant monitors which lined one great wall, showing each monkey camera's image. Bob led Richard to a control panel with many dials and switches. Printers spewed bits of information and thousands of tiny red and white lights blinked, their language incomprehensible to Richard. They seated themselves in hi-tech leather swivel chairs. Around them, people in headsets swirled about, speaking into tiny microphones next to their mouths, tapping away on keyboards, turning the mysterious dials.

"You see, while you've been in your lab working on the cells, I've been getting to know these people. BioSys does all their animal work right here, and so naturally, they have every toy imaginable, all at their disposal."

Richard gawked at the images of the monkeys, his eye roving from screen to screen—there were twenty screens in all. Taken together, the individual images made a story of the life of all the vivarium's monkeys. It was like watching a live movie. What would Hazel do next? What about Cirrus? He watched one eating, one playing, one grooming a friend, one playing with the camera itself. It was instantly intoxicating.

"We'll video-phone Stuart now and speak to him through one of the monitors, here," pointed Bob to a smaller monitor encased in the console. Richard was astonished to see his own father, aged seventy-seven, push a series of buttons, click with a mouse, and then switch on a light above them.

"What's that for?" asked Richard, who had just gotten used to the cozy darkness of what he now deemed a movie theater.

"So he can see us, my boy."

Richard furrowed his brows. It wasn't until he saw the image of Stuart on the screen that he understood. They were speaking on a videophone. But where was the camera that would transmit their image? Richard looked around, trying to figure it out.

"Just look here, Richard," said Stuart from the monitor. Richard saw Stuart on the screen, sitting at a desk somewhere.

"Oh, I get it now. Hello, Stuart," he said, just a little too loudly, as if talking to an elderly person.

"Hi, guys. What's news? Tell me something good, please. It's been a helluva day."

Bob began talking. It seemed to Richard that, from their way of speaking, the two men must have been in close contact over the last month.

"Well, great results on the four-week tests. We saw a lot of progress in just one week, especially in Hazel, the monkey with the most Alzheimer's-like damage. The cells have differentiated as we expected. I plan to do a biopsy tomorrow, which Richard can then analyze. In six weeks, as we expected, we'll know everything we need to about the rate of differentiation and proliferation."

"And, you, Richard?"

Richard leaned into the monitor, still unused to the device.

"I received the human cells from the cadaver and am conducting the necessary tests now. I am testing the differences between the cell line I arrived with and the one from the adult human. The adult human neuron stem cells are very encouraging. Between the two samples, we have a very solid study. I agree that we can begin on human subjects in six weeks. We'd like to do four patients, each two to receive different cell sources."

"Sounds logical," nodded Stuart. "But can we move my surgery up? Six weeks from now is an eternity."

"There are risks, Stuart, with any new procedure. I'd like to lessen that risk before we perform any of this on a human. I know you're anxious," said Bob. "We all are. This is the chance of a lifetime, however, and we want to get it right. How are you feeling? Do you have any new symptoms?"

Stuart sighed and looked away from the camera's lens. "Well, whatever you gave me for the depression is helping. I was really incapacitated for a few days there. Putting the keys in the same place every day has helped, also. New symptoms? No, none that I've noticed. I've got to go to another meeting now, so over and out."

Richard and his father made their way out of the den of technology into the corridor. A wave of excitement passed through him, and Richard realized the trial was really going to happen, and even though at least one monkey had developed a small tumor, he had foreseen that, and the good results of the adult neural cells fired him up. For the first time in years, he saw the fruit of all his labors maturing before his eyes. Bob read his mind. He patted his son on the back firmly and turned to face him. Richard saw tears in his eyes.

"You know it's all I always hoped for you, son." Bob put his arm around him, and they walked out into the stifling afternoon air.

Stuart was pleased that all was progressing, but could not imagine how he could hold up for another six weeks—ten, if you counted when he would see results from surgery. Although it was true that he had no new symptoms, the simple tasks of each day were becoming more of a struggle. He was embarrassed to admit this fact, so he didn't, not even to Bob. The lack of control just made him feel more desperate. He looked out the airplane window and saw the runway recede at a rapid clip. Soon, his favorite blue waters would welcome him to Anegada. He closed his eyes as his corporate pilot banked elegantly eastward.

The board was becoming more of a worry than usual. In the past, he had been a firm leader, a confident captain. But now, every time he had to face them, he felt he might slip up, perhaps even be overruled. He was sure they sensed his failings. He would do anything to be his old self again.

He'd had no trouble getting away from the States. He had simply told his staff that ABT-55 needed his constant attention, and after all, what better way to monitor the drug's progress but to be on-site? They had understood, unquestioningly.

A terrifying surge of emotion in his throat gripped him. This time, it came with a memory, a picture, of Rita. He missed her! His wife, Rita. He had been so absorbed in work for so many years—he had buried her and those feelings long, long ago, but he did still remember that day, the pool of blood beneath her face. What had been left of her face.

He shook himself, straightening in the seat. It was not normal to be missing his wife; that was ancient history. Her killer, a drugged-out burglar, had been found two weeks later, dead himself, just evidence at the scene of a drug deal. No, he must carry on as if everything was normal, for soon, it would be. He was sure of that. Thank goodness he'd found Bob and Richard.

And thank goodness for technology. Stuart's schedule in the islands was as demanding as it was in North Carolina, and he could not have kept up appearances were it not for his videophone, a very expensive prototype that a major computer company was trying to bring to market. There were numerous problems with transmitting real-time video over a cell signal, so this company used a combination of cell and satellite technologies. It worked most of the time, better when the plane was taxiing than flying, for instance—but it heated up like crazy from the massive processing power it drew. He set the videophone on the seat next to him, on its side so it could ventilate.

For years, BioSys had been conducting trials and testing outside of the States. It was common knowledge that British laws catered to the drug industry, unlike in America, where progress took years and years. And the British were happy to have the rent, the licensing of the patents, and the employment for their citizens. BioSys employed two thousand locals on its Anegada campus, most of who commuted back to Tortola every day on a BioSys ferry. Between the three twenty-four-hour manufacturing plants and the administrative offices, there were always new challenges for anyone with enough ambition—not to mention all the service-oriented job slots.

Stuart's videophone beeped. Its frequency did not interfere with the pilot's instruments, so he could easily converse while in-flight—if the satellites could keep up. He quickly flicked the screen's power on.

"Stuart here," he answered. As he did, he saw Paul, barely, from the office on the screen. After their last exchange, Stuart was anything but pleased to receive his call. It was a good thing he had a poor signal. Stuart saw the screen trying to resolve and not doing a good job. Despite the poor quality of the video, Stuart could make out Paul's smug smile. Wait, was Paul in his own office, or in Stuart's? It was hard to tell. The audio was sketchy as well.

"Hi there St…. Just chec…in latest with ABT…. I heard there was some new—"

The video cleared for a split second, and Stuart felt ready to explode.

"What the hell are you doing in my office?"

"Woah, Stuart. Calm…I'm in your office because my…broken. The new admin tripped…it and…bent. It's being repair—"

"Right. And the dog ate your homework, too, I imagine?"

"Look, Stuart, it's the truth. I…to see if I could be of any assistance with ABT-55." The picture was entirely gone now, and Stuart rubbed his eyes in agitation.

"And I'm telling you to mind your own business and get out of my office, Paul, before I have you thrown out."

"Stuart, I've got a lot…ABT-55. You know that."

It was true that Paul had a lot to lose if ABT-55 did not go as planned. Paul owned more stock than did any other board member, except of course, for Stuart himself.

"And you know that ABT-55 is going to be just what we planned—the least toxic chemo drug to ever be developed. So stop worrying about your stock and get back to work, please. While you're at it, I'd like a report from you about the predictive numbers you tried to pass off for the third quarter."

The video flicked back on, and Stuart could see that Paul looked genuinely shocked, if the weak video signal was to be trusted.

"What do you mean 'tried'? Those were goo…I spent quite a bit of time…Besides, I thought you'd be pleased. We're entering a great…trend."

"I'm not going to spend time teaching you Economics 101, Paul. Let's not pretend. Just fix it, and don't pull a stunt like that again, or I'll report you to Securities."

Paul started to speak, and then stopped himself, changed course. "Sorry to bother you," he managed to fit in just before Stuart quit the video connection.

Stuart sighed and looked out the window of the plane again. They were making their typical low approach over fields. Stalks of an exotic flower were blooming, their fruit being plucked by a crew of laborers.

Therese boarded the elevator at the Stanford Medical School, again. Although she'd been swept up in fundraising efforts at Culinary Classroom, she had been looking forward all week to the result of June Hamels' brain scan. She was now on the edge of her seat in anticipation of what that mysterious Tank file from the medical examiner's office would reveal.

Therese greeted the doctor she had met just seven days earlier. The doctor led her into her office, which was decorated with various framed degrees and a watercolor portrait of her family. Her two children, both under ten, had inherited the doctor's hair.

"Please, sit down," offered the doctor. They both sat—the desk between them. The doctor flicked on the lights of a film viewer mounted on the wall behind the doctor's chair. It filled the room with a fluorescent glow.

"What have you discovered about June, doctor?"

"Well, it turns out we've discovered a good deal. And I'm afraid what I'm about to tell you may come as somewhat of a shock."

Was June, after all, a drug-taker? Did she have a rare form of cancer? Of course, that must be the answer.

The doctor took a deep breath. Her jaw tightened visibly. "The scan we took of your brain shows that you are at a high risk for developing Alzheimer's. You have distinct neuro-anatomical signs of MCI, or mild cognitive impairment, in your left temporal lobe." Silence, then she cleared her throat and quietly uttered, "I'm terribly sorry."

"Me?" Stunned, Therese sat in silence, processing the news. "But I thought you were going to tell me something about June. I—well, I don't know what to say."

"I'm sorry to deliver such terrible news. I was surprised myself, seeing as we did not intend to diagnose you. We intended to use your data as a healthy control."

Silence reigned for a few moments. Therese heard a cacophony of internal voices. When would she start to show symptoms? Was she destined to develop the disease? What could she do to keep her brain healthy? She felt herself paling.

"Let me explain what we know about your brain," began the doctor. She assembled the films on the light box. Therese focused her attention, anxiously awaiting the details.

With a laser pointer, the doctor began to explain.

"Here, in the area of your hippocampus, we see a cluster of darker cells. This corresponds to areas of high activity. Can you see the area I mean?"

Therese nodded.

"If I didn't know from your blood work that you carry a gene called APOE-4, this scan wouldn't bother me. APOE-4 is a gene we know pre-disposes people to Alzheimer's. The combination of your genetic code and your scan indicate you're quite high-risk. Does anyone in your immediate family have Alzheimer's?"

"No, of course not."

"Well, I mention it because you inherited the gene. Why don't I take some family history down? Maybe we can begin to see you regularly, if you'd like. There are great strides being made the area of gene silencing." The doctor took up a pen.

The doctor took down all of Therese's information, and Therese found herself struggling to think of any disease she knew of in her small family. Her mother's mother had died in the burglary, but had been healthy, and her father's parents had died naturally, albeit senile, after a long life. Her maternal grandfather was still living, retired, in Key West. Her mother's siblings were all healthy, and her father had no living siblings. There was no trace of Alzheimer's that she knew of, but then again, perhaps everyone in her small family was too young to exhibit symptoms. The thought of what could be lurking in them made her shudder. With a start, Therese remembered June.

"But what about June? Did you learn anything?"

"June had some brain surgery, certainly. Our interpretation of the Tank imaging was able to determine, with impressive accuracy, the surgical margins. We saw a small hole in the frontal area, and it appears that one of her olfactory bulbs is partially missing. The computer was able to interpret the path of the surgeons. It also made a detailed analysis of the surrounding tissue, which was healthy and normal, but there were signs of inflammation and possible hemorrhage. Her memory, however, was probably completely normal. We know that by comparing her data to yours."

When the interview concluded, Therese made her way out of the office, but later, she wouldn't be able to recall her exact movements, not due to an ailing memory, but shock. She went back to the parking garage to get her car, and then? She drove around downtown Palo Alto aimlessly, then parked and wandered into a café on University Avenue. She stared out of the window at the sunny day, thinking, until it was dark. She ate dinner alone in an Indian restaurant, but she couldn't enjoy the Punjabi meal. She ate because she needed fuel, not because she appreciated the complex tastes, her mind elsewhere.

Therese tossed and turned in yet another hotel room bed. At four a.m., she finally got up and got dressed. She strode down Palm Drive towards the Stanford quad, its street named for the giant palm tress that lined it so regally. The sky turned from black to blue, and a foggy breeze made the palm fronds above her head dance. She walked on, her head pointed at the non-native, imported tropical trees, the fresh, moist air clearing her head. It struck her that her behavior now—the sleeplessness, the distractedness—reminded her of someone. Her father. He always got like this before a big project began. She hadn't thought about that in so long. Well, she hadn't seen him in so long. A big project...

Of course. He could help her. Who else could? With new energy, she jogged back up Palm Drive. Now there were people out walking their dogs or jogging themselves. She felt she could rejoin the world of the living.

By that afternoon, she was back in a plane, but this time, the jet would take her away from work, not towards it. Fancy dozed across three seats on the other side of the aisle. A quick call to the Culinary volunteers was all that was required—they were in a fundraising mode, anyway, a perfect time for a break. She had spent so much time running and planning in the last five years, without ever stopping to catch her breath. The results of the fMRI were terrifying, but at least they had provided a wake-up call. She had never planned to work herself to death when she started her organization, and she certainly didn't want to end up like her father. She rubbed her eyes and lifted her to-go coffee mug to her lips.

My father, Stuart Franklin. In a moment, Therese found herself gazing at a wallet picture she kept of the two of them—taken on the day she first opened the foundation's office. They were standing outside, and above their heads, two workmen were hanging the new Culinary Classroom sign that had just been delivered. Her dad was making a goofy pose, as if the sign might fall on him. She was so proud that day! She smiled at the memory.

From the outside, it appeared he had given her everything; she'd had every opportunity in life, which had been like walking a path through an enchanted forest carpeted with rose petals. She had all this, and yet, she had never had his presence. He had always been too busy for her, too absorbed in a new drug, too busy making money. Sometimes, she felt she would have given up every cent in exchange for a life spent living together. Maybe this was why she had developed a life of flurry, constantly going here and there, changing careers, stopping and starting. Being at home just made the absence of both parents loom larger. As an adult, Therese had filled the empty shell of a house in the canyon with furniture to dampen the echoes, but that had only made the house feel small.

How had her mother coped? What had it been like to be married to one of the richest men in the world? Of course, he hadn't been at all rich back then, when Therese was just born. Rita had had a baby to look after, and then, once Therese was in kindergarten, her mother had gone back to work at the paper. Had there been fights, tension? She couldn't remember.

Therese gazed out the window, and the sight below filled her with a strange optimism. She was going home—not to Santa Monica, but her childhood summer home, in the British Virgin Islands. She saw a tiny island surrounded by startlingly blue waters and populated with lush forest. It appeared uninhabited and perfect in every way. This aerial view of earth's bounty delivered a short wave of peace, and for a moment, she glimpsed the vast order of life on this planet—its pain, its ecstasy, its sorrows, its exultations. For a moment, she actually felt that this was all part of some plan.

Therese and Fancy landed at BioSys' private landing strip twenty minutes later. Therese stepped out into the steamy island afternoon; the dog loped down the stairs behind her. Dusk was falling, and from her memories of being here as a child, she knew it would be quite dark quickly. She had arranged for a BioSys driver, and after stowing her carry-on bag in the trunk, they were off. The ocean breeze rejuvenated her airplane-dry face, and Fancy enjoyed the air by sticking her head out of the sunroof. As they drove away from the landing strip, she thought she heard the roar of a plane's engine. Surely, her plane wasn't taking off already, she thought. She turned to look out the rear window, but saw nothing save a stunning sunset.

The last light of the day made her face sparkle like a precious jewel.

Stuart was entrenched at his desk at Eastwind when he heard a commotion through his open window. He abandoned his stack of paperwork and reading glasses and moved into the hallway and the large living area, which was cheery and homey, with a large breezeway that brought in fresh ocean air. He immediately recognized the voice in the driveway. Therese was here, god damn it! But why? he wondered in a startled panic. What poor timing! He would have to keep her at another house. Stuart walked out into the drive.

"Therese!" he shouted in greeting. Despite his anxieties about her sudden presence, he was overjoyed to see her helping the dog unfold its giant frame from the hired car. They embraced on the porch.

"What on earth are you doing here?" Stuart stood back to survey her young face. To be so young and energetic again! Her face clouded slightly when she replied.

"I've decided to take some time off from the Classroom. I've been working too hard, and I haven't spent any time with you in years." She paused, and a smile brightened her face, but he could see something was eating at her. "So, surprise! Here I am."

Stuart had to force his own smile this time. He led her into the house.

"You can stay at one of the beach condos. You'll have more privacy there, and you can take morning swims. And Fancy will like the sand." Hearing her name, Fancy put her giant paws on Stuart's thighs and craned up to kiss him on the chin.

"I'd love that. Thanks, Dad. It's just what I was hoping for." She righted Fancy, and they all proceeded into the house.

"So, sit down and tell me about your travels."

At the word "sit," Fancy climbed up onto the oversized leather couch and sat in the very middle. Therese squeezed in next to the giant dog as Stuart moved to the wet bar. Fancy closed her eyes almost immediately—she was no pup anymore, and the day's travels had worn her out. Stuart opened a bottle of chilled white wine and passed Therese a glass, which she nearly finished in a gulp. Therese asked her father about his latest workload, although she knew the answers already. She was trying to lead into her most important question.

"Tell me about the drug that's brought you down here. It's a new—"

"Chemo drug, going to be very, very big. Can I get you another?" Her father motioned to her empty wine glass, and she nodded. Stuart moved back to the bar, his back to her. She sensed he did not want to discuss the drug, and there was a palpable tension in the air. What was so special about the drug that it required his full-time presence in the islands, she wondered? She decided to drop it and get right to her question. She knew if she didn't, she'd be up all night thinking about it, and she had already been thinking about it constantly for twenty-four hours. "I was wondering—" but her father had already begun to speak.

"It's a revolutionary drug," he passed her the glass, unaware that he had cut her off. "It uses a special new biochemical approach which causes much less damage to the cells of the body. There's never been anything like it. It uses an enzyme called—" Stuart paused, remembering. "Phytonzonase, that's it," he continued. She saw his brows furrow; he had always struggled with the technical side of his business.

"This enzyme is biochemically smart. It can actually determine which cells are disease cells, which are cancer cells. It only kills the cancer cells! It works by meeting one cell and actually penetrating it, and in the process, it transmits a biochemical signal, then waits for the biological equivalent of an answer, like a phone conversation. If the answer comes back 'healthy,' it moves on to the next cell." Stuart smiled and paused to see the effect on her face at the news of such a miracle of science. Therese had been the audience for many of these speeches. She didn't mind listening to them—they displayed her father's best traits: enthusiasm and magnanimity. He had a way of translating even the most complicated scientific methods into lay terms. Of course, he oversimplified the science, but no one cared. They wanted to believe in the ultimate power of facts and data. Therese was a believer, too, but often these spiels left her feeling like her father was more salesman than CEO, but was there even a difference? She listened to more details about ABT-55, but then felt she might burst. A craft-brown corner of the large envelope containing her fMRI films in her brushed against her leg. It occurred to her then that other adult children, at this stage of their lives, might be anxious to deliver good news—a wedding, a baby, maybe.

"Dad, I know BioSys is a leader in oncology drugs, but are you investigating other areas of medicine—say, for instance, neuro-degenerative diseases—maybe Alzheimer's?" She cleared her throat. Maybe using the word 'neuro-degenerative' was a bit much. Therese hadn't expected what came next. She jumped slightly when he raised his voice.

"Alzheimer's? Of course not!"

"Why not? Has your company considered it? You know, it could be a great money maker," she added, trying to deflate his odd reaction. Her voice was as calm as his was agitated.

"We're a cancer company. It'd be next to impossible to branch out. Besides, there are no exciting avenues of research regarding Alzheimer's now. It's considered a hopeless cause in the research world, and speculative drugs never make any money. You know that."

Therese had never dreamed her father would utter the word "hopeless." She couldn't believe it, and his manner and attitude did not compute. Her adrenalin level dropped; she was now exhausted. She began to cry, the sudden tears catching her off-guard. Fancy awoke at the sound; her father went ashen.

"Why, darling, what is it?" He sat on the coffee table across from her and reached out his arms to hug her. Fancy stuck her snout on Therese's lap. "Whatever would you have to be so upset about? Therese?" He lifted her tear-streaked face to his, looking for an answer. She hated to upset him, but whom else could she tell?

"Dad, I've got early Alzheimer's." She looked at him. There was nothing else left to say.

"But that, well, that's impossible. Who told you that?"

"It's a long story, but I found out at Stanford that I carry an inherited gene that predisposes me to the disease."

"Well, someone's obviously made a mistake." Stuart smiled. He got up and moved to the wet bar for water. "On the other hand, I suppose you could have inherited such a gene from your mother."

"You couldn't carry the gene yourself?"

"Therese, that's absurd! Look at the man standing here before you. I have access to the best minds in the business. Don't you think I've had all my genes mapped? Of course, I have. I did it for you, a few years ago, in case you decide to have a family one day."

Therese slouched back into the cushions of the sofa and closed her eyes, dry now.

"I guess it was Mom, then."

"Of course, it was, darling. But listen," Stuart brought Therese a chilled glass of water and sat on the coffee table across from her. "I promise," he said, "that you will not be a victim of this disease. You have my word."

Therese couldn't see how this could be true, after his remarks earlier, but she said anyway, "Thanks, Dad."

Richard sat up in bed, startled by the shrill noise, alarmed and disoriented. The ring of what, though? The smoke alarm, again? No. The phone. It stopped. His t-shirt was damp with sweat. He'd been sleeping soundly. Was he sleeping still? His heart raced as he leaned over to see the clock: 4:13 a.m. He hated loud noises, and hated even more to be caught off guard. *But who would be calling now*?

Richard stumbled out of bed and into the hall, tripping over his shoes in the process. His room was on the second floor, and the hallway overlooked the great room below. He leaned over the balcony.

"There's no problem, Richard; you can go back to sleep," Bob called up to him. Richard saw he cradled the phone between his neck and ear, as if his hands were not free. What could be so urgent at this hour? Bewildered, he waded back to his bed. He half-heard snippets from downstairs: "second subject," "rate of infusion" "non-invasive." But the sound of waves, floating in from the cracked window, soon blanketed the murmurs from downstairs, and Richard was asleep again.

Chapter Twenty-Eight: *Fox Alzheimer's Hospital, Ypsilanti, Michigan*

THE NURSE WHEELED THE TROLLEY down the hall. She was tired. And she was tired of administering this so-called "vaccine." She could see it didn't work. It just dragged things out longer, made things harder on everyone involved. Not that there were many involved, not at this dump. No family visits, no friends. The people here were mostly poor, left for dead.

She arrived at her last room of the evening: 212, Tony Rossetti and Vic Stevens. Tony had been nice to her, but that didn't make up for the hours, the smelly rooms, and the thanklessness. *I hate this job*, she thought to herself as she prepped the IV. Mr. Rossetti was sound asleep, as usual. Could you blame him? In a matter of months, he would be a complete mental vegetable. I'd want to sleep through it all, too, she mused. She injected the vaccine. *Thank you for not being one of the belligerent ones, Tony.*

Tony's chart was a mess, thanks to one of the lazier day nurses. She had to dig around to find the drug orders page. Some days she wondered why she even bothered. No one ever read the thing anyway. She flipped through the chart from back to front. In the back, she caught a glimpse of the press clippings from when Tony had been admitted. He'd been a noted organized crime leader—Mafia, she supposed that meant. Didn't much matter now, did it? He certainly couldn't do anyone any harm in this sad state. She finally found the page she was looking for and made her entry. She didn't bother to creep out of the room quietly. Tony was totally out.

Now she just had to sign out. A little early, she thought, but her boss would never know. The boss only worked three days a week—cutbacks—and in any case, didn't have much contact with the staff nurses. So, she'd made a habit of leaving early on Tuesdays to meet her friends at the bowling alley. She was organizing their league's new season. She made her way to the main nurses' station, which was dark except for one overhead lamp. She wondered where the other on-duty nurse was. *Probably watching TV in a patient's room.* She entered her name in the OUT section of the nurse's log and wrote in a corresponding time of departure—6:30 p.m.

She left as she always did, right through the front door. She passed the security desk. Usually she felt obligated to chat a bit with the night guard, but he wasn't at his post yet. She was relieved to gain another few minutes. The girls at the alley would be so surprised!

At dawn, Stuart paced in his living room in front of the oversized leather couch, where Bob sat in sweatpants and sneakers. Stuart was still wearing his clothes from the previous day. Suddenly, Stuart stopped and pounded his fist on a wall, making the whole room shake. An original Miro painting on an adjacent wall sloped sideways. Bob held his head in his hands, nonplussed by the display of frustration.

"Stuart, you have to calm down. We're working as fast as we can. It's barely been four weeks, and we have to test the cells on humans before we administer them to your brain. It's as simple as that."

"Don't tell me that. I'm not your university paper-pusher administrator. I'm not the FDA. Hell, I've made billions by doing things faster. I know it can be done. You have everything you could ever need. I don't want to hear any more excuses." Stuart flung himself into an armchair chair like a petulant schoolboy. His necktie was tied incorrectly, and his hair was unruly. Bob heard desperation in Stuart's voice, but he had heard it all before. No one wanted to die, especially slowly.

"Listen, Bob, I don't care what you have to do to make this happen, but we must move the trial up. I want those new damn stem cells put in your four goddamned Alzheimer's patients immediately. We've no time to waste; do you hear me, Bob? No time! We're talking about my daughter, here, for chrissakes!"

Bob didn't have the will to fight him, and after all, Bob had felt that way himself most of his career. Doing things "correctly" took too long, procedures could never be approved, and no one could agree. Committee, committee, and more committees. It was maddening. *Those patients are doomed anyway*, he thought. Why not move up the schedule? Hadn't he taken these risks before and been rewarded? Well, yes, except for that one instance. Not bad for fifty years in practice.

Bob held his hands up, his St. Francis ring gleaming in an errant beam of morning sunlight. "Stuart, leave it to me."

"We need to know everything about them first," Richard began. "How long they've been on the Alzheimer's vaccine, if they've been in any other experimental trials, and so forth. That's number one."

"Agreed. We also need a record of every surgery and all the films." Bob helped himself to another cup of coffee. He and Richard stood in the condo kitchen. After a short breakfast at home, they were making a revised plan based on Stuart's early morning outburst. If four patients were about to arrive, they would need to completely redirect the two labs this afternoon.

They made some quick notes about what tasks to give to whom. They both took large swallows of coffee and left the condo in a hurry. As they climbed into the car, movement from beyond their driveway caught Richard's eye. As he backed away from the house, he glanced over at the next unit, where he saw a beautiful young woman walking an enormous dog.

"So, we have a neighbor after all," mused Richard aloud. He'd assumed the units on either side of theirs were uninhabited. He was glad to see a neighbor. He'd seen or heard no other people in the vicinity, just the roar of the ocean and an occasional plane overhead. There was an oddly disturbing silence on the island that had at first been pleasing, but that now—with the thought of that camera—gave him an uneasiness.

"Be sure to keep your lips sealed around the 'neighbor' about our mission here."

"I certainly won't go divulging our secrets to a tourist, Dad!"

But, Richard noted to himself, he would indeed like to talk to someone. What an odd feeling! Maybe all those years around all those people had changed him. With this observation fresh in mind, he looked around the streets as he drove on to BioSys. To his surprise, he saw no one. Stuart had told him there were only about two hundred permanent residents on the island. Two hundred! Richard was used to two million, all very close to him, all the time. So why did it seem like the extra space he's always craved was somehow smothering him? Richard did what he could with such a thought—he ignored it. He couldn't think about it now. Not now. If you let them, those things could take over. Thoughts, noises, numbers, fans, colors. He had to focus.

Richard approached the entrance to the facility. As usual, at the secured gate they were required to show their BioSys badges, which the guard ran under a bar code scanner. An affirmative "beep" sounded, and the guard returned their badges and pressed a button that controlled the large, metal gate, which was more like a wall of steel. As they meandered through the complex to their designated parking space, a thought struck Richard.

"Dad, do you suppose anyone vacations here?"

"What do you mean?"

"Well, I mean, I've assumed since we arrived that this was a vacation destination. But there's no one here."

"I think the people who can afford to come here are paying partly for seclusion. They don't want to be found."

"I suppose. I'd like to explore and see where they all are someday."

"Well, in a couple days time, you may as well. Once we implant the cells, we'll have to sit back and wait."

"True. I hadn't thought of that. Of course, I will always be working on the finer points of the cells—there's always work to be done."

"You've worked hard," said Bob as they entered their building on foot. "It might be time you took a break."

Fox Alzheimer's Hospital

Tony stirred in his bed and struggled to see the clock. The illuminated alarm clock that he and his roommate shared declared the time to be 1:12 a.m. That meant the nurses had already come and gone. Later today, his wife was scheduled for a visit. She came about once a month, bringing reports about the declining status of the family business, and his favorite pasta. Tony had been the kingpin of a few local lucrative operations in his sixty-seven years, and the Westside of Chicago had been good to him. Before he had been cooped up in this place, he'd had a community he could rely on, a large extended family, and an even larger degree of power. Now his rival had taken over his slot in the warehouse district, his drivers, and his routes, and Tony could do nothing about it. That son of his had never visited, not even once. Wanted out of the business anyway and worked as a chef at some faggot restaurant. He was a wimp, that's what his son was. His wife didn't trust the kid, either, for that matter. Tony was embarrassed that his own son had become a servant, when he should have been keeping his eye on the inventory for the sake of their family. And he hated how everybody treated him like a helpless cripple just because he had some memory problems.

This was the stuff that kept him awake at night—anger. He was mad at everything, thanks to this damn disease! If only he wasn't so far away from everybody. They thought they'd been smart to tuck him away in Michigan, thought he'd be safe from harm here. But it frustrated him to be so out of the loop. He felt the loss of his emotional will and wanted to scream with anger, but knew he would awaken the poor soul sleeping next to him. And now he felt a headache coming on. He turned over, sighing loudly. He had to get out of this joint, but how? It was making him crazier than any of the Alzheimer's loons in this lockbox. The docs had told him he was a burden to his family now, in this "stage," but Gina, his wife for over fifty years, had never complained when Tony was at home. Now, she made homemade pasta once a week and sent it to him, along with a letter about the sad state of the house and her lack of grandchildren, not to mention that stingy son of hers who was too cheap to fly her to see her beloved husband. It was plain to Tony, even in his condition, that Gina had nothing to do.

To Tony's surprise, what appeared to be a male nurse approached, but it was someone he didn't recognize. Or did he? He wasn't sure. The man opened his mouth to speak, but Tony got there first.

"Who the hell are you? You ain't my nurse."

"I'm an orderly, with papers here to take you to radiology this morning." He waved the official papers in the air, legitimizing his task.

"They don't let me go anywhere, doc, it's like a prison here. And besides, it's one in the morning."

"Well, this is a good time—less traffic. And today we get to see how your brain is looking. We'll take a scan again, like we did last week, remember?"

Tony couldn't remember any such scan. "What about Vic over there?" Tony motioned to his roommate, still fast asleep. "Does he get to play hooky, too?"

"Not Vic, but some other patients. You'll see."

The nameless orderly unlocked the wheels of Tony's bed and wheeled him out of the room. Tony felt that going anywhere was better than hanging around that dumpy room, so he didn't complain. In moments, the motion of the wheels brought on the sudden pull of sleep.

Therese settled into the waterside condo for the night. Fancy collapsed her long legs under her and immediately began to snore loudly at the foot of the bed. Therese watched her and a smile appeared on her face—some guard dog she had turned out to be! Her father insisted years ago that Therese have an obedient and fierce dog with her for protection. He probably had a German shepherd or Doberman in mind, but Therese had fallen for a rescued ex-racing greyhound instead. Over the years, Therese had made friends with every islander and was never afraid. Fancy, too, knew almost everyone in town. When she encountered them, she would attempt to strike a menacing pose—her silky fur on end—until she got a good sniff and recognized the person as a friend, at which time she became as playful as a puppy, especially if there was a couch nearby for lounging.

"Good dog!" murmured Therese as she leaned down to pet her. The dog opened one lazy caramel-colored eye in response. Therese laughed at Fancy's exhaustion and went to the kitchen to put on the kettle.

She stood at the kitchen sink with her tea and looked out the window into the moonless black night. These were the moments that were hard—moments when she surveyed her life and thought, *If it were all over tomorrow, would I have done everything I wanted*? Since she had told her father about her pending disease two nights ago, the reality of her future mind—potentially as empty as the black night she now surveyed—had plagued and inspired her, all at once. She knew that feeling sorry for herself was a waste of energy, so why not use her smarts and money to help others? Or even to help find a cure? Surely, this was a healthier approach.

But as she made her way through the big, empty beach house, a condo intended for ten people, she realized she hadn't fooled herself entirely. She was scared and lonely. Her father's strange reaction added to the fear. He had tried to reassure her, told her he would do everything possible for a man in his position. "I promise," he had said, "that you will not be a victim of this disease. You have my word."

But still, his use of the word "hopeless" earlier in that same conversation disturbed her. Could she believe him? Perhaps she could do her own research. The task was daunting. While she was excellent at researching other people's concerns, she didn't relish the idea of searching out information for her own good. Why was that?

She would simply have to trust her father. She knew this catastrophe would bring out the best in him, and it felt good to realize that he might even be working on a solution this very minute. But still, the fact-finding side of

Therese nibbled for a bite. She sat in the rocking chair across from the bed, listening to Fancy's deep breathing. She closed her eyes and pictured her mother sitting on the edge of the bed. *Mom*, she'd say. *I got some bad news the other day. It seems I inherited a gene from you.*"

Wait. Therese opened her eyes, the illusion shattered. The Stanford doc said Therese had inherited the gene. Her father had implied that the gene must have come from her mother. Her mother, the dead one. The somehow faulty one. But of course, it could just as easily have come from her father. Why hadn't she pressed him on this before?

"C'mon, Fancy." Therese gestured to the dog, whose ears perked up at the sound of her name. "We're going for a walk." She had to know. As soon as possible.

The giant animal made her way to the floor slowly, limbs creaking. Therese located her leash and they left through the front door. A car was pulling into the driveway next door. For tourists, they were certainly returning home late, she noticed.

Fancy and Therese headed for Eastwind—a half-mile walk. Although it was pitch dark and moonless, both sets of feet had made this journey many times, so the going was peaceful. Tiny pebbles crunched under their feet and cicadas hummed, their nocturnal search for a mate in full swing. The scent of night-blooming jasmine wafted in and out, carried by a gentle breeze.

The estate of Eastwind was soon before them. Therese and Fancy headed up the tree-lined drive. The house looked dark—perhaps her father had already turned in. The front door was locked, so Therese knocked. Hattie, their longtime maid and cook, a backpack slung over one shoulder, answered the door.

Hattie, normally subdued and shy, broke into a giant smile and opened her arms for a hug, which Therese returned warmly, Fancy barking in excitement.

"I didn't see you last night when I arrived," smiled Therese.

"Your father, he like for me to take nights off now. In fact, I was just going home. But it's so nice to see you again!"

"Thanks, Hattie. It's nice to be here, where I can relax a little."

"You been busy, I know. The Mister tell me. All over the place!"

"And where is Father?" Therese looked into the den as Fancy scampered around the entryway, sniffing the ground for any treats that may have fallen from Hattie's apron.

"He's not home yet. No. He's been working late most nights. He should be home in not too long, I think."

"Okay. I'll wait for him, then. It's been so long; we have a lot to catch up on."

Hattie took her leave, and Therese settled onto the couch in her father's study. His desk was disheveled, as it always was when in production of a new drug. There were many journals on the coffee table, and she found herself flipping though all of them, hoping to find something about Alzheimer's. There was nothing obviously about the disease, though. She thought about looking through the stacks of papers on her father's desk; she might find the answer to her burning question. But she decided against this drastic measure—she would simply ask him again in person when he returned home. To pass the time, Therese picked up the local paper and began to read. An hour went by with no Dad, so she tried one of the medical journals. And then another. Outside, the cicadas buzzed rhythmically. A fountain trickled water. Therese struggled to keep her eyes open, but soon they closed, against her will.

Richard consulted his white board yet again. On the wall behind the worktable, he had diagrammed the molecular phases that the cells would undergo once they were implanted. Although rushed, he felt it was the most thorough science he had yet conducted. He was ready for tomorrow, when the first four patients would undergo the procedure. Two would receive human embryonic stem cells, two adult neural ones.

Next, Richard turned to the slides prepared from the monkeys' four-week biopsies. He had samples of the tumors and samples from the other parts of the brain. The slides would be the basis of Richard's molecular conclusions. Did the cells differentiate as hoped? How far did they travel within the brain, and what was the status of the damaged cells? Had the stem cells spawned duplicates of themselves, as they did in their normal *in vivo* environment? He had a feeling the news would all be good, but to be sure his hopes didn't influence the outcome of what he saw, he implemented a control—a sample of healthy monkey brain that had not received any stem cells, already prepared.

At the end of the long day, he had all the conclusions he and his father had expected. Both of the monkey cell sources had differentiated nicely. Richard was easily able to identify the new cells that had been produced. The growth factors he had predicted were within an acceptable margin, at least at four weeks. In four more weeks, a monkey would be autopsied so they could perform a fuller examination of the movements of the remarkable stem cells.

Bob and James were seated in Adirondack chairs on a large deck overlooking the ocean. James was the experienced neuro-radiologist they'd enlisted from the States for this very special human stem cell procedure. They'd had to get James here fast, since the schedule had been moved up so suddenly. James was an old colleague of Richard's who Bob had respected for his Marines service as a decorated Battalion Surgeon who had seen just about everything imaginable in *Operation Desert Storm* in the nineties. Bob knew James had seen things that recalled the worst of his own battlefield experiences. Having both worked under extreme stress, they were innovators who had been forced to take great risks to save their men. James' post-war career spent specializing in advanced imaging techniques for surgery had seen its ups and downs—it turned out retirees in Florida were not as willing to bankroll his electronic tools as he'd expected. "It's a stupid case," explained James on the phone days earlier. "The woman was ninety-three, and now that she's dead, the family wants to know why I didn't recommend traditional surgery for her tumor!" James admitted, he could use the money, paid in full up front, and in cash. He had flown in yesterday.

Bob said, "We've got three options, as I see it."

"And those are?" James took off his glasses off, which had drops of sweat on them, and cleaned them on his shirttail. A pleasant breeze evaporated the small beads of moisture on his tanned forehead. He was glad of the fresh air, a refreshing break from the mind-numbing air conditioning he was accustomed to in Florida. His mind raced ahead, anticipating Bob's proposed scheme. James knew Bob well enough to guess that he was in for some kind of inventive medical practice.

"Well, there's the traditional route, and two innovations I've been working on. Why don't you tell me which you think is the safest?"

"Shoot."

"One approach is a trans-nasal one. We'd go in via the nose and plant the stem cells there. These cells take root and travel easily, so we only have to get them close. The second idea is a trans-ventricular one.

We'd go through the back of the skull with a cannula outfitted with fiber optics. We could drive the cells to the wall of the third ventricle and drop them there, where we know they'll flourish. They might even revive any remaining stem cells in the area, since we know they are produced there."

James exhaled. "And the third way?"

"The traditional way—a twist hole through the dura, straight into the temporal lobe." Bob pointed to the side of his own head to illustrate the area. A stranger watching might have misunderstood his gesture as someone holding a gun to his own head. "We could even do it without shaving their heads, leaving only a tiny scar."

"How stable are the patients?"

"There are four patients, and they are all under seventy, with early-to-medium Alzheimer's. None are advanced, in other words."

"So a small operation should not have any unintended effects—cardiac arrest, for example."

"Exactly my thoughts."

"If there are four patients, why don't we do two each with different techniques—the trans-nasal, as you say, and the trans-ventricular? We can leave the traditional as a last resort."

Bob smiled, pleased. "I like the way you think, James. I like it. That was my approach with the monkeys."

"I've been shown the facilities here, and as you promised, they're absolutely state-of-the-art, so for any procedure, I can get you an incredible picture. We can map out the entire procedure first with new CT software that BioSys just patented. I got the tour of the machine and software today. You'll never be blind. The imaging will be real time." James was pleased to notice his own enthusiasm was growing, realizing the significance of such a procedure, especially the third ventricle approach. He continued with renewed vigor. "I can attach a special, microscopic fiber optic line to your canula, as you suggested. As you pass it through the ventricles, I can get a high-resolution color image. You'll be very pleased with the results."

The next day, Bob retracted the cannula from the fourth patient's skull with precision and care. As he had hundreds of times before in his long career, he employed an advanced sewing technique that left only a very light scar, one that would never be noticed, except perhaps by another surgeon. The cannulas had implanted the cells Richard had delivered to surgery fresh that morning.

As with the monkeys, he'd had no unexpected surgical problems or issues. Once the patients had been sedated, James and he had targeted the area of transplantation using stereotactic imaging—imaging that allowed them to pinpoint an area of the brain's interior using x, y, and z coordinates with millimeter-sized accuracy. The relatively simple procedure had only taken about one hour per patient—and what an hour! Wouldn't they be thrilled twelve weeks from now, when they suddenly remembered their spouses' names! He and James shook hands and moved out of the operating room.

Now, Bob reflected, all he had to do was wait. The patients would be monitored for twenty-four hours, and then a CT scan would be performed to make sure there was no hemorrhaging. He didn't expect any. Business as usual, he mused as he removed his scrubs. Wouldn't he love it if this *were* business as usual? *Think of it*! he mused. *Saving a life every day!*

Richard jogged heartily as the sun rose in the sky, his sneakers leaving deep prints in the damp sand. Following his father's suggestion, Richard had decided to take the morning off. Now that the patients were safely recovering back in their own beds at the Alzheimer's hospital, Richard could breathe more easily.

And breathe he did—he was astounded to realize he could barely jog one mile. He stopped to catch his breath and he felt his limbs trembling from the unusual effort. A sudden chill swept over him and, still breathing heavily, he struggled into the sweatshirt that had been tied around his waist. A stretch was in order, he figured, so he dropped to the ground. His heartbeat echoed in his ears, its beat in his chest louder than the waves.

It felt so good to be sitting that he lay down and shut his eyes, listening to the morning sounds and the ocean. He could feel the early sun beginning to warm his legs. It was so peaceful. He must do this more often, now that he could, he thought.

A sudden wetness and stinky hot breath on his face startled him, causing his heart to start racing again. His eyes popped open to find the giant snout of a dog looming over him, licking his face. Richard sat up and tried to subdue the dog.

"Fancy, Fancy-pants; come back! Faaaancy!" Therese ran from the promenade down to the water, and the dog immediately sat at attention, waiting for a scolding.

"I'm so, so sorry," Therese gasped, out of breath. Richard began to laugh.

"No problem. I was just startled. I had nearly collapsed overdoing my morning run. Maybe he just wanted to help a poor old guy like me?" Richard stood and brushed the sand off him. The sunrise was shining directly into his eyes and he could not see the dog owner's face, so he held his hand up to his forehead, blocking its angle. What he saw took his breath away for the second time that morning; it was a young woman with long auburn hair, jeweled eyes, and a face like porcelain. The woman he had seen next door! He was stunned.

"It's a she. And I hope she didn't bother you. She's a big beast, but she's got a heart of gold, don't you Fancy-pants?" She leaned down to pet the animal, which was panting wildly and looking up at its master with an expression that seemed to say, *Wow, look what I found!*

"She is imposing, I'll say that! How on earth did you get her here? She must be," Richard put a hand to his own body to help estimate the height of the dog, "nearly four feet high!" He bent over to pet the dog and looked into its big, intelligent eyes. Animals, Richard could understand. But when it came to people, or women…

Therese laughed. "Four feet, three inches, to be exact! She travels well. She has to go everywhere with me or be with someone she knows well. She's very sensitive and gets lonely easily." Therese turned slightly so the man could remove his hand from his head.

"You live here?" Richard said, half to the dog, half to Therese.

"Well, actually, I live in LA. But we have a residence here, yes. Fancy lives wherever there is a nice big couch."

Hearing her name mentioned again made Fancy rise and begin galloping around the area. Richard's eyes followed the dog.

"She looks like she wants to play."

"She always wants to play—when she's not sleeping, that is! She acts like a puppy by the water, but she's actually about seven, and that's old for a big dog." Therese looked at Richard, but he was looking away. "Do you have any pets?"

Pets? The idea had never even crossed his mind, he thought. Richard stole a glance at her and saw the clear sunlight sparkle in her eyes.

He turned back to the water, wishing the dog would return so he could hide behind it.

"Oh, no. No. We had a goat growing up, though."

"A goat! I can't really see you with one of those things, with their floppy years."

Richard was pleased that she'd pictured him at all; it seemed such an intimate gesture. Richard was suddenly aware of his lovelessness. Who was the 'we' this woman spoke of? Must be married. "They're very smart. And devoted to their owners. Pack animals." There was a pause. Now, they both watched Fancy frolic in the ocean foam, emitting small snorts at each wave as it broke and crashed at her paws.

"You get 'em, Fancy," joked Therese. "Maybe she'll make herself useful and catch us some dinner, what do you think?"

Richard turned to Therese, but found it hard to concentrate. He wanted to watch the dog. The dog was easy to relate to. He looked at her quickly, then back at the water. "Is the fish here good?"

"Oh, yes! Have you just arrived? My name's Therese." She held out her hand. She had an innocent, yet worldly, air about her. He took her hand for a quick handshake, and then replaced his hand quickly.

"Richard. Richard Weigand. You know, I believe we're neighbors. And your hand is awfully warm."

"Is it? Well, I was running."

"You run?"

"No, I was running to get here from the street, when Fancy slobbered all over you."

"Oh, right."

"So, is that you staying next door at #5? I think I saw your car last night."

"Yes, and I saw you leaving your place. With the dog. You know, you shouldn't walk the dog so late. Something could happen. I mean, it might not be safe."

"Thanks, but we're okay. We know everyone here."

"You didn't know me. Until just now."

"That's true. But, let's see—you must be working for BioSys. Scientists tend to be pretty harmless."

"Oh, really? You don't know some of the people I used to work with at the NIH. But yes, I am now working with more harmless folks at BioSys." At that moment, Fancy began barking wildly at the ocean.

Therese moved to see what the fuss was about. Before she could stop her, Fancy had picked up a dead fish in her mouth.

"See how smart she is? She heard me suggest she get dinner. Fancy, no, put that down. Drop it," Therese commanded. The dog, to Richard's surprise, immediately opened its oversized jaws and let the fish drop. "Good, Fancy. Good!"

"Well, seems she's hungry. We just came home from a long walk from across the island. I'd better get her back and make her breakfast." Fancy seemed to understand these words and began a rapid trot toward home. Therese began to follow, and as she did, looked over her shoulder and called to Richard.

"Want to walk with us?"

Richard's smile seemed as bright as the sun itself. He trotted ahead himself, falling in line next to Fancy.

"I'd be delighted. C'mon, Fancy, let's race."

Richard spent the next morning looking through the paper for a dog to adopt. Curiously, he could not stop smiling at every one he encountered. Richard could not explain this odd behavior, so he attributed it to having made a connection with the dog, whom he was surprised to find he seemed to understand in some deep way; he longed to see the dog again.

Fox Alzheimer's Hospital, Michigan

A man motioned to the other men in black clothes. Everything was ready inside. All they needed to do was return one more patient. It was well after midnight. The man figured that, even though the higher-ups at the hospital had been well compensated for their troubles, the fewer people who saw them come and go the better. There was no night guard now—he was out getting his lunch. The place was bathed in moonlight and so silent he heard his leather jacket crinkle with every move. In thirty minutes, it was over, and he could plan what he was going to do with all that fresh cash.

Therese paced the villa. Her brain felt like gravy. If this was how people relaxed, she'd never understand. It had become clear that she had two settings: ON and OFF. How many more days could she sit and read on the beach or play with Fancy? She was going crazy. She had to get out of the house and do something.

She decided a brisk walk to BioSys might do her good. Perhaps she could catch her father and question him about the Alzheimer's gene, or at least he could give her some work to do. Although she thought she'd needed a break, all this time to think just made her anxious. Surely, he of all people would understand. She gave Fancy some fresh, cool water and set out.

The moment Therese stepped out of the house, she felt the blazing sun overhead. It was obviously well after noon. Although she had done nothing all morning, the day had sped ahead without her. She knew it was foolish to make the four-mile walk in the treacherous heat, but something in her insisted. After all, she had her hat.

She walked along the gravel road headed toward the city's main road, which was loosely paved. She seemed to hear each tiny stone whimper under her step. There were no sidewalks here—hedges and tropical plants lined the streets instead. The sweat had begun to pour from her temples. Why hadn't she brought a water bottle? *Her mind really was turning to gravy*, she chastised herself.

She was so absorbed by the heat and gravel that she did not hear the approaching car.

"Therese!"

With a start, she turned. She saw her neighbor, Richard, in a BioSys Land Rover, waving to her from the passenger window, which had just been rolled down. Misty clouds of condensation rolled around the window as the hot humid ocean air met the car's dry air conditioning. The prospect of relief drew her to the car like a magnet, and she realized with a start, so did the face of its passenger. She could see a BioSys driver at the wheel.

"Hop in; we'll give you a lift," he called through the open window. She did.

"Whew!" she exclaimed as she slammed the rear door closed behind her. "It's beyond hot out there. I don't know what I was thinking." In the frigid air of the car, she could feel how sweaty she was. She attempted to dab her forehead with her shirt. Goosebumps lined her arms.

"Do you always waltz into town when it's 101.7?" Richard smiled and pointed at the car's digital temperature display. He looked at her briefly in the side mirror.

Therese laughed. "It's just that, well, I wanted to get out of the house. I felt a little stir crazy. I was going shopping." Therese lied without meaning to. She was so used to hiding her Franklin identity that she didn't even notice her automatic white lies anymore.

They approached the town square. It was deserted. In the noonday heat, the market was usually closed: siesta. Therese had not thought of that possibility, but she quickly recovered.

"I was going to shop, but now I realize that a nice cool drink of iced tea would be better. There's a place just around the corner there, you see it?" The driver slowed the car down. Richard saw a weathered, hand-painted sign that read Ferdy's Tropical Tea Cafe.

"This place has always been here. It's the best tea. Grown here, Indian-plantation style. You might have tried it at BioSys. It's the island's best-kept secret. When I try to make it at home, it just doesn't taste the same. Do you have time to try one?"

Richard was befuddled by her easy social skills. *How did she do it*? he wondered. And with such a casual air? *Maybe she wasn't doing anything but being a good neighbor*, he warned himself.

"I'd like nothing more. I'm not needed at the lab now; I was just going in to work on something for the future. Let's go." The driver let them out, explaining that he would return to fetch them later.

The cafe was a dark, cool, cave-like place with adobe walls painted a deep cobalt blue. The only illumination came from the sunlight that bounced off the floor from the doorway and onto the blue walls, giving the place a watery glow. The proprietor came out from behind the counter when he saw Therese.

"Ferdy!" Therese held out her arms for an embrace. "It's been so long!"

"Yes," began the dark-skinned man, with a heavy accent of some kind. "You have been away too long, child. Who is your friend?" Ferdy held out his hand in greeting. Therese stepped back and motioned behind her. "This is Richard, ah, Richard—"

"Richard Weigand. Pleased to meet you," interjected Richard, who stepped forward to meet the cafe man's hand. Richard discreetly wiped his hand on his trousers.

"Please, sit down, and I'll bring you some tea. We have nice cold chai today. I'll bring some snacks, too. Sit, sit!"

The place was deserted, since the custom was to nap—or at least seek refuge—in the hottest part of the day. Richard and Therese sat at a table next to one of the clay blue walls, which threw off a pleasant coolness. Richard looked at Therese. The soft ambient light of the cafe bounced into her eyes, and he could make out flecks of green he'd not seen before.

Ferdy appeared with a tray full of shiny items. There was a large, frosted, stainless steel pitcher and a series of small silvery dishes. He began by placing the small snack dishes on the table. Each container displayed a riot of color and shapes—Richard identified them as West Indian snacks. He immediately recognized the bhel puri, which Raj had often brought to the lab in Bethesda. It was a rice and potato dish, spicy and salty at the same time. Ferdy set each dish on the table with ceremony. An assortment of chutneys appeared in smaller metal saucers. Then a small cup of cane sugar. Lastly, Ferdy presented a vase with a small bunch of daisies towering over the rim. He smiled down at Therese as he poured the chai tea, which was caramel colored and thick, and emitted a complex dark aroma.

"Where have you been? I have not seen you or your father in too long, now."

"I've been working with schools in Los Angeles. I've been helping kids learn to garden. It keeps me busy!" Therese didn't know how to answer the question about her father's whereabouts in front of Richard. She hadn't yet decided what to reveal.

Come to think of it, what had her father been doing? It struck her now as odd that he had spent so much time in the islands. In a flash, she was sure he had lied to her about his reason for being here. But why?

Ferdy let her off the hook. "Well, I'll let you two young lovers have your tea. You come back more often, okay?" Ferdy smiled, and Therese felt herself blushing. *Lovers*?

"Oh, no, I'm not her lover," clarified Richard with a totally straight and unembarrassed face. He was simply correcting the man. Ferdy just smiled and walked away.

"I don't know why he said that. Do you?" asked Richard. Therese just laughed and mixed some sugar into her tea. *What an odd man*, she thought.

Richard did not tell Therese that he was actually delighted at Ferdy's assumption. Was Therese embarrassed? She must be single! He imagined her blushing was a good sign. Although he had only met Therese twenty-four hours ago, he had been preoccupied with her since. And now here he was, sitting in a small, charming, island cafe with the woman! His life was becoming too good to be true. He took a sip of his tea, planning what to say. But Richard was too naive to try to hide his enthusiasm. He watched her drink.

"You know, I've never seen anybody with eyes like yours."

Therese began to cough violently, her eyes filling with tears. She waved her hand in front of her face as if to say, "I'm okay; it's okay."

"Oh! I'm sorry."

"It's just—it just went down the wrong way. I'm fine. Thank you."

"But your eyes, they're quite different, I meant. I mean, they're very—" Richard struggled to think of what someone else might say—someone's normal words—not something about rods and cones. "They're very pretty."

Therese stared back at Richard, unaccustomed to unveiled compliments. "Well, thank you. They're my mother's eyes." Therese smiled. Although flattered, she was uncomfortable with open attention. She changed the subject. "What is it you're doing for BioSys?"

Richard's gaze returned to a more conversational one. "I am working on—" Richard hadn't been prepared with an answer, as his father had warned him he should be. "I'm working on a new chemotherapy drug."

"You must be quite important to be staying at one of the villas. Are you a researcher?"

"Yes, yes, I am. I've been here a month."

"Where did you come from?"

"Bethesda. From the National Institutes of Health."

"This town is a little more charming than Bethesda! A little smaller, too, I'm afraid."

"Oh, yes. But I don't mind that. I was fed up with the traffic and the big box stores. The sprawl. This place is a dream come true, actually." Richard swirled the tea in his glass and peeked up at Therese. "The other great thing is, I'm enjoying having money. At the NIH, we were always strapped for money. We had so much red tape. You can't imagine. It took me six months just to get light bulbs changed in my lab. Here, you simply ask, and like magic, there it is. It makes a big difference in productivity."

Therese thought of all the times her father had lamented government research for just that reason. She thought about bringing him into the conversation, but was still leery.

"Yes, I can imagine. I'm always struggling with money myself. With a not-for-profit, you can never pay anyone back. Of course, the payback is the contribution."

"And what, exactly, does your not-for-profit contribute?"

"As I was telling Ferdy, we build gardens in public schools and teach the kids how to grow their own food. My foundation is called Culinary Classroom. We try to instill sensitivity about the land and its cultivation. Classroom-as-a-lab, that kind of thing. Lots of hands-on. Sometimes we bring in speakers to expose the kids to the latest ideas in sustainability and the environment. We also help other non-profits by providing catering. We use only local food supplies and try to support local farmers as much as possible."

Richard was intrigued. Not only was she smart and beautiful, but generous as well. The photographic soft-box effect of the room began to give her an angelic glow.

"You mean botany lessons."

"Yes, but it's more than that. We cover biodiversity, preserving heirloom species, organic methods. But mostly, we try to emphasize the treasures that we can find or grow locally in our own backyards."

"You mean like eating bugs? Like on those reality shows?"

"No, I mean eating wild clover that happens to be growing in your yard, for instance, or growing your own garden to feed you and your family year-round. That's easy in Southern California, but you'd be surprised how many people there have never even plucked a tomato off a vine."

Richard had never really thought much about the food he ate. It was fuel, pure and simple. It had never occurred to him to harvest his own food. He took a bite of the bhel puri, which was delicious.

"Add me to the list of those people."

"Really?

"Really. Fast food is my main food supply. When I wasn't fed by people at the lab, that is."

Therese laughed. "Well, you won't find any fast food here."

"So I've noticed. To tell you the truth, I've been so hungry that I've had to resort to cooking my own meals. I bought some snapper the other day—I believe it was local—and tried to cook it."

"And how did that go?"

"Terribly. I set off the smoke detector." Wanting to change the subject fast, Richard continued. "But anyway, what brings you here to Anegada? Are you gardening?"

"I'm just taking a break." Therese paused to take another sip of tea. "Taking a break so I can figure out—I've been so busy working, I hardly know myself anymore. I've lost focus."

"Hmm." Richard knew the feeling she described. When was the last time he had sat this long just talking to someone new? Well, that was easy. He never had. Generally, he avoided people. But this person…

Richard looked down at his tea, where tiny particles of tealeaves swirled. He looked back up at Therese. "So, what's there to do around here on the weekends?"

Therese felt completely exposed; he didn't take his eyes off her. This was flattering, but unnerving. It'd be so easy to just offer her company; it was so easy for her to be the ultimate hostess. He was good looking, and no doubt a brilliant researcher. However, they were neighbors. *Careful*. But then, he spoke up.

"Maybe we could take a hike or go to the beach. I'm sure you know all the best places."

"Anegada is full of wonder. Not to mention the other islands, which are all easily accessible by boat. There's cove scuba diving, rustic hiking trails, and hidden grottos tourists never see."

"Sounds like we need a series of weekends to see it all!"

She got caught up in his enthusiasm. And those eyes of his; they were glued to her, as if he'd never seen another human before. "I can show you the most dazzling highlights first. I have time to plan outings. I'd be pleased to be your guide."

The ring of a cell phone startled both of them. Therese looked down at her handbag and saw the glow of her phone, alerting her of an incoming call.

"I'm sorry, but I need to answer this."

Therese accepted the call, and Richard stood to give her some privacy and explore the rest of the café. He strode to the far wall, where a series of framed photographs of people posing with steel drum sets was displayed. As he crossed the room, he noticed an aging piano in the corner, hidden by the lack of sunshine. A dusty mirror hung above the piano, and in it, he saw Ferdy at the bar behind him, drying cleaned glasses.

"You play?" asked Ferdy of Richard's image.

"Well, I used to," Richard looked down and struck a few simple chords. The sound filled the room with a deep, warm tone, thanks to the thick clay walls. He pulled the stool from under the piano and sat, poised to play. Therese walked up behind him.

"Everything okay?" asked Richard, referencing the phone call. Richard played a few notes, almost absentmindedly. He was well out of practice, and the piano needed tuning.

"Just my father." Therese looked down at Richard's hands hovering over the keys. "Will you play something?"

"Oh, I don't know. I don't know too many songs anymore."

"That's okay. Play anything," Therese smiled and pulled up a chair.

"Well, if you insist," smiled Richard. "This is a song my mother taught me when I was little." He cleared his throat and looked down, took a breath, and began.

"Let's see if I can remember."

Therese watched in surprise as Richard began to play and sing. She listened, rapt. She recognized the tune, but couldn't place it.

"*That's all; that's, all.*" He stopped, finding the notes and remembering the words. "Okay, I got it. Boy, it's been years. *I can only give you country walks in springtime and a hand to hold when leaves begin to fall. And a love whose burning light will burn, warm the winter nights, that's all. That's all.*"

As he played, she watched him, relaxing now that she was unobserved. He had a perfect nose. His dusty blond hair was swept to one side, his skin still pale from life in the city. He had handsome hazel eyes. Most surprising was the tenor of his voice, which was full and strong, yet not overpowering. He seemed to be a natural musician. She had a vision of the two of them walking along Crow's Reef, where she had spent many happy afternoons. For a moment, time stood still, while the music did what it did best—transform a room.

The short standard was reaching its conclusion.

"*So if you're wondering what I'm asking in return, dear, you'll be so surprised to know that my demands are very small. Just say it's me that you adore, for now, and evermore, that's all. That's all.*" His voice didn't quite hold the last notes, and he laughed, making the last piano key linger in the air. In the sudden silence, the hum of the ceiling fan was heard. A clap of applause came from Ferdy, and Therese joined in.

"That was beautiful!" exclaimed Therese.

"That's kind of you. I'm very rusty! It's odd how you can remember segments of a song, and then if you get enough of them, the song is back. Completely. Every note."

There was silence for a moment while Richard looked down at the piano. Therese thought about what he'd just said, and it sparked something. "I read recently that people with amnesia can often remember music. Entire scores of music."

He turned to her suddenly.

"Do you play?"

"Oh, no. No. I've never been any good at that sort of thing."

Who was this Richard staying at villa #5? Surely, he knew her father. Therese made a decision, the mood of the piano sound still alive in the room, a thought about therapy for Alzheimer's in her mind.

"Well, I suppose I should be getting to BioSys," Richard said, replacing the piano cover. He turned to her, their knees nearly touching in the small corner. Richard moved back, discretely, out of habit, and the front door opened. The driver had returned, and started catching up with Ferdy. "Can we drive you somewhere?"

"Sure, why not drop me at BioSys? I'll pop in and see my father. Maybe he can put me to good use." They stood to go.

"Your father works at BioSys, then?"

"Oh, yes." Therese paused slightly, choosing her words. "Actually, he runs it."

Richard's eyes widened, and they both laughed. "Stuart Franklin is your father?"

"Yes, it's true. Are you shocked?"

"Not shocked, exactly, more like—well, I don't know. You don't really look much like him and—" Richard struggled.

"I take after my mother. And yes, we're nothing alike. It's true. But I did inherit some great traits from him. I can work an eighteen-hour day and not bat an eye, for instance."

They laughed together as they left Ferdy's Tropical Tea Café. Richard hoped he would one day look back at this moment as his first day with Therese. It was with an odd certainty that he opened the car door for her. A new confidence had overcome him, but he could not yet name it as such. He was just very, very happy.

Stuart knew he looked terrible. With a lazy hand, he adjusted his hair across his forehead. He was due for a haircut, not to mention a thorough shave. It was more and more difficult to hide his erratic mood swings, which were getting more alarming by the day, it seemed, although Stuart could not be sure. All he wanted to do was relax—maybe on his yacht? He could hire a captain and simply sit, fish, and dive. He longed to rest, but he knew he wouldn't. There was still too much to be done.

He found his eyes shutting, but a knock on his office door brought him back to wakefulness. He adjusted his tie and cleared his throat. "Yes, do come in," he called.

"Hello, Dad." It was Therese. She appeared before him as a ball of energy, her smile as wide as a mile.

"Hello, darling." He stood to kiss her. She took a seat across from his desk. "I'm so relieved to see you so full of life. You look positively radiant."

"Well, I've vowed to not worry about the early Alzheimer's as you suggested." Therese smiled. She had to tell him. "And I met a friend of yours."

"A friend?" Stuart couldn't think of anyone on Anegada he would call a friend.

"Well, a special employee. I suppose he must be special, since he's staying next door to me at the villas."

It'd been years since Stuart had been to the BioSys housing units, so he hadn't even considered the possibility that his daughter might cross paths with his prized stem cell scientists. He mentally kicked himself. The thought of Therese knowing anything about their venture made his muscles tighten. He was suddenly very alert.

"You met Bob?"

"No, I met Richard." Therese looked puzzled. "Who's Bob?"

"Oh." Stuart tried to hide his relief. He wouldn't want Therese to stumble onto Bob; at least, not before Stuart could warn him of her presence. "Bob is Richard's father."

"His father?"

"Well, yes."

"Do they both work here?"

"Oh, yes, they're a team. In research."

"Are they working on the new enzyme?"

"Enzyme?"

"You know—the one you told me about the other night. The chemo agent that only kills cancer cells."

"Oh yes, ABT-55. They are. Quite right." Stuart stared back at her. He felt blood rushing to his face.

Therese noticed her father's hair was askew and that there were no papers on his desk. Odd. She had caught him off guard, but why? He was clearly distracted.

"Well, I just wanted to tell you we've met, and I enjoyed his company."

"Yes, yes, well, he's quite brilliant, quite, yes; I can see why you'd like him." Changing tactics, Stuart's expression became serious, and he leaned back into his leather swivel chair. "You know, he's a good man, Therese."

"I'm sure. I'm sure he must be." Therese could see the idea in her father's head, and she didn't like it. She'd make her own matches, for herself—not strategic ones that might suit her father. And besides, she'd only just met the man. Seemed a bit presumptuous. "Is everything all right, here?" Therese gestured to the large, empty desk.

Stuart stood, hands in pockets, and sat on the edge of the desk, on Therese's side. "You know, Richard could sure use a break," he said, ignoring Therese's attempt to change the subject. "You should take him over to Blue Grotto, show him the coral reef. There's not one like it in the entire world, you know. And, listen, why don't we all meet for dinner this weekend? Get to know each other better. I'll have Hattie make her barbequed Anegada lobster. What do you say?" Stuart smiled his charming smile.

"This weekend?" It was all happening too fast. Therese didn't want to disappoint her father, but still, the whole conversation rubbed her the wrong way; she didn't like being manipulated.

"Sure, why not?" said Stuart, still smiling.

Maybe it had been a mistake to come down to the islands. She could leave. She would leave, after the weekend. No harm in accepting, then. No choice, really, either.

"Okay, that would be nice, Dad."

Stuart stood, the deal sewn up. "And now, why don't we head into town for some lunch? Just talking about Hattie's cooking has me starved!"

Stuart was glad to have pleased his daughter; it made him feel he had a grasp on something again. He was feeling much more like his old self. As they left the office, he put his arm around her. With confidence, he said, "Darling, everything's going to be fine, just fine."

Tony sneezed. As he did, he felt a slight tingling in the back of his neck. He reached back to rub the area, which felt like an irritated bug bite. It was tender where he rubbed it. He sneezed again.

"This damn, dirty place!" he hollered to no one in particular. His roommate was gone. He looked around. It was only now that he noticed he was in another hospital room. There was no second bed to his left. The windowsill to his right, something he had grown so used to in his old room, was somehow different—dustier. He sneezed again.

"Nuuuuurse!" He called as he always had, not really expecting anyone to respond. But a woman surfaced almost instantly.

"Yes, Tony, what is it?"

Tony looked up at the nurse. To his utter surprise, she was lovely; her face was confidence inspiring, unlike any nurse that he had ever seen.

"Do you work here?"

"Well, yes, I do."

"How come I never seen you, then?"

"I'm new on this floor." Tony contemplated this. As far as he knew, the building only had one floor. He watched the new nurse smile.

"My name is Nancy Wilkins. Is there something you need?"

"Yeah, a Kleenex. Got one?" The nurse reached into a cabinet against the far wall and pulled out a box of facial tissues.

"Here you go. It is a little dusty in here, isn't it?"

Tony blew his nose heartily. "How long you gonna be 'on my floor'?"

"What do you mean?"

"I mean, how long am I gonna be so lucky to see your pretty face?"

"Probably for the next few months. You're enrolled in an Alzheimer's research study, and I'll be making sure you get the experimental medicine and watching over you, collecting data and measuring your responses," she said casually.

"Hmm. Where's my buddy?" Tony blew his nose again and motioned to where a second bed could have been.

"I was asked to move you to your own room. Aren't you happy?"

"Happy? Listen, honey, I don't get those kinds of emotions anymore, you know what I'm sayin'? And why was I moved? Am I getting looney? Dangerous?"

"Oh, no. Nothing like that. We've gotten more funding, thanks to the drug trial, and now we can spread people out more and take more scans, more tests, that sort of thing. In fact, you're scheduled for a CT scan this morning—says so right here." The nurse picked up his chart and thumbed through it.

"Tests, tests, and more tests. I don't understand it. What are they looking for, anyways?"

"Beats me, Tony. Maybe you just have a special skull." The nurse smiled a soap-opera smile.

"Hey, you got some good work in there."

"Where?"

"In your mouth. I can tell. I used to know a guy, Guy DeFalco was his name—isn't that a great name?—and he was a great capper."

"Capper?"

"You know, dentist. He specialized in, whaddaya call it, cosmetic dentistry. He could fix us all up good after a tough night out, you know what I'm sayin', doll?"

The nurse clearly did not know what he was saying. But she nodded anyway, clenching her teeth at her new charge's choice of words.

"Listen, Tony, I'll be back in a while to take you over to radiology. Why don't you rest until then? You'll sleep better in a room of your own."

"Rest? I just woke up. How about providing some—well, some entertainment?"

"I can bring you a book, if you'd like. I'll look around for one. In the meantime, try to get some rest. See you later." The nurse turned and left the room abruptly. *A book*? Tony was picturing a deck of cards instead. Or a nice video, *On the Waterfront,* maybe, or *The Hustler*. Now that he was in a room alone and there were more 'funds,' Tony didn't see why they couldn't set him up with his own DVD player and TV. Maybe even surround sound. He hated going over to the rec room with all those depressing old guys. But he did like his new digs and his new nurse.

But if she thought he bought her act, she was dead wrong. She was no nurse. Maybe his son was behind this. Was it possible that fruit had turned around? He must be sure to ask him.

Despite himself, he fell asleep.

Therese had been relaxed, but now she was on guard. After a tense lunch with her father, who acted like a host on a game show, she retreated to the privacy of her villa, pulling the draperies closed. Her father had told her more than she wanted to know about Richard over lunch—about what a brilliant man Richard was and how brilliant it was to snatch Richard from the NIH and all about chemotherapy. The fact was she didn't want to hear a word of it. She wasn't going to be an item on her father's projects agenda.

Why did it bother her so much, she wondered as she filled the teakettle. She didn't have to ponder that one very long. It was simple; it was the same thing it always was. She wanted to be her own person, doing things for herself, not handed everything and everyone on a platter. It irked; it made Richard or anyone associated with her father very unattractive.

But that wasn't Richard's fault. And she had to admit, she was thinking about him. Too much. And she didn't like that, either; it wasn't healthy. He was practically a stranger. A distraction. Time to think about what matters, what's real, she chastised herself.

She set her tea on the coffee table and retrieved June Hamels' file from her nearby briefcase. She crouched on the floor and spread the meager evidence out before her. She sighed and vowed to at least come up with a hypothesis about June. Greg was waiting.

She reviewed the facts she knew about the case. The girl had been seventeen and homeless. She had been smart and good-looking. She had no living family. She was last seen in her squatter's apartment four days before her death. Where had she gone and why? She'd had surgery, but her ailment was not known. June had appeared at her door one afternoon and collapsed. Was she driven there? By whom? Therese again listed these facts on a legal pad, hoping that writing them down would make something more obvious. Perhaps a detail she had overlooked would reveal its importance.

She looked again at the report labeled 'TANK, PRELIMINARY, NOT TO BE USED FOR OFFICIAL RECORD' and reread the conclusion aloud. “Scan with contrast of head reveals an abnormal gap (2.5cm x 1.5cm) in the frontal lobe, cause unknown. The margins of gap are clean and well-healed.” A gap, yes.

A scenario appeared. Could June have perhaps donated part of her brain to science for money? What would June be willing to do for money? Probably a great deal, Therese suspected.

But what part of a brain would be useful to someone? Was it for a transplant? Was there a part of the brain that was discrete—like a liver or a kidney? And if it were like an organ transplant, wouldn’t this Tank thing know what had been taken? The report only said “abnormal gap.” And the Tank did imply it was surgical in nature—the word “margins” gave that away.

Could the surgery have been a botched attempt at saving her from the effects of the aneurysm? That seemed very possible; there might have been a reason to remove a part of the brain in an attempt to save her life. However, if that were true, why didn’t the coroner mention the missing section of brain? Wouldn’t that have bolstered his explanation for June’s death-by-aneurysm?

Therese got up, paced, and thought more about the gap in June’s brain. It occurred to her that she still hadn’t seen the pictures from the big file on the Tank disk! She had been so shaken by the bad news about her own health that it hadn’t occurred to her to ask to see them. What had the doctor at Stanford said about June? She couldn’t remember. Think! Of course—her olfactory bulb was missing! Had she said ‘missing’? Yes, ‘missing, or partially missing.’ She was sure.

Then it dawned on Therese, just as she had hoped something would. Search the Internet for medical uses of the olfactory bulb! It was so simple she nearly slapped her forehead in disgust. She moved to the computer.

Therese paced as the computer booted up, envisioning the results of her search. Genetic testing? The Genome Project? DNA? She racked her brain over the latest medical advances she’d read about in the papers.

Finally, the machine was ready for her input. She opened her Internet browser, ready to type in the URL of a good medical search engine she’d become acquainted with in her short stint at medical school. But something was wrong with her connection to the Internet. She wasn’t online. She checked the wires leading to the satellite modem. Everything seemed intact, but Therese knew that satellite service on the island could be spotty. She attempted to reset the satellite and restarted the computer, hoping for a connection. Nothing.

Now that she had an idea of how to solve the mystery, she couldn't stand to wait for the machine to be up and running—it might not even be working tomorrow morning. She wanted to do the search this very minute. Impulsively, she walked to the dining room windows and looked out from the drawn curtains. A heavy rain was falling and she hadn't even noticed, cooped up inside. Across the way, she saw a light on in the villa next door—just what she had hoped for. She grabbed her raincoat and was out the door before she could think twice.

He opened the door.

"Hello, Richard," she said with what she hoped was a simple, neighborly smile from beneath the beak-like hood of the raincoat. His eyes were shining. She was glad he was happy to see her, but still. *Keep your eye on the ball*, she thought.

"Therese! How wonderful to see you. What—"

"Is your satellite working?" Therese stepped into the foyer, ignoring the puzzled look on Richard's face.

Fox Alzheimer's Hospital

Nancy Wilkins, RN, stood in her office. Seven o'clock approached—the hour they had arranged before the surgeries. She was not surprised when the phone rang at 6:59. She lifted the receiver on the first ring.

"Is this a good time?" the caller asked.

"It is, Dr. Weigand." She listened as the surgeon cleared his throat.

"Very good. Any signs of trouble? Nausea? Bleeding?"

"None. All four patients are healing perfectly."

"And the scans?"

"The post ops were sent yesterday by courier, and we plan to do another head CT scan in a few days, as we discussed."

"Bloods?"

"All normal."

"Excellent. Keep up the good work, my dear." Nancy winced at the inappropriateness of the doctor's tone, but still, she was lucky to have gotten this job. It paid more than she'd ever dreamed of making on the stage, and she felt oddly proud to be involved in such cutting-edge research with a company like BioSys.

The doctor disconnected, and she took the hint. Odd, how they were so confidential about this trial, but she supposed what she didn't know couldn't hurt her. An errant hair flopped down into her eye, and irritated at the distraction, she moved into the bathroom.

Inside, the mirror, like the patient Tony, liked what it saw. A natural blonde, Nancy Wilkins stood almost six feet tall and had what people nowadays called an "athletic" body. Deftly, she adjusted her long hair, fixing it back into its tight bun at the back of her head. She had been lucky to inherit her father's fine skin—she didn't look nearly thirty-five. And now that she was making a cool $250,000 for this Alzheimer's study, she felt even younger inside. An irritating old man wasn't so much to put up with considering the cash—and that just two months ago, she'd been doing dinner theater. Well, she figured, now my cheekbones can charm worried patients, not to mention important scientists.

Nancy left the bathroom and settled down at her desk to some paperwork. Now that Dr. Weigand had made contact, she was required to begin filling out the study's case report forms, which would give her a format to record each patient's progress. She looked over the instructions in the front of the binder for the trial. The title page read: "ABT-55: A Phase I Double-Blind Study."

She read the instruction booklet late into the evening and learned all about her responsibilities, many of which she was familiar with, having spent a few weeks observing a real clinical research nurse. What she didn't understand was why her Alzheimer's patients were receiving an oral chemotherapy agent, but she obviously wasn't a molecular biologist, now was she?

She was, however, financially stable for the first time in her life. The feeling of worrying about where the next meal would come from was fresh in her mind, and now she was putting in a bid for a condominium, while she could.

With a yawn, Nancy Wilkins, MS, RN, PA-C, gave her office a cursory tidying and left the building, looking forward to a good meal at a fine restaurant in Ann Arbor.

Richard led Therese to the cozy library. She unzipped her raincoat and began to explain.

"You see, there's someone I owe a favor to, and it just struck me that I could do an Internet search to help solve his problem."

"Oh." Richard was crestfallen at the mention of a "he," but tried not to show it. He stood with his hands stuck firmly in his jeans pockets.

"And my satellite connection seems to be out, and well, I wanted to get to the bottom of the matter while I was still in the groove."

"Of course, I understand, and I'm happy to help. Have a seat. Can I get you something hot to drink? It's getting a bit nasty out there." The verandah doors that faced the ocean were beginning to swing from the breeze that had now picked up considerably. Richard pulled the doors shut.

"Some tea would be lovely, but please, don't go to any trouble. I'll only be a few minutes. I don't expect to find much."

But her first search for "olfactory bulb," performed on a medical database library, returned a daunting three-hundred fifty-two research articles. Apparently, there was something to write about this smelling organ! Richard returned with the tea and glanced at the screen.

"Oh, my," he began, looking over her shoulder at the words on the screen, which displayed the first twenty citation titles returned by the search. "'Transcription from the gene encoding the herpes virus entry receptor nectin-1 (hvec) in nervous tissue of adult mouse.' That's quite a research topic!" Therese could see the wheels in Richard's head spinning. She almost blushed at the misunderstanding.

"No, that wasn't the kind of article I was looking for; I'm not sure why it came up at all, as a matter of fact."

"What are you looking for?"

"Well, here, you see—the article just below the herpes one; I think this is more like it."

Richard's eyes lit up when he saw the second entry on the list of articles retrieved.

Therese read the entry aloud. "'Neurogenesis in the olfactory bulb of adult zebra fish'. Well, 'fish' wasn't exactly what I was looking for, and I don't know what 'neurogenesis' is, but—"

"Wait, wait one minute." Richard got up and closed the library doors that led into the foyer. He returned and sat back down. He spoke quietly.

"Therese, what on earth are you researching?" He looked distressed, and he knew it. He read another entry on the screen aloud, attempting to veil his reaction to the word "neurogenesis."

"'Genetic dissection of the olfactory bulbs of mice: QTLs on four chromosomes modulate bulb size.' Are you trying to get me to hire you?" To his relief, Therese smiled at the joke.

"I'm just trying to learn about the olfactory bulb, that's all." She also spoke in hushed tones, following Richard's lead. She wondered if she had done the wrong thing by coming here—she seemed to have alarmed Richard. But she had been so sure she would find a simple explanation for the missing bulb. She began to print out the articles anyway.

Richard knew stem cells were found in the olfactory bulb, but they were also found in other parts of the brain. Was Therese learning about stem cells? He must do something to stop her, before she found one of his own papers.

"But why the olfactory bulb?"

"I'm trying to help a poor homeless kid find out why his girlfriend died in a county hospital. I met him while I was catering an event in New York City. When I looked into her death, I discovered that a section of her brain was missing, apparently from surgery. But no one can explain to me why this poor girl had brain surgery, if she did."

Richard hadn't expected that kind of angle. With a sigh of relief, he realized he and his stem cell research were off the hook. And he'd no need to be jealous of the "he" anymore. Clearly, Therese's sleuthing was unrelated to his own work. He was obviously paranoid from all the security measures surrounding their study.

"Well, why didn't you say so? I can help you decode some of this science, if you'd like."

"That'd be great. Let's start with 'QTLs,' then. I suspect she may have been a subject in some bizarre clinical trial. Maybe they paid her money—she was homeless and desperate for college money."

"Well, that's illegal. You can't pay human subjects."

"Well, maybe it was illegal. But she wouldn't have cared. She just wanted the money."

"Nonsense. No one would leave her to die in this day and age."

"I didn't say someone from the medical world killed her or left her to die."

"Okay, I jumped to a conclusion when you said she might have been a subject in a 'bizarre' trial. It seems unlikely, is all I meant. She probably had some kind of life-saving surgery. That's very likely."

"In what scenario?"

"Well, she could have had a stroke, a seizure, or an aneurysm."

"That's what the coroner said."

"Aha. You knew more than you let on!"

"I was just testing you!"

"And I passed?"

"I'll give you an A- for not asking what she died of first."

Richard smiled. "What did she die of?"

"According to the coroner, cardiac arrest caused by meningitis." They both smiled.

"Well, Watson, that's not much of a case, then, is it?"

Therese sighed. "I suppose you're right. Maybe I've been overanalyzing. Maybe I've had too much time on my hands."

"There's nothing wrong with healthy curiosity." There was a pause while they both concentrated. Richard spoke suddenly.

"Speaking of the coroner, is it possible that he removed the bulb?"

"I thought of that, but I can't imagine why he'd remove it. Can you?"

"Well, I'm sure young, healthy organs are hard to come by. Perhaps, knowing she was a Jane Doe, he removed it for students to dissect or for future study. Perhaps he intended to remove the entire brain and ran out of time or money."

"Hmmm. I wonder." Therese gathered the printed pages from the printer and perused the titles of the articles. "Here's one I didn't notice. This is interesting." Therese paused, processing what she had read. Could memories be related to the case of June Hamels? "'Activation of GABA(A) receptors in the accessory olfactory bulb does not prevent the formation of an olfactory memory in mice.' I don't understand some of those words, but I happen to know June had a perfectly functioning memory."

"That article is just about a basic science application of a molecular way of triggering an event in the mouse brain."

"Basic science?"

"Yes. I mean, it doesn't really have any clinical application, not yet, at least. It only concerns laboratory learning. Important learning, but you can't really apply the knowledge to a subject with an illness, for instance."

"Oh."

"Why is that article interesting to you? You can come to my lab and learn about receptors whenever you like! It's fascinating—one cell talks to a protein, and one doesn't. One protein talks to a gene, and one doesn't. How can I make a cell or protein talk to a new gene or new chemical? It's great stuff!"

Richard was a scientist through and through. His face shone proudly as he spoke. Therese liked that he did not dumb the subject down for her, but used elegant examples with basic words. He would be a perfect speaker for a Culinary Classroom event. His manner was not in the least intimidating, and his face was open and kind.

"Tell me more about what you're doing for my father."

"Well, as you know, chemotherapy works by killing off cancer cells. It's as simple as that. And, in the last few years, the big pharmas, like BioSys, have been working on improving that idea by adding some benefit to the chemo treatment. So, instead of killing all the cells—including the healthy ones—you could maybe figure out a way to spare the healthy ones and compromise the immune system less, so the patient has a better quality of life, and his or her own body can do more of the killing of the cancer cells. So the idea is: okay, we kill the bad cells, but while we're bothering to inject this stuff, why not give the patient something good, too—something like a vaccine? This area of therapy is called chemo-bio."

"I've heard of that."

"Right, it's very popular now. The problem is getting the 'chemo' part targeted enough and getting the 'bio' or vaccine part to be effective."

"I can imagine it's very complicated."

"Yes. But your father's company is leading the fight and getting closer." Richard stopped there, afraid to give much more detail on an idea in which he was well versed, but by no means an expert. Therese stood.

"Well, I should be going. I've taken up enough of your evening." Therese gathered the pages she had printed and closed the browser program on the computer. Although she was enchanted by Richard's enthusiasm and felt she could listen to him speak about anything, she didn't want to wear out her neighborly welcome. And besides, she did want to read over the articles anyway, even if it now appeared that June's death was nothing out of the ordinary.

Richard let his disappointment show, since he knew no other way. What luck that the lovely Therese had shown up at his door—and in need of his assistance! He wasn't ready for the evening to end. Inexplicably, he just wanted to be with her. *Damn!* Had he been boring her?

"Know that you're welcome. I mean, you can come over anytime. And I'd also be happy to give you a tour of the lab."

He walked her to the front door and helped her on with her enormous raincoat. The foyer was tiny, making them both aware of their physical closeness. He looked down at her.

"When am I going to see you again?" He saw what he hoped was interest in her sparkling eyes.

"Oh, very soon, I expect. Dad mentioned he'd like to host a dinner in your honor soon. Thanks for your computer."

"Anytime. See you soon!" Richard waved goodbye and watched the hooded figure of Therese Edwards Franklin make her way across the flagstone path, through the rain, toward her own front door. At the same time, tall headlights appeared on their narrow street, and Richard watched his own father approaching in the BioSys Land Rover. Although the two had not met, he saw Therese wave to the man pulling up in the driveway at villa #5. And then she was gone.

After a few words exchanged with his father, Richard went straight back to the library computer. He re-opened the browser application and pointed it to the last web pages visited. He read the abstract for the article about neurogenesis and the olfactory bulb with interest. Of course, it was well known in his world that neurogenesis continually took place in the healthy human olfactory bulb throughout life. This article pointed out that the growth of the new cells—derived from stem cells—could be identified using a specific type of marker, a variation of the ones Richard himself had used. He did a quick survey of the other literature found in Therese's "olfactory bulb" search, and thankfully, did not find anything surprising. But the fact that she had made the search at all did make him wonder.

He walked into the kitchen absentmindedly and poured himself a glass of water. If the homeless girl's olfactory bulb had been intentionally removed, it could be for harvesting stem cells. But who was doing that kind of work in New York? There had been no harvesting of human neuronal stem cells that he knew of—and he was sure if it existed, he would know all about it; it would be all over the medical journals, not to mention the popular press. Was there a private company collecting human adult stem cells? It was very possible. But very disturbing.

Back in the quiet of her own living room, Therese saw the array of June Hamels' documents and was uneasy again. Although Richard's explanation was reasonable, she still felt something wasn't right. If her search had turned up only three or four papers about the olfactory bulb, she could have let the matter rest. But three-hundred fifty-two papers represented a lot of research, she told herself. She sat down on the floor again and read the citations and their abstracts, of which she had only printed a few. It was well after midnight when she turned out the lights, but when she finally did, it was with the knowledge that the olfactory bulb produces and stores stem cells, the very popular "precursor" cells that had the medical world in the spotlight now. She guessed she had found her answer.

Fox Alzheimer's Hospital

The patients were all gathered around backgammon tables. The blinds were drawn, bright sunlight struggling to seep into the dank room through the slats. Tony took his turn, and then watched his opponent consider his next move. It'd been two weeks since he was moved into his own private room, and he missed his old roommate, Vic, who now made his move and looked up at Tony. This was the first group activity in which the new nurse had allowed him to participate. Around them sat dozing dementia patients. It was noon.

Vic surveyed the board. "The way I see it, you got about two moves before I crush you."

"I see three, at least. Don't put me in my coffin just yet, buddy." Tony rolled, and then made a definitive move on the board, removing himself from immediate jeopardy.

"You're pretty good, for a sick old guy," retorted Vic, stifling a yawn. "Hey, the last time we played this game, you didn't even want to think a few moves ahead. That new nurse is working wonders, huh?" Vic nodded to Nancy, who loomed near their table, keeping a close eye on her charge. Tony looked over his shoulder in confirmation.

"Oh, yeah. I think my loser son finally pulled some strings for me. It's about time, too! What's a guy gotta do to get a little R & R in this joint, I kept asking myself."

"I thought you liked my snoring? Said it reminded you of your wife!" They both belted out hearty chuckles at Marie Rossetti's expense.

"Okay, buddy, looks like you're about to lose your twenty bucks." Vic made a critical move. On the wall above the table, there was a dusty old sign that read, "No Gambling."

"I think not, Vic old boy." Tony performed a bait-and-switch move, and the game swung far back into his favor.

"Oh, no!" cried Vic, surprised.

"That's a trick Bessie taught me."

"Bessie? You mean Bessie the Blue Hair, over there playing with old what's-her-name?" Vic pointed across the room.

"That's her. She's a character."

"When did she teach you that?"

"Uh, I dunno. Just before they moved me, I guess." With a final roll of the dice, Tony won the game. The two sat back in their chairs, much the same, Tony realized, as they might have done in his own living room back on the Westside of Chicago. With a jolt, he remembered the squeak that those old chairs at home made when you really leaned into them.

"Hey," Vic interrupted his thoughts. "Your blonde is coming our way. What's her name, anyway?"

"I don't remember," Tony began, automatically. She stood at their table, and he looked up at her and added, "Wait, scratch that; sure I do. Vic, meet Nancy. Nancy Wilkins."

Richard was nervous. In fact, he paced the villa like a wild animal. Stuart would be expecting them for dinner in just one hour, and he still had no idea how Stuart had reacted to his flirting with Therese. If he knew at all. He knocked on Bob's bathroom door, which was slightly ajar. His father was shaving.

"Dad, I—"

"Now, look, son. I've got two things to say, and I'm only going to say them once." As he spoke, he continued to shave, staring intently at his own image in the mirror. "I want you to play it cool. Very cool. I understand you like this girl, but—"

"I'm crazy about her, Dad!"

"Okay, crazy, but the point is—point number one—Stuart is the boss. Whatever he says goes. Son, he's going to make you fabulously famous if you'll just be—"

"Famous? Who said anything about fame? I just want to—"

"Quiet now. Point two is a golden rule. A *golden* rule." Bob patted his face dry with a hand towel and turned to face his son, looking him in the eye. "And that is, work and home must remain separate, my boy. The lady of the house must remain shielded from the work of the office. Although you may at times be tempted, you must never share with her any of the ideas from the lab. That's true in real life, but especially true down here. Why? Because Stuart owns us, let's face it. And what she doesn't know can't hurt her. You understand?" Bob gave Richard a buddy-to-buddy pat on the shoulders. "Now, let that be the end of it. I've already spoken to Stuart for you. He won't bring it up. The secret-keeping, I mean." Bob sighed and moved into his adjacent bedroom. He looked over his shoulder before he disappeared into his enormous walk-in closet. "Let's have some fun tonight, okay?"

Richard turned to face his own empty bedroom. He went and sat on the bed and looked out the window, as he had as a child. Why was he being treated like one? He'd done nothing wrong. But he had to admit, Therese's stumbling onto the concept of neurogenesis had rattled him. Thank goodness, his father didn't know about that.

With a sigh, he got up and went to his own bathroom. He studied his face in the mirror. *Not too bad*, he thought to himself. He looked a little pale. He had been feeling so good just yesterday, energized by Therese's surprise visit, and now he felt a terrible pressure. He squinted and watched his crow's feet appear and disappear. Was his life different now, justifying that his private life be public knowledge? That would be odd, since he now worked in the private, not public, sector. Did Stuart's cronies follow Therese around? What exactly was that damn smoke-alarm-slash-camera for, anyway? He felt confined, an unwitting lab rat in a maze.

He closed the lid of the toilet and sat down on it. If he had to leave Anegada tomorrow, could he? But why would he leave? His life was here. His old life in Bethesda had been erased; at the time, it seemed the easiest way to move in secret. He'd no bank account there, no address. He'd kept a PO box for their remaining bills and necessities, but that was all. The friends he once had never bothered corresponding.

He was beginning to wonder if the sudden move had been worth it. He would know if it had once the four patients started improving. If they didn't, at least he had met Therese. But what then?

Bob called out from downstairs. "Richard, come on; let's get going."

Richard stood and checked his countenance again. He remembered he would soon see Therese. He was relieved to see a layer of happiness in him bubbling again to the surface.

The crisp white wine and chilled melon soup worked wonders to break the ice. Stuart surveyed his guests. He was pleased to be holding court—it'd been years since he'd had a proper dinner party at Eastwind.

"Friends," he began, raising his goblet a little too dramatically for his daughter's taste. He had worn his favorite tie for the occasion, which she bought for him in San Francisco. She also noticed an errant hole in his shirt—a button missed in haste. She refocused her attention on her father's face.

"I know we have only known each other for a short time, but I look forward to many more dinners like this one. Bob and Richard," he swung his arm to his right and left, "are very special people, Therese. I know you already have an inkling of how special Richard is." Richard smiled widely; Therese looked only at her father, waiting for the end of the speech. "When we are done here, we'll have designed the most sophisticated chemotherapeutic agent the world has even seen, a scientific achievement that will affect millions of Al—er, cancer suffers." Therese watched her father as he cleared his throat. "What I'm trying to say is, Bob, Richard, thank you very much for your hard, hard work—and Richard, watch out—she's a heartbreaker!"

Everyone laughed, and Hattie, their longtime chef, entered with the main course—lobster barbequed over an open sand pit with a traditional West Indies sauce called callaloo, full of okra and chili peppers. Bob, on her left, began to speak, and Therese was thankful to hear someone other than her father engaging the table.

"I hear that this kind of lobster is specific to this region. I've been reading books on the local fishing industry."

"It's true," Therese responded. "I'm an avid fisher, as is Dad. This lobster breed wasn't always native, though; the Spanish brought it with them."

"You fish?" Richard couldn't hide his incredulity. He smiled across at her, picturing a blue-sky day out on a boat—just the two of them.

Bob and Stuart began to discuss yachting, and Therese let her guard down. "I'm full of surprises," she said quietly, and wondered why she'd actually said that aloud. She hoped Richard hadn't heard her.

As if in a theater production, a sudden crackle of thunder and lightning joined the dinner party, like a new character. Therese laughed at the drama as the bright light splashed into the dimly lit room. "Speaking of yachting!" added Stuart to the interlude. "It is nearly monsoon season. If you'd planned on working on your tans, I suggest you do it soon."

"Are the rains very severe?" Bob frowned, his vision of endless days on a boat evaporating.

"They can be, yes. Therese is the expert in that area."

"Why's that?" Bob turned to face her as Hattie entered the room to clear the plates.

"Well, one year, when I was nineteen, Anegada—and the entire region—had a devastating rainy season. The small populace of this island was completely displaced. The other islands, which are volcanic, suffered badly since there is little terracing to accommodate the run-off gushing down from the volcanoes. Anegada suffered the worst, again due to its geography—this island is made almost entirely of coral and limestone—and not long ago, geographically speaking, it was underwater. Today, it's only twenty-six feet above sea level. Well, that spring, it was looking like it was going to be underwater once again. Evacuating people—even the island's two hundred—was a nightmare. Local residents hadn't ever lived through such a flood, and they didn't know what to do. And because the island is basically a giant coral reef, sailing around it can be treacherous. One of the evacuation boats, carrying twenty people, was grounded, and the sharp reef tore a hole in its hull. The boat took on water quickly, and soon everyone was swimming. Although the water is warm, its eddies are powerful, and some passengers panicked before help could arrive. Tragically, three people drowned, including a baby girl who was too small for a life vest.

"So, that year, I put off going back to college for a semester and stayed here, working with the neighboring islands to develop more foolproof evacuation procedures. Between the British governor, the British Coast Guard, and volunteers from the villages, we came up with something satisfactory. In a way, that was the beginning of Culinary Classroom. You see, many plants were so eroded we couldn't figure out how to reseed them. Their varieties—lost. Now we have a seed bank."

The table was silent. Therese looked at Richard and saw him giving her that stare of his. Bob, who'd been following her story closely, jumped slightly when the next crash of thunder announced itself. She laughed and put her hand on his.

"But you don't have anything to worry about. This year's supposed to be very light, thanks to El Niño."

After-dinner cocktails were served in the library, which had a big screened-in verandah, perfect for watching the storm. Bob and Stuart poured over a coffee- table book of famous yachts at the far end of the room, while Richard stood with an oversweet brandy and gazed out into the blackness. The wind was picking up, and random detached banana tree fronds blew past the terrace below. Therese approached him from behind, a tray of chocolates in her hand.

"I wouldn't want to be out sailing tonight!"

He tuned to face her. She was beautiful in the lightning flashes, her eyes electric green, as if charged by the sky's ions.

"No, indeed." He popped an offered sweet in his mouth and was surprised how well it went with the brandy. He couldn't remember ever having been served brandy in a library before, and it made something in him twitch, slightly. He realized it might be *nervousness*. The whole thing made him uneasy. Yet it all seemed…easy. "You can't even walk me home in this dreck."

Therese smiled at the role-reversal joke. "Why not? I have my giant raincoat. And after all, I know the evacuation route!"

"This island means a lot to you."

"Of course. It's where I got to roam free, discover things, wander. I think all children should be outdoors to fulfill their sense of wonder and curiosity, don't you? I remember once, I got bitten on the toe by a jellyfish, and I didn't even feel any pain at first because I was so intrigued just looking at the glob next to my foot!"

"You were just open." He stared at her deeply; it stirred her. She took a seat in a club chair, moving away from him.

"Yes, like a clam feeding," she joked.

"Are you still?"

"A clam?" Therese smiled, enjoying their repartee.

"You've a few more curves, now." Therese felt his eyes move over her from where he stood.

"Yes, and a few leaks. The old mouth doesn't always seal like it used to."

"Doesn't it?" The rain came down louder outside, and Richard was aware that they were now alone in the room. He studied her, and was not aware that he did this with an utter lack of self-consciousness—her mouth, her lips, the way her eyes lit up in the occasional lightning. It was like studying a specimen, and it was easy because she wasn't looking at him. He realized he would like to study her more—her face, her hands, the way she walked.

Therese got up. "I should help Hattie in the kitchen," she said, and then she was gone. Again.

Chapter Twenty-Nine

THERESE SLEPT FITFULLY and awoke unrefreshed. She wondered if she'd slept at all. She glanced at the clock, which gratefully no longer hovered in the three a.m. area. Between the tension of those moments alone with Richard and her newfound knowledge of stem cells being produced in olfactory bulbs, she knew she had little chance at sleep for today. She stretched and climbed out of bed, stepping over Fancy's huge figure, sprawled out on the floor at the foot of the bed.

A glorious sunrise greeted her in the kitchen. She stood at the kitchen window, watching the morning emerge. She heard the welcoming hiss of the morning sprinklers starting, despite last night's rain, and soon a fine mist was re-soaking the banana trees and gardenias. She started the kettle, and was again faced with the early hour—5:05 a.m was displayed on the range's clock. That meant she would have to wait at least two more hours before she could call Greg in New York City and tell him her new theory about June. The poor man had waited long enough.

Over her mug of steaming tea, it occurred to her that she'd left her address book at Eastwind last night, and she'd need it to phone Greg. A walk sounded nice anyway. Maybe she could work out some tension. She pulled on a sweatshirt, laced up her sneakers, and left the house, Fancy still soundly asleep. Knowing her father, he'd be out golfing or at the office already. And if she remembered correctly, Monday was Hattie's day off.

Outside, the air was fresh and cool from last night's storm, and as she expected, the brisk walk did her a world of good. She reflected on what she had leaned about stem cells being produced and stored in the mysteriously important olfactory bulb. Therese knew from just reading the papers that stem cells were coveted, since they could be the source of medical solutions for Parkinson's, diabetes, heart disease, or even cancer. For months now, stem cells had been all over the newspapers. They were controversial, so therefore, she concluded, difficult for scientists and doctors to obtain.

Before she knew it, three miles of grass and gravel had elapsed, and the massive estate of Eastwind stood before Therese. She made her way up the long drive, waving to the guard as she passed. The wooded drive always gave her a chill, and she pulled her sweatshirt around her. She walked around to the back of the house, headed for the back kitchen entrance. To her surprise, she heard voices from an open kitchen window above her.

"I told her to take another scan."

Since she had not expected to find anyone at home, she stopped to listen, alarmed at hearing the word "scan." But then she heard her father's voice.

"Is it possible the memory is coming back already?"

"I didn't think we'd see any clinical results before at least six to twelve weeks, Stuart."

Therese recognized the voice from dinner last night. Bob Weigand. What were they doing up at this hour, and in the kitchen?

"Is this really a clinical result?"

"I would say we should treat it as one. These subjects have trouble with their recent memories, that's what's so interesting about his sudden recall of the nurse's name; he had only met her two weeks previously, and he'd heard her name just after surgery to boot!"

Surgery for Alzheimer's? In her studies, Therese had not read about any surgical approach for Alzheimer's. Suddenly, Therese recalled her father's dramatic reaction to her Alzheimer's study suggestion. But if her father was running a study, or following one, why was he discussing it with Bob? At six in the morning?

She made her decision quickly. She moved swiftly and quietly to the front door. She rang the front bell. She felt silly eavesdropping, and it seemed more appropriate now to announce her arrival. There was no movement from inside, so she rang the bell again. The door was abruptly opened. Her father stood there, his tie tied sloppily. His hair was rumpled and his clothes looked slept in. Why was he letting himself go?

"Therese! Sorry it took me a while to get here; I forgot Hattie isn't here today."

"I'm sorry to show up so early; it's just that I forgot my address book, and I need to make an important call this morning. Am I disturbing you?"

"Good lord, no. Why don't you come in and we'll have some breakfast. In fact, Bob and I—" Bob appeared from the kitchen and moved forward to greet her. “Bob and I were just getting started with a breakfast meeting, but we’d be pleased if you’d join us. There’s plenty of time for work today, and the eggs are ready!” Stuart smiled from ear to ear, evidently pleased with his explanation. Therese moved into the house, too curious to decline the odd invitation.

“Go sit in the sunroom, you two, and I’ll bring out breakfast.” Therese followed Bob into the sunroom, which was filled with plants. A bubbling fountain provided a soothing atmosphere, but Therese did not feel soothed as she looked at Bob, who was sipping his coffee. She studied him casually. His silvery blonde hair was impeccable and neatly groomed. His skin was healthy and lightly tanned. He must have been in his seventies, but he didn’t look it. His hands and arms showed no signs of aging, and his blue-gray eyes held a youthful glimmer. He wore a pink golfing shirt and a golden ring on his pinky. It seemed out of place on a surgeon. It had light etching on its face that Therese could not make out at her distance.

“I see you’ve noticed my ring,” Bob began, and Therese looked up in acknowledgement.

“Yes, I had.”

“It has an interesting history. Let me tell you about it.” He took another sip of coffee then cleared his throat loudly. “About twenty years ago, I was having dinner with my wife Esther at our favorite neighborhood deli on the Upper West Side. A man at the table next to us began to choke. I attempted the Heimlich maneuver, without success. I had very little time—the man was turning blue. I called for a knife from the kitchen and some boiling hot water. I cleaned the knife in the boiling water and used it to perform an emergency tracheotomy, opening the throat about here,” Bob illustrated an area on Therese’s own throat, leaning over to touch her, “and removing the jammed pickle slice. I had to devise a way to seal him temporarily until the paramedics could get him to the OR, so I used a few cloth napkins!” Bob paused to chuckle at the memory. “He lived, thanks to God. And when he recovered, he tracked me down. I don’t know how, since he hadn’t even gotten my name in the chaos, and he gave me this ring. It had been in his family for generations. It is believed to have come from the original Franciscans of Italy, as in St. Francis of Assisi. The picture on the ring, see,” Bob took it off and handed the ring to Therese for closer examination, “depicts St. Francis receiving his divine orders from above.” Bob smiled as he concluded the story and leaned back in his chair. Therese could see the story on the ring. There was St. Francis with his arms outstretched to the horizon, from which light shone down, forming a spotlight on humble St. Francis.

The significance of the story had not eluded Therese. Its pompousness irritated her, and she responded accordingly. "Is medical science a divine order, Dr. Weigand?"

"Well, of course my dear. Of course."

Stuart arrived with a tray containing breakfast. Therese stood and helped her father serve.

"So, Therese, darling, what is this important item on your agenda this morning?" Stuart's voice sounded oddly theatrical to Therese, and when she looked at him, she saw what she could only described as a wild look in his eye. She doubted he'd slept at all last night. He sat down and began to eat quickly and voraciously, like a five-year-old who'd been out playing all day. What was going on?

"I have to call a donor for Culinary Classroom. She asked that I call her this morning, before she leaves for a long trip, and she wanted to give the donation in the new quarter, apparently. It's a quite sizable amount—" Stuart looked up from his food, suddenly alert, like a wolf that smelled the presence of his prey.

"How much?" Stuart nearly shouted. Therese looked at her father, puzzled. Although Stuart had helped her get the seed money for the foundation, he'd left all other financial matters to her and her financial advisors.

"Well, $350,000, actually." Therese was not lying; she did expect this donation sometime this month.

"Wheeeeew!" whistled Stuart, awestruck. It seemed a mysterious reaction, since the amount was practically pocket change to the multi-billionaire. Therese began to eat, not sure how to react in the face of his odd, childlike behavior. Without looking, she popped a forkful of eggs into her mouth. They were burned. She washed the crunchy eggs down with orange juice and stood.

"Well, I must be getting back. Fancy needs her breakfast."

Stuart nearly jumped out of his chair. "You should stay a little longer. Richard will be here soon," smiled her father.

"Maybe some other time, Dad." She kissed him on the check then leaned over to shake Bob's hand in farewell. "It was nice chatting with you. Goodbye."

Therese let herself out of the front door and walked swiftly away, her mind racing; soon she was running.

At the kitchen table, sweating now, Therese made some notes on her trusty legal pad: Dad acting odd. Overheard Bob and Stuart discussing "memory" and "scans" this morning at Eastwind. Then, a new paragraph: June—her death corresponds to coroner's explanation, but her olfactory bulb could be missing or partially missing for its stem cell value. She put down her pad and picked up the phone to page Greg to the payphone.

"Hi, Greg. I'm sorry it took me so long to contact you."

"That's okay. I understand. I've been trying to keep busy, just keep my mind off it all."

"Well, here's what I've concluded. Are you ready?"

"Ready."

"June must have had some life-saving surgery, obviously unscheduled. She couldn't phone you from the hospital because you have no phone and she was barely conscious. Erroneously, the hospital assumed there was no one to contact. All alone, she presented to the ER with an aneurysm, a severe one. She would have been in great pain and perhaps delirious. The doctors performed an operation to reduce her intracranial pressure, which was threatening the flow of oxygen to her brain." Therese paused to catch her breath.

"Okay. Go on," reassured Greg.

"She was probably in recovery for six to twelve hours. She was released when it appeared everything was fine—again, no one to call to accompany her home. Next thing I can gather is that she collapsed at your door from the effects of meningitis, which had set in quickly. She no doubt had a raging fever as her body fought the infection. Apparently, meningitis is a known risk of any brain surgery."

"And I know the rest."

"Well, not quite. Your instincts about information being withheld were not wrong. When I read June's records, I discovered that a section of her brain had been removed, and I assumed this was due to the life-saving surgery. But then, after I brought her records around to experts, I learned that what was missing in her brain was precise, specific. An imaging expert confirmed this. But no one could explain why this specific section, the olfactory bulb—"

"Olfactory bulb?"

"That's what I said, but I did a little research, and I've put it together. The olfactory bulb produces and stores progenitor cells or 'stem cells.'"

"Stem cells? I've read about them in the newspaper."

"Right. I think the coroner removed the olfactory bulb to study the organ, dissect it, or perhaps give it to students. That explains his evasiveness. I happen to know he is not very well funded—his department just suffered a big funding cut."

"That adds up. Sounds just like what a public worker would do. He'd be driven to desperate sources—all that red tape."

"Exactly. And since she was considered to be without family, the coroner, no doubt, figured he wouldn't meet any resistance." There was a pause while Greg digested this idea. She hoped he wouldn't suggest they track the bulb down—what use could it be now that June was dead?

"And there's another thing. June had an excellent memory."

"Is that related to her olfactory bulb?"

"I'm not sure. But, as far as I can see, the trail ends there." They were both silent for a few moments. "I'm very sorry about this terrible experience, Greg, and I hope we can keep in touch." Therese didn't know what to do, other than wrap up the conversation. "I can send the records to you, if you'd like."

"I would like that. And thank you for your hard work. But, actually, the trail hasn't ended."

"No?" Therese was puzzled. The idea that the mystery was solved had been sitting well with her; she now had her own mysteries to solve.

"No. I've spent the last two weeks on the streets looking for more information. I found a street kid who said he saw June get into a fancy car four days before she died."

Therese gasped. "A limo?"

"Maybe. The kid showed me where he saw her, and I staked it out for a couple days, waiting to see it again. But I never did."

"Is there more information about the car?"

"He didn't know the make or model, only that it was a long black sedan of some kind. Said it looked old and he heard somebody on the street call it 'Eating our,' whatever the hell that means. He obviously doesn't know much about cars. I think he meant it was a vintage car—he mentioned chrome—but I can't be sure."

"Plates?"

"He didn't know. He didn't notice; he just figured June was going on a hot date."

"I see. Is it out of the ordinary to be picked up by such a vehicle?"

"I suppose not. She could have been a hired escort for some corporate guy. Who knows?" There was a moment of long silence while the possibilities were considered. Greg spoke first.

"How do you feel now about the case being closed?"

"Well, it's a lead, I agree, but I think my scenario could still account for her cause of death—emergency surgery, surgery complications arise, meningitis sets in, June dies, coroner takes liberties."

Greg sighed. "Now that you've framed it that way, I have to agree."

"My advice to you is that I think it's time for you to start healing and stop investigating."

"It's out of my control, anyway, is that what you were going to say next?" Greg's voice was suddenly hostile, a pot of water nearing a boil.

Therese was suddenly very tired. "Well, more or less. Look, I know you're frustrated, and I know it's not easy—your instinct is to react—"

"Thanks for all your help, Therese."

The line went dead, and Therese stood with the phone next to her ear, in shock. She had hurt him—but how, when all she'd wanted to do was help? She felt guilty, and then angry; he had been wrong to try to make her feel that way. June was *his* problem, not hers, she reminded herself. She didn't like knowing someone was angry with her, and it didn't feel good to be curtly disconnected. She considered paging him again.

It didn't take her long to decide against it.

Therese collected her June Hamels papers and walked to the trash. Since Greg had been so rude, there was no reason to consider the matter further.

"Why bother?" she said aloud to the empty villa. With a sigh, she let the papers fall into the dustbin.

The entire day stretched before her. It was not a pleasant feeling. Although she did her best to ignore it, she felt hurt by Greg—why? She sought to keep her mind off the unpleasantness of their conversation. She paced the kitchen without realizing it. She considered going back to bed. Then, she took a deep breath. It was obviously time for a swim. She changed into her swimsuit and headed outside to the surf.

At nine the same morning, Richard and Bob stood over the CT scans, which were illuminated by a portable light table set up in Stuart's Eastwind study. Bob addressed Stuart.

"Just as we figured," he began, "small teratoma tumors are forming in the two patients who received the embryonic stem cells. Our expert James pointed them out to me." They studied the scans more closely.

"And the other two?" Stuart leaned in to see the pictures Bob described.

"Well, neither James nor I see any change on their scans, which is what we expected at this point."

"Is there any way we can see what the stem cells are doing?"

"Well, probably not now, unless we did a biopsy," Richard replied. His statement was met with an odd glare from Stuart. Richard studied him in response. Today's Stuart was clearly a different man. He was a man on the edge. His voice was haggard, as if he'd not slept. His unshaven face seemed to confirm this.

"So, Bob," Stuart began in a caustic tone, turning away from Richard, "how will we know when the cells are working?"

"The two patients, ah, let's see—" Bob, unruffled by Stuart's behavior, leafed through files in his briefcase and read from some notes. "Yes, here they are. Marvin Glen and Tony Rossetti. Well, the best way to know how the stem cells are thriving is by watching these two men. I have our planted nurse at the Alzheimer's hospital sending daily reports directly to my office. You already know about the one tidbit of encouragement—"

"What tidbit?" Richard looked at Bob in surprise. Bob raised a hand to Richard.

"I'll tell you later. Stuart, the only way to really see the effect of the cells is to wait a few more weeks and watch their progress." Stuart suddenly slapped his hands on the table, so loudly that Bob and Richard jumped involuntarily.

"I'll go see them!" Stuart shouted.

"You'll what?" Richard volunteered, caring less and less for guarded words. He didn't like being startled at all.

Stuart pointed to Richard with a long finger, punctuating the air with his words. "You'll stay here and work on converting these cells to avoid this mess," Stuart held up the CT scans, indicating the small tumors forming in the two less-fortunate patients. He was suddenly as sharp as a decorated admiral—his tone authoritarian and exact. He turned to Bob. "You will relax and rest your hands for my procedure, which will take place very soon. I will travel incognito to the Alzheimer's hospital and keep my eye on our two heroes. I will report back when I have new information." Stuart paused and tossed the scans on the large table. "Richard, you are dismissed." Stuart placed his hand on his waist in a distinctly Napoleonic fashion.

Richard was happy to leave the Eastwind estate, which was starting to give him the creeps. He made his way though the long, winding hallway that led to the front doors, his shoes making loud echoes on the stone floors. As he approached the front hallway, he noticed a surveillance camera perched over the giant wooden doors with a notable lack of discretion. He paused to get a better look at it, and wondered how he had missed it previously. Pondering again the fact that they were under constant surveillance, he left the mansion and went to sit in the garden to wait for his father.

Fred Thiessen watched the image of Richard looking into the Eastwind front door camera, #121, with great interest. Fred noted the day and time, and then refocused his attention on his desk, where he was repairing a panel of electric circuitry. Behind him, his security staff busied themselves preparing for today's drill on securing the facility in the case of a fire or a dangerous chemical or radiation leak.

Back in the cool and order of his lab, Richard drew a schematic on his white board. He'd spent the entire morning trying to shake off the odd treatment he'd received at Eastwind by launching a series of experiments. The point of all of them was converting embryonic stem cells into properly functioning neuronal stem cells, this time using cells derived from the bone marrow of adult primates. These cells had the potential to differentiate into many different cell types, but the most important kind for Richard's use was neurons. He sat back and gave a deep sigh. Now he would have to wait again.

Richard was tired of being uninformed about his cover job. Twisting the truth to Therese had made him uncomfortable; he couldn't stomach lying to her. Lying in and of itself was completely unnatural to Richard. Now that he had some free time, he intended learn everything he could about the ABT-55 drug trial, which would be relatively easy since the lab next to his did bonafide BioSys work, preparing the drug for its upcoming clinical trial. But before he spoke to them, he wanted to be informed. He logged into BioSys' secure document library, did a search for all the documents he thought relevant, then clicked Check Out. Copies of each document were downloaded as files to his local computer. He then logged out.

As he read the tables of data on his computer screen, he let his mind wander to the day he could tell Therese about his real work here in Anegada. Then something in the data caught his eye. It was a diagram of a complicated molecular structure, one Richard read like written language. But what caught his eye in the diagram was the scientific equivalent of a typo. He looked closer, zooming in to 150%. He considered that what he had labeled an error could perhaps be a novel molecule. He sent the paper to the network printer so he could study the document more carefully.

As he munched on an apple, Richard went through the entire monkey study document and began reading the beginnings of three other papers. The more Richard read about the miracle chemo project, the more he questioned its validity. He had confirmed one major molecular error easily, so why hadn't someone else?

It was lunchtime at BioSys HQ in North Carolina when Paul Westin's computer email program signaled to him. Ten new emails in his Inbox. He dropped his fork in his low-cal cafeteria salad when he saw the subject lines of the ten new messages in his Inbox. He opened one of the emails, not quite believing as he read.

> To: Paul Westin, Document Owner 45137
> Cc: Richard Weigand, Ph.D.
> From: BioSys Document Library v2.001.245
> Subject: Document Activity: 45137
> -----
> This is an automated email message; do not reply.
>
> Dear Paul Westin,
> Your document, 45137, Pre-clinical Studies of the Novel Molecule ABT-55 in Primates, has been checked out to user no. 309876, Richard Weigand, Ph.D.
>
> This document is in Published status and may not be edited.
> -----

Paul clicked on the hyperlink for User No. 309876, which brought up a company database record locator for Richard Weigand, PhD. He was in Anegada—in the manufacturing group, of all damn things! Building 7, floor 3, room 412. Why the hell had Paul never heard of him?

Paul locked his computer, locked up his office, and ran to Fred Thiessen's security office.

When he arrived, Fred was nowhere to be seen, thanks to lunch or luck, Paul wasn't sure, and it didn't matter. An underling was there who responded as desired to Paul's authoritarian voice and title.

"I need you to bring up this location, now—and fast!" Paul's tension was not lost on the underling, who typed with all his might. He used a GPS-like interface to locate the building in Anegada that Paul specified, and then he switched the screen to a database that listed all the rooms and their camera numbers. It had only been about three minutes, but Paul was starting to sweat.

"Hurry, this is important!"

"Okay, okay; we're waiting for the data to load. The computer has to locate all the cameras in that building then filter by floor, and then we can get to the room."

A progress bar onscreen showed they only had "a few more minutes."

Slowly, a picture resolved onscreen. It was a workspace, a large lab table in the middle. There were no people there, just computers. The lab table had a lot of stuff on it, some of it documents. The image was black and white.

"Here—can you zoom in? About there?" Paul pointed to an area of the screen.

The underling punched in a command on the keyboard and the image redrew, slowly, and then again.

It was all Paul needed to see. Even with the poor resolution, he recognized the page that had been left open from one of his large, outsourced monkey study documents. He saw handwriting on the image—*shit*!

"Okay," said Paul, attempting to mask his alarm. "That wasn't what I was looking for. Can you switch to—"

Paul had the underling go to another building and room, which he picked randomly, and pretended to have found the source of his panic there.

"No big deal. I was wrong. Thanks for your time, kid."

"Sure," said the underling, who went back to his ramen noodles and Su Doku puzzle, unphased.

Richard stood at the white board, about to redraw the molecule correctly to examine it at a distance. At that moment, there was a knock at the lab door. Richard looked up to see Dr. Ling, a molecular biologist Richard had scarcely met, gesturing to him to come into the hall.

"Fire drill!" called Ling in a muffled shout from the other side of the thick lab door glass, gesturing wildly at his ears. Funny, thought Richard, he'd not heard any alarms sound. As he moved toward the door, however, they began. And they were deafening. Richard was instantly reminded of his incident with the fire alarm in his villa. He ushered out his six lab workers then walked swiftly down the hallway to the stairwell with Dr. Ling and the other scientists, all covering their ears to block out the clamor.

Outside in the parking lot, Richard introduced himself properly. Although Richard knew he was not to consort with the other scientists, he also knew that isolating himself from the other scientists at this facility was shortsighted; he'd gain nothing from this experience. If he adopted such a firm policy, he might as well have stayed in the cloisters of the NIH.

Near the building, the BioSys Fire Task Force conducted their drill. There were now about two hundred workers gathering under the red "Muster Area" sign.

"Dr. Ho Ling," the other scientist said, after Richard offered his own name. Dr. Ling then introduced him to his staff members and explained that they were all part of the ABT-55 group. What luck to have a chance to speak to the original ABT-55 authors! Now Richard could get more information about the molecule. He studied Ling. He was short, with tanned skin and a bowl haircut. His dark bangs were parted against his long forehead. Dr. Ling was curious about Richard, too.

"Dr. Weigand, what are you working on?" This was an inevitable question, and he hadn't been fully prepared to summon a foolproof response in the surprise of the fire drill. Richard surprised himself with a quick recovery.

"I'm working on an off-shoot of ABT-55, the next generation."

"Oh, well then, we should talk! I didn't know that was in development yet, but it makes sense, since the drug is going to be a big hit after Phase I." Dr. Ling smiled widely, quite proud of his lab's work.

"I'm glad you offered," began Richard as the fire marshal started waving everyone back toward the building. It would take ages for them all to reach their offices, he noted. Most of the crowd moved forward en masse anyway, but Richard lagged behind, hoping Ling would do the same. Richard couldn't handle large groups of people; they made him claustrophobic and panicky. And it would be quieter here—a safer place to talk. "I have some questions about the placement of one molecule."

"Oh? Which one is that?" Dr. Ling's eyebrows heightened in wonder.

Should he continue or do more research first? Richard decided to dig. "Well, the L-isomer of Alanine in ABT-55 seems like it should be the D-isomer, not the L-isomer."

"I don't believe it is an L-isomer.

"Oh, no?"

"Oh, goodness, no. If that were the case, the L-isomer of the amino acid would cause the ABT-55 to fail. It would be a disaster."

"That was what I thought. Could the diagram I read contain an error? 'L' instead of 'D'?"

"Well, it's possible. What did you read?" Richard and Dr. Ling moved under the shade of a large palm tree.

"I read some monkey studies from the document library system. I've only just begun to research what's already taken place."

"Oh, well, the monkey tests; that may explain it."

"Why's that?" asked Richard.

"We didn't do those. Oh, no. Not BioSys."

"What do you mean? I thought everything was done here."

"No, we got a notice that said we should let another company conduct those studies." Dr. Ling squinted back at Richard, the sun in his eyes.

"What lab, if I may ask?"

"I don't recall, but I'll look around our office and try to find out. Somewhere on the east coast. New Hampshire, maybe?" Richard pondered this, and Dr. Ling continued. "But we're doing more monkey trials now. I can pass the data along to you, if you'd like, or perhaps you'd like to join us in the lab at your convenience?"

"Yes, I would like that very much. Thank you, Dr. Ling."

"You're welcome. Goodbye." Ho moved to join his colleagues in the sea of people anxious to get back to work. Richard crouched underneath the tree and waited.

It took twenty-two minutes for the crowd to clear. With a clearer head, Richard re-entered the building, hoping most of the people had reached their offices already. He took the stairs, even though the elevators were operating. At his office door, he fished for his keys, placed his hand on the knob, and was about to insert the key when the door gave way. It had been unlocked. But surely, he'd locked it when he left for the fire drill. He had been the last one out of the room, as was standard procedure in any emergency.

Richard's staff began to arrive. How had he beaten them? They all had coffee cups in their hands; that explained it. The lab staff reconvened the work they had stopped a half-hour earlier. Richard went to his private inner office and closed the door. He sat down and looked out his giant window, which faced one of the many BioSys fields that grew the blue cornflower the lab used to manufacture their most famous drug. The grounds looked more like a farm than an institution of science.

Hadn't he locked that door? He couldn't be sure now. He supposed he could have been so surprised by the drill that it slipped his mind. But that would be a breech of the most common lab operating procedures—procedures that were second nature to him. It occurred to him to take a good look at the lab, make sure nothing was amiss. He opened his inner office door and took a long, hard look at the central lab station. But now, with the lab staff moving around and chatting, it was nearly impossible to determine whether anything was out of order. He had been the first one in the lab. Had anything looked odd? He was so distracted by the open door he didn't notice! *Damn!*

In frustration, he plopped back into his inner office chair. He couldn't seem to think straight here in Anegada. Was he losing his mind, like Stuart? He felt like he had been doused with a doping potion. He had never been forgetful or distracted in his life! It was unnerving. He must be more conscientious of security, he reminded himself. Stuart had been smart to base their operations in such a remote place—but still; he shouldn't let himself get careless.

He looked again into the main lab, and that's when he noticed what was missing. The monkey studies he'd been reading on the lab table were gone. He stepped into the main lab and looked around, but didn't see them. He questioned the staff, but no one remembered seeing them, and no one had moved them. He must have absentmindedly put them away. But, no. Not in his desk, not in a filing cabinet.

A quick search on the computer was all he needed to do—he'd simply retrieve his downloaded copy. He logged into the document system and repeated the search he had done yesterday. He used the same keywords, but instead of the system returning ten documents, as it had earlier, it returned only nine. Richard, who thought mostly in pictures, instantly saw that the monkey study document was not there.

But it must be! Richard did another search, this time explicitly for Document No. 45137. *No records found.*

He should tell Dr. Ling. But tell him what? Dr. Ling had said more monkey studies were being done. Perhaps the older study had been so problematic it was just being repeated? Yes, Dr. Ling had probably removed the old document because it was going to be replaced with the newer, more accurate study.

That was a reasonable explanation.

He looked again out the window, over the fields, and toward the ocean. He could make out the villas where he lived, although he could not see his unit.

He decided to reward himself later in the day with a phone call to Therese. He stood and headed into the main lab. But even with the thought of Therese to look forward to, an odd sadness arose and made itself known, one that cast a dark shadow on the stem cell mission. For the first time in his life, he moved to his white board with a sense of duty and noted lack of passion. He could not explain it, so he ignored it.

He erased what he had written on the white board before the fire drill, and instead began to draw a map, from memory and to scale, of all the places he knew on Anegada, starting with Therese's villa.

It was well after five p.m., and Therese's swim had cleared her mind enough to allow her to nap for several hours on the couch with Fancy nearby. She decided to visit her father again—get some perspective. She took a leisurely stroll to Eastwind, Fancy galloping elegantly beside her. A breeze was building, and the wisteria scented the fresh evening air. Therese planned what she would say. *I know you've been under stress. Let's talk. Dad, I am worried about you.* None of it sounded right.

She needn't have worried, for when she arrived, the house was dark, and there was no one home, not even Hattie. The door and windows—all locked. This did nothing to assuage her fears; Therese and Fancy ran the entire way back to her villa, trying hard not to picture her father lost inside the dark house, wandering from room to room, alone.

Fox Alzheimer's Hospital, Ypsilanti, Michigan

Stuart tried to munch his grilled cheese sandwich like the others, but just being present in the Fox Alzheimer's Hospital made him want to retch. Thank goodness, he was not going to end up like these poor people! He looked around the lime-green lunchroom with its windowless, cinder-block walls and humming mercury vapor lights. Certain patients were being fed, others were feeding one another, one was hysterical, but most were half-asleep. The hysterical one was yelling about the food being poisoned. Stuart put his sandwich down for the final time and rose from his seat. One of his future friends was just making his way out of the lunchroom and into the hall, and he intended to follow him.

Stuart stood, tightening the baggy mint green hospital pants around his waist. He should try to remain calm, although he felt like breaking into a run, so excited was he to introduce himself to a brother-in-stem cells. He entered the hallway and caught sight of his man shuffling down the corridor with the aid of a blond nurse. *That'll be the plant,* he reminded himself. She should be expecting Stuart's arrival. As he trailed behind at a cautious distance, he vacillated over how much to tell Mr. Rossetti when he finally met him. He rounded a corner, following their lead.

He watched the two make their way down another corridor, this one filled with bright sunshine from the large, leaded glass windows. Finally, some natural light in this prison! This wing, no doubt, was the only original part of the building, which had obviously been modified from another purpose, perhaps having once been a school. He studied his trial Alzheimer's patient. Although he walked slowly, he had an air of determination about him. He wore a raggedy old sweater and leisure pants, the kind with a polyester sheen. Stuart watched the nurse guide Tony into a room off the bright hallway. As she did, she turned and caught sight of Stuart, who now felt a fool, lurking and not making his presence known. What on earth had he been thinking? After all, he practically owned this facility! No need to sneak around. He strode forward with confidence, employing his CEO stride while his pants loosened again.

"Hello, you must be Miss Wilkins."

Her initially perplexed expression gave way to one of distinct awe. "Oh, yes, and you must be Mr. Franklin." Her face lit up and she stretched out her hand, which he received like royalty. This was the type of welcome he had come to expect in years past, but which was now, he reflected, less and less common. An image of Paul suddenly sprang to mind, and all at once, he saw the many ways his colleague had been undermining him. And it wasn't just Paul. There had been general insolence all around in the past months at BioSys headquarters. This lack of control over his company made him frown.

"Mr. Franklin?" Nancy's toothy grin stretched widely in politeness. He had missed something, and erased the almost involuntary grimace from his face. He was the CEO again.

"Oh, yes. I'm sorry. What were you saying, dear?"

"I'll meet with you in my quarters after you've met Mr. Rossetti. Why don't I introduce you? Now is a good time." She smiled like a movie star, and when Stuart made this connection, he felt on very solid ground again. He and Nancy Wilkins, he could plainly see, thought the same way.

Inside the patient's room, Stuart was pleased to see the face of his beloved guinea pig. He immediately registered the bright, shining eyes, the large hands, and the capacity for physical intimidation. Stuart saw the aura of the power this man had once held, and the thought made him pity his own situation, since he had also once emanated such an aura. Perhaps it was not all gone. Yet.

The introductions were made, and Nancy left the room. Stuart sat in a chair next to Tony's bed. From his position, Tony looked grand, propped up and almost regal, not unlike Stuart's own image of himself whilst sitting in his office. The afternoon light poured into the room, casting a healthy glow on his olive complexion. Tony spoke first.

"Damn sun, makes it impossible to see the TV!" Tony gestured to the TV, which was suspended above them in the corner. Stuart looked over his shoulder to assess the situation, and in a stab at camaraderie, he moved to draw the curtains.

"See, they moved me. I used to be in the other section of the building. I had a roommate there. But, my kid," he lowered his voice conspiratorially, "he got me a private room, see. And a hot nurse!" Stuart took a seat next to Tony's bedside.

"But how are you feeling, Tony?" Tony retracted his head and leaned again against a deep pile of pillows.

"Well, doc, I just figure God put me here for a reason, right? I mean, I done some things in my time. You know what I'm sayin'? Maybe this is payback. I dunno." Tony looked suddenly exasperated and leaned his head back, closing his eyes.

Stuart didn't care about whatever Tony was talking about. "No, but how do you feel? Physically, I mean?"

"Oh, I feel great, actually. You know, to tell you the truth, I don't really know why I'm here. I was doing fine at home with Marie." Stuart nodded, in an attempt to gain Tony's trust. What was he talking about? Who was Marie?

Fully alert again, Tony's eyes popped wide open, and he exclaimed, "Hey, who the hell are you, anyway?"

"Oh, well, I'm Stuart Franklin. We met a few minutes ago. Miss Wilkins introduced us."

"Oh. You aren't a doctor?"

"No, I'm a businessman."

"Ah-ha! A businessman. I catch your drift." Tony paused, smiling and sizing up his new friend. Then, his face clouded over. "Do I owe you money?"

"Oh, no. No. It's nothing like that."

"Why are you here, then?"

"I'm here to visit you and see how you're doing. To watch you."

"Watch me? Why? Does this have something to do with why they moved me?"

"Well, yes, actually. Hey, listen, if I let you in on a secret, do you promise to keep it to yourself?"

"Sounds like money's involved. And I don't make promises to nobody, you hear? Nobody except my dear dead mother, God rest her soul." Tony crossed himself.

Stuart remembered the details of Tony's livelihood, and he was struck with an idea.

"Well, you're right, Tony; money is involved."

"See?" Tony stuck his index finger in the air, gesturing heavenwards. Stuart, baffled, continued.

"What I mean is," began Stuart, leaning closer, "there's money to be made. You see, there's a goldmine for us, and it's sitting inside your brain, right now. But we have to protect it."

A few hours later, Tony was in Stuart's car, with instructions about when to return to the Fox Alzheimer's Hospital for tests.

Bob fished in his wallet and retrieved a thick wad of bills.

"This will do, I believe?" He looked into the face of the young boatman. The two men stood on a dock in the colorful bay, the clangor of colliding masts and sea birds providing an ambience Bob had only dreamed of. The sun shone with a brightness that made one squint, even with the best sunglasses. The water beyond was mint blue and crystal clear.

"Oh, yes, very good, Mister," the man said with a heavy local accent. "Thank you very much. You'll find the papers in the hutch by the ignition key, and there's petrol in the tank. You know how to find me if you have any problems."

"Indeed. Thank you, young man." Bob patted the tanned and brawny man on the shoulder and watched him wave goodbye. He studied the man's bright, cropped pants, his fine muscles, and his kerchief; the sight pleased him with its storybook enchantment. Barely containing his glee, he turned back to admire her—his very own boat—*The Emerald*, its name painted in Celtic font. Bob hopped aboard.

Chapter Thirty

TWO WEEKS LATER, Tony took his rightful place at the head of the table. They had all gathered at Rossetti's Dry Cleaners in the back room, just as the old days, all the old guys from the neighborhood. He was feeling good, thanks to a new suit and recent haircut. The cash advance from Stuart had helped smooth the path back into the old business. He surveyed his friends and family. His fruitcake son was missing; but then again, that was nothing new. He cleared his throat.

"Thank you all for coming," Tony began slowly, with a touch of drama that put him back on familiar ground. He had been away for two years, after all. He studied their faces as he continued. They expected him to slip up, have some kind of episode.

"I want you all to know that you don't need to worry about my health. I want you, in fact, to put the matter of my absence out of your heads. Permanently." Tony paused to light a cigarette. "Any questions?" The blank faces affirmed that there was no dissent. "Good. Then lemme tell you all what needs to be done."

Chapter Thirty-One

BOB WALKED FROM THE MARINA into Stuart's waiting Land Rover. He had spent an entire two weeks exploring the British Virgin Islands on *The Emerald* and felt a career's worth of anxieties melt away in the first week. Sleeping on the boat under the stars and breathing in the ocean air had rejuvenated him to such a degree that he had made a decision. After the stem cell trial, and after delivering lectures about his innovative surgical techniques, he would retire. Perhaps he would spend the rest of his years on the boat, penning memoirs, and living off the fruits of the sea.

These pleasant thoughts nearly vanished after he climbed into the Land Rover and took a good look at Stuart, who appeared Bob's exact mental opposite. He was on fire with manic energy. His pupils were dilated, and Bob could see the whites of his eyes. Stuart shook slightly and spoke in quick, rapid fragments.

"Bob, old man! Great to see you. Hey, listen; wait 'til you hear about Tony. Are you ready? Are you?" Stuart looked at Bob with wild eyes and drove towards the lab, not keeping his eyes on the road for more than a few seconds.

Tony? It took Bob a moment or two to recall—one of the Alzheimer's patients.

"Well, sure I'm ready to hear all about Tony. You've been hiding your progress reports!" Bob decided to play along, lest he anger Stuart at the wheel. He studied Stuart some more. He wore an unseasonable long trench coat, and underneath, a gaudy, striped golf shirt. He caught a glimmer of something around his neck. Was that a gold necklace? Had he always dressed this way? Well, it wasn't any of Bob's business. Best to focus on the procedure. The sooner it was done, the sooner he could begin planning the lecture of his life.

"Oh, yeah, buddy; you won't believe it! The man is back; I mean, he's out of that facility!"

"Really?" exclaimed Bob, now quite interested, despite Stuart's alarming behavior.

"This guy, he's something else. He can remember things—short term things—again. He had lost some motor skills, and that is improving. Most importantly, he plans to be back at work next week. And you know what? Turns out, he's Mafia; can you believe that? Not just any Mafia character—he's a Don. You know what that means?" Stuart's face was illuminated with glee. Bob felt his heart race.

"Mafia, huh?" he tried to play it cool, as if having cured a mobster were a brilliant idea.

"It means, Bob," said Stuart, with the excitement of a child, "that we and stem cells are officially in business."

Bob stared out the window, speechless. He didn't savor getting involved in a business now—his boat was waiting for him. But then again, he supposed, more money couldn't hurt their venture, as long as it was he, and no one else, that got the credit.

They arrived at the lab, and Stuart brought the hulking piece of metal to a lurching stop. Bob escaped the car gratefully as Stuart rambled on. They discussed when Stuart could undergo the procedure, Stuart nearly begging for the earliest possible date. Bob conceded, willingly.

"I don't see why we can't operate within the week. That would be about a week ahead of schedule. The first thing we need to do is give you a full exam."

Stuart's eyes lit up with fear. "An exam? What do you mean?"

"Well, just basic pre-op stuff, nothing out of the ordinary. Why don't you meet me at my office tomorrow morning, and we'll do everything then?"

"Great!" squeaked Stuart with a hint of a New Jersey accent. With both of them standing, Bob saw Stuart's full regalia and recognized the costume. Tony the mobster'd had some influence on Stuart, it was clear. How much influence beyond the attire and street language was yet to be determined. He must be sure to examine him thoroughly tomorrow; he wanted to be sure nothing stood between him and a 100% success in this venture.

Richard was leaving Dr. Ling's office for his own when he saw his father approaching.

"Dad! What brings you in off *The Emerald*?" As Richard said this, he realized he already knew the answer.

"Let's go into your office, shall we?" Richard led his father to his private office within the lab. They took their seats, and Richard switched on his desktop coffee maker.

"How soon can you be ready with a batch of cells for Stuart?"

"Oh, they're ready. I take it you mean the cadaver cells."

Bob paused, almost too long. "Of course."

"Well, they're at the ready, in the freezer. I only need a heads up to defrost them the morning of the procedure."

"Well, heads up. We operate in seven days."

"Understood. But what have we learned from the patients in Michigan? I haven't heard anything, and I've been on the edge of my seat. Are the clinical results promising?"

"Oh, yes. In fact, I expect the latest films to arrive this afternoon by courier. Stuart tells me that the two hero patients have a clear reduction in their plaques. And their outward behavior shows a marked improvement."

"Dad, that's astounding! Why aren't you more excited?"

"I'm a little worried about Stuart, that's all. I am very encouraged about the results, certainly. But Stuart—well, he's awfully manic. I want him more relaxed on the day of surgery."

"Is he manic, as in manic-depressive?"

"He's very keyed up; he almost appears strung out. It is a common symptom of all dementias, but his is most extreme."

"Hmm. Well, Therese tells me that Stuart tends to get like that when he's anxious, but anticipating a triumphant outcome."

"Well," said Bob, rising, placing his hands in his lab coat with a shrug, "I'm sure that's all it is then." He turned to go.

"Dad," Richard began.

"Yes," said Bob, turning back.

"There's something else."

"What's that?" Richard noticed the lack of enthusiasm in his father's eyes.

"Well, it's this ABT-55 molecule. I've been working on it with Dr. Ling across the way, and—"

"You've been what?" interjected Bob, his fiery sprit resurrecting itself.

"Well, yes, I've been working on it. You see, my cover was nearly blown, so I had to get involved. But the point is," Richard continued in a quieter tone, "the point is, Ling and I discovered that someone made a terrible mistake on the molecule. If it had gone to Phase I in its present condition, the trial would have been disastrous. The drug would have been very unsafe."

"What are you saying, Richard?" Bob's full attention resided in every word.

"I'm saying two things. One, somehow, a very sloppy drug was moved ahead, and I don't know why. Two, we fixed the molecule. We came up with a novel configuration that may be even more effective than the original was supposed to be." Richard smiled. He had put in many hours with Ling over the last weeks on just that, and was proud of his work.

"My boy," began Bob. They were on familiar ground once again. "Don't get involved in the 'sloppy' part. It could do us in. Two," Bob paused for effect, "I'm very proud of you. Does Stuart know?"

"I left him a voice message. But more importantly, Ling is sending the documentation needed for the Phase I FDA paperwork to the Bio-Sys review committee today."

Bob smiled widely, and Richard joined him.

"Now, most importantly," Bob began, a sheepish grin forming, "how's Therese?"

Richard shook his head. "No progress to report there. On good days, I run into her when she walks her dog."

Bob laughed and turned away.

Later that day, at his lab, Richard knocked on the door to Dr. Ling's lab. He wanted to check on the progress of the documentation. He knocked twice before a lab assistant opened the door.

"Oh—hello. Dr. Ling around at the moment?"

"Oh, no. Didn't you hear?"

"Hear? Hear what?"

"Dr. Ling got moved to an urgent assignment."

"Moved? But we were in the middle of something—"

"Big job. Very important. In Hong Kong."

"But what about our data?"

"I don't know. Come in and see for yourself."

Richard stepped into the large lab, which contained many workstations, and went directly to Ling's desk, which like his own, was housed in a private, inner office. To his shock, Ling's desk was completely cleaned out. There were no papers. The computer was gone. The file cabinets—empty. The diplomas on the walls—removed. You could see the outlines of where they had been just—yesterday!

Stuart waved his hands above his head, as if conducting an orchestra. His eyes were closed, and his body lay in a large hospital bed in a BioSys recovery room. At his side, various monitoring lights blinked, and an IV dangled precariously from his roving left arm. He hummed.

Bob entered the room and looked at his patient's dance. He gently reached out and quieted the arm. The gesture was not lost on Stuart, and his glassy eyes opened slowly, like a toddler just wrenched from a nap.

"How are you feeling, old boy?" smiled Bob.

"Did you hear that song?"

"No, Stuart. You're just coming off the drugs, that's all."

Stuart's face lit up in wonder. "It was a lovely swing riff, one of the first I ever heard Eve play."

"Eve?"

"Yes. Surely, I've told you about her? Oh, Bob, she is a goddess. When she sits at the piano, she casts a spell over the audience. You can't imagine how potent it is." Stuart closed his eyes again, ready to return to the world of memory and dreams.

Bob patted his arm and took a glance at the readouts on the machinery. He pulled up a nearby stool, removed the chart hooked to the foot of the bed, and began to make notes. He monitored this most-valuable patient personally as much as possible; he didn't want to miss one moment of the transformation he was sure would take place. He closed the chart and turned his attention back to Stuart, who dozed peacefully. In a few weeks, mused Bob, Stuart would sleep easy without the aid of drugs, for the greatest problem of his life would have been eliminated.

Stuart was oblivious to the world outside his bubble as he recovered. Very few major newspapers circulated on the island, but of course, it was the major story on every cable news network, so it was hard for the waking to avoid. "Massive explosion destroys crowded church," was how CNN lead the story, while the more sensationalist media outlets ran with phrases like "Terrorist attack of 2008 kills hundreds of the holy." Ten city blocks of Chicago's Westside were temporarily off-limits to civilians while the National Guard aided the bomb squad and firefighters and cleaned up the mess. Many of the bodies inside the Catholic Church had been burned beyond recognition; others were crushed by falling stone. The building, a Chicago historical landmark, was left a heap of rubble.

When Carlo picked up the late edition of the *Los Angeles Times*, he tried not to read it. Like the rest of the world, he had heard the story on the news—seen the carnage on the monitors at the gym. He'd not really paid much attention until he'd heard who was among the dead. It got his stomach churning, just as it used to feel when he was about to storm the house of an armed drug dealer. But then, you had backup—more guys on your side, with more guns, a bulletproof vest. But all the backup, training, strategy, and planning failed when it came to some people, because no matter how hard you tried to outsmart them, they knew you too well. They were three steps ahead. People just like his father, Tony Rossetti.

EXPLOSION STRIKES CHICAGO. 217 DEAD,
INCLUDING ARCHDIOCESE. POLICE RULE OUT TERRORISM

In the worst explosion to strike Chicagoland since 1929, over 200 people perished when bombs exploded during Sunday Mass at the Immaculate Conception Church of Flossmoor Village.

Eyewitnesses from the neighborhood reported anywhere from two to five explosions heard and felt in rapid succession at approximately 11:15 a.m., just after Mass began on Sunday. There was a distinct smell of cordite in the air after the explosions, and screams were heard coming from inside the church, then people starting running to safety. Dust clouded the area for many minutes in the chaos that followed.

Local firefighters were assisted by inner-city stations in the four-alarm fire that destroyed everything inside the church. Approximately seventy-five people were treated on the scene for injuries ranging from broken bones to third-degree burns. The injured were transported to St. Thomas Hospital for further treatment.

Police will hold an official press conference this afternoon at city hall. After many hours of work, Police Superintendent Foley stated, "The scene is still under intense investigation. We're working with the FBI and not able to say much [this afternoon]. We have evidence that the bombs were remotely detonated; however, we have ruled out political terrorism. That is all I can say at this time."

The visibly shaken mayor, a practicing Irish Catholic, made a statement outside the roped-off crime scene. "The immediate danger in the area is being negotiated with professionalism and speed. We have five stations reporting, and our local personnel were on the scene within minutes. The SWAT team has pronounced the area explosive-free. We rallied our resources using new disaster communication tools, a locally funded bond effort put in place after 9-11. I am impressed with the efforts of all our fine people, none of whom, I am happy to report, have been injured or killed. We'll be assisting federal law enforcement personnel 24-7 to root out who committed this hideous and hateful crime."

In perhaps a related development, Church sources reported late in the day that the church had experienced a break-in the previous Thursday, in which minor artifacts had been stolen. Father O'Hara discovered the artifacts the following day in a nearby dumpster. The event was not reported to the authorities. Said O'Hara, "We have trouble with neighborhood kids once in a while—drugs and so on. We have an outreach program to try to bring these kinds into the arms of the Church; only the Lord can turn them around."

Services for those killed in the explosion will be organized by the city; details will be provided as they are released. Among the dead was the honorable Archdiocese James Finney (see sidebar *In Memoriam*). Other victims include the entire Flint Girls' School Catholic Choir, University of Chicago Professor Emeritus Dr. John Ryan, who is survived by his family, and noted local businessman, Francis O'Malley and his wife, Sheila.

Even if the article hadn't mentioned Tony's long-time rival, Francis O'Malley, Carlo would have recognized his father's hand in the matter. It was the grandness of it. The spectacle. His dad just couldn't let the matter of Francis O'Malley alone, and he had to make sure everyone got it, loud and clear. A twenty-year war was finished.

His dad was, of course, the reason Carlo had joined the force. For one thing, he'd had to get away. For another thing, he knew the business—the crime business. At fifteen, Carlo left home for good and joined the police academy under a new name. He sent the occasional post card, although rarely. When he was in the academy, he wrote to Tony to let him know he was in culinary school, because in a sense, he was. He'd been a 'private chef' ever since, too busy traveling with celebs to stop in on the old neighborhood. In his short time on the force, he'd helped take down many organized crime operations and gathered evidence for the larger stings done by the FBI. He had been working on a big case when his father disappeared from the crime radar.

He was obviously back.

Carlo folded the newspaper and tossed it in a trash receptacle on Westwood Boulevard. He tried not to gag on the rank smell emanating from within.

Chapter Thirty-Two

STUART WAS MORE THAN RELIEVED—he was triumphant. Two weeks after surgery, he felt better than ever, but that was only because the procedure had been completed. He did notice improvements in his thinking. Details were less muddled. He suspected this tiny improvement was only the beginning of his miraculous recovery. And so it was with great confidence that he strode into BioSys headquarters in North Carolina.

He was greeted with the smiling faces of his staff, most of who had been informed of his arrival after many weeks away. He went straight to his office; today, he had a very special meeting. He was at his desk, preparing his thoughts, when there was a knock at the door. The surprise visitor did not wait for a reply.

"Stuart?" Stuart looked up from his desk to see Paul's face peering at him, unnervingly disembodied by the bulk of the door, which was slightly ajar.

"Paul, come in," answered Stuart with a thinly veiled lack of enthusiasm. Stuart readied himself in the face of his problem underling. Then again, he was a new man these days. His adrenaline surged as Paul crossed the room, headed for his desk. Paul stretched out his arm for a friendly shake; Stuart obliged, but did not stand.

"Good to have you back, Stuart."

Paul took the opposite seat at the commanding desk. Stuart was determined to make quick haste of the visit, and then get on with the more important meeting yet to come.

"Thank you, thank you. As you know, my absence has not been in vain. A new-and-improved ABT-55 is going to Phase I, as scheduled, in September."

"Yes, so I've heard," replied Paul, with what stuck Stuart as condescension. "What got it moving on the right track again?"

"Our brilliant Richard, of course," said Stuart.

"Richard Weigand?"

"He's the rising star I discovered at the NIH."

"Well, I'll say. The new tests of the molecule are astounding." Paul had seen the tests before he shredded them, but after he sent his future partner's loyal Dr. Ling packing.

"Yes, aren't they?" added Stuart as he absent-mindedly opened some mail. He hoped his body language communicated the right level of aloofness. Paul did not deserve an audience with him. But Stuart had his wits about him, he was pleased to notice.

"And what have you been up to these last weeks, Paul?"

Paul stared at Stuart, apparently taken off guard. But only momentarily.

"Well, as you can imagine, there's been business matters to see to—purchases, accounting, managerial staffing, and the like. I've been working on projected sales of ABT-55, as well. And, as usual, meeting with the sales staff—educating them, informing them." Paul smiled, satisfied with this detailed answer.

"Good, I'm glad to hear it." Stuart decided to play a new card. "I say, I haven't even had a moment to thank you for all the extra work you've no doubt performed in my absence. Thank you, Paul."

"Oh, you're welcome, Stuart, really. I didn't think twice about it. I'm happy to wear whatever hat is required of me, you know."

Don't I know it. There was a distinct pause in the flow of conversation. Stuart let it rest on Paul's shoulders and affected a nonchalance he knew would make such a weight heavier.

"Well," Paul rose, without visible irritation, "I'll let you get back to your business. You must have a lot of catching up to do."

"Yes, I appreciate that. Goodbye, Paul."

Paul was nearly out the door when he replied, "Goodbye, Stuart," with a smile thrown over his shoulder. The door closed behind him.

Stuart allowed himself a sheepish smile. The conference phone buzzed with an announcement. "Mr. Rossetti to see you, Mr. Franklin."

"Thank you, send him in," replied Stuart.

Tony emerged presently. Stuart rose to meet him, and they embraced like old friends.

Fred had been making his rounds, as he did every Monday, doing an employee count within the executive office. Since so much information processed in the group was proprietary, he made it his habit to verify that the people logged into the computer network were indeed the people supposed to be hard at work. His presence had the added benefit of discouraging insiders from getting any ideas about divulging company information. He reached the end of the hall, Stuart's corner office, and heard voices inside.

He thought Stuart was absent, as he had been for many weeks now, so he walked closer. Through the cracked door, he saw Stuart talking with someone, so he was relieved. He was about to turn away and continue when he heard the stranger say, "He's on ice now; problem solved," and the two burst into laughter.

Fred crept away quietly and headed for the reception area, where he intended to review the visitor log.

A flashlight scanned an empty kitchen, then an empty living room, early daylight coming through the drawn blinds. Two men came together at the fireplace.

One said, "What about the car in the drive?"

The other replied, "Check upstairs." One of the men disappeared up the loft-like flight of stairs, but he returned in a just few moments.

"Well?"

"Just the old guy."

The flashlights were extinguished, and the men slipped away.

Fred performed a simple search on the stranger in Stuart's office; it hadn't taken long to discover his identity. What the hell was Stuart doing taking a meeting with a Mafioso? It troubled Fred, so he decided to watch the activities of Stuart and his friends more carefully.

Fred knew the ABT-55 mission was critical to the success of the company—the project could not be jeopardized. He had put the BioSys security staff on high alert since Stuart went to the British Virgin Islands, knowing his presence there indicated that the production of the drug was sensitive.

That was why he'd had special surveillance placed on Anegada weeks ago and had been monitoring the island for anything suspicious. Today, his extra work had paid off. He turned his attention to a transmission sent from a BioSys boat in the harbor. A new, small boat had arrived in the harbor, but no one had emerged from it in two days. Fred punched some numbers into a videophone terminal, placing a secure, encrypted call, and breathed a sign of relief when Stuart's face appeared.

"Where are you?" blurted out Fred.

"I'm lunching at the club. Why? What's happened, Fred?"

"Nothing, yet, but I'm concerned about strangers on the islands."

"Oh, Fred, you've been reading your spy novels again!"

Fred saw Stuart being served a huge plate of lobster.

"Stuart, you need to tell me why you have been monitoring the operation in Anegada so closely monitored. I have to know."

"Fred, to tell you the truth, I only went there because I needed to get away. In fact, I'm returning for the weekend. You see? A real vacation!" He began to pierce the lobster. Stuart's nonchalance was no act today; he really couldn't understand what all the fuss was about. BioSys manufactured new drugs constantly, and each one was important, but on the other hand, there would always be another drug. They were a healthy company. Lightness overcame him and jolted him into the realization that his old self had resurfaced, as if it had never left. He smiled widely.

Fred pondered this possibility. Stuart never took vacations. "Well, is the drug on schedule?"

Stuart looked into the video monitor with surprise. "What's all this about, man?"

"Strangers are lurking on Anegada, and there may be reasons to tighten local security."

"Fred, you secured the facilities there yourself. And pre-production of the drug has begun—it's not as if someone can steal a vat of it during the night, now, is it?"

"I suppose you're right," said Fred, agreeing to disagree, as they always had in matters of security. But there was a reason Stuart had hired him, and he intended to keep close watch, regardless of Stuart's optimism.

"Say, how's that lobster?" Fred added, to clear the air. Stuart pretended to feed Fred a bite, moving a forkful toward the monitor.

Part III

Chapter Thirty-Three

PAUL WESTIN, VP OF BIOSYS OPERATIONS, stood in a dark BioSys office, a mobile phone at his ear, a panoramic window at his back. The window overlooked an industrial park, lights blinking, smoke coming from the stacks, and in the distance, the faint outline of mountains poked through a polluted haze. The sharp lines of an expensive new suit silhouetted him against the waning light of day. He listened to the speaker and paced the room in a controlled manner, like a cat surveying its prey before pouncing. Then his voice filled the empty room.

"I sent the coordinates in three separate encrypted transmissions, each from a different source, as we discussed. You know that. No, we only need to wait a little longer. You need to guarantee to me that your people are in place. We're only going to get one shot at this."

Paul flipped the small phone closed. Then he sat down at the desk before him and turned on a small desk light. From his blazer's inside pocket, he removed a floppy disk and inserted it into a laptop computer. He began to type.

Fancy trotted along with her usual morning glee. The early sun shone dimly through a patch of clouds, softly reflecting in Therese's eyes. Richard jogged alongside Fancy, having met up with them—a lucky day.

"Brrr!" exclaimed Therese. "I knew I should have worn my shoes!" Therese wrapped her sweater around her more snugly. Richard caught his breath; Fancy barked at the waves.

"I wonder why she does that," said Therese as they both watched the dog.

"Hmm. I guess she wants to protect us from the advancing water." Richard scanned the horizon as he spoke. "Well, actually, today, I see something besides the waves. Look." He pointed to their right, where a fishing boat bobbed.

"Huh," replied Therese. "Someone's fishing, I suppose."

Richard thought for a moment. "I thought you told me there was no fishing out there because of the reefs?"

Therese yawned and wrapped her arms around herself for warmth. Richard wanted to put his arms around her, but instead put his hands on his hips. "Yes," she said sleepily. "You're right. I'm just not awake yet. Poor boat's probably stuck."

Suddenly, Fancy ran up to them and barked fiercely, then ran past them at full greyhound speed, hunched down, all four limbs practically airborne, barking all the way. Therese turned from Richard, recognizing Fancy's protective bark. They turned to follow Fancy, and as they did, saw her collapse in the sand mid-run. Therese ran to her.

"Fancy, oh my god!" she screamed as she ran, but as she did, Richard grabbed her arm and pulled her back.

But it wasn't Richard.

A black net fell over her. She screamed wildly.

"Richard! Richard!" Someone tied a rope around the net, forcing her hands behind her back. She screamed louder. Through the net, she could barely see movement. The mesh was thick, but let light through a series of interwoven fibers. "Richard!" she screamed again, just as a cloth was wrapped around her mouth, stifling her cries. A scratchy rope quickly bound her bare ankles. A moment later, she was horizontal and being carried away at an alarming speed.

She tried to calm her breathing and stay alert, although tears poured from her eyes. It was difficult to breathe because of the gag. She listened to her captor's breath; he was almost panting. He carried her as one might carry a child, and something in his right hand rubbed painfully under her knees. He must be very strong to have carried her this far. How tall did she think he was? She thought hard, trying to place the events. What had they done to Fancy? And why? Where was Richard? Had he been captured, too?

Then, it dawned of her. Of course—she was being kidnapped. They'd want money, that's all. All her life she'd been aware that this was a possibility, being the only child of a multi-billionaire. Her father had always emphasized safety and protection, but having Carlo as a bodyguard just made her uncomfortable; she hated to stand out. But how she now wished she had listened to her father and not let down her guard!

The man carrying her slowed. She heard other voices, but the gag had wrapped her ears as well, and the sounds were muffled. And then, a sound she recognized—the engine of a Cessna turbo prop.

Then, like a sack of potatoes, she was hoisted into the plane and propped up against a wall. There were no seats; this must be the cargo area. The floor was ice cold, and the ridges in the wall dug into her back. Light streamed through the net thanks to the open cargo door, and she could make out movement. She strained for a clue as to her captor's identity, but then the cargo door was slammed shut, leaving the area in darkness.

"Therese!" A faint gasp came from the other side of the black pit. She felt the rumble of the engine course through her bare feet.

"Mmmm," replied Therese, unable to utter a word through the confines of her gag. Was that Richard?

A shuffling sound ensued; perhaps Richard was trying to get to her? She kept making noise through her gag to indicate her location.

"Hang on, I'm coming," she heard clearly. It was Richard!

She heard him inching closer; he must also be bound. He finally reached her. The engine of the plane revved. Were they going to take off? As if in answer, the plane began to slowly roll. Her tears streamed again, involuntarily. Richard continued to inch, and then he reached her, out of breath.

"Therese, are you alright?"

"Mmmm!" was all she could reply.

"Hang on. I've nearly got a hand free," Richard wrestled beside her as the plane gained speed. In a few moments, Therese knew, they would begin the ascent.

"There, got it," said Richard. "Hang on, just got to untie everything, now that I can." Just then, the plane began to take off, the sharp incline shoved him against her, and she tipped over. Richard managed to steady himself with his free hand, which he used to remove the knots from his right hand and his netting. The shock of seeing Therese bound, gagged, and toppled over nearly made him sick.

He began at once to untie her, starting with her gag.

"Richard! My God!" she gasped. He quickly removed her binding and net. Their feet were still bound, but without thinking, they embraced.

"What the hell's happening?" Richard blurted as they went to work on their feet.

"I suppose this is a kidnapping," Therese replied, fighting with a monstrous knot. Richard freed his feet and assisted Therese. In a moment, they were completely free. The plane leveled off, which, noted Therese, meant they couldn't be flying at more than three thousand feet or so.

"A kidnapping? If that's true, why take me, too?"

"I'm not sure; I hadn't really thought it through yet. Maybe they didn't plan on you being on the beach." Therese ran her fingers through her hair, removing pieces of twine that were stuck in her long mane. Her hands shook with fear.

"Perhaps," said Richard, making a cushion out of all the netting. "Here, sit on this, might be more comfortable." Therese moved to the pile of kidnapping accoutrement. Richard crouched beside her.

"Well, let's think about what they might want."

"And what we can do," replied Therese. "And where we might be going." They looked around the cargo area, but it was windowless and provided no clues.

Stuart walked along the pier with Bob. "Well," began Bob in a proud father's voice, "there she is." He gestured to *The Emerald.*

"Wheeeeeew," whistled Stuart in admiration. He ran his hand along the letters painted on the boat and the expert detailing of the wood trim.

"Hop aboard, my friend," Bob jumped onto the deck. Stuart climbed aboard with equal aplomb. Bob dried off the wooden deck chairs, and the two took seats. The sun shone with almost religious clarity, typical of mornings on the island, and Bob soaked up the sun in silence for a moment, his eyes closed. Waves lapped against the docked boat; the slight rocking always made him sleepy.

"So, what's on your mind, Stuart?" Bob asked, turning his head to face his companion.

"Well, I've got an idea. Do you have a stereo on this thing?" Stuart reached into the breast pocket of his suit coat—the pinstripe one that he had donned nearly every day since his return from the Alzheimer's hospital.

"Well, yes, sure," replied Bob, taking the CD from his hand and rising.

"Track seven," commanded Stuart.

Bob placed the CD in the stereo system and reached for his reading glasses, which were, for once, conveniently poking out of his shirt pocket. After some effort, he advanced the songs so that the tiny LED lights on the display read "7."

A jazz song poured out of the small yacht speakers. Bob returned to his seat, remote in hand. He began to speak, but Stuart said, "Listen to the entire piece first, please," holding his hand in the air to signal quiet. Bob, resigned, laid his head back on the deck chair and listened.

As he did, he watched the sea birds and thin clouds painted across the canvas of shocking blue sky. He did not know a sonata from a concerto, Mozart from Bach; that had been Esther's interest and hers alone. Certainly, he knew zero about jazz. Although, he now recalled, hadn't Richard been involved in music somehow? That must have been many years ago, when Esther was still alive.

Bob watched a small blue fishing boat pass, and he made out two persons aboard. Although his distance vision was impressive, considering his age, he could not make out the name inscribed on the hull of the small vessel. As it passed, he noticed a glimmer from the vessel, something like a mirror catching a ray of sun. And then another flicker. A moment later, the boat was out of his sight.

Track seven concluded with a rousing cacophony of horn notes. Stuart's eyes popped open, and he turned to Bob.

"Well?" he asked, as if he'd been waiting for a response for days.

"Oh, yes, well, it was lovely. I—"

"It's not lovely, Bob, come on! Weren't you listening?"

"Well, I confess I heard it, but I'm not much of a jazz music aficionado. What was I supposed to hear?"

"I just wanted you to hear," sighed Stuart, with a lecturer's patience for a slow student, "the genius. That's what I wanted you to hear. You see, anyone can play that piece, anyone. It's practically a standard. But when Eve plays it, she infuses it with a tone, a style that is simply astounding. She's beyond brilliant, you see."

"Who is this Eve you keep referring to?"

"Eve Klein, of course. She's a famous jazz pianist—a diva, an ingénue. But what makes her sizzle in performance is her interpretation of the music." He dragged out the word "interpretation" as if sounding out notes. "She hears it like no other, and so she plays it that way. She's inspired with an almost divine sense of music."

"You're in love with her," remarked Bob, softly.

"You don't get it, do you?" retorted Stuart sharply. "This is about genius. Being a genius!"

The CD was now well into track eight. "You see—there," began Stuart, picking up on a bar of music. "That could so easily be 'dah, de dah da da' if played by a less gifted, mechanical pianist, but to Eve's ear, those notes are 'daaah deee daaah daaa daaa'; consequently, they have meaning."

Bob turned his attention again to the water. The small blue boat was coming this way again, but from the opposite direction.

"Okay, I think I understand," said Bob, absentmindedly.

"But there's more. You see, I'm suggesting an idea."

"Okay, what is it?"

"If my brain can accept healthy stem cells, why not give it the stem cells of a genius, too?"

Bob turned to Stuart, his mouth agape. And then, a smile crept over his lips, slowly.

Therese and Richard steadied themselves in the plane's dark belly. Richard rubbed the irritated flesh around his wrists, where the ropes, though hastily tied, had dug into him without mercy. Therese rubbed her jaw, bruised and sore from the gag.

"Did you feel that?" Therese motioned to the cockpit.

"Barely. What do you make of it?"

"We're headed down. Somewhere. We have to think, and fast. I can't imagine we'll be alone when we land."

"I could use something as a weapon, maybe," Richard picked up the ropes they had discarded and looked around the cabin. It was dark, but he was fairly certain there was nothing useful around—a sledge-hammer, for instance.

"We should probably lay low when we land. Then, when the cargo door is opened, we could at least give a firm kick to whoever is behind the door."

"Right, I agree. But on the other hand—"

Richard was interrupted by sharp bank and drop in altitude. They were going down, and fast. Richard's heart skipped a beat, and it suddenly occurred to him that perhaps this was not a kidnapping. Therese gasped and slapped her own hands over her mouth.

"Richard. We have to move, now. Do you realize what's happening? Who knows who is flying this plane? They don't seem to know what they're doing. We could be in trouble. Get up!" She stood as high as she could, which meant being bent over, her head shoved against the roof of the plane.

"What are you saying?" Richard rose into a crouch, although it was difficult due to the sharp angle of the plane's nose. The small cabin seemed smaller now that his eyes had adjusted to the dark, and he felt panicky, short of breath. He saw terror in Therese's eyes. He received Therese's thoughts as if by telepathy, and remembered her mentioning having logged thousands of hours on her father's Cessna. Adrenalin rose in him that was almost inhuman, and he saw what he had to do.

"There's a latch on the cockpit door. I'll open it; you be the strong man. There are probably two of them. We only have one shot, so give it all you've got. They've got to be out cold." Therese crept up to the cockpit door and placed her hand on the latch. She gave Richard a look, and he moved forward behind her.

Later, he would remember an exaggerated image of Therese's fingers on the dark metal latch, and the blinding light that poured out, and then the terrifying sight of the ground from the plane's windshield. It was hard to remember exactly what had happened after that.

"Pull him harder; hurry, Richard!" Therese's voice was sharp and high, but she didn't notice how much it sounded like someone else's—a stranger's—as she slipped into the pilot's seat.

She clutched at the controls and struggled to breathe. Thank God, there was only one of them. Thank God, thank God. Her mind raced as she attempted to stabilize the plane; the altitude had just reached 1500' when she grabbed the controls. She moved the plane up quickly and assessed the other controls. She was aware of movement in the cargo area, and wrenching one hand free of the stick, she slammed the cockpit door shut behind her. *In case Richard doesn't win*, she thought, she could buy herself a few more seconds. 3000', 3500', 4000', 4500'. She watched the altimeter to keep her hands from shaking. She forced herself to breathe regularly. Her cheeks were burning from the adrenalin. 5000', 5500', and rising.

As she ascended, she began to think of where to land safely. The coordinates in front of her didn't add up in her brain—she had no idea where they were. She suddenly heard the radio crackle next to her, and the most obvious plan of action presented itself. She glanced at it and to her horror, saw a hand on it, and screamed. The pilot was back!

"It's ok, it's ok; it's me," screamed Richard over the cargo area noise. He placed his other hand on her shoulder and patted it. He had opened the cockpit door, and she hadn't even registered it. She tried to calm her breathing as Richard spoke into the tiny white receiver.

"Mayday, mayday, can you read me? This is—" Richard broke off and sat in the co-pilot's chair. He turned to Therese.

"How do I identify our plane?"

"Tell them—" Suddenly, the radio sparked to life and a crackly voice emerged from what seemed like another world.

"Roger that, 6543-S. What's your position? Over."

"Our position is—" Richard's eyes followed Therese's gestures to the coordinates grid. Surprising himself, he figured out how to read it instantly. "Our heading is 190 and altitude is 5750 feet; speed, 108 knots." Richard replaced the radio with a shaking hand. Therese looked at him, as if to ask, "How did you know?"

"The kids called me 'parrot' in school. Enough said."

Stuart ambled off *The Emerald*, leaving Bob to contemplate his suggestion. The dock felt warm through his thin leather shoes. He looked down at his feet, studying their movements, and began to count the number of steps between planks. The cracks between the planks were distressingly uneven. He took two steps backwards, keeping his head down, absorbed. Perhaps he could make two entire steps fit inside of one beam length? Lately, he had seen numbers and patterns everywhere; they surrounded him as the night sky surrounded the stars, or as white sheet music held notes. What would Eve say, he suddenly wondered, when she found herself on stage with Stuart Franklin, performing duets?

"I'm telling you, he didn't see me," Paul sighed, exasperated. He held the cell phone to his head and stood below deck. "Look, the guy is batty, remember? That's the reason for this entire operation. We have a bigger problem, in case you'd forgotten. What the hell is their position? And why hasn't the plane arrived yet?"

The voice from the other side of the line replied. "I wouldn't know. It was your job to move him to St. Martin, and then we would take over."

"Look, don't get snippy with me. I lived up to my side of the bargain. You have control of the monkey studies, and soon we'll have the scientist out of the way. We're going to pull this off."

"And don't you get snippy with me, young man. Remember who's making those large deposits on your behalf."

"And remember who got you the data to begin with! Without me, you have no business plan and no way to fund the 'new-and-improved' ABT-55. Don't call this number again."

Paul closed the cell phone in a rage. True, it had probably been a mistake to hire Francis' people to get Richard away from BioSys. *Incompetent baboons*! Paul cleared his throat and adjusted his silk tie, which was limp from the heat. Only Francis himself could have pulled this off correctly, and now Francis was just a memory. Paul made his way above deck and tossed the phone into the water below. He shouted to a man, "Okay, send the plane, as scheduled, to meet us in five minutes."

The man nodded and buried his head in a laptop, typing furiously.

"I see the runway. See it? Right there," motioned Therese out her left window.

Richard leaned over to get a better look, but it all just appeared to be farmland to him. He did see something that looked like a dirt road. "Are you sure that's a runway?" Therese banked left while dropping altitude at a steady speed.

"Absolutely. This position matches the coordinates the other tower gave us for landing on Anguilla. Now, don't get upset, but I need to tell you something."

Richard looked at Therese, the blood draining from his face. "What do you have to tell me?"

"I'm not IFR certified."

"What the hell does that mean?"

"Instrument flight rules certification. I've never needed to be. I don't fly at night, and I always use the Cessna turbo prop."

"Oh my god. Are we going to crash?" Richard was ashen.

"No. It's broad daylight, Richard. And I know how to use the instruments; I just can't use them legally. And these are a little different. See, since there is no tower here, we can't get someone on the ground to verify that it's safe to land. I need you to help me make sure we don't land on another plane, or worse."

"How am I going to do that?"

"I need you to open the door and look. Seriously. I'm not going fast, and your harness will keep you in, I promise. I've already got the plane in the correct position."

"Therese, I can't. I can't open a plane door midair! Are you out of your mind?"

"Richard, you have to. And you have to do it right now."

"How will I close it again?"

"Just open the goddamn door. Now!"

Chapter Thirty-Four: *Anegada*

CARLO DROVE THE CAR around the neighborhood one more time. Since Fred had sent him down to the islands this morning, he'd been reacquainting himself with the tropical paradise from the comfort of a BioSys Land Rover, trying to forget about the fire and the fact that there was nothing he could do. He could not reverse time. He could not re-invent the law enforcement system, or make it actually work. Oh, the cops, the Feds, they all knew about Tony Rossetti and others like him. They just couldn't make the case happen. *I gave up,* thought Carlo. The paperwork. The mindlessness. The clock-punchers. The appeals for improvements and streamlining that went nowhere; meanwhile, bodies showed up in dumpsters and now, bombs in churches.

Carlo was surprised that the island hadn't changed much, but then again, his memory was probably failing him. Therese had been a just a high schooler when he'd first come here with the Franklins—at least fifteen years ago now. He watched the people on the streets and looked around carefully for suspiciousness.

Fred had not been able to provide any specifics, but thought the marina might hold a clue. All Carlo had seen there were Stuart and an older man shooting the breeze on a small boat. That must be the doctor, he surmised. *What a life these people had!* Sometimes, in nice, sunny places like this with the Franklins, he got a random vision of some of the cases he'd worked on—a dismembered leg, a charred arm, the beaten face of a child. It all seemed so disconnected from this world. He couldn't match them up, and he wasn't sure why he even tried.

Carlo ended his Anegada tour by turning onto Corniche Lane, which dead-ended at the BioSys villas, the sea breaking below the bluff. He would visit Therese, put Fred's mind at ease, and then maybe he'd go down to the beach for some fried plantain tacos. After all, it was nearly lunchtime. When he saw Therese's car safely in the driveway of villa #4, he parked the Land Rover in the street and slipped off his shoes. He walked to the cliff edge and looked out over the water.

He could see Enrique's Tacos! He was delighted it was still there, after all these years. He made his way down the bluff.

As he descended the rickety stairs and felt the sea breeze on his face, he remembered one night, when he had crept down these exact steps to meet a local girl. The moon had illuminated his path—he saw the scene vividly. He had met the girl, and they had kissed a little and planned to meet again. But she stood him up, he now recalled, and he laughed softly to himself. *Married.* He should've known! He reached the end of the stairs and gazed into the water, taking a deep breath of island air. He shut his eyes again to the sunlight, blinding as it bounced off the sand. He began to walk toward the taco stand, hypnotized by the sound of the water. And then he saw something incongruous, something awful, and his instincts took over. A large thing, ambling awkwardly along the water.

He was running before he knew it, using every muscle to its fullest, although he seemed to be in slow motion, the weight of his body tripled in the deep sand. He reached the giant dog, finally. Fancy was panting hard, and her rear leg was covered in blood. The dog looked close to collapsing and could not put any weight on the leg. It wasn't easy, but he got Fancy to lie down on her good leg. Carlo ripped his shirt into a tourniquet—he couldn't bear to see the blood, so he worked fast.

Where the hell was Therese?

Carlo surveyed the scene. "Therese!" he called, his voice barely traveling across the sprawl of the sandy beach. "Therese!" He looked up and down the beach for signs of life. There was no one about, and the taco stand was boarded up. He saw signs of a struggle in the sand. Two sets of footprints, maybe three? The intense sun made it difficult to be sure. The angle of the sun would make an investigation impossible at this time of day—he would have to come back later.

He lifted Fancy in his arms, and the dog began to whine and cry in distress. His strong biceps bowed from the strain. In the dog's neck was a tiny arrow. Could that little arrow have been the dog's downfall? This giant powerful dog? Had Therese received one, too? It didn't bear even thinking about. He pulled the arrow out of the animal's neck and shoved it in his pocket for further study later. With a massive heave, he lifted the dog higher, being careful of the leg, and headed towards the steps once again, struggling in the sand, breathing heavy, dripping with sweat, trying to see the way in the blinding sun.

Richard unlatched the plane's door, his hands covered in sweat.

"Now, you have to hang on to it and lean out."

Richard managed to open the door about three inches before Therese leaned over and swung it out further, Richard screaming.

"Look down as I circle!" Therese shouted over the air noise.

Richard looked. There was no way not to, since he had a death grip on the Cessna's door. To his surprise, looking down was not terrifying, except when he saw his sweat fall from his face into the air. The dusty runway was deserted. For good measure, he looked behind the aircraft before slamming the door shut with all his might.

"It's just us," he said placidly, the shock taking over.

Therese guided the small plane down, in spite of what seemed to Richard like heavy winds. The plane jostled about and then, suddenly, the landing gear met the dirt runway, and Therese clutched at the controls. They were down. The engines wound down and the plane slowed, coming to an inelegant, but complete, halt.

Therese unbuckled her seat belt an instant later. Richard stopped her as she began to rise.

"Have you forgotten about our guest?" Richard motioned to the back of the plane, beyond the cockpit door.

"Well, he's out, isn't he?" A worried look formed on her face.

"Well, as out as possible. But who knows what's transpired since then."

"You mean, he could be awake?" Therese looked at the door.

"Well, yes."

"Then let's get the hell out of here!"

Richard looked at Therese, confused, until he saw her unlatch a small door next to the pilot's seat. He seemed to have forgotten how to open his.

"Come on," she said as the small door swung free. "We have to climb down. Hurry!"

They scrambled away from the plane towards a small office connected to the unmanned control tower. It was only about three hundred yards, but the distance between Therese and the shelter was made infinite by the thought of imminent pursuit. The mid-morning sun beat down overhead. Therese's legs felt like jelly as they reached the office, panting.

"Help!" she blurted, to no one. Richard was next to her, less winded. But the door was padlocked.

A loud whizzing noise distracted Therese from her pleas and what sounded like an enormous bug passed her ear. A bullet hole bloomed in the door before her.

"Get down! Run!" shouted Richard, pushing her into a crouched position and towards the rear of the small building.

"The gun? The man? My God, he's armed, Richard!" Therese muttered as she put the clues together in a delayed shock.

"I know; just go, go, come on!" shouted Richard, and they ran down a dirt road lined with palm trees. *It must be the airport access road*, she figured. As they ran, they looked over their shoulders for their kidnapper-turned-murderer. Therese saw he had given chase and picked up her speed to catch Richard. "He must have had the gun hidden somewhere. I didn't feel it when I roped him up."

"He's coming! He's coming!" shouted Therese in his ear, as Richard grabbed her arm and made a sharp right turn onto a smaller path in a copse of thick palm trees, which provided some cover.

"This way!" Richard guided them down yet another trail. The forest of trees became thicker, and they were now sheltered from the sun, but running was difficult. There were rocks, vines, and enormous tree roots to maneuver around. Therese became aware of her heart thumping away, but she did not notice that her feet were deeply scratched and bleeding. Her limbs brushed against fronds as they flew by, tree after tree. Her hearing was amplified; she swore she heard the footfalls the tiny creatures around her and the deep thrashing of the heavy boots of their pursuer close behind. Her mind began to race. What to do next? A car? A phone? She had absolutely nothing with her. Richard led them in a succession of quick turns, and then they emerged from the copse and found themselves on another dirt road, this one wider than the last.

They surveyed their possibilities—across the street, a mature cane field, a tractor buried deep within it or down the road, no cars this way, no cars that way. "Shit!" muttered Richard. But he made the decision for them. He grabbed Therese's hand and they scurried across the road, keeping low, weaving themselves into the tapestry of cane stalks.

"Whoa, oops! Ouch!" Therese landed with a thud and Richard leaned down to help her.

"What is it? What hurts?" Richard asked between heavy breaths. Therese pointed at her ankle.

"Something tripped me. Ow!" She moaned when Richard touched the ankle, which was already beginning to swell. "We have to keep moving, though. Let me try to get up."

"I agree. Here," Richard put her arm around his neck and helped pull her up. "I'll support your bad side. If we can just make it over to the tractor, we stand a chance of out-running him."

"It sounds as if he's lost us, for the moment."

"I think he has, but this island isn't very big, right?"

Therese concentrated on moving forward instead of replying. They continued their journey, but at a slower pace, hobbling through the dense field.

"Do you see it? The tractor, I mean?" gasped Therese as she laboriously placed one foot in front of the other. She looked down at her scuffed and bleeding feet and noticed, for the first time in many years, how much they resembled her father's.

"Yes. It's a great big John Deere. Now, let's pray that its owner has left the keys in the ignition," groaned Richard, heaving Therese's body alongside his. Grains of long wheat whipped his sweating face, lashing him with their fine petals.

"C'mon now, just a few more paces," said Richard encouragingly. Therese could see the great green machine now, parked in a small clearing. Richard moved her legs into the passenger's side, and with a heave, helped push her into the seat. The plastic seat was blazing hot; the tractor had been there for some time. Richard ran to other side and hopped in, searching frantically for a key. There was none.

"Damn!" shouted Richard, slamming his hands against the steering wheel. In the next second, the unmistakable sound of metal impacting metal burst into their ears.

"Jesus, get down!" managed Richard, who instinctively grasped Therese's neck and pulled them both down into a crash position.

"The key! There it is!" cried Therese, spotting an upside-down sparkling key, not so much hidden underneath the driver's seat as placed there for convenience. Richard plucked it, mated it with the ignition from his crouched position, and with little grace, flung the tractor into gear, hoping the pictures in his mind of a person 'driving' would be adequate and quick teachers. A giant plume of black smoke emerged from the back of the tractor, and they were off.

"Stay down, stay down!" shouted Richard to Therese, who bobbed her head up anyway to get a position on their attacker.

"I said, stay—"

"He's fallen! Thank God, because he's only about two-hundred feet away!"

The tractor trudged forward, at the alarmingly slow rate of about twenty miles per hour.

"I have something to tell you," Richard yelled over the engine.

"Oh, God. What?" Therese lifted her head from the floor of the tractor.

"I don't know how to drive."

It might have been funny if Therese had been listening.

"He's up again!" she reported as Richard maneuvered the tractor onto a gravel road. "Okay, let's come up with something, and fast," she added, turning back around to face the road.

"Well, I'm in the highest gear, and the pedal is all the way engaged. I think that means I can't go any faster. But listen, I've put something together," shouted Richard over the din of the tractor's engine.

"What's that?" asked Therese, turning around again to gauge the man's distance.

"If this were a kidnapping, why shoot to kill? Why the daredevil plane ride?" When Therese did not reply, he continued. "I mean, if the kidnapping didn't go as planned—presumably to capture you safely and collect a ransom—why continue to pursue you after you've seen his face? And why attempt to harm you? I can't imagine there's anything like a bounty out on you, right?"

"Well, of course not; I mean—what on earth for?"

Richard turned the tractor down a smaller street, and suddenly, a small town square emerged. A few townspeople milled about a tiny outdoor produce market, as did a spattering of tourists in colorful shorts and visors. One turned and gasped, having found herself, quite unexpectedly, next to an idling tractor. Richard allowed the engine to sputter and grabbed Therese's hand.

"Let's go. He won't dare fire near these people, if he even comes any closer."

Therese looked dubious, but limped from the tractor anyway. Richard supported her with his body again, and they began to hobble. By now, all eyes were on them. Who were these frightened people who had driven into town on a tractor?

"Where should we go?" asked Therese, as quietly as possible.

"How about into a shop? We can play tourist, perhaps hide behind the flag display—there." Richard motioned to a stall selling various items bearing the island's name and flower.

"Can I be of some assistance? The lady there looks like she's in pain." The man who spoke to them emerged from behind the tourist stall. He wore overalls and a large brim hat. His eyes were old and tired, but warm, his skin leathery from years spent outdoors.

"Yes, we need some help, maybe a way off the island. You see, we're being chased." Richard scooted Therese behind the flags as he spoke, attempting to hide her from view.

"He's got a gun, and he's dangerous," whispered Therese from her camouflage of flags.

"Well, in that case, we'd better move. I'm glad you got some use out of that old tractor; she hardly moves for me anymore," the man said nonchalantly as he placed large hats on Richard and Therese. Therese managed to smile despite the circumstances. This was a small island.

"Come on now, and follow me. I got a pickup 'round back." He ushered the two through the back of his stall. "My name's George," he said as he opened the creaking truck doors, "but you can call me Red. Everyone does."

The three squeezed into the front seat of the old Ford pickup truck, and in a moment, they were speeding away from the town square, a trail of dust behind them.

Since his arms were not free, Carlo kicked the front door of the emergency vet's office. "Help, help!" he cried, then turned his back to lean against the door for support, and to protect Fancy's leg. The tourniquet had done its job—just. Blood was beginning to seep onto Carlo. He couldn't manage the door with the giant animal in his arms—he'd have to use his back. Someone responded from the other side, and Carlo felt the door open.

"We're closed for lunch, sir."

"Oh, no, you're not," Carlos shouted, pushing open the door and backing inside, turning once he was in the threshold.

"Oh, my goodness!" gasped the technician, seeing the blood and the exasperation of the man cradling the dog.

"This is Stuart Franklin's dog, so you are now officially open."

"Oh, of course. Of course!" gasped the technician, who ran to get a gurney.

"Goodbye, Red" called Therese from the edge of the pilot boat, waving her arms. The small boat pushed away from the shore, Richard coiling its heavy ropes on the boat's floor. Red waved back and tipped his large hat. The whole procedure hadn't taken more than twenty minutes; Red had thought on his feet. Therese collapsed on the small boat's floor and watched a wake emerge beneath them. They were gathering speed. Richard placed his hands on her shoulders, and she nearly gasped.

"Shhh," he whispered. "Just me." He slid down beside her for a much-needed rest.

"What did you tell the skipper?" mumbled Therese, just now, it seemed, grasping the need for secrecy, her eyes on the shore, which fell farther and farther away.

"That we had been mugged. That we had no money, but we'd pay him for his troubles back in Anegada."

"Anegada? We can't go back there!"

"Well, we have to. We'll get to a phone, let your father know—"

"My God, Richard! They'll be waiting for me there, don't you see?"

"Well—" Richard sighed and turned to her. The porcelain wall of the tug felt like a slab of cold marble against his sweating neck, and he relished it as he chose his words.

"Well what?" Therese turned to him now, too, taking her eyes off the hypnotic waves.

"It's like this. As I said earlier: who would want to harm you?"

"I don't understand. You mean someone might want to harm *you*? Is that what you're implying?" Therese was incredulous.

"This doesn't add up. It's not about you."

"But what would they want with you, Richard?" Therese turned his head towards her; he had been looking out at the water. He made no move to speak. "What is it, Richard? Have you done something? Has something happened?" Her voice rose in pitch with each successive inquiry.

"Well, you see, I—well, I work for your father, you see, and—" A loud boat horn sounded, making them both jump up. The skipper waved hello to a passing boat. Therese sighed with relief, and they resumed their seats.

"Yes, you work for my father," prompted Therese. "Since when was that a crime?"

Richard cleared his throat; she couldn't imagine the weight of what she had just said. He had been involved in crime; he could see that now. Who, what, how? He wasn't sure, but he'd sensed it—just hadn't faced it; the pictures just a jumble in his mind. He improvised, which took all the effort he had. Words were never easy for him. He could have drawn a picture on a white board with much less struggle. The pictures he would have drawn would have been of the camera in his villa and the ABT-55 molecule.

"You know I'm working on a very important cancer drug, and the drug industry is in trouble—more trouble than they've seen in decades. People are scrambling for an innovation to boost their stock value; you know that. You've read about it in the papers."

"But what's this got to do with you?"

"The industry is very cut-throat right now." Richard paused. "People will go to great lengths for an advantage."

"Espionage, you mean?"

"Perhaps."

"What does this cancer drug do that's so special?"

"Well, it could be innovative for people who don't respond to traditional chemo, and it will have fewer side-effects. But here's the thing—it doesn't do that right now."

"What do you mean, 'it could'?"

"That's just it, you see. The data's been doctored, but not in the usual manner."

"Not to make the drug look better, but worse?"

"Exactly. Someone or something does not want that drug to work."

Therese sighed and leaned back, trying to make a connection. Did her father know?

"So, what's your role? My father's?"

"I don't think your father is involved in the specifics," began Richard. At least this was true, thought Richard, hesitant to lie to Therese, or anyone. But hadn't he been lying all along?

"Let me cut right to my involvement. From the beginning, things have been odd. For instance, did you know there are cameras in my villa? And all over BioSys."

"I didn't know that," said Therese slowly, unbelieving almost, shaking her head slightly.

"Well, there are. I understand those at the lab—they've a good bit of intellectual property to protect—but in my home?"

"Well, if what you're getting at is corporate espionage, wouldn't those cameras have been installed by another company?"

"Yes, true. Or someone within BioSys. Or I don't know whom. But we're getting off track. You see, Therese, it is possible that it is me these men are after, and you just happened to be in the wrong place at the wrong time."

"And that explains the bullets?" Therese said, wild-eyed. "They would shoot you for this information? Can't they get it off a computer or via paperwork?"

"Well, that's just it; none of this is very well documented. And that's not unusual, at least, not in this early phase. Right now, the goal is not to make the drug work—on people who won't die of the disease anyway. The goal is just to get the dose right. Certain aspects of the process are documented so we can learn, but there's no paper that puts it all together. At least, not yet."

"But you have it all? In your head, you mean?"

"That's another thing. I don't. They've got the wrong man." Richard rubbed his neck and leaned back, closing his eyes. At least, he thought again, all of that was true. But now that he had posited his espionage theory aloud, another thing became clear. It probably wasn't the chemo drug they wanted. They'd want the stem cells. Or—wait—not the stem cells at all.

"That's it, Therese."

"What?"

"I'm not the man, like I just said, with all of it written down."

"Which man are you, then?"

"I'm the man with the fix."

They were both silent for a long, few moments. The water lapped the sides of the boat, a drop or two making its way to their faces.

"So," Therese began, the gears turning. "I guess we rule out calling the police."

"Naturally. We need to protect BioSys, and the less publicity, the better."

"It would be a PR snafu, I can see, if the whole idea is to get the public excited about drugs so the company's stock soars. A story about a kidnapping to cover up bad data could not be good."

"Right. We don't for sure know that's happening, but yes, speaking out would make BioSys look very foolish. And as I said, the industry is rocky now. BioSys needs a big hit with ABT-55."

"Is that why you think it's safe to go back to Anegada? I mean, will the bad guys have fled to keep things quiet?"

"I think so. I think they'll try again, but not now. Besides, I need to get back to the lab to make sure everything is intact." That, he reflected, was also quite true.

"Richard. Think about it. We can't go back. There's no place to hide! It'll be obvious we're there. Sitting ducks!"

The two sat in silence again, listening to the engine and the waves. Therese mused cynically on the ugliness of the drug industry. She knew the companies did everything to make a fast buck, but thought her father's company was at least invested in cancer research for the right reasons. She hoped they still were. Had her father been working hard all his life at manipulating consumer confidence? It could not be true. Perhaps he had been pressured to play a numbers game, but he was a purist. He really did believe in science, that life was simply a series of mysteries to be unraveled. If this was not true, she realized, an image of deadly, intertwining plaques building up in her brain over time, she and many others like her, had little hope of a cure.

She turned to Richard, her face betraying her new fear—for her own brain. Involuntarily, wells of tears formed in her eyes. She whispered, "What if you knew—if you knew," she labored, attempting to keep her voice from cracking, "that you were going to die of a very specific thing? And you had only to wait for its symptoms to show? What if you knew," she took a deep breath, "in advance?" Her fair skin was flushed, her skin taut.

"I—I don't understand." Richard shook his head, looking at her in confusion.

"What would you do, Richard? My God, what would you do?" She nearly whispered the last words, then her face collapsed into her hands, and she wept openly. Richard placed an awkward arm around her and called out to the boatman.

"There's been a change of plans," he shouted above the roar of the engine. "Take us to the nearest major island, please—but not Anegada." The skipper waved his hand in acknowledgment, and the boat turned sharply starboard, away from the bright sun.

"Damn it!" screamed Paul as he slammed his fist against the side of the plane. "You're telling me you lost them? A woman and a puny scientist?" The two planes sat parked—one Paul had arrived in, and one Therese had landed.

"Look, the boss told me to be quiet about it, and I tried. I didn't expect them to know how to fly a turbo prop cargo plane. I could barely fly it myself—something was wrong with the controls." The would-be kidnapper's voice rose. "You tell me what I should have done!"

"Quiet down, now! Jesus!" whispered Paul. "Okay, so you lost them. Did they get a good look at you?"

"No, I stayed back until we hit the town square. They could have seen me then, but I doubt it; they were too worried. I headed back here to rendezvous, but not before I saw one thing."

"Yeah, what was that, smart guy?" Paul leaned in close; he could smell the cane field on the man.

"The guy whose pickup truck they got in."

"Take me there; let's go. Now!" howled Paul, already running to the car.

The pilot boat's engine slowed as the skipper navigated a channel. Therese saw stunning islands to either side, green and forested with plants different from those on Anegada.

"We're at Nevis!" said Therese incredulously. She picked herself off the floor of the small boat, and Richard followed her. Therese moved next to the skipper to get a better look.

"And St. Kitts, of course," the skipper replied, motioning to his right.

"I've never heard of these islands," said Richard.

"Many people haven't, save the rich and famous." The skipper turned the helm quickly, making a sharp turn.

"That's good," Richard said, standing next to Therese. "We're looking for a private spot." If the circumstances hadn't involved being pursued by gun-toting assailant, and if he could get Therese's attention, the remark might have implied romance. As it was, Richard was simply stating a fact, and facts were his specialty.

"Well," continued the skipper, rotating his wheel, and maneuvering the breakwaters, "you'd probably like to explore Nevis. I was born there, and I can tell you it's not on the map the way it should be. It is a very special and beautiful place. You'll see."

"How big is it, actually?" Therese asked, looking out over the stern.

"Oh, about forty square miles, at most. It's only seven miles across. But for being so small, it used to be pretty important. For sugar, you know."

Richard and Therese watched the skipper guide the boat into the small bay. Its bumper hit the dock with a gentle thud.

"This way's Pinney's Beach," motioned the skipper to his left. "That's where most of the hotels are; it's just a few minutes' walk."

"And that?" pointed a wide-eyed Therese to a mountaintop rising on the horizon behind them, the most lush she had ever seen. She hadn't been to Nevis since she was a small child.

"Oh, that's Mt. Liamuinga, on St. Kitts. You can take a boat there and hike it. Let me know if you want to go. You tell Ricky there—see him?" The skipper pointed to a man securing a yacht to the dock. "You tell him if you need me, okay?" The skipper smiled.

Therese and Richard alighted from the ship and moved down a small plank dock. A tropical mist materialized and enveloped them; a comforting breeze stirred the smell of the sea. Therese breathed deeply—the oxygen revived her. She took in the unfamiliar trees with enormous fronds, the call of circling birds, and grains of sand digging into the gashes on her feet.

"Well," Therese sighed. "Where to?" The faint sound of jazz music drifted toward them, its source hidden by the breeze, which was picking up.

"We need a bath and a rest." Richard nodded toward the music and led Therese in that direction.

"And first-aid," she mumbled, looking at her wounds.

"Here, up we go," replied Richard, scooping her up in his arms, cradling her tired body. "We'll pretend we're honeymooners; that way, I can carry you across the threshold. Sound good?" He smiled down at her through the mist, and Therese tried not to smile, but did anyway. Richard walked for a few minutes in silence. A large, colorful bird flew beside her for a moment, twittering long enough for Therese to see its yellow and aqua streaked feathers.

"But, my feet—and your clothes. We're a mess."

"We'll think of something," panted Richard; although he was strong and relatively fit, walking in the sand with Therese in his arms was a challenge. He moved toward the trees, and stumbled onto the pavement.

"That's better." Richard increased his speed, no longer sure he was leading them anywhere. He strained his ears for the music, but it had stopped.

"Oh, no!" cried Therese suddenly.

"What? What's happened?" started Richard, alarmed.

"We don't have any money!"

A tiny hotel came into view in the same instant—the pavement Richard had discovered, it seemed, was a driveway. A golf cart sped soundlessly past the lobby entrance. A regally uniformed porter, complete with cap and boots, approached them.

"Checking in?" he asked, a warm smile on his face. Richard began to put Therese back on the ground and heard the jazz music again, no doubt drifting from a nearby verandah.

"Well, actually, if we could just use the phone—"

"Yes, we are checking in," interrupted Therese, righting herself. Richard looked at her, stunned. Before he could protest, she continued, "But we'll need to speak the manager about some rather delicate, uh, arrangements. You see, we've been robbed."

Therese flashed the porter and Richard a dazzling smile, reached up to her earlobes, and began to remove her flawless and rare diamond earrings.

Carlo reached the front door of Eastwind and stopped a moment, catching his breath. He adjusted his tie and smoothed his jacket, which he had sweated through. He cleared his throat then put a hand on the wrought iron doorknocker, giving it a firm bang. He would never forget this awful moment, just as he would never forget the tortures he had been through before. Carlo shook the ghosts from his head and gave the knocker another firm shake.

"Well, Carlo, what a nice surprise," smiled Stuart. "Come in and join me. I was just finishing lunch." Stuart motioned Carlo inside and closed the door behind him.

The hallway was filled with what could only be described as junk. Papers, pens, empty cereal boxes, apple cores, and unopened mail. Something smelled distinctly burned. Furniture had been moved out of the large kitchen—the outlines of where pantries and shelves once stood apparent on the old walls. A huge white board was leaning against the wall where something used to be, and its surface was covered with markings.

Stuart pulled something unrecognizable out of the oven. Carlo thought about sitting down, but there was no free space on any surface. He clasped his hands in front of him and took a deep breath.

"Mr. Franklin, she's missing."

Stuart started to hack at the thing, which appeared to be a pizza.

"What do you mean? Hattie? I let her go a while back. I needed some privacy. I know I'm not too competent in the kitchen, but—"

"Mr. Franklin, Therese is missing."

The baking tray in Stuart's hand collapsed to the floor, and Stuart turned away to the window.

"The bastards drugged Fancy on the beach. They must have been out walking. From the quality of the footprints in the sand, I put it between 7 a.m. and 9 a.m. There was a struggle—probably two assailants. I hoped you would know something, but, well—"

Stuart turned back and moved close to Carlo. "Are you sure?"

"I'm not; that's why I'm looking for her. When did you last hear from her?"

Stuart stood, perplexed. "Well, let's see—" A silence settled over the room. "Why don't we sit down? There must be a simple explanation." Stuart's voice trailed off as he disappeared behind the sliding glass doors that connected the hall to the kitchen. A dazed and sweating Carlo trailed behind and took a seat.

In the den, Stuart stood in front of him, as if leading a meeting of the board—calm and collected. "Okay, tell me again, everything you know, from the beginning."

Therese collapsed on the luxurious bed in the suite. She was swathed in a lush bathrobe and her long hair was wrapped in a fluffy towel. Richard leaned over and began applying an ointment to her feet. Therese wriggled in discomfort.

"Just a little bit more on this one, then the bandages," soothed Richard. From the other room, the opening and closing of a door could be heard, then the clank of a silver tray meeting a marble tabletop.

"Thank you," called Richard. They had arranged for food and supplies to be left quietly in the adjoining room, requesting the level of discretion afforded by the deposit of Therese's very valuable earrings.

"I'll phone my banker on Monday," offered Therese, but the hotel manager had been more than flexible after Therese pointed out the well-known logo on the two-carat gems.

"Of course," he had replied and, accustomed to special requests, made the necessary phone calls to his first-rate staff. Richard and Therese requested two rooms, the delivery of food, clothes, and first aid, and most importantly, assurances that their identity not be disclosed to anyone who might "call" on them. The manager simply nodded. Celebrities and dignitaries routinely required the same discretion. He did not ask about police, but merely handed them two keys and escorted them up a private elevator to their suites.

"Ouch! That side hurts more," winced Therese as Richard secured the last bandage.

"Oh, they'll be healed in no time. Just like new." Richard straightened from his crouched position on the floor and then sat, exhausted, on the bed next to Therese.

"If only all ailments were that simple to correct," sighed Therese.

"Yes, I know, I know." Richard let his eyes close and became aware of what seemed like every muscle in his legs trembling from the day's events.

"Richard?" She wanted to explain about her episode on the boat. But, then again, with everything else going on— Richard cut her off, anyway.

"I'm beat, and we need to rest, especially if we don't plan on staying long. I should get to my own room."

"I was going to say that I was thinking of renting a car first thing in the morning, just to stay on the move."

"Good idea." Richard stood to go.

And then, Therese bolted upright.

"My God," she gasped.

"What is it?"

"My poor father! He must be worried sick! Pass me the phone." He did, and then retreated, casting a look over his shoulder, as if to assure himself that Therese would be okay.

When the phone rang at Eastwind, Stuart was standing next to it, facing Carlo. Carlo had just concluded his story, not including the part about the blood on the dog, which he could still not explain—perhaps

Fancy had gashed it while struggling. Stuart placed a hand on the receiver. "Okay," he almost whispered. "If this is them, I'm ready." He took a deep breath and picked up the receiver.

"Stuart Franklin," he said into the phone, attempting to make his voice sound normal. Carlo rose and stood next to Stuart, trying to overhear. The voice on the line was loud enough; he needn't have bothered. The caller sounded like he was in a plane or a car with the windows rolled down. He was practically screaming.

"Ten p.m., the dock, by your friend's boat. One million in cash, unmarked bills. Don't worry; she's alive. You cannot overtake us, so don't try. No police!" The line was immediately disconnected.

Carlo sunk his face into his hands, his worst fear a reality. At least he knew exactly what to do, thanks to many late nights on the drug-bust squad.

"We need to call the local constable. Immediately. Place two, maybe three men around the boat, and—"

Stuart slapped the palm of his hand on the desk. "Oh, no; no way. It's simple. We deliver the money."

"But," Carlo stalled, trying to keep Stuart out of the matter and get Therese back safely. "Today is Sunday. How will we get that cash?"

"Never you fear. I want this matter considered closed. I will handle it. I will bring the cash to the dock tonight—"

"But, Mr. Franklin, they'll be armed. You can't go alone! I'll join you—"

"Nonsense."

"Mr. Franklin, please let me help, I've got more experience, and I feel responsible—"

Stuart howled, "You've got no experience in this world, Carlo, and you know it."

Carlo was stunned at the recrimination, and color flushed his face. It was true; he had walked away from that world, scarred, scared, overwhelmed by what he could not fix. But still, Stuart's jibe hurt. He felt terribly guilty, and he was worried about Therese. It had been his job to keep an eye on her, for this very reason. He sat in silence, his heart pounding.

"I'll go. On my own," boomed Stuart, back in CEO mode again. "Now, off with you. I've got some banking to see to." Stuart took a seat at his desk and watched Carlo exit. He sat for a moment, listening to

Carlo letting himself out the massive front door. And then he rose quickly and with deft movement, reached for a book on a high shelf. In the next second, he had a small key in his hand.

The trunk was, today, in the closet of a rarely used spare bedroom. Stuart crept up the stairs, reminding himself that he would have to move the chest later, but not now. He was in the habit of moving it, and thank God, had never once forgotten its location. The door of the bedroom creaked open, but he ignored the sound. He had done this before; he had practiced. He opened the old closet, shoved aside a stack of old blankets, and inserted the key in the rusty old trunk lock. His mother had once used this trunk to move everything she and her poor family owned to the United States of America. The stamps on it still showed the trunk's ports of call: Skye, London, Dover, and finally, Ellis Island. He opened the hinged lid, and there, in conveniently "unmarked" bills, sat exactly one million dollars.

He kept such a box at every residence.

Then Stuart disappeared so deep into the cave that had become his existence that he could not hear the phone when it rang insistently, over and over.

Therese replaced the receiver and collapsed into the feather bed. She could not remember a time when each fiber of her being felt so utterly crippled. Just the effort of moving her aching feet to a pillow for elevation seemed a daunting task. She would phone Eastwind again first thing when she awoke. Odd that the phone had rung and rung. Where was Hattie? At that moment, she felt she could sleep for days.

With a thought, she sprang out of bed and double-bolted the main door, wincing from the pressure of her own body weight on her feet. Then she dragged the coffee table and side tables in front of the doors. Just in case.

She was asleep minutes later.

The day's dusky last light hung heavy below deck, casting a warm glow over the interior of the small boat. Bob sat at his typewriter, plucking away at the keys with a smile on his face. He typed, "A Novel Surgical Approach to Early Alzheimer's Using Stem Cells; a Phase I Clinical Trial." Bob hit Return, and the small machine "dinged" a confirmation, as if showing satisfaction at the confident words. Bob paused to shuffle through the stacks of data on his desk. First, he would cite the monkey work in the Background section of the paper, then the data from the live patients at the Alzheimer's hospital, and then, well, when Stuart agreed—which he would, eventually—he would cite his most important case: Stuart Franklin, CEO. Then a voice from the night called, "Bob?"

Stuart's voice! As if on cue. He must have been absorbed to not hear Stuart's heavy footfalls on the dock. He yanked the paper out of the typewriter and stowed it in a drawer.

"Coming," he called. He ambled to the bow and walked up on deck. There was Stuart, a silhouette against the darkening sky, looking more eccentric than ever, wearing a tracksuit and headphones, and carrying a briefcase.

"Well, hello, Stuart. What brings you—"

"I haven't time to talk. And not out here." Stuart walked past Bob and headed below deck. Bob followed, alarmed.

"Is something wrong?" Had Stuart been spying on him? Not possible on this small dock, thought Bob. They took their seats, and Bob switched on a small lamp.

"Something is very wrong." Stuart took a deep breath. "Therese has been kidnapped."

"My God!" spurted Bob. "But why on earth? And what do they want? Money?"

"Of course. It's right here," Stuart patted the briefcase. He looked solemnly at Bob.

"But when? Are they coming here, for chissakes?" Then things began to add up. He saw it in Stuart's eyes.

"Someone kidnapped Therese, but they didn't want Therese."

"Exactly."

"And Richard? Shit!"

"Of course." Bob and Stuart sat in silence and listened to the waves lap against the boat. Its mooring ropes creaked eerily. "I've been all over your villa. He's not there, and he hasn't been into BioSys in days."

Bob paled. "What are we going to do?"

"We give them the money, that's first. Then we find out what they know and what they don't know."

"Who cares what they know? What about my son, damn it?"

"Whoa, whoa, Bob! Listen to yourself!" Stuart got up and walked closer to Bob, leaning on his hands on the arms of Bob's chair. "You have to tell me if you leaked this, Bob. You have to be straight with me. You see what's at stake. Don't try me, Bob. Don't even think about it." Stuart's face was nearly touching Bob's. Bob shoved him away and stood up. The weaker man fell easily into a chair.

"That's craziness, and you know it. I cannot believe you are implying that I would let our study, or its findings, out to anyone. I agreed to absolute secrecy when this started, and you know I want success just as much as you do." Bob quieted himself and pointed a long finger at Stuart. "Don't you dare accuse me of such a thing!" Bob turned away and began to pace.

"Okay. I had to ask, don't you see? If it wasn't you, who the hell was it?"

Bob brought over two mugs and filled them with coffee, then handed one to Stuart and sat down again.

"You have more people to worry about. We have no one. Not a soul! My life is my dwindling career and my boy. You know that. You, on the other hand, have a staff of thousands, a driver, and Lord knows whom else. What about that piano player you were telling me about?"

"Eve?" whispered Stuart tenderly. At the mention of her name, he remembered he was wearing headphones and removed them from his head, then switched the portable CD player on his belt to OFF. He looked down at the player and murmured, "No way. Not her."

"What time does the deal happen?"

"Ten p.m. That gives us about an hour and a half to come up with a strategy."

"Are we sure she—and Richard are—"

"Alive? The caller said Therese was. He didn't mention Richard."

"Well, then why don't we start by looking for him?"

"Would he crack?"

"What do you mean?"

"I mean, would he crack, Bob. Jesus. Would he tell them anything?"

"I doubt it. He worked with sensitive information at the NIH; he could never talk to the press, that sort of thing. Besides, he likes rules. If the rule is you don't talk, he won't."

"If there's a pistol at your head, you might. You might tell all."

"Well, we don't know that. We don't even know who these people are, do we? Do you? Have you told me everything?"

"Of course I have! All I know is what he said in the call—the time, the place, the amount, and that Therese was alive."

"Let's hope Richard is, too, my God."

Ten p.m. arrived too soon, and things happened too quickly. A hooded figure appeared at the boat, a .45 held out in front of him. He motioned for the briefcase, and Stuart, terrified despite having coached himself in bravery, passed it over. He watched as the hooded figure opened it quickly, then closed it and fled. Stuart saw no one else in sight. Should he pursue? He felt stupid now for not allowing Carlo to help. Stuart sighed and paced, and that's when he noticed the prone, motionless figure on the stern. "Oh, no! Please, God, no!" he cried, and he jumped to the top of the boat and started running, jumping over rope and anchor ties. Bob rushed out of the boat to see Stuart crouched beside what was obviously a body wrapped in a shroud. Bob felt his heart stop until Stuart called, "Jesus, Bob. It's Paul. Paul Westin."

Nearby, Carlo sat in his car, hidden by a copse of small palm trees, and watched as a man in a hood hurried along the road, lit only by cloud-filtered moonlight. He got out of the car silently and followed him.

Therese slipped out of bed. It was still dark; no sun slid under the light-blocking velvet curtains in the suite. A digital clock read 4:45 a.m. Asleep for nearly twelve hours! No wonder her back ached. She switched on a table lamp and rubbed her lower back.

Therese looked around at the stacks of supplies that had been sent to the room yesterday. The leather armchairs overflowed with piles of clothes—sarongs, wraps, tank tops, shorts—a case of bottled water, two robes, slippers, chocolates, fruit, and bathing products. The hotel's logo was stamped or embroidered on everything. To her delight, she saw the one thing she had hoped to find: a bathing suit. She undressed and shimmied into the suit. A little small, but it would do. Her feet, although swollen, bruised, and aching, fit snugly in the slippers. She plucked an apple from the fruit bowl and let herself out of the room, weaving through the furniture she'd placed in the doorway yesterday. The heavy mahogany door closed silently behind her. Barely detectable Musak greeted her in the hall, and the thick wool carpet absorbed her footfalls. She smelled sea air.

The pool area was deserted, not a surprise considering the hour. Empty cabanas awaited the day's customers and drink orders. A thatched snack bar, clean and orderly, rested before the lunch rush. The pool was the area's centerpiece, however. It was an "infinity pool"—its edge appeared continuous with the sea—and Therese was happy to see it was a fifty-meter one. The weather was perfect, about 65 degrees. Half indoors and half outdoors, the pool was stunning, lined with cobalt blue tiles that made the water feel as deep blue as the twilight horizon. She spotted an abandoned swim cap and goggles and decided to borrow them. Therese sat on the pool's edge, looking at the sky while adjusting the goggles. There were some stars low in the sky, but the darkness was making way for the coming day. A slight breeze carried in the smell of the tropics: nutmeg and sugar. She took a deep breath and slipped under the surface, barely disturbing the still, warm water. She'd be hidden here. Safe and hidden.

She stretched every limb as she made her way down the lane, every ache in her battered body making itself known. The chlorine stung her feet, but that would pass. She felt the oxygen circulating from the tips of her fingers down to her toenails. She had traveled almost to the end of the lane before she came up for air. She drifted to the pool's edge on her back. And then, she began.

With a vigorous push off, her arms stretched forward, she swam freestyle—right arm up, then down and next to her body, displacing as much water as possible. Kick, kick, kick, then left arm up, down, next to body. She took breaths every third stroke and turned her head opposite directions each time, getting air deeper into her lungs at every round. She continued, back and forth, back and forth, until her mind was quiet and open. Her bad foot began to throb, but she was too invigorated to pay attention. Her pace was steady, and at each flip turn she noted the sky brightening, bluer and bluer each lap.

She flipped over for backstroke. A loud bird flew overhead, looking down at her. Its belly was bright yellow. The bird flew back and forth for a few laps of Therese's, as if mimicking her movement, and then flew away. She was alone again.

Yes, she was alone, wasn't she? She stopped using her arms and made the next lap on her back, kicking gently, using her abdomen to hold her up. *She was indeed alone*, she thought. It occurred to her again, just remembering, that she was being hunted and must rent a car immediately; as soon as she left the pool, she would speak to the hotel manager about a rental. But a thought surfaced. She wasn't being hunted. Richard had hinted at this, and now, here in the quiet pool, she saw that this was more than a hunch. She was sure Richard was right. She was just an innocent bystander.

But why? What did he have that someone wanted? She turned at the end of the lane and began more freestyle. She really didn't know Richard, after all. They had only known each other a little more than a month. She assumed he was a good person; he seemed capable, smart, and trustworthy. She couldn't imagine a neighbor—or an employee of her father's—being guilty of any wrongdoing. But he had not wanted to talk about his work…

Another lap, then another. The sun peeked out from the horizon, and it instantly warmed the air. On her mental table, Therese laid out the cards in her hand—some facts, some glimpses of intuition. She had learned the hard way about intuition—one mustn't ignore it; although one couldn't prove it, it was often the truth. Love was that way: a leap of faith.

No, she couldn't prove this thought—not now, at least. But she knew—she couldn't say how, exactly—that Richard was lying to her about his work at BioSys. But why? She needed to find out what he knew.

She climbed out of the pool, head clear, and examined her ankle wounds. The swelling had gone down, but the bruising was just beginning. Big purple swatches covered both ankles. Her legs were scratched from the running in the cane field, and her wrists were swollen and bruised from the ropes. But she stood with new energy and reached for a towel, the sun enveloping her. She must wake Richard; they had a long way to go today. A long way to go.

At the front desk, there were only boats for rent, so with the help of the night staff, Therese booked them on the longest local cruise available; they needed time to work everything out, and she knew they could, together. They were to sail south to St. Guadeloupe, but the small cruiser left from Basseterre, the main port on the neighboring island of St. Kitts. The concierge kindly arranged for a ferry crossing and the Guadeloupe tickets. The man at the front desk smiled profusely and retrieved Therese's earrings from the safe, informing her that the wire from the bank was in the computer system.

"Come and stay with us again, Madame," smiled the man. Therese waved goodbye, her slippers making tracks in the deep pile. She disappeared into the elevator.

Her next stop was the business center, which she was pleased to see had computers with a fast Internet connection. In three minutes, she had logged onto the members-only medical search engine to which she still belonged. She typed in Richard's name under "Author" and waited.

Stuart knew just what to do with the turgid body of Paul Westin.

He gave exact instructions to Bob, and they navigated *The Emerald* out to the reef.

"How can you be sure we're not going to bottom out, Stuart?"

"Trust me, Bob. It's worked so far."

They made tiny adjustments, Stuart taking over near the end since Bob was new to sailing, and the reef was treacherous. It was famous for the drowning of many boats and sailors. However, the wind tonight was steady and in their favor.

"Okay, now come help me." Stuart and Bob heaved the body of Paul Westin, former BioSys VP of Operations, over the edge of the small vessel. A splash followed, and Bob waited to see the body floating, under-confident in Stuart's plan.

But to his surprise, the body did not re-surface. The coral enveloped him, and it would hold him down until the sharks arrived.

"Now, let's get the hell out of here," said Stuart, returning to the wheel. Bob followed. "I've an important phone call to make. I have a bad feeling we gave that money to the wrong people, Bob."

"Oh, thank God!' shouted Richard as Therese stood at the open door to his room, a refreshed and relaxed look on her face. Richard's face could not have been more tense.

"What? What is it?"

"I was worried. I woke up and knocked on your door—no answer. Then I phoned and phoned. I figured you'd gone for food, but now I see." He looked at her still-damp body. "You went for a swim; that's all." He wiped his hands on his pajama bottoms. Therese laughed with relief.

"Yes, I needed time to think." She began to towel-dry her hair in the hallway. "And I've got a plan. We sail at 8:30, so we'd better get a move on."

"Sail? Well, that's a good idea."

"Yes, and we're traveling under assumed names."

"Even better," replied Richard, shifting his weight, wondering if he should invite her into his room. "That was a stroke of genius. But how on earth—I mean, what's this going to cost?"

"Oh, there's no need to worry about that. That's the least of our worries. And besides, I'm supposed to be vacationing, remember?"

"Well, I suppose. I just—well, I feel funny about you paying for things."

"We're in an emergency situation. Besides, even if we were on a real vacation together, we certainly would not stay at such an upscale resort in private suites with private elevator access on a remote, star-studded island, now would we?"

"No, you're right; of course we wouldn't. I'm sorry I brought it up at all."

"Don't worry. We're both a little stressed, wouldn't you say?" They both laughed at the understatement.

"I guess I'd better get a move on, then."

"Agreed. See you in the lobby at 7:00 a.m. sharp."

Richard listened to the soft patter of Therese's slippers retreating before closing his door and heading into the shower.

The ship's horn blared as it moved away from the white shores of St. Kitts. Therese and Richard made their way to their two cabins—modest staterooms with tiny portholes offering a mere slice of a view.

"Now this makes sense," uttered Richard as he opened his door, surveying the dollhouse-like quarters. They kept their doors propped open so they could hear each other. They had no baggage to stow, save for the small items they had decided to take from the hotel: a change of clothes, a swimsuit, toothpaste. Therese began to unpack, anyway.

"I know it was exorbitant, but we hadn't much choice in the matter, did we?" Therese wondered if their friendship, like others she'd had, would suffer due to inequality. Richard had never struck her as the insecure type, but, she mused, he was after all, a man.

"I didn't mean it that way," sighed Richard, popping his head into her room, standing in the threshold. Therese pulled the tags off a men's swimsuit. "Just because you are an heiress, and I am a poor working man—" Therese and Richard both broke into smiles.

Therese joined in the sarcasm. "Yes, I'm sure you're barely making ends meet working on a top-secret drug."

"Doesn't mean we can't be blissfully happy, forever and ever," he finished, then paused, and his smile turned thoughtful.

Therese stared back at him, her smile disappearing like the sun behind a cloud at a family picnic.

He had made her uncomfortable, he knew that much. He had such limited experience with choosing the right words—he really could only express simple things, despite his vast intelligence. After the teasing he'd gotten as a kid, he had become very good at changing the subject.

"Are you going to wear that?" He pointed to the men's swimsuit.

She tossed it into his hands. "It was in the package of things sent up to my room. I thought you might need it on this trip."

"Good. I could use a change of clothes about now."

It was already seven a.m. by the time Stuart had a usable signal again on his mobile phone. He left Bob on *The Emerald* at the dock and looked around. It was quiet—no one was around—the fishermen had sailed hours earlier. But still, he wasn't taking chances. He drove back to Eastwind, watching his rearview the whole way. No one.

In his study, Stuart pondered the possibilities. Had Paul been in Anegada to check up on him? Or on the production of ABT-55? What about the stem cell study? There was no way Paul could have known about that. Stuart was sure. But Paul did know about Richard's ABT-55 fix. Why hadn't he phoned Stuart to let him know he'd be arriving? That proved it, he thought. Paul had been trying to move in on Stuart's position. But how? Was he trying to take credit for ABT-55? Why was he murdered? Was he the kidnapper? Or was he trying to sell BioSys secrets? He was shocked at the thought; even though Paul had plagued him, it was hard to imagine, but it made the most sense. He was surprised to find he felt betrayed by his long-time associate.

Perhaps Fred was correct after all about security in Anegada. The ABT-55 facilities must be secure—even from nosy subordinates. If Stuart was right about Paul, it meant someone had insider info on his company. But what did they have?

Stuart moved to the couch, thinking to place a call regarding the securing of ABT-55. But to whom? He laid his head on the armrest to think. Who was running the production? He had been so wrapped up in using ABT-55 as a cover trial, that he had nearly forgotten the drug was actually being produced and that people were overseeing it—head scientists and quality assurance people and so on. But who were these people? And could they be trusted?

He could make another call, instead. And he would. He could trust his new brother. Tony would find out who stole his company's secrets, his million, and find Therese and Richard along the way.

Then, he could work on Eve.

After the ship embarked, and they had attended the mandatory safety drill, Richard and Therese removed their life vests and set off to explore the small vessel. The narrow hallways were empty, save for a few passengers finding their cabins. This was not a giant cruise ship—the kind that typically sailed with thousands aboard. Their vessel slept about fifty, and a local family managed the voyages. A skipper greeted them by tipping his hat and then disappeared behind a corner. At the end of the corridor, a turquoise sea greeted them. They stepped outside onto the open deck, the ship's speed apparent by the gusty breeze. They found shelter on two cushioned wooden chaises. Richard turned to Therese.

"What is it, Therese? I mean, besides the obvious. You look anxious."

"Well, it's just—I'm not sure how to begin, really, except to say that I know why you're here. I found you out." A smile crept across her face. "As Monsieur Poirot might say, 'The little gray cells have been working.'" She paused and turned serious. "What I'm trying to say is, I know about you and the stem cells."

Richard reclined back onto his chaise and looked out at the sea. The land they had departed was barely visible already. A woman and her small child toddled past.

"It's not what you think; I mean, it can't be what you think."

"Well, let me tell you what I think. I think my father recruited you, a noted stem cell expert, to come down here and work on some therapy—not chemotherapy. He plucked you from the corridors of the NIH easily; perhaps you needed money or a change of scene. Am I getting close?"

"Yes, Inspector," smiled Richard. "And what else do your little gray cells tell you?"

"Well, I have stewed for some time, and I still cannot come up with a reason—a motive—to explain why you would choose to lie to me, or others, about your true mission in Anegada." Richard turned quickly to her, his smile gone, replaced by a graveness in his eyes.

"I didn't lie, Therese, you must understand—at least, not in the traditional sense. I did not lie to you. I'm not capable of lying. Oh, damn it!" Richard stood, moved to the deck's rail, and looked down. Therese followed him.

"Now, you're scaring me. What have I dug up? Please, tell me, Richard." He turned to her slowly. "Please."

"Well, Dr. Holmes, you're correct about some of your deductions." He looked behind him, and then, satisfied that the deck was empty, continued quietly. "It's true; I have solid experience with stem cells. I wouldn't call myself an expert, exactly; no one could be at this stage. Your father had a theory about Alzheimer's—"

"Alzheimer's?" Therese's eyes widened.

"Yes. Please, don't interrupt; it really sets me off."

"Okay. Sorry. Please continue."

"Your father had some theories he wanted to test, based on our research—mine from the NIH and the work I've done with my father. Yes, he recruited me, and yes, I suppose I needed the money. But that's wasn't the reason I decided to get involved." He turned again to the sea. He wasn't sure he could look her in the eye. "There was more at stake. A big opportunity. You see, he wanted to use stem cells to stop the spread of Alzheimer's—on himself."

Richard turned to Therese, preparing himself for the worst. She clapped her hands over her mouth in surprise and muttered, "Of course! That makes perfect sense. Oh, father! My poor father. No wonder!" The hands on her mouth moved to her eyes, and she began to cry softly, leaning on the ship's railing.

"What have you done to him? Has it already—"

"Yes. You see, the trial is surgical. My father performed a surgery he'd wanted to try, but for which had no outlet or support. It's very novel, very cutting edge—"

"But what's involved, for God's sake?" Therese was upset, understandably, and Richard led them back to the chaises. Therese blew her nose with a cocktail napkin.

"You can speak to my father about the surgical particulars. It's almost non-invasive, and your father had little to no discomfort. It was practically outpatient. We're seeing some progress on his scans. The surgery was about a month ago. It's remarkable."

"How far along is his Alzheimer's?"

"Not very far, and that's one reason for the success, I'm sure."

"Tell me more about the stem cells. I thought the federal programs using them had been banned."

"Well, it's a bit more complicated than that; there are many sources of cells, and some work better than others. Some may not work at all. It is all very new, and there's no one experimenting on the human brain with them."

"But on the ones in your papers? How were those tests performed?"

"Some used tissue donated from reproductive clinics—"

"You mean fetuses?"

"Yes. And those were all legally acquired. But the other sources I mentioned are much less controversial—umbilical cord blood, bone marrow, heart tissue, even skin cells! It's almost like a transplant. Picture a suffering heart, for example. Fresh stem cells, to use an unscientific term, can be introduced to that heart and can thrive, defeating the dying cells and returning the organ to health—almost reversing its aging."

"That would be like a miracle, like a fountain of youth."

"Exactly. We are on the threshold of one of the most exciting advances in medical science ever."

"If it's so exciting, why aren't all the bio-med companies jumping on it? Because of the controversy with the stem cells themselves, I suppose."

"Of course. As a scientist, I try to stay out of the moral debate, especially because we've shown—your father, my father, and I—that even more benign stem cell sources can be effective. By the way, we've shown so in more cases than your father's—we've treated four other Alzheimer's patients."

"What was your 'benign' stem cell source?"

"Cells from a fresh cadaver, a patient who had donated their organs to science."

"I see." Therese shivered and held her arms close to her body. She blew her nose again. "It sounds like fiction, like *Frankenstein*, what with you mentioning fresh cadavers and all."

"That's nothing new in medicine." He placed his hand on hers. "Shall we go inside? You're shivering like crazy."

"Yes, but there's one more thing." She took her hand away gingerly, to catch tears with her balled-up napkin. She bowed her head, shaking it in frustration. "Poor Dad! How desperate he must have been to undertake something so radical!"

"Yes, I think he was. But we certainly did him no harm, and he may even beat the disease. But he—well, maybe he wanted to be a pioneer. After all, he's spent his life introducing live-saving drugs to the world. Life-saving drugs! Really, you shouldn't worry about his health, not now, anyway."

"But his behavior! It's been so wretched! He's been cruel, strange, and short with people, even me. I wondered what was wrong with him. Is his behavior a side-effect of the surgery?"

"I have no idea; I'm not a clinician. We could speak to my father about that. I noticed he has been irritated, but I figured that was his way of dealing with stress, and perhaps he'd always acted that way. He is, after all, a man with great, great responsibility. Perhaps that power was threatened—"

"By what? Disease?"

"Well, yes, or who knows what else, and it's making him depressed. That would make sense."

"Yes, I suppose." Therese looked out at the sea, and the boat turned slightly, so that a pool of sun warmed her chest. She leaned her head into it to collect its energy and took a deep breath.

"I have it, too, you know. Early Alzheimer's. They called it MCI, mild cognitive impairment. At Stanford, they saw it on a new kind of scan."

Richard sighed and leaned on the railing, taking one step closer to Therese. He didn't know what to say.

Therese continued. "They said that in combination with my blood work—oh, Richard! Of course, it's genetic! They asked if anyone in my family had—and well, I didn't know. I didn't know."

It took all of his courage to face her. "Therese, the work we've done here is going to pave the way for a whole new family of drugs, drugs that work on a molecular basis. They're being born, right now, today. I may not know many things, but I do know what I've seen in my lab, and it is astounding. We—you and I, and your father and my father—will see it along. Don't you see?"

Therese smiled, thinly. "You're the second person to try to reassure me…to tell me science will save us all. How do you know if I'll die of it or not? Science may have some answers, but not all of them. Why do you doctors and scientists think you know everything? You don't know—"

"It's our job to know. It's my life's work." He spoke, but then realized how hollow his words sounded. He couldn't promise, but he could intensify his research work.

"You're wrong. Not everything is quantifiable like that." She took a long look at Richard, then at the sea. "Your dad thinks he's been chosen by God to be a surgeon. To save people."

Richard looked at the water, and then back to Therese. "Well, how do you know he hasn't been?" Richard winked, Therese's point taken.

"Touché," Therese sighed.

A sea bird landed on the rail next to them and squawked loudly, as if weighing in on the discussion.

"But, seriously, is it all numbers for you? Facts and hypotheses?"

Richard avoided her eye. Because he was uncomfortable talking about emotions, and he didn't understand his own, he was easily angered. He was frustrated with people so often! Why couldn't she just let it go? "More reliable, yes. Better than people, most of the time, if that's what you mean."

"Well, I didn't mean—"

"All the noise, and interruptions, and confusion—all those things, the wrong words—they're caused by people, you know. They get in the way."

Therese touched Richard's arm, an offer of truce. He jumped slightly, and she withdrew her hand.

"I didn't mean to upset you, I just—" Therese noticed he would not meet her eyes and looked panicky.

He knew what she wanted him to say. The whole world wanted him to think as they did—why? Why couldn't they just accept him for who he was? People had asked him all his life about his opinions, his feelings, on matters. Of course, he had feelings—too many for his own comfort. There wasn't an animal he didn't empathize with, a detail on a passing tree he didn't appreciate, not a day went by in which he didn't automatically count the things around him, without even noticing, just to have something to focus on so he could avoid looking at all the other things that surrounded him.

"It's just that I prefer the facts. That's all." He exhaled deeply. Therese looked at him, waiting for him to look up at her, and he finally did.

"You know, I think I'm overwrought. I should really go and take a nap." He turned and retreated, and Therese watched him disappear inside a corridor, leaving her alone. She slapped herself on the forehead, fitting punishment, she felt, for the stupid dunce she had just been.

Carlo slammed the door of the Land Rover and cranked up the air conditioning. All he was thinking was, *After all this, after all this! Incredible.* It went against every instinct he had to stand up to his employer, but the last thing he was going to do for Stuart Franklin was kidnap a famous jazz singer for some wacked-out medical experiment. He started the engine. He caught a glimpse of Stuart in the driveway and saw him duck back into the house. The bastard thought about apologizing! Too late. Carlo put the engine in reverse.

He just wanted to help people, as his company BioSys did every day, Stuart had explained. But would the 'treatment' Stuart spoke of be permanent or have dangerous side effects? The whole idea of medical experiments made Carlo sick. Absolutely sick.

How could the guy be thinking about anything but Therese's safe return? It burned him up.

The sun was just peeking out over a cliff as he made his way out of the quiet residential neighborhood. The SUV's hot tires squealed beneath him as he cut the switchback turns too sharply. *The nerve of that man!* He was furious, and he didn't mind taking it out on the car. And what about the million bucks Stuart blew? Who had taken it? It was clear, even to "inexperienced" Carlo, that a third party had stepped in and taken advantage of the situation. Carlo had followed the hooded guy long enough to see that he didn't have Therese, but he did have information. Carlo watched the man ditch the gun and then get in a plane.

A savvy guy, too—looked experienced. Let's face it. The guy had "mob" written all over him. He had tried to explain it to Stuart, but Stuart didn't want to hear he'd been conned. Carlo rounded a blind corner, accelerating.

A millisecond later, he slammed on the breaks and just barely avoided smashing his nose on the steering wheel. "Of all the damn things!" he shouted, although the mother duck and her ducklings, six inches from his front bumper, could not hear him. They waddled across the street in an orderly fashion, the smallest at the end of the line, struggling to keep up. He pulled the car onto the sandy shoulder and took a deep breath, watching the ducks disappear through a swampy hedge. On their way to breakfast, he supposed, and immediately his own stomach grumbled. A warning tone sounded from the dash, making Carlo jump in his seat. He looked down to see the engine light flashing red. A computerized voice announced, "The engine has overheated. Please attend to this matter at once. I repeat, the engine—" Carlo got out of the truck and kicked the door closed behind him. He would leave the damn thing to talk to itself!

On foot, he headed into town. To his relief, Ferdy's Tropical Tea Café was open, and he smelled eggs frying. He took a seat and waved hello to the ever-friendly Ferdinand. The cool, thick adobe walls seemed to create a breeze against his skin, and he sighed deeply, trying to let go of his anger.

After friendly banter with Ferdy and a bite or two of food, reason returned. Where the hell was Therese? That was the most important thing. When he followed the hooded guy to the plane, he'd gotten close enough to determine they didn't have Therese. Hell, they'd never even seen her. Another guy—another professional, had flown them away after Carlo overheard, "Francis' brother won't mind seeing this," patting the briefcase, and, "fifteen-dollar bug made him a cool million!" Laughs all around. Carlo had heard enough to be sure the mob was involved. Francis's gang excelled at the double-cross. Perhaps they'd done the kidnapping, but let Therese go, or something went wrong, but they made the call for the ransom money anyway. That sure sounded like how Francis used to operate. But try telling Stuart that! *Of all the stubborn, arrogant…*

Therese would need things—money, clothing, maybe even food. Stuart seemed to think she was with Richard, thought Carlo as he took another swig of the deep-roasted local coffee, but he was a scientist, not a bodyguard. If anything else was going on, Therese could be in danger. Of what, he couldn't say. In either case, Carlo had to find them, before someone else did.

He had never made use of the personal data accessory Stuart had given him, but fortunately, he had it with him now. He took it out of its stiff leather holster and turned it on. It beeped reassuringly. The one thing he remembered Stuart showing him was the local listing feature. This thing could give you phone numbers of restaurants, travel agencies, hotels, and other local services. He used the touch pad to start finding information on the web.

Up popped all the local information Carlo wanted—and not only for Anegada, which was, of course, very small, but all the surrounding islands. Even Florida! Ferry times, hotel phone numbers, he had it all. He laughed aloud. He would find Therese in a few phone calls!

In fact, it took a few more. Therese had been clever, using a false name that perhaps only Carlo would have guessed—Marie Duchampes, the name of the baby girl who drowned in the tragic flooding some years back on Anegada. After the flood, Carlo had helped Therese with her evacuation plan for the island, and he, too, had grieved for the little girl ever since. Carlo paid the bill and bid farewell to Ferdy, who asked about Therese and why she hadn't been in the café lately. "I think she's off having fun," replied Carlo, immediately regretting the white lie. He was superstitious about such things—say one thing, and make the opposite happen.

"Those were the days," lamented Ferdy as he flicked a dishtowel over his shoulder and laughed.

Stuart also sped in a fury down the switch backed roads, heading for his office. He, too, slammed on the brakes at the blind curve, but only because he wanted to reverse the car. He was delighted to see the unmanned Land Rover on the shoulder. With a swiftness that surprised even him, he retrieved a long hunting knife from the glove compartment, leapt from his own vehicle, and plunged the knife into the front left tire of the Land Rover. For good measure, he slashed the front right tire, as well. Then he hopped into his own car and drove away, this time observing the speed limit, a gleam of satisfaction in his eye.

That afternoon, after getting Tony settled into Eastwind ("Nice digs," Tony had exclaimed when he'd entered the mansion), he flew to New York.

The first thing Tony did once he was alone in the house was look around Stuart's den. He'd been briefed on the previous night's events—the visit from the incompetent bodyguard, the ransom call, the money handover, the dead stiff, the dumping of the body. Tony had complimented Stuart on his presence of mind with the body. Turned out the dead guy was an asshole, anyway, so Tony decided not to work that angle just yet. The key was to get the million back and find the daughter before the trail went cold.

Tony sat in Stuart's office chair and looked around. The call seemed like the best place to start, so he looked at the phone's incoming call history. Many local numbers—one that corresponded to the time Stuart received the kidnapper's demand, but then another call, a bit later, from a non-local number.

At 4:30, Richard knocked on the door of Therese's cabin. To his relief, she answered right away. Her hair was wrapped in a towel, and the smell of flowery bath water filled the corridor. Richard tried to hide his natural reaction any intense smell, which was to cringe and flee, and smiled.

"I'm glad you're here."

"Me, too. I mean, I'm glad you're here, too," said Therese, awkwardly.

"I was hoping you'd be hungry; maybe we could have an early dinner? I'd like to explain some things. About the stem cells, I mean."

"Great," said Therese, thinking this was the information she needed to help her father. "I just need a few minutes. I'll meet you in the restaurant, okay?"

"Ms. Duchampes, right this way, please." The maitre d' led Therese and Richard past a sumptuous seafood buffet to a quiet corner of the dining room. The table was large, as Richard had requested. Richard turned to the host. "May we have some extra paper napkins?"

"Of course, sir." The host's evening wear indicated his island homeland: an elaborate chocolate-brown design, reminiscent of fern leaves, hand printed on a long, crisp, white cotton shirt, tied with a hand woven leather belt. He returned instantly with a stack of paper napkins, a contrast to the linens already set on the table.

Richard pulled a hotel pen from his pocket. "I'm going to explain all this to you, in pictures as much as possible. No more secrets," smiled Richard.

Therese's eyes lit up. "I'm ready. Hit me."

And so the long, but interesting evening began. Between ceviche and lobster salad, Therese watched Richard sketch on the napkins. She learned about mitosis and necrosis, then cell markers and mutations, plaques and proteins. Then coffee and crème brulee, neurons, and neurogenesis. Richard cited experiments done in primates that showed where new neurons, or brain cells, had grown and for how long. He spoke of the concept of replacing non-functioning neurons with new ones and the process of differentiation and proliferation—getting the good cells to mature and spread. He went on to tell her about the exciting work that had been done with embryonic stem cells—startling work that showed progress for patients with heart disease, diabetes, and possibly Alzheimer's and Parkinson's. For instance, he explained, an injection of embryonic stem cells into the coronary artery after thrombosis could escape into the heart muscle and change into adult myocardial cells, rebuilding the damaged area to near-normal function. He discussed the different kinds of stem cells—from different sources—and framed the controversy over cloning. He even spoke of the idea of cancer stem cells—stem cells so powerful that they could take over and cause cancer themselves. Therese was so engaged, she was surprised to see the sun setting in orangey beams across their table, as Richard made another drawing to illustrate a point.

A new maitre d' appeared, his predecessor having been replaced hours ago. "We'll be arriving at the port shortly," he announced. "There will be a shore-side soiree this evening, which you are invited to attend. I highly recommend it; it's quite entertaining."

Therese stood, looked out the window, and gasped. The island of Guadeloupe loomed, covered in lush greenery, volcanic peaks emerging from the western side. In the last light of day, it glowed, like someone shining a flashlight on a pile of emeralds. She'd been so engrossed in Richard's primer on stem cells that she'd not taken in the scenery. Standing now, for the first time in many hours, her ankle throbbed, reminding her that this trip was not a sightseeing tour. She limped back to the table, where Richard popped up to assist her.

"Your ankle, it's—"

"Yes, starting to bother me again. I thought I had it licked."

"Well, it's not even been twenty-four hours. I'll get some ice."

Richard disappeared, and Therese managed to turn her chair to face the view without using her foot and dragged another chair alongside to prop her leg on. She sighed and was suddenly aware of the hour. She'd been awake over fourteen hours, but it felt like twenty-four now that her brain was filled with the complex issues surrounding stem cell technology. She watched the island's vegetation get closer and began to see shops along the dock. Then she saw a flock of bats emerge, black dots against the deep blue sky, flying with orderly speed, out for their nightly hunt.

Stuart emerged from the jet onto the landing strip at White Plains, NY. Night had fallen. *So early*, he thought to himself. *What was the date*? He glanced at his watch. Of course, it was already July, and the days, like his short-term memory, were getting slightly shorter.

His stomach grumbled and his ears rang as he let himself into the car he always kept in White Plains, the key conveniently taped to the rear license plate. *Now that, I remembered*, he congratulated himself. The car roared to life, and he began the trip into New York City.

Unfortunately, he wasn't feeling well. He would admit that to himself, but only to himself. For about a month, he had felt quite well, and saw his memory improving. But now, well—the treatment was obviously wearing off. That's why he was on this mission tonight. Bob said the treatment couldn't "wear off," but what did he know? The man was guessing. That's what he paid him to do, wasn't it? He could guess some more, as soon as tomorrow, if things went as planned.

He crossed into Manhattan and headed south, the twinkling lights of the city calling him like a beacon. In the Eighties, it occurred to him. He had no supplies. What was he supposed to do if there was a fight, resistance? He pulled over at a random spot and jumped out of the car, causing much honking and yelling. He saw a corner convenience store and entered. The door's bell clanged loudly behind him, announcing his presence.

"Hi there. Where's your duct tape?"

"Duck tape?" answered the elderly Korean woman behind the counter. "Duck tape. Hmmm, try back there." She motioned to the back of the store, and Stuart went. When he saw the small hardware section of the store, other ideas popped into his head. Was this what thugs always did? What a job! Why had he ever bothered involving another person? This could be done by anyone, and so innocently. Adrenalin began to flow through his body and he felt better, encouraged, even, by the hum of the fluorescent lights, and instant access to everything he assumed he needed.

Stuart purchased three rolls of duct tape, two packages of laundry line, three rolls of toilet paper, and four packages of Tylenol PM. He said goodbye to the shopkeeper and ran to his illegally parked car.

"The Indian people who first inhabited this land called it *Karukera*, or 'Island of Beautiful Waters,'" explained the guide as the ship guests hovered around the bonfire, which was just sparking to life. The sand still held the heat from the day, and Therese dug her stocking feet into a pile of it. The effect was like a warm massage. A man with a glamorous tray of hors d'oeuvres bent and offered her a Creole conch fritter, which she devoured, even though she had just eaten. The guide continued, speaking from a small stage, the ocean behind her. The palm trees swayed in the slight breeze.

"As you probably know, this is not really an island, but an archipelago, comprised of two main islands and three lesser ones: La Desireade, Marie-Galante, and Les Saintes, which is itself a group of islands. Perhaps the first settlers were inspired by the three waterfalls that dot the Western half, known today as Basse-Terre."

Two local women in native dress began to mingle with the crowd, handing brightly colored masks and headscarves to the ship's passengers.

"Being a French *departement,* or state, Guadeloupe is a great culinary center. If you visit the markets in the morning, you may think you are in a tropical arrondisment of Paris, seeing the array of fresh produce, local meats, and shellfish. You will see women, mostly, haggling for a fair price. The Guadeloupians take their cooking very, very seriously, and in August, have a national holiday to celebrate this extraordinary local art. It is called the *Fete des Cuisinieres*, or "Festival of Woman Cooks," and we are going to reproduce it for you this evening!" The crowd cheered, apparently having been anticipating this treat. A local woman approached Therese and held out a bright red headscarf. Her skin was as black as night, and her giant bosom was lined with shiny purple beads. Huge gold hoops hung from her earlobes, and a scarf covered her head. Therese held the scarf and attempted rather gracelessly to wrap it around her own head, studying the woman before her. The woman chuckled. "No, no, cherie. I do. I do." She grabbed the scarf and leaned over Therese, tying it efficiently and quickly. Therese watched the woman's hands, silky from cocoa butter and fast as lightening.

"The festival honors the Christian martyr Saint Laurent, who was the patron saint of cooks. The ladies in the group are now be given a costume fitting for the event, so that they, too, can assume the role of guardians of Creole cooking. And the men—well, it's your job to don a mask, and most importantly, pour the rum." A wine cart was wheeled toward the crowd, covered in jars of brightly colored rum in wide-mouthed jars, some of which held suspensions of fruit. A steel drum band appeared and struck up a festive Caribbean melody. It was an instant party.

Therese was draped in a generous apron, and plastic shiny bangles now lined her arms. The woman added the finishing touch—a garland of beads around her neck. Then all the women were herded to a cooking area set up behind the stage—and what a setup it was. An outdoor brick oven formed a center island, and stainless steel workstations had been placed around its perimeter. Water boiled in a giant pot, heated by a small fire pit in the sand. The countertops were stacked with piles of brightly colored chilies, limes, coconuts, and glistening bunches of cilantro and parsley. Piles of freshly grated ginger and coarse sea salt sat in hand-worked wooden bowls, a mortar and pestle nearby. Therese looked up and saw Richard waving to her, his mask slightly askew, the bonfire behind him, and she laughed aloud at the silly sight. She noticed he stood slightly outside the group.

The women from the cruise ship were given small tasks, like chopping garnishes, while the real Creole ladies finished already-prepped delicacies. Therese was given a pineapple to dissect. Thanks to years of watching Hattie whip up tropical foods back at Eastwind and her own cooking acumen, Therese knew exactly what to do. She adapted quickly to the bustling outdoor kitchen and assisting other women with the parsley and cilantro, allspice, cloves, and garlic. Blenders whirled, choppers chopped, and soon the hallmark smells of the island wafted across the beach. Therese turned to the center of the kitchen in time to see a small family of crayfish doused in the pot of boiling water. Next, land crabs were added to the same water, and then both entrees were pulled out and splayed onto a cutting board.

The pace was very fast, and Therese was energized. The land crabs were expertly chopped, seasoned, and then put back into their original shells for serving. The crawfish were doused with rum and flambéed over the open fire. Another group of ladies assembled small trays of condiments: fresh ginger, dollops of various chutneys, lime wedges, and okra. It was a dizzying array of sights and smells.

Then, just as suddenly as it had begun, the steel drum beat ceased, and the Creole women gathered the cruise women together, and they all joined hands in a circle around the fire. The Creole women began to sing softly, using a mixture of Carib and French, and the singing got louder and louder. The ladies formed a procession, each holding a tray of food. The cruise women caught on and grabbed trays. The woman who had tied Therese's scarf led the line of woman cooks out to the waiting men and concluded the song. Then there was silence, save for the crackling of the bonfire.

It was a prayer, Therese saw, a blessing for the food about to be served, and perhaps an ode to Saint Laurent. Therese took a deep breath and closed her eyes as the Creole women did. A deep feeling of sadness surfaced in that moment, for her father. *He should be here*, she thought, *enjoying this with me, enjoying his last years, if they were indeed his last. Not meddling in some lab, not worrying about money, or the company, just simply here*.

The steel drum band struck up, and everyone cheered. Two long wooden dining tables were carried into the center of the group, the trays of food were arranged on them, and Therese was reunited with Richard. He passed her a small glass of rum, and they toasted. But Therese's face grimaced upon tasting the heavy, fruity rum.

"What, you don't like it?" laughed Richard. "I'm on my second round!" Therese handed her glass back to him. "Well, then, you're welcome to mine. Let's grab a plate; I'm dying to try the land crabs!"

Their plates filled to the rims, Richard and Therese turned away from the buffet line and came face to face with a brightly colored blue mask. Therese nearly spilled her plate.

"Oh, I'm sorry, sir; I didn't see you—"

The man reached and pushed up his mask. "But I saw you, Marie."

"Carlo!" gasped Therese, as he removed the mask.

"You know this man? How extra—"

"Well, of course, I do," Therese put her plate on a chair so she could embrace her old friend. "My hero! You found me!"

"You must be Dr. Richard Weigand," began Carlo, holding out his hand for a vigorous shake. Therese asked wildly, her face flushing, "Is Dad all right? Is he ill? Has something happened?"

Carlo didn't answer right away. "Let's go somewhere more private, where we can talk."

Carlo moved Therese away as a trio of musicians wove their way through the diners, and arrived at their spot. The song they sung was obviously a serenade, accompanied by an acoustic guitar and a small conga drum. The woman's voice responded to the man's, and they looked into one another's eyes with love and smiles. It was quite a performance. Therese wished she understood the local French, but it was so mixed with Creole she could only guess at the song's meaning, catching an occasional "l'amore" and "lumiere." Through the gaps between the musician's bodies, Therese saw Carlo look towards the buffet. He suddenly looked stricken, such a dramatic look that Therese also turned towards the buffet line. A few people were mingling there. One was a beautiful, tall blonde, the other a short, squat tourist, the third a tall man with a panama hat.

The song concluded and they all gave a hearty applause and tossed coins into the band's collection hat. The band moved on to the next group of revelers.

"C'mon. We have to get away from here, while the band hides us, at least for a few minutes. Richard, c'mon; follow me, discretely."

Carlo led them, food and drinks in hand, into the dense forest that rimmed the shoreline. From the other side of the trees, the bonfire could still be seen, but the foliage provided a screen that Carlo hoped would give them enough cover.

"You've got me worried, Carlo."

"You should be worried. If I'm not mistaken, you were recently kidnapped."

"No, you've got it wrong," interjected Richard, a little too loudly.

"Sssh, keep it down," warned Carlo, making a dampening gesture with his hands. Richard took another large swig of his rum drink.

"Is my father okay?"

"I wouldn't say 'okay' by any stretch."

Therese gasped in alarm. "What do you mean?"

"He's fine, outwardly. I mean, he looks normal, but he's acting weird. And he asked me to kidnap someone."

"What?"

"He said it was for a medical experiment."

"That doesn't make any sensssss," slurred Richard, clearly drunk. Therese took the drink out of his hand and tossed its contents onto a plant.

"He wanted you to kidnap a sick person?"

"I have no idea. I don't think it matters now, though. I told him, 'Hell, no.'"

"I'm getting vrrry confusssd," mumbled Richard, plopping his rear down in the brush.

Therese contemplated this news. "Does this mean you've been to Anegada? Oh, Carlo, did you find Fancy? Is she okay?"

"Recovering at the emergency vet."

Therese sighed. "Thank God. Don't tell me what happened to her; I couldn't bear it right now."

"Here's the thing; we have to get you to safety."

"What are you saying? Am I in danger?"

"Depends how you define 'danger.' The mob is here; I can tell you that much."

"What? Why? How do you know?"

"Because I already saw him. He's over at the buffet, and he's seen you."

"What are you talking about?"

"Listen, Therese, you know how we trust each other and always have?"

"Yes, of course." Therese's tone was barely contained.

"And you know how when I was a cop, I worked extra hard and found myself promoted and promoted?"

"Yes, you're scaring me again, Carlo."

"Well, I had a pretty good motivator. That's him, over there." Carlo pointed to the man in the Panama hat, who was looking around rather conspicuously. "My father."

"He's your—your father? And he's—"

"A major criminal, yes. Armed, powerful, influential—yes, all that. Therese, he's a killer. His name is Tony Rossetti. Remember that church fire last week in Chicago?"

Therese's face went completely blank. "Why did you never tell me this?"

Richard interjected from the damp ground. "Cured!"

"What?" Therese looked down at Richard, deliriously rocking back and forth on his haunches.

"We cured 'em."

"Of what?" demanded Carlo.

"I know his name from the daaata. Cured."

"What is he talking about?"

"Here's what we're going to do. You two need to go back out to the party and try to act normal. I need to get my father away from here and find out what his involvement is. We'll meet up again before the ship sails." Carlo dragged Richard up off the ground.

"But, Carlo, I don't know what to—"

"Just do what I say. And fast. Before he notices you've been gone." With a gentle shove, the two were back in the sand. Richard, knees wobbling, said, "Can you get me some more of that rummum?"

Therese took his hand and led him to join the others, who had just started doing what Therese assumed was a local dance. The bonfire was raging now, and Therese's eyes had adjusted to the island's darkness.

"Whoa!" Richard stumbled, his foot caught in a sand drift. Therese clutched his arm instinctively.

"Boy, this rum is strong! I nearly fell on my rear end, darliiiing," said Richard, regaining his footing. "Whoo! Me oh my," he continued, to no one in particular, his head bobbing.

"Richard, keep it together!" Therese held his head in her arms as they attempted to sashay in the sand with the others.

"I am not...I am not..." His eyes were slightly glazed. Had he only had two rums? That didn't seem too much. Just then, Therese's eye caught a glimpse of the man in the Panama hat among the dancers. She looked over Richard's shoulder, trying to follow the hat.

"Look, it's—" And then she lost sight of him as a man in a flowered shirt blocked her view. In the next moment, Richard's head collapsed on her shoulder. She gasped.

"Richard! What is it?" She sat him in the sand; rather, he brought her down to the sand with him, his body losing its strength. She examined his eyes, which rolled back into his head. His face was clammy and pale, his body like jelly. She slapped his face smartly.

"Richard, Richard," she coaxed. A small crowd gathered, but the music went on, the festivities heightening, the native women singing and clapping loudly. Richard's tongue slipped out of his mouth, apparently involuntarily. This alarmed Therese, and she looked at the gawkers.

"Help me, please. Can someone find a doctor? Oh, hurry, please!" She gently laid his body in the sand, resting his head on her lap. She leaned in to listen to his breathing, a challenge with all the noise, and took a quick survey of his vitals. She knew CPR, but that didn't seem to be the right thing to do. He wasn't choking, nor was he having a heart attack. He was getting paler and beginning to drool.

"Richard, hang on; help is coming!" With unexpected speed, Richard's hand reached up and grabbed her hair, pulling her toward him.

"What? What is it?"

Richard cracked his eyes and breathed heavily and with effort, like an asthmatic having an attack. She put her ear to his lips.

"It's—it's—poison."

Therese gasped.

"The rum. In the rum."

With surprising speed and dexterity, two medics in white uniforms appeared, apparently ship staff, stretcher in hand.

"Oh, thank God," began Therese as the men lifted Richard gently onto the stretcher.

"Drink too much, Missus?" The medic smiled and spoke with a broad Cockney accent.

"Um, what?" Therese stood, thinking what to say.

"It's a common problem, here, Missus," he continued, as his assistant began to administer oxygen.

"Well, no; he only had two. He said he'd had two."

"We'll take him back to the ship, to the infirmary."

"The ship? Well, I—" Her voice trailed off. The last place she wanted to be trapped was on the ship, for the poisoner must also be there, or would be later. But what choice was there?

"But he's been, he's been—" She lowered her voice, suddenly aware of the crowd that formed; the music had stopped. "He's been poisoned, I believe."

The medics looked back at her, quizzically. "Alcohol is poison, Missus. But we'd better get a move on. You can follow us." The men assumed a light jog en route to the ship, Richard bobbing slightly on the stretcher between them, and Therese followed, instinctively looking for Carlo the whole way.

Finally, the shore ended, and they ascended the planks of the ship. It sat empty, its lights on, like a forgotten jack-o-lantern. Therese tripped on a small step, her bad ankle reminding her of her limits.

Stuart slammed on his brakes. *If he wasn't damned!* There was his subject now, walking out of her brownstone. He watched, as he imagined a good detective would, as she fastened her light coat against the evening chill and tossed her hair over her shoulder, a movement she also made at the piano. Her shapely, pretty bare legs skipped down the steps. Her presence was lighthearted, and she was smiling like a schoolgirl. He turned the volume down on the car stereo, suddenly aware it was very loud. She might hear. Hear her own music!

This made Stuart giggle a little, and he didn't know why. The laughing seized him and avalanched into a full belly laugh, the likes of which he had not known in many months. He collected himself and continued to watch Eve Klein as she loitered on the corner. She was waiting for someone. Why? Wouldn't her driver escort her anywhere she would want to go?

Stuart had forgotten how bright city nights were. He could see practically everything, down to the color of her shoes, which were green, and she was an entire block away. He must be careful, very careful. This was not Anegada, where the dark of night was a heavy cloak. It had been easy to hide Paul's body there, for instance. Ah, but the sounds! The music of the city! He held his breath for a few seconds and heard at least four radios, doors being slammed, car horns blaring, a loud TV, and a couple fighting. While he might not have darkness as a cover, he had sounds. No one would hear. It was that simple.

If all went as planned, there would be very little to hear anyway. Stuart smiled to himself at the simplicity of the plan. A red sports car pulled up to the curb at an obnoxious speed. He watched as Eve collapsed her tall frame into the tiny car and heard her laugh. She was off with a young Turk, was she? Off for an evening of romance, was she? Well, no matter. It wasn't her love Stuart wanted, after all.

He alighted from his car, pulling his bag of supplies from the back seat, and headed for 82 Central Park West.

Carlo knew how to get his father's attention and take him away from the crowd—police lights. As it happened, he carried on his key-chain a small L.E.D. that was specular and blue enough to strongly resemble a police vehicle bulb. From a clearing, he used a shiny key and the blue L.E.D. to flash the lights in a way that looked like they could be coming from just offshore, as if from a Coast Guard ship.

Even Carlo was impressed with his father's reaction time—it was practically Pavlovian. Carlo watched as Tony made a comment to the blonde—probably some off-color remark about having to urinate, then skirted into the trees, out of sight.

Carlo was waiting for him.

"Hold it right there," he said, close enough to reach out and put a strong palm on his father's chest.

It was dark in the copse, so Carlo did his old man a favor and shined the L.E.D. on his own face.

"What the—" Carlo knew Tony would go for his weapon, but Carlo was ready with a strong arm to stop him.

"Relax. Even you wouldn't kill your own son. Or would you?"

In two seconds, Carlo had spun his father around and handcuffed his hands behind his back, the element of surprise working for him. He then proceeded to remove the pistol from his father's blue jeans and patted him down for other weaponry.

"You ain't no cop. Why you tryin' to act like one? Always were a fruitcake."

Silently, Carlo led Tony into the forest. It was very dark; the moon, which had shone brightly earlier, was being overtaken by clouds. Tony stumbled twice before Carlo forced him to sit on a log.

"What are you doing here, Dad?"

"I should ask you the same thing," panted Tony, his Panama hat askew.

"I used to be a cop, Dad. Now I protect Therese."

"Hah! Damn fine job you've done of it."

"Actually, I am pretty good at it. I figured out, for instance, that your old enemies attempted to kidnap her. I know from the arrow they used in her dog. Traced it back."

"Oh, did you, now? Well, they fucked it up, that's for sure. They ain't got nobody with any experience left over there, if you didn't notice."

Carlo took a deep breath. "Of course, I noticed. And you'll see; they'll get you one day."

"I don't know what you're talking about, son. Now why don't you uncuff me, so we can have a civilized conversation?"

"Let me remind you, then. Toddlers gasping for breath, trampled beyond recognition in the mayhem. Old ladies, dead from black smoke inhalation before they were charred. Bits of arms and legs in the air. Is this ringing any bells?" Carlo was trying not to scream, but it wasn't easy.

"Son, you're dreamin'! You made a lotta assumptions just now. How could I pull off something like that, anyway? Think about it, fruit! Just an old, sick guy, like me? You better let me outta these cuffs before I start screamin' my head off. Then the real police'll come runnin', and it won't be me they want."

Carlo moved behind his father and put the pistol to his temple. "Don't think about going anywhere until you answer my questions." He uncuffed his father and stepped in front of him, aiming the gun with a steady hand.

"What is it you want to know?" Tony asked, standing and rubbing his wrists—as if there were no gun pointed at him and they were at a cocktail party. He was fearless.

"What's your involvement with BioSys?"

"Oh! Is that all?" Tony started to chuckle. "My involvement is that Mr. Stuart Franklin gave me my life back."

"How?"

"Yeah, you been too busy slavin' over a hot stove to know that I been locked up in a hospital for Alzheimer's patients for four years. And then one day, my luck turned, and I got picked randomly to undergo a new procedure. And here I am. Checked outta that dump for good."

"Are you joking?"

"Could I make this up? Long story short, I was back in business. I gave Stuart some seed money, some cash to start a new enterprise centered on this treatment. Least I could do, seeing as the man saved my life and restored my mental faculties. It was getting harder for him to use his cash, so I helped him out. Nothing new there; it's my area of expertise, moving the stuff around. But then we got a little problem when the floater showed up in Anegada."

"What floater? Who was it?"

"Guy inside BioSys who got a little too talkative."

"And he involved Francis' guys, and then there was a screw up."

"Bingo. Francis' brother thought he could make off with some cash, at least. Then he had to get rid of the middle man."

"The BioSys guy." Tony nodded. "But what did he want? Who did he talk to?"

"That's what I'm here to find out—and who was backing him."

"And let me guess—reclaim your unmarked cash."

"Of course! It was stolen from me. I'm out a million bucks, maybe more; who knows what else has happened. I intend to get it back and protect my investment."

"Don't you dare go near Therese."

"She ain't my investment. Richard is!"

"What do they want from him?"

"I'm not sure. He's a very talented man, however, and he's the secret to this whole thing coming off. We just want him back in his little cage, all safe and sound. And you, my son, are going to make up for lost time and help me get him there before someone else grabs him."

Carlo stood. The moon was barely a sliver now, but it was enough to see the smirk on his father's lips.

"I came here to bring Therese home safely, not get involved with your scheming. I won't help you. Ever."

"Well, it's too late for that. I believe you're already involved in this 'scheme,' as you put it. Do I need to remind you that the prosecutor will call your involvement 'kidnapping'?"

"I didn't kidnap anybody!"

"Stuart told me today that that's what he'll say in court. You shouldn't have made him so mad, son."

"This is insane. I didn't do anything. I have witnesses that saw me here."

"Carlo, we're talking about Stuart-fucking-Franklin here. Get real! You don't stand a chance."

"I don't believe you."

"See what the judge says, then."

Carlo was aghast at his father's baiting. "Judge!"

"See, you need me, son. Stick with the plan, and there will be no judge. By the way, I saw a picture of you at Therese's. On her mantle. I've been watchin' you all night. A chef, my ass!" Tony slapped Carlo's face and laughed, then turned away. Carlo watched him cross the sand on the now moonless beach.

Therese looked back at the festivities on the shore. From where she sat on a deck chair on the docked boat, it all looked so innocent, so beautiful. Yet, out there, somewhere, was someone who wanted to harm Richard. She began to hobble in the direction she had seen the medics heading, using the guardrail for support.

First, the poison. If it was poison, why? If the person after Richard needed information, why try to kill him? He would be no good to them; unless, of course, they didn't actually want information. *Maybe they wanted less.*

Therese turned the corner and was relieved to see a sign that read "Medical Centre," with an arrow. She continued to hobble, her ankle smarting. Perhaps he wasn't poisoned, her reasoning continued. Perhaps simply drugged—to facilitate taking him away?

Who had she seen at the party tonight? She searched her memory, but had trouble pinpointing anyone as out of place. Besides, she was preoccupied with her kitchen duties and absorbed by the display of local culture. She hadn't exactly been aware of her surroundings.

She neared the Medical Centre door and heard loud moans emerging from beyond its walls. She quickened her pace, anxious to be of assistance.

She turned into the doorway just in time to see Richard vomit violently all over the floor. The medics nudged him back onto the makeshift hospital bed, and he groaned. Therese approached.

"Oh, Richard!" She rushed up to him. He was very pale and shaking.

"Probably more coming up, Missus; you might want to stand back. We've given him a stomach cleanser to get the stuff out of him."

Therese stepped back into the hallway. She had to close her eyes and think. Perhaps the poisoning was only meant as a distraction. But from what? Or whom? Therese began to pace in the narrow corridor. She stopped at a porthole window and looked though it, though not really seeing. Dark figures danced along the shore—her fellow cruisers, she supposed—although they were hardly more than shadows thrown from the firelight. Then there was Carlo's father. What was he doing here?

Her thoughts were interrupted by the painful noise of violent retching. She left her thoughts and rushed to Richard's side.

"Oh, Richard, I'm so sorry!"

"Don't worry, I'm—well, I'm coming around, at least." Richard slouched in a chair as the medics mopped the floor. The smell was almost unbearable. "At least I made it to the wash basin this time." Richard looked up at Therese. His eyes were rimmed with tears, his face pale and sweaty. She consoled him with a hug. "What the hell did I drink?"

"I've no idea," began Therese. The medic with the Cockney accent interjected.

"Simple herbs 'round here cause all kinds of reactions. It's witch doctors we got here, mate. Old ladies fix up potions—hell, all of them do it. It's their religion, like."

"You mean, like, voodoo?" asked Richard as he wiped his brow on his shirt.

"Suppose so. Anyone can get their hands on 'em; they just ask their grans. Part of the culture, you might say."

"How did you know what to give me?"

"Good guess. We gets lots of these cases round Carnival, so we know it when we spot it."

"What should he do now?" Therese asked.

"I imagine he should sleep and keep himself hydrated. There's nothing we can give him; just got to let nature do its thing, so to speak. It'll be a couple days—"

At that moment, Richard turned even paler and dashed to the sink for another episode. Therese stood, helpless. As he emerged from the sink, she bolstered him with her shoulder.

"Let's get you back to your room. There's plenty of bottled water there, and I can get a nice, cool compress for your face."

The two hobbled back into the deserted ship corridor, one limping from injury, one from utter weakness.

"Well, we make a sorry pair, don't we?" Richard tried a faint smile.

"It's not so bad, now I know that you'll recover." She glanced at Richard for confirmation of this assertion, but he still looked pale, and his limbs trembled involuntarily. "Any guesses about who might have—"

"None. I'm getting nervous; we obviously haven't lost this person. And now it's clear that the target was me."

"Yes, although I did hand my glass to you, remember?"

"True, but maybe I'd already had enough poison."

"Don't worry about the poisoner now. We have to get off this ship."

"When?"

"As soon as I find a way. In the meantime, you need to rest." Therese propped Richard against the wall and turned the key in Richard's door slowly. What she expected to see when the door opened, she wasn't sure, but she hesitated on the threshold, anyway. Richard flung himself on the bed, and Therese entered, switching on the lights. She opened the tiny closet door, then the bathroom door, even pushing aside the shower curtain.

But the room was untouched. Richard's few belongings appeared intact. Therese fluffed the pillows and rested Richard's head on them, caressing his forehead. He closed his eyes.

"Sleep now; I'll watch over you," she whispered.

After she had fetched a damp washcloth from the bathroom and placed it on his forehead and eyes, she took a seat next to the bed, and spotted the sketches Richard had drawn earlier that day, the ones that illustrated the points he had been making about biochemistry. She picked them up and began to study them again. Richard began to breathe deeply; he was already asleep.

Therese stood up quietly, not wanting to wake the patient. She had the urge to pace. The room was small, however, so she found herself at the porthole window instead, where she saw that a fine mist was beginning to envelop the ship. She watched the fog swirl in the light thrown from the hull's lights. She had a nice view of the gangway and observed that people were drifting back to the ship, their faces distorted by the fog and harsh sodium vapor lighting along the dock. She tried to study each one as they ambled aboard, jolly from rum and dancing.

One could be their adversary, but which one? It was almost two in the morning; the party had evidently been a success. Had anyone else ingested the poisoned rum? No, the herbs must have been slipped into just one—or two?—glasses, glasses the person knew were intended for Richard and herself. And now, here they were—sitting ducks.

She focused her attention on the faces boarding the ship. Perhaps a list of passenger names would reveal something, but she had no idea what. She spotted the man with the Panama hat—Tony. Tony Rossetti was boarding the ship, followed by the other two she had seen with him earlier. They must be a group, or family. They didn't resemble each other at all, however. The tall blonde woman was laughing. She was quite lovely, with striking features and a slim figure, handsome, with stylish clothes. She looked like a starlet or a model. In fact, she looked like someone she couldn't quite place. Perhaps some star she had seen on the cover of a magazine.

Just then, there came a giant sneeze from underneath the washcloth. She retrieved a series of facial tissues from the bathroom and sat next to Richard, who was attempting to prop himself up on his elbows. He blew his nose heartily and made a disgusted face. "The smell is atrocious," he said from behind the tissues. He collapsed back on the pillows, exhausted from his effort, and closed his eyes. "The damn smell may be forever lodged in my olfactories."

Therese resumed her seat at the room's small desk and looked at Richard, who pulled the blankets up almost over his face. Therese shuddered and realized she, too, was chilled. She got up and went to the thermostat. She switched it on, and it made a clanking sound, but Richard did not stir. Therese glanced at the bedside clock. If it was two a.m. now, they could probably get some form of transport by six or seven a.m. Best to let Richard sleep and see about getting a car or boat and finding Carlo, while avoiding Tony.

His olfactories?

Renting a car was the best idea Therese had. At least that would take them further from the ship that was making her feel more preyed upon each moment. With a sigh, she slipped out of the cabin and headed to the concierge. The door made a reassuring *click* as it locked behind her.

There was a chilling breeze in the open-air corridor, and Therese removed her apron and wrapped it around her like a shawl for extra warmth. The wet fog doused her face and made her instantly more alert. She walked quickly. At the end of the corridor she looked behind her to be sure she was not being followed, and saw the hallway awash with fog; her own cabin door was invisible.

She reached the concierge's desk, which thankfully, was located in an interior corridor.

"Hello," she began, removing the apron from her shoulders. Her cheeks were red and glistening.

"Well, good evening, Madame," beamed the older gentleman behind the desk.

"I'm glad you're still here. Can you help me to rent a car on the mainland?"

"Well, certainly. In fact, you needn't rent one. We have two cars on shore for day excursions, and you may use one, but of course, not tonight."

"Not tonight? But I need it tonight."

"Oh, Madame, haven't you heard? There's a mighty storm approaching."

"Nonsense. I've lived in these islands throughout my life. I can drive in a storm. If you'd like, I can leave a healthy deposit—in cash—"

"I don't mind the car, Madame, but you don't understand. The roads have been closed, since they will certainly be flooded."

Therese stepped over to the window and looked outside. "But it's not even raining!"

"No, but it will be. We have very sophisticated tools to gauge the weather because we cannot sail under certain conditions."

"Oh, of course. Do you think you will sail on schedule?"

"Certainly not."

This was good news in a sense; maybe she could get Richard off the ship on foot, if she had to.

"Thank you for your help."

Therese wrapped herself up again and pushed open the swinging door, where the cold air greeted her with a slap. It had begun to drizzle. She heard the drops hit the water below—*pling, pling*. How could she find Carlo? Maybe he was staying on the ship? *Let's hope*, she nearly said aloud, and she reversed course to the reception area.

As she approached, she realized it was doubtful the ship would let her see a list of passengers. In hotels nowadays, Reception wouldn't even give out room numbers. Offering money, her natural plan of attack, didn't seem to affect the ship's personnel. She quickly worked out a story in her head.

"Good evening," the young woman behind the desk greeted her. "Or should I say, 'Good morning'?" The woman glanced at the clock above her; it was going on three, and perhaps she did not welcome a visitor at this hour. Therese cleared her throat and attempted to lie.

"Hello. I'm in an awful bind; I do hope you can help me," Therese began, putting on as pathetic a face as possible. Perhaps she could make the clerk feel important and needed.

"Well, of course. Is something wrong?" The young woman looked concerned. *Good work so far.*

"Well, you see, this is quite awkward for me, and I'm a bit embarrassed."

"Oh, Madame, you needn't be. We're here to serve you. How can I be of help?"

"Oh, you are sweet, thank you. You see, there's been a strange coincidence. Years ago, I fell in love with a wonderful man, and he—well, he left me in quite an awful way," Therese let tears well in her eyes and decided to really go for it. "He left me after we got engaged, at the height of our love for one another. At least, what I thought was love." Therese saw sympathy on the young woman's eyes, and was encouraged. "I got over it, of course, after a year or so, and the man married a woman who had been in both of our social circles, but I hardly knew her. And they're here! On this ship! Of all the luck. But I can't remember her name! I know it sounds silly." Therese gave a little embarrassed laugh to keep up the charade. "I must have blocked it out. We were forced together tonight at the shore dinner, and I was just mortified to not be able to recall her name! I listened to try to hear him speak her name or introduce her, but he didn't. Surely, I will see them again on this voyage, and I just won't be able to sleep knowing I could be that embarrassed again. I wonder if you'd be so kind as to let me glance at the names of the people aboard—"

"Say no more, Madame! But let's keep it between us, if you don't mind." The clerk winked, and Therese mock-wiped her teary eyes in preparation to read. The clerk swiveled a computer monitor around. A quick scan of the names showed her no Carlo aboard. The name of the blond was immediately apparent, however, and Therese recognized her as an up-and-coming actress. But no other names looked familiar. Therese feigned relief and bid the clerk a good evening.

When she turned on her heels to go, she noticed a stack of complimentary newspapers. She grabbed one, realizing she hadn't had any news in over seventy-two hours, and curious to see if her kidnapping had been reported. Once safe from the eyes of the clerk, she opened the thin local paper.

The paper was a daily one, but it was already two days old. The lead story was about parliamentary actions in France and their potential impact on the island. There were many ads for local restaurants, but no mention of anything having to do with the Franklins or BioSys. But then, on the last page, was a headline that made her heart race. "Body found off Anegada—boating accident blamed." Therese covered her mouth when her eyes landed on the name of the body identified: it was her father's long time business associate, Paul Westin.

Therese sprinted as best she back to her cabin, each step becoming more painful on her damaged foot. She had to find Carlo; he was her only resource. Perhaps Carlo had left a voice mail iterating a plan. She hurried back down the exterior corridor, checking the posted signs to be sure she was in the right hallway. She had to get quite close to the signs to read them; the fog now coated everything in opaque white.

A quick stop in Richard's room was in order. She found his door and opened it, anxious to be warm again. She flicked on the lights—hadn't she left them on?—and walked to the bed.

Richard was gone.

The door to the penthouse unit swung open, and Stuart stepped inside. He had eluded the doorman and the neighbors; his pace had been swift. With a sigh of relief, he closed the door behind him and switched on his flashlight.

He stood in an opulent hallway covered with framed photos and paintings, all arranged salon-style, crowding the walls with mismatched frames hung at artistic angles. The cornices were painted gold, and a chandelier dominated the tall ceiling. A quick scan of the entrance area led Stuart to believe there was no security system in place. "Incredible!" he whispered to himself, and marched into the next room, where he gasped at a grand piano framed by a giant window overlooking Central Park.

He leapt across the room and sat on the leather bench in front of the revered instrument. He placed his hands on the keys, tossing the flashlight to the floor. He breathed deeply, imagining he could smell the great pianist in the air. And in fact, he could smell her. Her scent lingered in the recently abandoned apartment like an echo. He cleared his throat and rubbed his hands together. Sitting in the dark in the penthouse, passersby could not see him, but he gazed over the park as if facing a black sea of audience members, blinded by the city's lights as one might be blinded by stage fresnels. With a triumphant smile, he cleared his throat and rubbed his hands together, and then, gingerly, he let his hands pluck out the first notes of the only song he had ever come close to playing decently, "Ave Maria."

He first learned the traditional hymnal in church, where he had played the Schubert version for piano with a sloppy hand, accompanying his mother's voice. The irony was not lost on him; he was certainly no Catholic, at least, not anymore. Music had become his only religion, and in its grasp, he played, even humming along quietly. After Eve's cells had begun to grow in him, he, too, would become a piano virtuoso. Of course, it would take practice—years, even, but he would be diligent, obsessed, driven by the anticipation of the elation his own hands could produce. The power he held at his huge company and his massive wealth would pale in comparison, for he would have the greater power of making people weep at his whim. The power of music would be his, and he would love something again.

He played the hymn again from the start, and then played it again, and again. When Eve walked though her front door, he was still playing. He waited until she approached him, her face aflame with anger and disgust. Her mouth moved, but he didn't hear her words, only the notes ahead on the next bar. He stood and clobbered her over the head with a vase that had held the flowers adorning the piano, and it shattered to the floor, having served a different purpose.

Chapter Thirty-Five

THERESE SCREAMED. It was the middle of the morning, but she didn't care. She screamed again, but a firm hand silenced her. The hand turned her body around.

Carlo stood there, not smiling exactly, but with a warm expression on his face. He removed his hand slowly. Therese's eyes were huge with confusion.

"He's gone, I know."

"What do you mean, 'you know'? Is he okay? What the hell is going on here?"

"I suspect he's out cold and safe. I have a good guess about who took him."

"Who?"

"My dad."

"Your dad?" Therese was exasperated.

"He got to him before I could get to you both."

Therese furrowed her brow. "He wants Richard because—"

"Let's walk and talk. It's getting late. Gather your things, and we'll be off. Unfortunately, I know where they are."

"You do?"

"I'm afraid so. He made me help him."

"What?"

"It's a long story. You need to find a coat. Fast."

"Where are we going?"

"I'll tell you on the boat."

Stuart dialed a number on his cell phone and looked at Eve's body, slumped into a seat on Stuart's commuter plane. There was a small trace of blood on her forehead from the blow, but otherwise she simply appeared to be sleeping. They had departed from White Plains just over two hours ago, and she was still out. He breathed a sigh of relief when Bob answered.

"We're on our way," he said cheerily.

"We?" Bob sounded sleepy, as if the phone had woken him. "What the hell time is it?"

"We'll meet you in about an hour for another procedure. You remember? The one I mentioned on your boat."

Bob rubbed his eyes and sat up in bed.

"You've got an adult?"

"Oh, yes. And not just any adult—that was the whole point, remember?"

Bob switched on his bedside lamp then fumbled for his reading glasses. The clock read 2:45. What the devil was Stuart rambling on about now?

"But I don't have the lab ready. Richard's not even here! And what about some advance notice?"

"You don't need Richard; you said so yourself. All we're doing is grabbing some cells, for the love of God." God now on his mind, Stuart began to hum "Ave Maria" into the phone.

"Okay, but you know it's risky. This is an adult we're talking about. The cells might not even be viable, and then we're going to freeze them, making them even less reliable. I can't predict—"

"I don't care. I want it done." Stuart had steel in his voice, overemphasizing each syllable for effect.

Bob rubbed his eyes again and sighed. "Okay, you're right; it's worth a try."

"There's the spirit!" exclaimed Stuart, and then he hung up his phone, smiling to himself. Suddenly, his smile vanished, and he felt himself go clammy all over. His heart raced, and the back of his throat itched with alarming intensity. He wiped his hands on his trousers and dabbed at his face with a handkerchief, but then it was upon him. He rushed to the lavatory and threw up in the toilet. He sat down to rest on the bathroom floor, which swirled in front of his dizzy eyes. He closed his eyes, and the spins seemed to subside. He shivered and cleared his throat, trying to relax his heart rate. In a few moments, he felt semi-recovered, and he pulled himself up from the floor, using the washbasin to support himself.

He ambled back to the main cabin and hovered over Eve's aisle seat. She looked peaceful, and upon reflection, almost angelic. He took a handkerchief out of his trousers pocket and dabbed the splotches of dried blood from her face with a tender hand; it occurred to him that he hoped he hadn't hurt her brain, especially after he had gone to all this trouble to snatch her. He maneuvered past her carefully, taking the empty window seat beside her. Slowly, he leaned down and rested his head in her lap. He closed his eyes and fell instantly asleep.

Therese trembled from the damp cold as she followed Carlo into the early morning. The fog had begun to lift, but a determined rain had taken its place. She wished she had her trusty raincoat to keep her warm and dry, but then again, she supposed she should feel grateful to have survived the kidnapping and poisoning. She began to jog, to keep up with Carlo and to stay warm. They passed a crew stairwell, where Therese spied a white cotton coverall, probably used for servicing the engine room. She didn't think twice. She stopped in the stairwell and donned the coveralls, which were actually heavy-duty canvas. They wouldn't be waterproof, but they were better than the useless fete apron.

"Where are we going?" she asked as they exited the gangway and set foot on a muddy walkway. He held her arm when she nearly slipped in the muck and guided them to pavement of the quay. Carlo broke into a run, and Therese followed.

The marina was starting to awaken, and as the sky brightened, Therese could see, about 500 feet away, a series of yachts. Seagulls diving for dead surface fish and perching on boats squawked at them as they ran. She smelled coffee.

"Ah, here it is!" panted Carlo, jumping to the deck of one of the smaller fishing boats. "Get in; we need to hurry."

Carlo revved the engine and deftly maneuvered the boat toward the breakwaters.

"When did you learn to boat?" called Therese, moving away from the spray.

"I didn't. But an engine's an engine, right?"

Carlo put the boat into a higher gear, and Therese nearly lost her balance and grasped a rail.

Soon they were in open waters, heading south, the big island of Guadeloupe on their right. In a few more moments, Carlo made a sharp right, and they circled the south edge of the island before heading north.

"Anegada?" called Therese over the noise of the engine.

"Yes, that's the plan. Look—I can see their boat!" Carlo pointed at small boat that Therese could barely discern in the rain, which was coming down harder now.

"Did you know about Paul?"

"Who the hell is Paul?" he called back as he accelerated the boat, looking ahead.

"You don't know?"

"No. Never heard of the guy."

"He's my father's vice president. And he's dead."

"Oh, so that's the guy that died."

"There's a connection—between Paul and your father."

"I'm not sure, but it turns out my father has a financial stake in the work being done by Richard."

"Hmmm," murmured Therese.

"And since it was clear Richard's life had been threatened, he decided to safeguard Richard himself."

"By drugging him, nearly killing him, and then stealing his sleeping body?" Therese was angry now. "And he made you help?"

"He threatened Stuart would implicate me in a kidnapping."

"My father would never do that! What kidnapping? The one he asked you to do?"

Carlo shrugged his shoulders, letting the gesture say everything.

Therese was still trying to digest the news that Carlo—her beloved Carlo!—was the son of a violent gangster and that her own father was potentially involved with kidnapping, when it occurred to her—

"Wait, Carlo! When did he want you to do that?"

"Tonight!"

Therese paused.

"So, how is your dad involved, anyway?"

"I guess he had Alzheimer 's disease."

"Had?"

Carlo threw his hands up, as if to say, "I don't know."

"But how did my dad get involved with—"

"With who? The mob? Listen, Therese. Nothing's for free, and you, of all people, should know that."

Carlo went quiet, concentrating on steering the boat through the blinding rain. The small vessel was taking a beating, creaking and moaning, water lapped over its sides. "I'm not defending either of them; just telling you how it is." Therese looked into the murky sea, the small boat holding Richard coming into closer view.

"Listen, Therese; you know I'm not like my father."

Therese was quiet for a few moments. "I know."

"You trust me, right?"

"I do. I've known you for a long, a long time—since my father hired you."

"Yeah, that's right. Well, today, he fired me."

Their small craft was within visual range of the other boat. Therese saw lights on in the hold. Carlo's boat was more powerful, and soon they were close enough that Therese could make out Richard in the hold, sitting down. She couldn't see if he was conscious or not.

As they inched parallel to the other ship, Therese saw Tony inside, piloting the craft. She watched him try to outmaneuver his son, prevent him from getting closer, but soon they were right next to each other, nose to nose. The islands of St. Kitts and Nevis passed in minutes to starboard.

The image of Tony at the wheel made her think of it. She slapped her hand to her head in frustration, then turned to Carlo and asked excitedly, "Carlo, what kind of car does my father drive in New York?"

He looked at her, puzzled. "A Mercedes, 300d type, 1957. It was their fanciest limo-style car then."

"That's right! Also known as the Adenauer, because it was driven by Germany's then-president, Mr. Adenauer. Do you hear that? 'Add-en-auer' What a kid might hear as 'eatin-our'!"

"Therese, hang on; we have to make a sharp turn," called Carlo, careening the ship sharply to port. Anegada was coming into view, and Carlo now had a good lead.

Therese went to the hold. She opened each latched container she could find, one after another, in a flurry. She found life vests—handy to have, sooner rather than never. She donned one, just in case, as Carlo careened dramatically again. Three or four latches, and nothing, then, near the aft, she found it—a first-aid kit.

"Therese," called Carlo from deck, "we're coming into port. I'll need a hand!"

Bob was soaking wet when he reached the lab. How he had slept soundly through such a storm he couldn't say. He was still sleepy as he prepped the mini operating room for the procedure, knocking things over and stumbling. *Damn that Stuart*! Operating at four a.m.—who ever heard of such a thing? Still, this would be a good learning experience. No matter how the adult cells performed in patients, they would have more valuable data, more publishable data. And there was certainly no better way to get it! The thought of a trial with volunteers signing up to have their stem cells extracted was crazy. It would never happen—never! The absurdity of the scenario made him laugh aloud, and he was again very glad to have met Stuart. He completed his prep and scrubbed up, now fully alert, just in time for Stuart's arrival.

Bob rushed to the door to assist his friend and employer, who looked pale and tired. Together, they lifted Eve's still-unconscious body to the operating table. Bob leaned over the body and stood up quickly.

"My boy, she's got a serious concussion."

"Has she?" replied Stuart, collapsing into a chair, exhausted.

"Well, yes. What did you do, clock her over the head?"

"She wasn't exactly coming voluntarily," Stuart sassed, rolling his eyes in disbelief.

Bob sighed audibly and checked Eve's vitals; Stuart yawned and leaned his head back, staring at the ceiling, listening to the whir of the air conditioning, fighting sleep.

Satisfied that Eve would do fine with a mild anesthesia, Bob draped the patient and administered the IV.

Therese and Carlo disembarked on Anegada, just as a gigantic streak of lightning filled the sky. The rain continued to fall, pelting their bodies, and covering the dock in mud. The wind howled, and Carlo led Therese to a shelter as they watched Tony approach the port.

"This reminds me—"

"I know," said Carlo. Therese was thinking about the awful flood.

"We don't have much time. We need to hurry. But we need Richard."

Therese and Carlo waited anxiously as the small boat moored, and soon enough, Richard was running from the ship, Tony close behind.

"Richard!" called Therese, motioning. When he reached them he said, struggling, "We have to get to my office. I've worked it out from what Tony said. My new ABT-55 molecule—it's not in production! We have to get the molecule fixed, right now!"

Tony ran up behind him. "You're not going anywhere without me," he cried, handcuffing himself to Richard.

"Oh, God, get those off me!" howled Richard, whose dislike for other humans was growing by the moment.

Therese interjected. "There's no time, Richard. It's going to have to wait. There's a bigger problem, and I need your help. C'mon, let's go!"

The four made their way through the blinding rain to a BioSys Land Rover. Carlo drove through the mud.

Bob stood under the glaring lights of the operating table, steady and focused. He had removed both of Eve's olfactory bulbs, as instructed by Stuart, without any problems and was adjusting her meds so she would come out of the anesthesia as gracefully as possible. Stuart snored nearby, having missed the twenty-minute procedure entirely. Bob adeptly packed and stored the tiny organs in a nearby freezer.

That was when the walls started to shake.

Fred was home, asleep, when his modified clock radio began blaring at him. Since he had programmed it, he knew the problem must be a breech at BioSys, somewhere. In seconds, he had his laptop up and running; he could monitor every building on BioSys property worldwide. When he found the site of the alarm, he did not hesitate. He brought the firewalls down with remote-control software, and in less than three minutes, the place was sealed. It should keep the perpetrators inside. Since it was not yet time for the morning shift to arrive, there was little risk of trapping employees. Although the plant worked around the clock, the building was about a mile away, and not reporting anything out of the ordinary.

Where the hell was Stuart? wondered Fred aloud, as he autoredialed Eastwind, then Stuart's cell phone, then Stuart's videophone, then Eastwind again. Fred tried the twenty-four-hour manned booth, which appeared to be operating normally. The phone rang and rang and rang.

Carlo blasted through the security gates of BioSys, setting off multiple silent alarms, and headed for the main building.

"Why was no one in the booth?" Therese asked, but no one replied.

"Look! Lights!" called Therese, as the lab came into sight. Carlo brought the vehicle to a halt, and Therese jumped out, just as the building emitted an eerie, loud, mechanical creak. Walls came out of the sides of the brick building, covering the windows with plates of reinforced steel! It was as if the building had its own armor. The building—and those surrounding, Therese saw—were transformed into grey tanks, camouflaging them against the stormy sky.

Just then, around the corner of the main building, two figures were seen, a wheeled hospital bed between them, a white sheet barely visible in the downpour.

"C'mon, hurry, Richard!" called Therese, grabbing his free hand, and the two of them—and the tethered Tony—ran, switch-backing between massive concrete barriers that kept cars from getting too close to the manufacturing facility.

Therese shivered as her father came into view. People assumed the tropics were always warm, yet on Anegada, she always seemed cold. Richard tripped behind her then Tony righted him. They were covered in mud, but they were gaining. Therese could hear the wheels of the hospital bed squeaking from the water trapped in its casters. She saw Bob, stooped over as he ran, trying to cover the patient with a flimsy umbrella that had just worked itself inside out.

"Dad! Bob!" Therese cried, waving her hands, but they only quickened their pace, the hospital bed nearly airborne as the trio made for the service road, an attached IV drip bag swinging wildly. Where were they going?

"The airstrip," called Richard, who knew the intricacies of the BioSys Anegada campus well, having mapped them out of loneliness.

He was right. The three turned into the open road, and Therese spotted a Cessna landing—choppy, but steady, down, down, into the mud.

"Dad," Therese cried again, as loud as she could—hoping the rain would allow him to hear her. He turned, finally, and he held up his hands: stop. She shook her head vigorously and continued, her feet slipping on a saturated patch of grass. She fell, crying out in pain from her bad foot, which was now thoroughly swollen, and began to bleed from a graze. Carlo caught up to her and leaned down to grasp her by the armpits.

"Are you sure you want to do this?" he said, hoisting her up, although he realized his input would not be a factor. Therese had inherited all of Stuart's fierce determination. She ran out of his arms, and he squatted on the grass, watching her limp—still making impressive progress.

"Wait! Dad, wait," she called, and an instant later, she was upon them. She put her hands on Eve's face and started slapping it, gently.

"You have to revive her, Bob!" she cried, trying to get her hands under Eve's shoulders, attempting to lift her to a sitting position.

"Therese, you have to leave. We have a delicate situation with this volunteer, and she must get on that pl—"

"Not yet!" responded Therese, moving the sheet away. "Eve!" screamed Therese. It had the desired effect. Eve moaned.

"This is unacceptable, young lady." Bob tried to put his body between Eve and Therese.

"Why am I—" moaned Eve, her eyes slits, opening to the chaos.

"We've got to get her out of here," Bob complained to Stuart, shoving Therese away from the hospital bed. "She'll ruin this."

"Eve, Eve!" Therese continued attempting to revive the barely-conscious singer by tapping her face, wrapping her arm behind her head, like feeding a baby.

"Therese, you must do as we say. We are in the middle of an important transfer. This patient is the link to a great advance in healthcare, and we must get her on that plane. There's no time to lose!"

Therese called to Carlo. "Come help me," she asked, getting her arms squarely behind Eve's shoulders. Carlo arrived at the gurney. "Help me sit her up."

"Just what do you think you're doing to my patient, Ms. Franklin?" boomed Bob.

"You'll see. Eve!" Therese shouted over the thunder.

"Huh?" replied Eve, her eyes slowly opening—completely now. Once she registered that she was not where she should have been—in her luxurious penthouse on Central Avenue or the bed of her lover, she screamed. Very loudly.

"It's okay. Shhh!" cried Therese, patting her shoulders. "Eve, I just need you to tell me something."

Bob began to wheel the gurney again, and Therese followed, practically leaning on the bed to stop it.

Stuart trotted along. "Listen," he began, trying to get Therese's attention.

But Eve yelled, "What the hell is happening?" She looked down at her attire and up again in horror—and then she saw Stuart looking back at her.

"You bastard! I'll take you for everything you've got. I'll—" Dr. Bob Weigand grabbed Eve's IV and added something taken from a coat pocket: benzodiazepine. Not only would it make her sleep, it would hopefully make her forget.

"What are you doing?" hollered Therese.

"Stay out of this!" retorted Bob.

"Eve, Eve, listen to me," Therese cupped the singer's face in her hands. "I need you to answer one question."

Therese retrieved what she needed from her coveralls—a small white packet from the first-aid kit. Therese broke the packet of smelling salts in half and shoved it under Eve's nose.

"Eve, can you smell this?"

Even quieted down, looking at Therese, who still clutched her face.

"What is it?"

"Can you smell it?"

"No. I can't smell anything."

Richard ran to the gurney, having smelled the ammonium carbonate from fifty feet away. "Are you sure, Eve?" he asked.

"I'm—I'm—sure," she managed to reply before the drugs did their job, and Eve was lost to sleep. Therese and Carlo released their grips on Eve and piloted her back to a prone position.

Therese turned to Bob, her face covered in giant raindrops. "She can't smell—even something this strong—because her olfactory bulbs have been removed. Isn't that right, Bob?"

"Of course they have been. She's a volunteer." Bob spoke as if the procedure were a tonsillectomy.

"An expensive volunteer," added Tony, who retrieved the key to the handcuffs and unlocked his charge, pocketing the cuffs.

Richard rubbed his wrists as he looked at Therese, putting it together. "My cells from the cadaver—but that protocol was stamped and approved. It was signed by the review board."

"Richard!" blasted Bob. "Stop this nonsense! I want everyone, all of you, out of my way, this instant! I've had it with your meddling, and I've had it for this evening."

At that moment, there was a giant thunderclap, and a strike of lightning touched down, close enough to make the hairs rise on the back of Therese's neck. The Cessna cut its engine. Richard felt it, too.

"We have do something, before we all get electrocuted. This bed's a lighting rod," shouted Richard. "Come on; get her to the plane. Help me, Therese. Get up!" Richard began pushing the gurney through the mud.

Therese took her weight off the hospital bed, and Carlo helped Richard push the bed uphill, towards the embankment, Bob and Stuart following. Therese ran alongside them, keeping her body between her father and Bob, who was struggling in the mud. Stuart was wearing his tracksuit, and it was soaked through. She pulled the coverall closer to her body and tried to keep pace, a trail of blood following her, obvious as it seeped onto the tarmac.

"Listen! There was a young woman in New York, about seventeen or eighteen. She was tall, thin, and blonde—everyone's image of what a young, beautiful woman should be. Except she was homeless. She was saving up to go to school and trying to stay safe on the streets. She had friends, a small family of other homeless people—children she looked out for. When the coroner got to her, she was missing an olfactory bulb." Therese paused to observe Bob's reaction, which revealed nothing. Stuart looked at Therese, his dripping face betraying his age, for once. Carlo and Richard lifted Eve Klein's unconscious body into the Cessna, which had started its engine again.

"The coroner could not explain it, nor did he want to. Various specialists couldn't, either. Nor could I, until I found a paper by one of Richard's colleagues about the olfactory bulb and its stem cells. June did not die from having the bulb removed. She died from meningitis, an infection in her brain. An infection from surgery.

"I have evidence that June was seen being driven away in a postwar, vintage Mercedes 300d sedan just days before she died. There aren't too many of those around anymore, and I believe an eyewitness can identify it specifically." Stuart looked at her, nodding his head left to right. His CD player fell from his sweatpants to the wet ground, breaking.

"No, that isn't so!" interjected Bob. "We didn't hurt her. She was fine when I left her. I attended to her myself. Who knows what kind of trouble she got into after that? I can't be responsible for her—a girl like her, a street girl—a prostitute." Bob lifted his hands in disgust.

Undeterred, Therese continued. “So, Dr. Weigand, I suggest you tell me what happened in that operating room, and why you lied to your son about the source of the cells you delivered to him, which Richard then harvested to use in various patients, including this one!” Therese pointed to Stuart. Her voice had risen as she spoke, and she felt she would burst if Bob did not admit his role in the matter. Richard and Carlo jumped out of the Cessna, and Stuart and Bob climbed in, awkwardly, Bob leaning over Eve to check her vitals. Stuart turned back around inside the small plane and looked out, surveying the buildings, the sky, the plant fields—all his.

“Therese, let explain something.” He spoke louder, over the engines revving up to speed. “Look at all this! I worked hard for it, Therese. I’ve given my life to it. It’s everything to me. I know you don’t understand, but we have to stop. We can’t go on like this. Something has to change. You aren’t ready for it, I know. But you will be. You’ll see. The fact is, my life is worth more than that homeless girl’s.”

Just then, Stuart lost his footing, although the plane had not moved. It was as if someone pulled him from his feet on strings, a marionette. He fell to the floor of the plane, hitting his head on the door. Instinctively, Therese ran to him. His temple was bleeding.

“You don’t see it, do you? I give people their minds back, Therese. Think about it! I can give people their minds back! Is that not the greatest donation you can imagine?” Stuart closed his eyes. “But I’m so, so tired.”

“Back off, Therese,” yelled Bob from inside the plane. He leaned over, and with impressive strength, pulled Stuart completely into the plane.

Then he slammed the door.

Therese, Richard, and Carlo watched, and in a few moments, the plane was shrouded in dark storm clouds.

Epilogue

Chapter Thirty-Six

WHEN THERESE FINALLY WOKE, it was still raining. She was startled from a dream in which she was trying to hoist a dead body from the water, but it was too heavy. She forced herself into consciousness. It was dark, and for a moment, she thought she saw Richard beside her, asleep. But she was imagining things; she turned on the bedside lamp. There was no one there, only the lack of someone. She stood and stretched—her back throbbing from so much time in bed. Then, a loud throbbing from the front door; without thinking, she called, "Richard?"

She stumbled through the dark hallway, her foot protesting, causing her to limp. She flung open the door, and she did not see Richard, but his father, Bob.

"May I come in?" he asked, as if nothing had happened between them, as if a girl were not dead. She said nothing, but opened the door so he could pass, looking beyond him to be sure he was alone. Bob seated himself in the villa's breakfast nook, and Therese opened the French doors and let the sea breeze enter. She stood there, on the other side of the room.

"I want to say two things to you. And if you love your father, you'll pay attention."

Therese, though irritated, moved closer and took a seat next to the doctor. The fruit in the bowl on the table was rotting. She held her face in her hands, unable to look at him.

"You may think you know something about making things right in the world. But you're wrong. You're too young. You just don't know. You haven't seen what I've seen. The girl did not die in vain."

"But she did die."

"We disagree about that."

"A body in a morgue is not something that can be disputed."

"Did you see it yourself?"

"The body? No, but I spoke to the coroner about her, and—"

"It's hearsay. It'll never hold up. Forget about her."

"I won't. Ever." She stared at Bob, and he said, "Suit yourself. Quite a waste of your time, I'd say."

"And what about Eve Klein? When will she learn that her nasal organs have been removed?"

"Good God, Therese, they weren't entirely removed. She's fine. She's got no idea anything even occurred. In fact, she's on the schedule at Carnegie next month."

"So that makes it okay?" Therese stood. "And your second point was what, exactly?"

"Sit back down."

Therese remained standing and shook her head in a way that said, "I want you out of my house."

"Therese, your father's dying."

Therese threw up her hands. "I'm dying, you're dying; we're all dying, Bob. You can't save any of us, either. Do you expect me to thank you for all you've done?"

"I said, he's dying. Right now. And not of Alzheimer's. We'll get the tumor out and then administer chemo and radiation. But it's an aggressive tumor."

Now, Therese did sit down. "Where?"

"His brain, deep in the frontal lobe. A glioblastoma."

Therese exhaled loudly. "Why did you come here, Bob?"

"Because he wanted me to tell you. He's not feeling particularly well. We operate first thing tomorrow. We'll do everything possible—"

"What, to undo what you already did? Is the tumor a result of the stem cell procedure?"

"Possibly. Probably. But we can't be sure; there's a chance it's unrelated. But you must remember what I said today, Therese. Your father tried to eradicate Alzheimer's." Bob got up and made for the door. "You should be thanking me—and your father. We may be the reason you don't end up in a home, God forbid, sixty years from now." He winked at Therese. "And don't forget to marry my son." Bob turned and closed the door gingerly behind him, leaving Therese alone in her dark villa.

Therese watched from the far side of the recovery room. Her father was coming out of the anesthesia, still groggy. He made an effort to hold out his hand then gave up.

“How are you feeling?” Therese tried a smile, but it didn’t fit. Her father smiled, instead.

“I’m so glad you’re here. I tried to reach you, the phone rang and rang, and I wanted to say—oh, Therese, please understand. I’m a victim in all this.”

If only that were really true. “Can’t you just say you’re sorry? Sorry about that poor girl, Dad? Can’t you just pretend to care about her? For me?” Therese was surprised to find tears in her own eyes. She turned and looked out the window.

“Honey, we’re on the same side, okay? You know I’d do anything to make you happy.” *I did it for you*, is that what he meant? Stuart closed his eyes. Therese turned back to the room and envisioned her mother holding her father’s hand. “Your father needs to rest now, Therese.”

Chapter Thirty-Seven

THERESE WALKED FOR MILES that day, up and down the familiar beach and into less familiar places—into rocky coves and through fields, Fancy at her side. They passed lizards and orchids and water the color of lapis, but only her sight hound observed these things. To Therese, it was just stuff between her and her thoughts. All she could think about was how it all came down to money.

Money was at the heart of the entire disaster, and it was her own personal disaster, she saw that now. Since she was able, she'd been donating her time, efforts, connections, and influence just to give other people money, or help them make more money. That was about all it came to—all that work. It was useful, and it made her feel good, but something was missing. She remembered Greg making a jab about writing a check to solve a problem, and he wasn't wrong.

And then, for the first time in her life, it occurred to her that, although she had always been a philanthropist, she hadn't really known why. Perhaps she had given her money and time to others out of a sense of obligation, because that's what women in society's circles did. But no. That wasn't quite it.

Now she saw the real reason. She had given to get love. She gave time and money because she needed to feel appreciated, loved. Her mother was a distant memory—sometimes even an imaginary companion—and her father had never made her feel loved, only looked after. Her father talked about giving her everything she could have wanted, but how did that measure against taking someone's life?

But rules were rules, and try as she might, she could not break them. Her father was her father, and she could either accept him for who he was or not. He was unchangeable. It wasn't within her to convict him—that would be his own burden.

Therese saw now, with great clarity, that had she a million dollars or one dollar, she would have given it away, just to feel connected to someone. How lonely she had been! The revelation brought tears to her eyes.

But now, to her shock, it dawned on her. She had a person to love. And love him, she did. How startling a feeling that was! It surrounded her—a simple fact—one that had been staring at her for weeks.

It seemed like days since she'd seen him, and it seemed to take hours to find him, although the light in the sky told her it was barely evening as she drove through the gates at BioSys, the only place she hadn't checked. She only had a vague idea of where his office was, and as she cruised the laboratory halls, empty this Sunday, she wondered what he was thinking. Was he angry with her? Aloof? Was he missing her, too? Her shoes clicked on the industrial flooring, echoing against the walls.

She heard music—a single piano—jazzy, slow brush drumming. A woman's voice. "*He was too good to me, how can I get along now? So close he stood to me, everything's all messed up and wrong now. Making me smile, that was his fun, 'cos my baby was too good to be true.*" Therese walked closer, slipping off her shoes and listening outside the doorway. The piano played a solo, and Therese looked into the room through the half-opened door. Richard was leaned over a desk, his profile visible. He was alone and appeared deep in work. A CD player on the work island was the source of the music. Now Therese recognized the voice of Nina Simone. The CD moved to the next track, and Richard did not look up. "*Make him love me, the way he should. I got it bad, and that ain't good,*" crooned Nina. Despite the agony of the last few days, the lyrics made Therese smile, and she involuntarily let out a small laugh. It was a like a little miracle. Richard looked up, startled, and Therese clasped a hand over her mouth.

"Are you spying on me, Therese?" said Richard, a twinkle in his eye.

"Caught. Guess I wouldn't be very good at industrial espionage."

"Neither were our friends, thank goodness."

"Nothing's missing?"

"No, incredibly. And I've replaced all the bogus paperwork with the correct data—ABT-55 will be safe. In fact, I've created my own method of encryption so I will know if the data's been tampered with." He got up and switched off the music.

"Why did you turn it off?"

"I'm not sure. I listen to certain CDs when I'm working, trying to solve problems; they help me concentrate. I'm not working now, I guess."

"Because I interrupted. I'm sorry. Should I come back—"

"Are you kidding? I've been waiting to talk to you. Speaking of—why don't you come in? We have a lot to catch up on." He motioned to a chair, but he looked sober; the twinkle in his eye had gone. She tried to erase the smile on her face, feeling inappropriate, but bursting at the seams. She sat in a swivel chair; he took a deep breath and put his hands on his knees. It was quiet now—very quiet.

"I've been trying to figure out what happened. I wanted to call you. I wanted to come over, but I—well, I just needed some answers first."

"Is that part of the answer?" Therese motioned to the hand-written math on the pages on the desk.

"Yes. It's the beginning. There's a long way to go, though." Richard rubbed his neck and looked across the room, past Therese, at the sun setting—low enough to hit the lab's window.

"The cells I got from my dad, well, they weren't what I thought they were." The sun sank into the room and splashed his face, lending his eyes flecks of gold. He looked back at Therese. "That's when things went wrong. I had no idea about the girl. I was told the cells came from a cadaver, and I had no reason to check that they weren't. I didn't know, you know."

"I know," replied Therese, quietly. "Would you have been able to tell if you'd known to look?"

"I'm not sure; that's what I want to work on."

"Could you have changed—"

"I just don't know. Yet. It's like a place you've seen on a map, but never visited. You know there are mountains, but until you climb them…" He didn't need to finish the sentence; Therese was nodding. She felt, oddly, the same way. "Cells have certain rules, rules that they always follow, and this isn't really adding up."

"A mountain that turns out to be a lake, you mean."

"Maybe not quite that far. More like a mountain that's a hill." They were quiet, and both turned to the window. The sun was moving fast. Richard continued his thought. "It's been sobering. I knew before we began the trial that tumors were a possible side effect of the stem cells, but not this kind of tumor. Stuart wasn't hearing it; he just didn't care."

"He was desperate."

"Yes," sighed Richard, wrapping his hands behind his neck. "And it's my fault. I should have stopped him. I should have convinced Dad to stop the treatments. I can't tell you how awful it feels to think you have a good chance of helping someone, and then causing a worse problem instead. I should have listened to myself! I knew I was being rushed."

"I'm sure you tried to do something about the tumors."

"I did. I concentrated all my efforts to finding a molecular way to prevent tumor growth. But the bio-chemical reactions that make good new cells grow also give rise to dangerous ones, tumor-forming ones. It's very tricky. It'll take years, if not decades, to work it out, at least for the brain."

"You know what's odd? This problem sounds similar to the one you told me you were working on—for the chemo drug. A drug that would do less harm while still doing good."

"Yes, and in that way, I suppose, I was trying not to fib. Therese, please forgive me for not divulging the whole truth to you. I promise I will never ever lie to you again."

Therese smiled weakly, and nodded. "You're also a victim in this. You and June."

"Not you? You may lose your father." He turned to her.

She sighed. "I've been letting him go for awhile now; I just didn't really see it."

He nodded in understanding. "We have a lot in common in that arena." Richard smiled in resignation.

"Can you help him, anyway?" Therese's eyes welled at the thought of being an orphan.

"We're sure going to try."

Therese stood and wiped her eyes. "I'd better let you get back to that job, then."

"I didn't mean for you to go. You just got here." Silence. Then Richard stood. "Why don't we have dinner?"

"Okay," sighed Therese. "That would be fine." *Your life is about to change. Again*, she thought.

"I can wrap up here and be ready in an hour or so. I'll knock on your door."

At home, the hour sped by too fast. Therese had wanted to clean up the villa, maybe put fresh flowers around the place. But she barely had time to clean herself up before the knock came. She ran a hand through her hair and took a deep breath before she opened the door.

She had assumed Richard was at her door twice already today—and been wrong twice.

Carlo stood there, haggard and ashen. "Where've you been?" he uttered.

"Around. Come on in." Therese led Carlo to the veranda. It was stuffy in the villa, and the night air felt cooler, although it wasn't according to the thermometer. Carlo flopped into an oversized wicker chair and stared at the night. She passed him a large glass of iced water. "It's all I have."

"Haven't been shopping yet, huh? What's wrong with you?" Carlo smiled, coming back to earth. His smile didn't last. He set his water down and said, "My dad's disappeared."

"That's good?" asked Therese, taking a long look at Carlo. "But then what?"

"Then," he sighed, "I do everything I can to forget that I'll never be able to catch him."

"You want to jail him?"

"Only to protect him. You know he gave your dad a million bucks?"

Therese shook her head. "No."

"He did. Wanted to help him with the enterprise."

"And my dad needed the money?"

"Apparently. I think he was trying to run it all without involving BioSys, and together they hatched a plan to expand the program, offer it to other desperate people. 'Rich executives live forever—get stem cells!' That kind of thing."

"Is there any trail of that money that we should be worried about?"

"Not that I know of. Besides, the money went back to where it came from, in a way."

"Back to the streets, you mean."

"Yes—when Francis' brother stole it."

"He stole stolen money?"

Carlo laughed. "Exactly." He paused. "Although, sometimes, I'm not sure there's any difference."

"It's all stolen."

"In a sense, don't you think?"

Therese wasn't ready to talk about money issues now; her soul-searching abilities were worn out from the day's thinking. She studied Carlo's face. "Something else is bothering you—more than the money. Francis, the fire, and what happened."

Carlo nodded and looked down at the concrete. "I just don't know what to do about it." He looked up at her. "You can't imagine how wrecked I feel."

"Francis was eventually going to kill your father, or your mother, or you, even, if you had stayed with the cops."

"Self-defense and all that—yeah, I know." Carlo leaned back in his chair and closed his eyes. "Doesn't mean it feels good."

"There's not a part of you that's glad he's dead? Francis was a terrible man, Carlo."

"That's the problem. Not much difference between him and my dad, and now you can add me to that list, too."

"But you're different. It's not the same."

"Isn't it, though? What's the difference between letting a killer escape and committing a murder yourself?"

A knock at the door prevented her from answering. "That's Richard," she said, a smile forming as she stood. Carlo got up and followed. "Don't get up," she said. "You don't have to leave."

"Therese, seeing you smile like that just now, in the middle of all this, with your dad in the hospital—well, it made my day. Why end it any other way? Besides, I can see when three's a crowd."

Therese shook her head. "Not true!" she said, although she didn't really mean it. She was looking forward to seeing Richard alone. She answered the door. Richard said, "Fifty-nine minutes, exactly." His hair was glistening; it was freshly washed and combed, his face open and happy. He held up white bags. "I brought fish and chips from town." The bags were already greasy and smelled of vinegar and salt. He stood on the threshold, looking at Therese and Carlo.

"Come in, come in," she said, nervous now. She led Richard inside. Carlo took his place in the doorway.

"Richard, thanks for all you did, putting up with my dad. He seems cured."

"I'm glad, Carlo."

Carlo turned away and closed the door behind him.

"He's not staying?" He turned to Therese, who was setting out plates. *Not a good sign*, she thought.

"Well, I think he has a lot on his mind." Therese let her voice trail off, reprimanding herself for getting her hopes up about the evening. "Thanks for bringing dinner," she offered.

"Sure. This place has good take-out." He sat down at the breakfast nook. "I was thinking afterwards, maybe we could visit your father."

"Oh," said Therese, as she fished the greasy contents out of the bag. Her timing was obviously all wrong. Go to a hospital? Tonight? Oh, why, why hadn't she realized how she felt about him earlier! "That's a nice idea. I haven't been to see him since this morning."

They ate, and the food was delicious. Therese was surprised at how much she'd been craving salt. She helped herself to extra vinegar, too. They licked their fingers in delight.

"So what happens with Dr. Richard, now?" she asked.

"I'm not sure. I'd like to work on the ABT-55 team, and there seems to be an opportunity."

"You mean the chemo drug?"

"Yes. It's a good challenge, and your father really has a crack team of people working on it. It's exciting."

"So after all this, you want to work for BioSys?"

"Sure. Why not? There's no better company for cancer research. And what other company can you think of with a CEO and chairman who'd risk his own life to help fight a disease?"

Therese said nothing, despite all she was thinking. Her father may have risked his own life, but he did it out of self-interest, as much as for any public interest. But Richard wanted leadership—she could see that. "What about the stem cell work?"

"Well, that can be developed in a legitimate way, but it'll be tricky." He paused and looked her in the eye. "Besides, if I don't work for BioSys, how can I keep tabs on you?"

Therese smiled, glad he was flirting, or whatever it was in his mind. But was it any more than that? She couldn't be sure. And yet she had been so sure that he felt the same way she did.

They drove into town, picked up coffees from the island's main hotel, and then went on to the hospital. Her father was resting peacefully, surrounded by an outrageous number of flower arrangements, each overflowing with well wishes. Richard looked at her father's chart and gave a "thumbs up" sign.

They drove home in silence. Richard let her off in her driveway and waited in the car until she was safe inside.

The next morning, after all were rested, Therese, Richard, and Carlo walked into town. It was a perfect morning, not too hot, and the sky was crystal clear. Therese was happy to see Richard after last night's awkwardness. They breakfasted with Ferdy, who treated them, as always, to a fresh breakfast of fluffy eggs, toast, and pineapple juice. But although the sun was brilliant, the sea breeze refreshing, and the day new, no one was smiling. Therese could see something was bothering Richard, and her suspicions were confirmed when he stood at the end of the meal.

"I've got something to do, but I'll be back later." Therese and Carlo nodded, and Therese watched him go.

Richard walked all the way to the dock. He had many things to say to his father, and he couldn't put them off any longer. Last night, he'd watched each hour go by, worried about legal issues, money, the regimen for curing Stuart's tumor. Should he move back to the States now? Next week? What about the future? Therese had brought up a good point. How would the stem cell work benefit the medical community if it was not published? But how to publish it now, after the death of the girl?

As Richard approached the pier, he was surprised to see his father leaning down, pulling in the small craft's anchor, coiling the tie lines like an expert. Richard took shelter behind a large palm tree, where he could not be seen. His fears of the sleepless night before were confirmed, and with a sick feeling, he watched *The Emerald* move slowly away from the dock. He wanted desperately to run after him, to call out, "Father, Father! Wait! You've left without me!" but he was glued to the bark of the tree. The small sailboat gained speed and soon the green of its hull merged with the color of the sea. He knew with Therese and Carlo's help, he could find his father, but he also knew the man did not intend to be found. He banged his fists into the tree until its bark scattered from its trunk like pearls from a burst necklace.

The day passed laboriously; Therese was sure it was the longest day of her life. The hot villa made even the smallest movements feel like marathons, and the absence of a breeze left the day stale and motionless. Therese's heart had been broken as she had never imagined possible, and now, staring at the walls, utterly detached, she knew what it meant to be shattered. This was how her father must have felt after the murder. It was a delayed reaction to her father's crimes—she saw that. Try as she might to find it, there was no consolation in the fact that a girl had died heroically so that others might live.

The next days passed just this way. She and Richard hardly spoke, but saw each other from their windows, each watching as the other crossed rooms and turned on and off lights, like stray cats cruising alleyways at night. There was little sleep, due to worry and sadness. Therese visited her father every day and watched his face grow livelier. He was beginning chemo.

At the end of the seventh day, Therese came across Greg's phone number, and recognition shook her back into consciousness. She had been very, very tired, but now she felt almost caffeinated and admonished herself for her selfishness as she reached for the phone.

The pay phone number rang and rang. Greg did not answer; no one did. She let it ring anyway, then hung up and dialed again, hoping she had made an error.

No. She slammed down the phone, walked over to Richard's and knocked on the French doors on the ocean side. He was sitting at the dining room table, working. He looked up, startled at her knock. The two took a long look at each other, and Richard waved her in. Therese moved over to the table and sat down.

"What are you working on?" she asked quietly, as if doing so might erase her frustration in not reaching Greg.

"Well, I'm working." He looked down at his notes. "It helps, you know."

"Oh, how I wish I had something to get lost in! Anything! This is maddening, the way I feel; it's a prison!" Tears welled in her eyes, and she brushed them away. Richard took her hand in his.

"I think you're about to have something to work on."

"What do you mean?" His hand felt electric in hers.

A loud bird cackled outside. It must have been singing for some time, but Therese only noticed it now. It was perched on the tree right outside the window. How long had it been vying for attention? They watched the bird until it flew away with its mate, chirping incessantly all the way.

"He wants you to be the acting BioSys CEO."

Chapter Thirty-Eight

BACK IN NEW YORK, the first thing Therese did after being named successor to her father was track down Greg.

It had taken some detective work, but she finally found him working in an uptown café. He was clean-shaven and alert, so Therese almost didn't recognize him. When he saw her walk into the café, he smiled and nodded to his coworker that he'd be taking a break. They sat down at a table by the window.

"I've been trying to find you for two weeks now."

Greg nodded. "I didn't leave much of a trail, I know. I needed to make a fresh start; you were right. I'll never forget June, but I can't change much by complaining."

"Do you like this job?"

"It's fine. It's great to have a paycheck. I feel more in control of everything."

"I've got a lot to tell you about June. Can we, maybe, go somewhere more private?" Greg looked concerned and let his boss know he'd be taking an early lunch. They walked into Central Park—fitting, since that's where they met. Therese told him everything she knew about how June Hamels died half a year ago. Greg took a seat on a bench, sighed, and looked at Therese.

"My dad—he hurt people, too, swindling their savings out of them. From his fancy office on Wall Street he conned old people, made millions. He called it good business all the way to his grave." Greg shook his head in disgust. "I just couldn't handle knowing the money he fed us with was—"

Therese nodded. "There seems to be a lot of that going around lately."

"It really messed me up for a long time."

Therese sat down next to him. "Still, I'm so sorry. About June."

"Thanks."

They were walking back to the café when the idea struck her. She stopped in her tracks. "Greg, did you say you liked your job?"

"Well, sure, but—"

"But you said you'd been to school, right?"

"Yes, unfortunately; I have a Harvard MBA, believe it or not."

Therese clapped her hands together. "Will you come work with me? You could be my—how about you come on board as my ethical advisor? You know how businesses should run, and you certainly know a thing or two about fairness and morality."

"At BioSys? You must be joking."

"You said yourself that you couldn't make a difference just complaining, didn't you?"

Greg accepted the job and started the following week.

That week, Therese opened a new branch of BioSys—the Weigand Stem Cell Institute, naming Dr. Richard Weigand its chairman and chief scientist.

Stuart began his radiation therapy and settled back into the house in Santa Monica Canyon, where he saw images of his wife and held regular conversations with her. He moved there to retire, and still had access to his daughter whenever he wanted it, via his video phone. He still wasn't sure what he had done to offend his daughter, but he hoped he had begun to make things right between them.

It was not until many weeks later that Therese and Richard, finally out on a proper date, kissed for the first, but not the last, time.

THE END.

References

Allen, Jane. "PET Scans Highly Reliable in Detecting Alzheimer's." *Los Angeles Times*, November 12, 2001, sec. S.

Broe, G. Anthony, David A. Grayson, Helen M. Creasey, Louise M. Waite, Barney J. Casey, Hayley P. Bennett, William S. Brooks, and Glenda M. Halliday. "Anti-Inflammatory Drugs Protect Against Alzheimer Disease at Low Doses." *Archives of Neurology* 57, (2000): 1586-1591.

Byrd CA, and Brunjes PC. "Neurogenesis in the Olfactory Bulb of Adult Zebrafish." *Neuroscience* 105, (2001): 793-801.

Chantal, Sophie, Martin Labelle, Remi Bouchard, Claude Braun, and Yvan Boulanger. "Correlation of Regional Photon Magnetic Resonance Spectroscopic Metabolic Changes with Cognitive Deficits in Mild Alzheimer Disease." *Archives of Neurology* 59, (2002): 955-962.

Daly, Ella, Deborah Zaitchik, Maura Copeland, Jeremy Schmahmann, Jeanette Gunther, and Marilyn Albert. "Predicting Conversion to Alzheimer Disease Using Standardized Clinical Information." *Archives of Neurology* 57, (2000): 675-680.

Farlow, Martin, Steven Potkin, Barbara Koumaras, Jeffrey Veach, and Dario Miriski. "Analysis of Outcome in Retrieved Dropout Patients in a Rivastigmine vs. Placebo, 26-Week, Alzheimer Disease Trial." *Archives of Neurology* 60, (2003): 843-848.

Farrer, Lindsay. "Familial Risk for Alzheimer Disease in Ethnic Minorities: Nondiscriminating Genes." *Archives of Neurology* 57, (2000): 28-29.

Fox, Nick, Simon Cousens, Rachael Scahill, Richard Harvey, and Martin Rossor. "Using Serial Registered Brain Magnetic Resonance

Imaging to Measure Disease Progression in Alzheimer Disease: Power Calculations and Estimates of Sample Size to Detect Treatment Effects." *Archives of Neurology* 27, (2000): 339-344.

Fuhrmans, Vanessa. "New Scanning Methods Help Detect Alzheimer's Early Signs." *The Wall Street Journal*, July 18, 2002, sec. D.

Gage, Fred. "Mammilian Neural Stem Cells." *Science* 287 (2000): 1433-1438.

Gould, Elizabeth, Alison Reeves, Mazyar Fallah, Patima Tanapat, Charles Gross, and Eberhard Fuchs. "Hippocampal Neurogenesis in Adult Old World Primates." *Neurobiology* 96, (1999): 5263-5267.

Gould, Elizabeth, Alison Reeves, Michael Graziano, and Charles Gross. "Neurogenesis in the Neocortex of Adult Primates." *Science* 286, (1999): 548-552.

Green, Robert, Adrienne Cupples, Alex Kurz, Sanford Auerback, Rodney Go, Dessa Sadovnick, Ranjan Duara, Walter Kukull, Helena Chui, Timi Edeki, Patrick Griffith, Robert Friedland, David Bachman, and Lindsay Farrer. "Depression as a Risk Factor for Alzheimer Disease: The MIRAGE Study." *Archives of Neurology* 60, (2003): 753-759.

Guillozet, Angela, Sandra Weintruab, Deborah Mash, and Marsel Mesulam. "Neurofibrillary Tangles, Amyloid, and Memory Aging and Mild Cognitive Impairment." *Archives of Neurology* 60, (2003): 729-736.

Haarr L, Shukla D, Rødahl E, Dal Canto MC, and Spear PG. "Transcription from the gene encoding the herpesvirus entry receptor nectin-1 (HveC) in nervous tissue of adult mouse." *Virology* 287 no.2, (2001): 307-309.

Hotz, Robert. "Alzheimer's Study Yields Early Clues. *Los Angeles Times*, November 2, 2000, sec. B.

Johannes, Laura. “Finding Alzheimer’s Early.” *The Wall Street Journal*, October 16, 2003, sec. B.

Johannes, Laura. “New Study Finds Indications of Alzheimer’s Early in Life. *The Wall Street Journal*, August 17, 2000, sec. B.

Kinsley, Michael. “Bush’s Hypocritical Stem Cell Stance.” *Los Angeles Times*, October 24, 2003, sec. Opinion.

Liotta, Lance, Elise Kohn, and Emanuel Petricoin. “Clinical Proteomics: Personalized Molecular Medicine.” *JAMA* 286, no. 18 (2001): 2211-2214.

Lopez, Oscar, Stephen Wisniewski, James Becker, Francois Boller, and Steven DeKosky. “Psychiatric Medication and Abnormal Behavior as Predictors of Progression in Probable Alzheimer Disease.” *Archives of Neurology* 56, (1999): 1266-1272.

Luchsinger, Jose, Ming-Xing Tang, Steven Shea, and Richard Mayeux. “Caloric Intake and the Risk of Alzheimer Disease.” *Archives of Neurology* 59, (2002): 1258-1263.

Mestal, Rosie. “Key Brain Cells Emerge from the Shadows.” *Los Angeles Times*, Febraury 22, 2001, sec. B.

Morris, Martha, Denis Evans, Julia Bienias, Christine Tangney, and Robert Wilson. “Viatmin E and Cognitive Decline in Older Persons.” *Archives of Neurology* 59, (2002): 1125-1132.

“MRI Technique May Help Find Root of Memory Loss Earlier.” *Biophotonics International*, (March, 2001): 14.

Otsuka T, Hashida M, Oka T, and Kaba H. “Activation of GABA(A) Receptors in the Accessory Olfactory Bulb Does Not Prevent the Formation of an Olfactory Memory in Mice.” *Journal of Veterinary Medical Science* 63, no.7, (2001): 807-809.

Roses, Allen. "Genetic Testing for Alzheimer Disease: Practical and Ethical Issues." *Archives of Neurology* 54, (1997): 1226-1229.

Shaw, Jonathon. "Stem-Cell Science." *Harvard Magazine*, July-August 2004, 36-45.

Shihabuddin, Lamya, Jasodhara Ray, and Fred Gage. "Stem Cell Technology for Basic Science and Clinical Applications." Edited by Hassan Fathallah-Shaykh. *Archives of Neurology* 56, (1999): 29-32.

Shihabuddin, Lamya, Theo Palmer, and Fred Gage. "The Search for Neural Progenitor Cells: Prospects for the Therapy of Neurodegenerative Diesase." *Molecular Medicine Today* 5, no. 11 (1999): 474-480.

Specter, Michael. "Rethinking the Brain." *The New Yorker*, July 23, 2001, 42-53.

Sugaya, K. "Neuroreplacement Therapy and Stem Cell Biology Under Disease Conditions." *Cell Molecular Life Science* 9, (2003): 1891-1902.

Sugaya, K. "Potential Uses of Stem Cells in Neurodegenertaive Diseases." *International Review of Cytology* 228, (2003): 1-30.

Tsuang, Debby, Eric Larson, James Bowen, Wayne McCormick, Linda Teri, David Nochlin, James Leverenz, Elaine Peskind, Alfredo Lim, Murray Raskind, Mary Lou Thompson, Suzanne Mirra, Marla Gearing, Gerald Schellenberg, and Walter Kukull. "The Utility of Apolipoprotein E Genotyping in the Diagnosis of Alzheimer Disease in a Community-Based Case Series." *Archives of Neurology* 56, (1999): 1489-1495.

Ullian, Erik, Stephanie Sapperstein, Karen Christopherson, and Ben Barres. "Control of Synapse Number by Glia." *Science* 291, no. 5504 (2001): 657-661.

Williams RW, Airey DC, Kulkarni A, Zhou G, and Lu L. "Genetic Dissection of the Olfactory Bulbs of Mice: QTLs on Four Chromosomes Modulate Bulb Size." *Behav Genet* 31, no. 1 (2001): 61-77.

Wilson, Robert, David Bennett, David Gilley, Laurel Beckett, Lisa Barnes, and Denis Evans. "Premorbid Reading Activity and Patterns of Cognitive Decline in Alzheimer Disease." *Archives of Neurology* 57, (2000): 1718-1723.

LaVergne, TN USA
12 October 2009

160599LV00001B/188/P

9 781595 269034